Jameson

A Novel

Kristina Lowe

First Edition

Revised

ISBN 9781099483837

For Shoreman

And an afternoon spent building a dog house

JULY 1990

Chapter One

I was serving a life sentence in jail. Only I was serving my time on the installment plan.

I remember the first time I laid eyes on him, in the dim yellow glow of what was referred to in those days as the booking room. Back before the politically correct terminology; of intake areas and correctional facilities. It was a *jail*, and it was a booking room. Dungeon would have been a more fitting term. The place had been built in the 1850s and it still had a wooden cell in the basement, with shackles attached to the wall right beside it. Truly something out of the dark ages of 'correctional facilities'.

He stood just over six feet tall, solidly built but not bulky, a frame that belied the quiet strength of lean muscle, wrapped in a wool blanket with LPD stenciled across the back. I read his paperwork, a sentence of thirty days for public indecency. Scanning further down the paperwork, I learned my newest ward was named Kane Woods, and he had been found stark naked in the middle of the public park. That explained the blanket provided by the Lawrence cops. His dark hair was shaggy and disheveled, his fingernails were ragged and torn, but his jaw was clean shaven. The man was a vision of contradiction, and his amber eyes darted about the room.

I had three and a half years of experience under my belt by then, so I can spot a man looking for an escape route. His eyes were not searching for a weakness in security, nor were they motivated by fear. More he was absorbing every detail of his new surroundings in mere seconds. Almost like a cop, or in my case, a Deputy

Sheriff would. It gave me cause to wonder if he had law enforcement or military background. I guessed his age to be early 40s, which also gave me reason to wonder how the Hell he wound up naked in the park at his age.

No track marks so not a junkie, and he seemed a little too old to be a black out drunk with no prior arrests. Mentally ill people usually have had some contact with law enforcement by his age, but again, there was nothing indicating that on his paperwork. We had no computers back then. A fortyish jail virgin with no drug use was unusual, to say the least.

"Mr. Woods, step forward please." I said, motioning to the black line of tape on the floor situated in front of the height chart on the wall. He silently moved to the line.

"I'm going to take your picture. Face front."

He complied.

"Turn to your left."

After the photographs were done; I pointed to the chair in front of the desk, which he filled in silence. He didn't fidget, he didn't stare into his hands, or at the floor. He simply met my eyes with no emotion.

"Mr. Woods, my name is Deputy Sheriff Jameson. That's a mouthful. Officer Jameson will be fine. I am going to gather some personal information from you, explain the rules of the jail, both the official rules and the unofficial, 'How to Stay Out of the Shit' rules. I would advise you to pay more attention those ones. They'll keep you unharmed as much as possible in here, and hopefully prevent you from having to harm anyone else. You follow me?" He nodded that he understood.

"Mr. Woods, you have been sentenced..."

"Kane." He interrupted in a quiet but steady voice that made me look up from the papers.

"My name is Kane. I would be more comfortable if you called me that, Officer Jameson."

"Okay Kane, I can appreciate that. You and I are not at the point where you can call me by my first name. Not yet. Your behavior will determine when that happens."

He nodded again. I continued my speech.

"You have been sentenced to thirty days in our deluxe accommodations here at Lawrence Jail and House of Correction."

"I cannot do more than twenty-seven days." he said, in a manner and tone that made me look up again from his Court papers. It wasn't threatening, quite the opposite. He sounded nervous, maybe apprehensive; perhaps even fearful, but adamant at the same time. His eyes met mine, and I saw the same emotions in them as I heard in his voice. I'm sure my right eyebrow arched, like every woman's does when she hears words she doesn't like, or something that raises questions in her mind.

"Mr. Woods," I said, returning to a more formal, authoritative tone with him, "The Judge has sentenced you to thirty days in our care and custody, and there is nothing I can do about that."

"Kane, please. It is Kane.", he responded. "And I realize that you can't do anything about that. I just felt that in the interest of full disclosure? I should inform you that I cannot do more than twenty-seven days."

I stared at him for a good minute. Usually the weight of my green eyes makes an inmate look away in less than ten seconds, but not this one. He stayed with me for the full duration. I spoke first.

"Hot date?" I asked.

"Previous engagement. One that regrettably, I cannot break." was his reply.

"Look, Woods; thirty days is not a big deal. Really. You can do that standing on your head. I realize this is your first time in, and you may be a bit nervous or scared, but this place really isn't that bad. Sure, it's ancient, and it does have its own distinct smell, but really. Once you get into the routine; the time will be over before you know it. And, barring any incidents, you'll earn three and a half days good time. So, keep your nose clean and fly right, and you'll be out in twenty-six and a half days."

His eyes brightened at that, and the smallest of smiles crept into the corners of his mouth. He nodded ever so slightly, and I found myself grinning back at him.

"Well then Officer Jameson, perhaps you should fill me in on those 'How To Stay Out Of The Shit' rules you were talking about." he said, and this time a full smile captured his face. He had incredibly white teeth, nearly perfect. Yep, no drug use here; that's for sure. His skin was too healthy, eyes too clear, and his teeth too white. Even his mangled fingernails were not discolored, no nicotine stains on them.

"As promised. But first, the personal information."

"Fire away." He said, and we began the routine questions asked of every new inmate.

#

It took the usual thirty minutes to gather the pertinent data and in that time? I learned quite a bit about Kane Woods. As I had guessed, he was forty-two, and had never been in any sort of trouble with the law. He lived alone in a rural area of Essex County; a small town called Rowley. Apparently had about an acre and a half piece of property that backed up to state lands which was known for good deer hunting and long secluded trails that meandered down to the river. He lived a quiet life, worked as a custom cabinet maker out of a workshop behind his small house. He laughed and told me the soil was rich for gardening but he only grew the vegetables his chickens would eat; informing me he leaned more towards the red meat as most bachelors do. No history of alcoholism or hard drug use; the occasional joint in the 80's but nothing too serious. Never married, no children and no next of kin. Overall? A quiet and uneventful life; one that would have gone completely unnoticed save for his birthday suit debut in the park.

Once the official rules were explained; the usual bluster of chow times, rec times, what was considered contraband and lights out, we moved on to the nuts and bolts of getting through the days with minimal problems from inmates and guards.

"Keep visible as much as possible. Nobody likes to pull any shit out in the open. There's a lot of dark corners in this place, that's where they'll come at you if they do. This place isn't like the outside world; lines are drawn along race. The whites back the whites, the blacks back the blacks, and the Spanish back the Spanish, although they have a subset within them. Puerto Rican, Dominican and Cuban, and they'll sort that out amongst themselves, but if white or black have a problem with any Spanish guy? They will unite for that incident. Don't get too friendly with the guards or the inmates will think you're a rat. I am the first and only woman to work in this place. It's more accepted to talk to me longer than to the other officers. After all, most of these guys have wives or girlfriends on the outside; so they can understand wanting to be near a female even if she does have a uniform and badge. If you see something? If it's not going to get someone killed or hurt, the general rule is *Keep Your Mouth Shut*. You'll hear a yell of five-oh when an officer enters the cellblock; it's their code for watch out, guards are here. Cigarettes are used as money, there's no cash in there."

"I don't smoke." He said, and half smiled at me. "Guess I'm broke."

I continued to explain the rules, and Mr. Kane Woods nodded after every morsel of information I fed him. He digested it all, and I could see him planning his next twenty-six days so that they would be problem free and he'd get out for his unbreakable appointment, whatever that may be. Once he felt he had a general feel for daily life at Lawrence? He showered and made use of the booking room nail clippers while I located some clothes left in abandoned property that would likely fit him. In 1990; Essex County did not issue uniforms. Inmates wore street clothes, and Woods had been dropped at the gate wrapped in a police blanket.

"You ready?" I asked the now fully clothed Kane, and added, "You look almost human."

"I am starting to feel that way again." he said, and a crooked half grin captured his face.

"Well, then let's hit it. Don't stare anyone down. Meet their eyes and then look elsewhere; but not down. Keep your head up, they'll be sizing you up. Walk like you've got a purpose, but don't strut. Basically? Be confident enough to be left alone, without being arrogant enough to be asking for a challenge. Got it?"

"I'll manage." he said, and after a nod, I opened the door into Block One.

#

It was free time in the cell blocks so the inmates were roiling about; killing time as best they could. The sights, sounds and smell of the place had become normal to me, but then again? I was serving a life sentence here myself; on the installment plan. Since I hadn't had the misfortune of committing an actual crime or perhaps the pleasure of doing so; I got to leave the place every eight to twelve hours and visit the 'free world'. But even outside those walls? It felt like I'd left a part of me behind those bars and that I never really, *fully* left the place. Outside of those walls? I always sat with my back to the wall, even better if it's in the corner and facing the door. My eyes constantly sweep the room, watching everything; alert for anything even slightly out of the ordinary. I study the set of people's shoulders; it betrays their true intentions far before any words are spoken. I watch hands. I watch the center of their chest for elevated breathing, or a millisecond's warning for which direction they may suddenly move. I never stand directly in front of anyone. I'm always slightly off center in a diagonal manner; strong foot in back, ready to pivot away or strike first if need be. I'm sure even if I live long enough to retire from the department, I'll never be free of these survival mechanisms so ingrained in me I don't even realize that they're happening.

For a first timer in Lawrence? It can be overwhelming. Waves of voices crash down upon them from so many different directions it's dizzying. I've seen many cell block virgins stumble a step as they are assaulted by the smells, echoing mixed languages and slapping of dominoes in the poorly lit common areas. Their heads swivel and spin like a tilt a whirl at the carnival; and it is more like landing on a different planet. The Cantina scene in Star Wars ain't got nothing on the Flats of Block One. Kane Woods looked straight ahead, not looking directly at anyone but not looking away either. He walked silently through the churning sea of wretches. Yep, he was going to be all right. He was as alert as any man but never let it show, carrying his sheets, pillow and a blanket that read Lawrence Jail instead of the LPD he arrived in. He was aware of everything; probably more than our usual clientele who were either still high or getting dope sick by the time they reached Block One. We ascended the iron staircase and I reached through the bars of the cell block gate and unlocked it with my key, swinging it open to allow us on to the main floor

"Where's he going, Cap?" I asked of the shift Officer in Charge who was seated behind the bulletproof glass window of the Control Room. I ached for my poor flustered Captain, playing an unwinnable lottery of "find a bed" for a new inmate in a jail already near 200% capacity.

"Fuck, I don't know Jimmy. Get some Velcro and stick him to the goddamn ceiling." was my Captain's disgusted reply. He shifted nametags into spaces on an ancient slotted board we used as the cell assignment diagram. It was always an interesting game in the afternoons, awaiting calls from courthouses throughout the county if someone had been released from Court or sentenced to a different facility or to the state prison system because we had three more guys in line for that one bunk. Finally, he shuffled some nametags and jerked his head upwards.

"Three. Catwalk. 32." He scribbled WOODS on the back of an already used nametag. They were also in short supply for some reason, and he stuffed the name in the open slot for the cell.

"Got it. 32."

I turned back towards the open floor of the jail, which was designed in a T shape. There was a center open floor where the "guards" patrolled, and that level was called the Guard Level. The level below the Guard Level; reached by those iron steps we had just come up was called the Flats. The level above, reached by another flight of iron stairs outside of the bars was called the Catwalk. Each level contained 5 cells, and at the end of Block One and Block Two, there was a large shared room known as the Dorm. The Dorms ideally housed 8 inmates, but in our current bunk famine they now held 15. The individual cells, designed for 2 men now housed 4; three bunks high and one on the floor. It was a smoldering cigarette in a room of gunpowder; it was just a matter of time before the roof blew off, and every officer and inmate knew it which added to the tension of an already hostile situation. Sadly, even navigating that dangerous and ever shifting ground had become normal for me. I had become oblivious to the volatility of it.

Kane Woods took in the place by osmosis; nothing escaped his notice, but it appeared to be for him as natural as breathing. He followed me up the stairs, the sounds of my boots thudding loudly compared to the soft landings of his sneaker soles. The jail had a deal with Nike, and their irregular sneakers that couldn't be sold were donated for the inmates to wear. I had gotten him a new pair, but not too flashy so as make him a target. Just like in the outside world, people got jumped for their sneakers. And just like in the outside world, sometimes? They got killed for them. Something about him was different, and although I hadn't decided if I liked him yet or not? I did my best to make it a smooth integration for him. Give him a fighting chance at least. The rest was up to him and I must confess; I was curious to see how he'd fare.

"Jimmy, huh?" he asked when we reached the top of the stairs. The catwalk was just over 6 feet wide, 15 feet above the guard floor, and an iron railing with three parallel bars ran the length of it. The cell block doors were individually keyed, and their heft swung outwards on to the catwalk.

"Yeah. The other screws shortened my name. It has a dual purpose. Started as a joke."

"Joke? Screws?' he inquired further.

"Yeah. I am the first woman in the history of the county to be assigned in the cellblocks. The other officers were initially protective. They told the inmates not to be grabbing their Jimmy; meaning me. It wasn't long before they figured out I could handle myself and didn't need special protection, but Jimmy stuck. And Screws? Well, that's us, the officers. You have to have a screw loose to do this job."

Kane smiled that crooked half grin again.

"I will be sure not to grab any Jimmies that don't belong to me then." he said.

"It would behoove you not to, Mr. Woods." I said in my cold, Officer tone, and I smothered my smile before it betrayed me. Yep, I liked him. His quick wit and humor were familiar. Hell, he could have been one of us had he kept his clothes on and applied for the job.

"You're in 32. Second cell in from the gate. Probably going to be in the very top bunk, or on a mattress on the floor. You're the new guy. The others have seniority. But 32 isn't that bad; one dope dealer, one car thief, and one rape murder but he's tame enough. Apparently, he needs an eight ball of coke to bash a girl's skull in with a fence rail after tag teaming her with his buddy. You'll find that asshole partner of his at our sister jail down in Salem."

"How is a rapist and murderer still in this place? Should he not be in a prison? Walpole?" Kane asked, his brow furrowed. Oh yeah, he *WAS* new to the system. Didn't fully get how slowly the courts of law moved.

"Oh, he will wind up there, as soon as he's convicted, or works a sweet plea bargain. But technically? Right now? He's an innocent man." I said, the sarcasm dripping in my voice.

"Ah, right. Innocent until proven guilty."

"The American Justice system at work. There's a lot of innocent people in here; you'll see."

I swung the block door open jerking my head towards the tier. Woods stepped across the threshold, and I shut the door behind him. The bars shuddered as the weight of the door struck home, the latch sounding slightly louder than usual.

"You'll be fine Woods. Second cell in, the numbers are painted over the doors. Chow's in half hour. If you need anything? Just call CO; that's us."

"Kane."

"Okay, Woods. You can call me Jimmy."

"See you in thirty then, Jimmy." he said, that smile finding his features one more time as he turned and walked down the tier to his cell.

CHAPTER TWO

The next few shifts went as expected, nothing out of the ordinary. Pathetic that two large brawls that involved more than six inmates each night were now routine, but what can you expect with 250 men crammed into 60 cells? Still? It had become business as usual for us. We sifted through the bleeding combatants, sent those that needed it to the infirmary, and others to the ER for stitches or splints, and then locked the everybody else into their cells. Reports followed lockdown; an event that was starting a half an hour earlier each night because of the mounting paperwork each officer had to complete. The heat of the summer hadn't even started, it was only mid-June, but we all knew it was only going to escalate once temperatures and humidity rose. The longer the days? The shorter the tempers. The jail was built in the 1850s; air conditioning was nonexistent. It had only gotten running water two years prior; before that it was shit buckets. Self-explanatory, but no less disgusting. Shit bucket duty in the summer was reserved for the officers who had fallen out of favor, and I had pulled that duty myself on occasion. Sitting in a small room with an open drain, watching as the contents of the buckets were dumped by their users made you rethink your choice of profession; believe me. Still; we all survived it and had a true appreciation for running water. Even if was never hot.

Throughout the confined riot, which is exactly what the jail was; an ongoing riot contained within the granite walls; Woods seemed to have assimilated in to the population. He followed the rules, and the unspoken rules, and his first few days were remarkably uneventful. He was aloof, as most new guys are, but mostly unnoticed. Looking back? We were so busy putting out fires, both figurative ones and actual fires, we would only have noticed if he'd been shanked or tried to slice out. Slicing out is shop talk for cutting one's wrists; hanging it up was hanging yourself, and shanked is getting stabbed. Every profession has its own specific language and jails are no exception. The days blurred into each other as we were grossly understaffed; officers were working seven days a week, sometimes double and even triple shifts. Time takes forever, and yet Monday becomes a Wednesday before you notice it. A life sentence; served on the installment plan.

#

It was a warm afternoon with a soft breeze when Woods approached me in the yard. Yard time had become a precious commodity for the inmates, with the guard to inmate ratio so out of balance? It was hard to get them outside and still have the floor covered. We had started dividing the cell blocks within themselves to allow some vitamin D absorption for our charges, and honestly? For ourselves. I often entered Lawrence as we called the jail, before 7AM and left after 11PM, and I was not alone in keeping these hours. I was the palest blonde I knew, still using blush in the New England spring while all my neighbors had the gentle kiss of summer upon their cheeks. Still; I was banking a lot of time so it didn't occur to me to mind it much. I had sensed someone approaching a few seconds earlier, and recognized the voice when he spoke from beside me.

"Jimmy, you got a minute?"

"Yeah. What's up Woods?"

"Kane."

"Right. What's up?"

"I have a problem."

I glanced his way, scanning his demeanor to determine how serious it might be, and then returned to watching the inmates in the yard. Volleyball on a patch of more dirt and gravel than stubbles of grass. A dozen inmates just leaning against the wall enjoying the warmth; nothing out of the ordinary for an afternoon 'rec' time. I could tell by the way Woods stood something was amiss, and it wasn't a simple 'I lost my shoelaces in a card game' kind of problem. It wasn't life or death; but it was serious enough for him to approach me.

"Okay. Let's hear it."

"I've been in here a week."

"Yeah, give or take. So?" I asked, scanning the yard and watching every movement before me. The inmates were so thankful for any time out of the cramped quarters of the jail I didn't think they'd try anything outside to ruin their yard time, but you never can bank on them doing the smart thing. After all, we had a frequent flier who got caught his last time on an armed robbery of a liquor store because he left his wallet, complete with ID and home address, on the counter when he fled with the cash.

"Well? I have these chickens." He began, and I had to look directly at him to see if he was serious. He was. His eyes were steady on mine; no deception lay in them.

"Yeah?" I asked, curious as to where this was leading.

"I have an automatic waterer hooked up but I always check it daily; just to be sure it's working. It has been a week, and three days since the last rain."

"Un-huh." was my reply, and I could feel my right eyebrow arching up. I didn't know any chicken foster agencies.

"You booked me in. You know I don't have family. My nearest neighbor is over a quarter mile away, and I don't even know their names."

"Yeah, so?"

"You also know my address. Maybe you could check on them." he said. I turned to face him directly. No diagonal, bladed stance; I was flat footed and straight in front of him.

"You want me... to go check...on your chickens?" I asked incredulously. He nodded; eyes full of hope. I could not believe what he was asking. Not hey CO; can you bring me in some Q tips? Not, hey CO; can I get an extra five minutes on my visit? No, hey CO; let me bum a smoke? No this was? Hey Jimmy can you check on my chickens. Are you fucking kidding me? I would have been less stunned if he asked me to choke his chicken!

"I don't keep them in a coop, so I know they can find food." He continued. Jesus, he was fucking serious! "But the water? That's a different story. I don't have a pond or pool. They rely on that waterer to refill itself." He looked up to the sky, shielding his eyes with his hand. "And it's getting warmer."

This was an absolute first. I was speechless. For the first time in my thirty-three years of life? I did not have a thing to say. I didn't have a clue how to answer this request. Chickens? Fucking really? They do not pay me enough for this shit.

It occurred to me that my mouth was slightly open as I stood in front of him, and I closed it as casually as I could. I tried to regain my composure from my utter surprise, and realized I was scowling. I internally scolded myself for revealing a genuine emotional reaction. Such moments of human behavior are perceived as weakness; chinks in the armor to the harder inmates we held and I was not in the habit of allowing them to show.

"Why in the *HELL* would you ask me, of all people, to go check water for chickens?" I asked, regaining my professional stance and returning my eyes to others in the yard. Volleyball was ongoing, and the Sunshine Club was almost asleep against the wall. My moment of humanity had gone unnoticed; save for Kane. That half grin of his appeared again, but his eyes were sincere and hopeful.

"Guess I just figured you wouldn't let creatures die of thirst. Maybe? I just hoped it." he said, shifting his weight from one leg to another but never looking away. Well shit. He was right. Perhaps his surroundings weren't the only thing he took in that first night he arrived. He had absorbed a few things about me as well, although how I'll never know. I cursed in my mind, hoping my expression remained unchanged on the exterior. If it didn't? He never mentioned it. Wise man. Or just a man who didn't want dehydrated poultry when he got out.

"This? I have to think about. It is not policy to look after an inmate's livestock while they sit for sleeping naked in a park. Care, custody and control ends at the gate, Woods."

"Kane." he reminded me gently and stepped back to wander the yard.

My head was full of racing thoughts. Fucking chickens! Of all the shit I had ever heard? Chickens were unique. He caught me off balance, that's for sure! New one on me. As the sun warmed my skin; my mind turned to these birds and I found concern for them entering my head. Thirst was a damn horrible way to go out, second to drowning or burning alive I supposed. And they couldn't get too far looking for water; the woods were full of foxes, coyotes and raccoons that would just love a Sunday supper of Kane's flock. I had decided before I even knew that I had decided. Dammit, I was going to wind up watching chickens. Fuck. Really? I scanned the yard; spotting Woods watching me with a slightly amused look on his face. Yep, he had me pegged alright. I was not going to let the birds die, no matter how ridiculous this was. Just call me Frank Perdue. He was crafty enough to look away after a second. Smart guy. He knew he had me, but didn't want *me* to know that *he* knew, and risk my refusal because he had figured it out. That I was in fact? A human being.

The loudspeaker crackled, and the Captain informed us yard time was over. The inmates grudgingly lined up to be counted. Kane lingered towards the rear of the line and made sure he fell into step beside me. He glanced my way several times but didn't speak. This guy was smarter than most.

"I'll check them in the morning, before my shift. Any other critters I need to know about? A dog that needs a walk perhaps?" I said as sarcastically as I could muster.

"No dogs. Just the birds. They have nesting boxes along the shed. Probably over a dozen eggs in there by now. Take them all."

"Jeez, thanks Woods."

"Kane. And they are the best eggs you will ever eat."

#

The following morning found me driving up what some would call a road in Rowley. It was more, huge chunks of broken pavement that happened to lie close together than it was an actual road. Still, I maneuvered my Mustang along its length and came to the last house on the left. Fifty feet or so past this last driveway the 'road' did end; gravel turned into dirt which narrowed into a hiking trail.

I studied the domicile of Kane Woods. It was a small house; well built and maintained, with landscaping that blended naturally into the surrounding woodlands. The tree line was dotted with blooming dogwoods; tiger lilies had emerged from the ground and their orange blooms perched atop long stalks and beginning to spread. I looked across the grassy open area between the house and the workshop. It was just as he had described. The shed was smaller and to the left, and the nesting boxes ran along the east side of it. The workshop, a longer building to the right and rear of the yard was locked up and awaiting Kane's return. I followed the slate pathway to cross the yard and found a flock of mismatched chickens calmly wandering the grass, searching for insects and pouncing on any they found. They looked up as I approached, sized me up for a few seconds and after deciding I was no threat? Returned to stalking their prey. As I watched them move about, I couldn't help but smile. They were cool to observe, and I began to understand why people might want to live outside of city limits. It was quiet. It was peaceful here. It took me several minutes to realize what it was. The place was *soothing*. That was a new sensation for me, and I noticed the tension that had been so tightly coiled in my shoulders and spine began to release. Slightly; not more than a fraction of a coil, but it eased none the less. Interesting, and long overdue.

A short few steps found me at the automatic water hook up. It was truly ingenious. A float, like you'd find in a toilet tank, kept the bowl full; when the water dropped below a certain level, the pipe kicked on and stayed on until the bowl refilled. I played with it for about ten minutes; marveling at the simple mechanism and how perfectly it worked. The chickens eyed me curiously as I did this; seemingly amazed that I was so fascinated by this device they had known their whole lives. I thought about my armed robber who left his wallet behind and laughed at myself. Guess I'm not a rocket scientist either, at least not in the eyes of these chickens. I did a quick head count, a skill I had mastered, and determined that all ten hens were present. Kane had asked me to do that as well. I almost forgot to check the nesting boxes, but once I did? I left with 18 eggs. Best eggs, huh? We'll see about that. An omelet was the least I deserved, driving out to East Bumfuck to check chicken water for Christ's sake. I loaded the bucket of eggs in the hatchback and headed back to civilization, shaking my head in amusement of my own actions.

#

The start of my shift found Kane lurking around the catwalk gate to block Three. He looked bored to the casual eye; but I knew he was desperate for a report on his birds. I completed my initial cell checks, and told him under my breath the waterer was working for his 10 feathered ladies. His shoulders relaxed visibly, maybe not to a "normal" person's eye, but I had stayed alive and un-raped thus far by noticing the slightest changes in body language. He was more worried than I had realized, and his relief made me smile. A sincere, warm smile one would give a friend when you've located their lost kitten. He returned it with a genuine one of his own, but it was fleeting seconds as we both remembered where we were and who surrounded us. Jerking ourselves from this moment of shared humanity; we resumed the masks that our respective roles required. I continued my patrol as Queen of the Catwalk, and he focused on peeling some flaking paint from the bars. No further words were spoken between us for the rest of the afternoon.

#

The next evening, as I made my going to chow headcount, he stopped me on the catwalk.

"What did you think of the place?" he asked, his voice hushed.

"It's nice. Quiet."

"Almost makes you feel human again, huh?"

Looking into those amber eyes of his, I searched for the hook; waiting for the punch line to the joke that only he knew. Try as I might? I found none. He was sincere, as far as I could tell anyway. That, and a buck three eighty will get you a cup of coffee.

"Not to worry; there's no catch. I mean it Jimmy. You are spring loaded and on a hair trigger, and I cannot blame you; not after being in here and seeing it for myself. But you seemed a little *less* spring loaded yesterday when you started your shift."

"Whatever, Woods. Lock in until Block 4 gets done eating."

"Kane."

#

That night when I finally got home, it was after midnight. Exhaustion was beginning to set in, the endless days of keeping an explosion at bay had been taking its toll on me while I wasn't looking. I was hungry and tired all at once. Opening the fridge to grab a beer; I spotted the eggs. I smiled and took out three. Why not? I thought, cracking them into the bowl to whisk together. They growled as they hit the hot pan, solidifying into the base of my omelet. One flip to seal it, another two minutes to fully cook and I slid it onto my plate. The first bite made me chuckle softly in the empty apartment. Kane was correct. These were the best fucking eggs I had ever tasted. The son of a bitch was right.

CHAPTER THREE

The following week was violence met by violence again; but it had become my normal and therefore, unremarkable. The fights in the cell blocks continued; some sick quota of blood that had to be met daily and the inmates made sure to pay the tab. The mess was mopped up, doors were slammed shut, and the chaos reigned supreme. The bruised faces and split knuckles became so frequent we barely bothered to track who fought who, or when. It was a blur; a bloody, sweaty writhing blur of inmates trying to not get beat down by beating down on each other. Looking back? We were damn lucky it was only the inmates turning on themselves. We were outnumbered 60 to 1 on a good day. Thank God they hadn't turned on us yet. That knowledge gnawed at all of us in the uniform, though we'd never admit it to each other or even to ourselves. If they ever came at us instead of at each other? We were fucked. Hypervigilance was survival, and we were vigilant, even in our sleep at home; on those rare and festive occasions we could manage a few hours of that.

Kane's sentence had entered its third week; June had somehow become July, and he'd melted into the population. I had started out stopping by his place every other day or so, checking the water and chicken count as well as gathering the eggs. Each time I did, I found myself lingering longer each visit; savoring the quiet of the dappled sunshine in the woods. He knew, and although he never mentioned it again? My 'uncoiling' was noticed no matter how slight or fleeting, and he nodded every day I came from his place into work. By the time that third Wednesday came around? I was making daily visits and earlier in the day, exploring further down the quiet paths to the river with each step of my feet in my boots softened by the forgiving Earth beneath them. It was a stark contrast to the sounds they made on the catwalk and the iron stairs. There were a lot of tracks down those meandering paths; raccoons, skunks, squirrels, coyotes, cats and a very large dog judging by the size of the paw prints. I mentioned them to Kane one time, explaining the paw prints were the size of my hands and expressed concern for the chickens should they stray too far. He assured me that in all of the years he had lived there? The cats, dogs, or coyotes never approached too close to his home, and the chickens knew to stay out of the woods.

"So, the birds are smarter than I gave them credit for, huh?" I said, and he smiled and snorted a bit.

"There are many things in this world not as smart as a chicken." He exclaimed, raising his hands and shrugging his shoulders. "I am a prime example. A forty-two-year-old man who can't keep track of the calendar, and wakes up naked in a park surrounded by cops. Who now sits here, needing you to check on his birds."

His comment interested me but he offered no further details, and before I could ask another fight broke out in Block 2. All in a night's work. The violence had become so routine we expected it. There were no good reasons; a perceived 'punking off' of someone, a missing cigarette lighter, someone using the last of the toilet paper without telling his cellmates. The constant elbow to elbow, jam packed quarters of the inmate populace were sparks looking for a place to land; and the jail was a tinderbox.

#

The first week of July, twenty-five days into Kane's court ordered stay with us; New England found itself gripped in a strangle hold of an oppressive heat-wave.

Temperatures were hovering around 100 degrees, and the air was so thick with moisture it seemed to smother sound. The jail was too hot for daytime trouble. The inmates just lay in their cells, desperate to escape even for a moment and some even took to laying on the concrete floors for any respite. Once the sun went down? That was a whole different story. Tempers flared in the sardine can of a jail, and no sooner did one skirmish get broken up than another erupted on a different cell block. My evenings were spent running from one incident to another, barely having enough time to jot down the names of the participants in my pocket notebook before scrambling to stop another round of combat. It was exhausting and it wore everyone thin; inmate and officer alike.

That was also the week that Hector Martinez arrived at Lawrence Jail. At age 28 he had already done a six-year bid in Walpole for attempted rape and aggravated assault, and that wasn't his first time in prison. He strutted through cell block 4, casually dropping his towel on the way to the showers and leered at me. The kind of leering that makes a woman want to take a shower to scrub off the residue of filth his eyes left on your skin. He watched my every move, and although this was not the first time I had encountered a maggot like this? I had zero patience for this prick. It was too hot, the hours were too long, and I was too damn tired. He read my name off the uniform name tag.

"I always liked the taste of Jameson." he said, licking his teeth. I glared into the blackness of his eyes wanting to slap the shit out of him. Absolute fucking scumbag. Normally? I would have pretended not to have heard him, refusing to provide him the satisfaction, but it was not a normal day.

"Shut your fucking mouth, you maggot piece of shit."

He grinned, and looked me up and down, sizing me up.

"You're feisty. I like them feisty. The more fight, the better."

I whacked the keys against the bars in front of his face, taking a small pleasure in him flinching and stepping back. Still, he kept looking me up and down, eyes lingering on my chest, crotch and ass. I consciously wished he'd get involved in a fight, giving me an excuse to take him down a little harder than was necessary. Again, not my normal thoughts, but this was not a normal night. Just then, a small scuffle started on the flats of Block 2, and I was gone.

#

Several hours later, the Block 3 inmates were returning from the chow hall and the catwalk door of Block 4 was opened. I don't know which officer was responsible, but the results were disastrous. The Block 4 inmates spilled down the stairs and crashed into the inmates from three, and an absolute melee ensued. Punches were flying, shanks were used, and it was a miracle from God Himself no one was killed. Once we had most of them down, cuffed or otherwise corralled? The rest were stuffed into their respective cell blocks.

Over sixteen inmates required some sort of medical treatment, two of which were serious enough to need a hospital run; shop talk for putting the inmates in handcuffs and leg irons and driving them to a civilian hospital under armed guard. Word got down to the administration in Salem, and I guess the powers that be had about had it with the constant fights within the walls. Blanket discipline was ordered directly from the Sheriff; every inmate involved was to lose their good time and spend the next two days in lockdown. And in that group of parties involved, was an inmate named Kane Woods.

#

I learned of his involvement as I brought the third bleeding inmate from Block 4 to the infirmary. Kane was sitting on the exam table, two right knuckles split wide, and a mouse was forming under his left eye. I did a double take. I was honestly surprised to see him there. My brow furrowed as I looked at him. He met my gaze but remained silent. After the inmate I had escorted went in with the nurse and another officer, I cocked my head at him; a silent question of *what the fuck*?

"Martinez." was all he said, and he stared at the wall. He sat rigid and upright; jaw clenched in anger. His amber eyes seemed a bit brighter for some reason. In fact, the color of them had changed too. They were more yellow. Gold even. Maybe it was because of the adrenaline from the fight, maybe the lighting in the room, but I swear they almost glowed. I dismissed that detail and stepped in front of him, eliminating his escape of staring at the wall, which forced him to look directly at me.

"What the fuck, Kane?" I asked aloud this time.

"I have excellent hearing Jimmy. Excellent." Still, he smiled. Smiling? This guy's a whack job.

"What the fuck are you grinning about? You've got a nice shiner coming up there, and your knuckles are junk. You a nut job or what?" I asked him, and *Dammit* if he didn't smile wider! White teeth, eyes all lit up? Maybe he was crazy after all.

"Well?" I demanded.

"You finally called me Kane."

Jesus, Mary and Joseph! I had. He was right. Well, so what if I had? I looked at him; he was still smiling and I felt a pang of remorse for what I had to tell him. I let his smile stay for a minute, really wishing I didn't have to say what I was about to tell him the punishment was going to be and what it would mean for him specifically. It occurred to me that my feeling anything close to remorse was beyond out of character for me, but I stuffed that thought down for exploring later. I told him the news.

"The word has come down from the powers that be. The Sheriff himself ordered it, and he's got the legal authority to do it. Two days lock down for all of you."

"No sweat. Got this."

"Yeah, I know. But they're also stripping everybody's good time, Kane."

The color drained from his face; his shoulders slumped at my words. He hung his head for the first time since he had walked into the booking room, and slowly shook his head back and forth; as if refusing to believe it would stop it from being true. He looked defeated, and that took me by surprise; as did the fact that it bothered me that he looked that way. Oh yes, there were many things I was going to have to *explore* and *sort through* after this night was done but now was not the time. Finally, he raised his head just enough to speak. Quietly, but not a whisper quiet; more like a resignation.

"I can't do more than twenty-seven days, Jimmy."

"Diana."

He looked up, eyes squinted slightly in confusion; as if he was unsure what I had said or if he had heard it correctly.

"Diana." I repeated, "My name, is Diana."

A broad smile spread slowly across his mouth; the biggest one I'd ever seen on him. His teeth were not only white; they were big. The smile reached his eyes, which still seemed too bright, but I blamed the room's lighting and the roller coaster of events that had just occurred within the past two hours. Still wearing the smile, he nodded approvingly.

"Diana. Goddess of the Hunt. And of the Moon, and of all wild places and things." he said, softly chuckling. "Ironic, yet perfect."

Before I could ask what he remotely meant? My radio crackled and I was summoned to escort more of the walking wounded to the infirmary.

#

It was almost midnight when we all finally got into the control room to start the reports, and it was obvious we would all be writing many so the Captain put on a fresh pot of coffee. I grabbed a stack of blank incident reports and straddled a stool near the corner of a desk. Thumbing through the pocket notebook trying to figure out which report to start with, I overheard my fellow officer and friend Scotty talking about the hospital run he had just gotten back from.

"...he was fucked up man, Woods did a number on him." Scotty was saying, and I discovered I was listening intently to his story. "Broken nose, knocked out a tooth, cracked two more. Took four stitches to close the lip and another six over the eye to get that shut."

"Who did you take to Lawrence General, Scotty?" I asked

"Martinez. The fucking rapist. Block 4. He's back up there now; crying like a bitch and hurting like Hell I'm sure. His face is hamburger and his body took a good beating too. Next thing you know; Martinez is going to be plotting some payback bullshit. Just what we need, *ANOTHER* reason for these fucking assholes to start fighting."

"Took three of us to get Woods off him." Andy, another fellow officer, said.

"No shit, right?" Scotty retorted. "When those doors opened? Woods went straight at him; like it was a personal mission or something. Wonder if they know each other from the street. Maybe Martinez did something to his sister or something. I thought he was going to kill him right there on the floor."

"Who the fuck knows why any of these guys do what they do." I said, silently praying my voice stayed steady. Nobody said anything different, and I returned to thumbing through my notebook and clicking my pen. I took an extra-long time before I started writing my reports. I had to wait for my hands to stop shaking.

#

It was a long drive home when I finally started that way around two thirty in the morning. Thoughts raced in my mind. Kane almost killed Martinez; right there on the floor of Lawrence and with his bare hands. What the fuck was that about? *I have excellent hearing* he said. What? Jesus Christ! Tell me this guy is all psycho protective because I check the chicken water. Nah, knock it off; it isn't about me. Maybe he had heard the charges against Martinez. Violent assault and rape don't sit well with most inmates, that's got to be what Kane meant by *excellent hearing*. Those thoughts spilled into another topic. Why, did I feel bad that Kane lost his good time? Sure, he wasn't your typical inmate; but what the fuck did I really care? I chewed these questions the whole drive home and in the front door. Disgusted with the situation, the world, and even myself, I tossed my keys on the counter and grabbed a beer. Two of these, about three hours sleep, and start it all over again Jimmy.

Welcome to your life.

Your nightmare.

Your Hell.

On the installment plan.

Chapter Four

Strangely enough, when my eyes opened the following morning? The world seemed a little brighter. And strangely enough, my mood began to match it. While it was an odd feeling, and it wasn't close to being happy, for a few brief moments? The sun felt good on my face, the coffee was rich, and the eggs were good. Oh yes, the eggs. If nothing at all, at least I had good eggs, and that made me half smile, half laugh. I'd be missing those for sure once Kane got out. Any contact with inmates after their release was strictly prohibited by the department, and as the only female officer? I had zero wiggle room there. Still, thanks to the fiasco of last night; I'd now have five more days of eggs instead of one and a half. And while it was based on pure selfishness? It was my one glimmer of something not awful in this endless sea of terrible. Finishing the third cup of coffee and my fourth cigarette; I grudgingly donned my uniform. Back to the dungeon. Back into the breech; one more time.

#

I must confess; the lock down of all of Block 3 and the catwalk of Block 4 made the shift less chaotic. Not only had over 25% of the population been locked into their cells for two days, the word of the lost good time had spread and it seemed to make at least some of the natives a little less aggressive. No, it wasn't anywhere close to Kumbaya and holding hands; but one or two fights compared to seven? It made the night seem almost easy. I could get used to this.

Although they were locked in; the inmates of three and four still had to be counted. Being a creature of habit can get you hurt, or worse when you work in a jail. Inmates have nothing to do for twenty-four hours a day, seven days a week, but to watch you, study you, and see if there's a predictable pattern. If one ever emerges, they can exploit it against you; either planning a distraction to cover up something else, to plan an escape, or to plot your bodily harm. It was a daily conscious effort on my part to change something up every day, and each day make sure whatever I changed was different than the day before. Oh, they may still 'get over' on me, shop talk for get away with something, and they may still 'get' me; but I wasn't about to draw them a 'how to' map. Change up? Keeps them guessing.

This evening, I decided to change up the order of my count. I've done it before, but tonight it seemed a good variable to throw their way. I started my catwalk count from cell block 4 instead of the expected cell block 1. As I said, simple changes keep them from being one hundred percent sure of what you were going to do next, which in turn makes it harder to lay in ambush. They'll still come on a full-frontal attack; no variable in the world will change that if they decide they're coming for you, but you do what you can to prevent a well-planned sneak attack. At least you can see the frontal assault coming, even if you've only got a half second to see it.

It's better than the whack to the back of the skull you never saw coming, and at least you've got half a fighting chance. I threw open the gate to the catwalk of 4 and made my way down the narrow walkway, maybe four feet wide from the wall of the cells to the chain link fencing that stretched from the ceiling above to the floor of the guard level tier below. The fencing had been installed years earlier after a riot. The inmates had been dropping TVs, bed frames, burning mattresses and even other inmates that they hated off the upper levels of the jail onto the heads of the responding officers below them;

clearly injuring some and reducing the effectiveness of the officers' response to stop the riot. Lessons learned; precautions taken. Never a safety guarantee, but it's better than it was.

Cell 41 had a count of five, cell 42 had five as well, but it was cell 43 that made me stop. Martinez was in 43. I stood by the barred doors, counting, and he slowly stood up from the bunk and stepped into a better lit part of the cell. Wow, Scotty was right. He *was* fucked up. Six stitches over his left eye, which was swollen almost completely shut. Under both eyes was blackened like a raccoon thanks to the broken nose that was quite swollen as well. His top lip was split with four tidy little stitches holding that together and though he wore a tank top in the steamy air, I could see four separate clusters of bruises on his torso. Jesus. Kane really was trying to kill him. Martinez took another step, wincing in pain, and narrowed his eyes at me. I simply continued to count heads out loud as if nothing was different. When I reached the number five, I jotted it down in the trusty notebook and moved down the tier to the final two cells. I exited the cell block, stepped out of sight of Block 4 and smiled. Couldn't have happened to a nicer guy.

#

Breaking up any pattern yet again; I descended to the guard level, crossed the floor and came up a different flight of stairs to count Blocks 2 and then 1; in that order. These are the little shifts in behavior that can keep you alive, and I had been doing them for so long they were second nature now. My final cell block to count was now Three. Instead of starting at cell 31 and moving down the tier, I entered the tier and went fully down the end, starting at cell 35 working back to cell 31. Again, little things really, but little things can add up quickly in a place like this. Each cell had five inmates in it as well, pathetic that jail cells built for three inmates maximum, now housed five. But that's the hand I was dealt. When I reached cell 32, the residents were playing spades, save for one Kane Woods. He was sitting quietly over in the dimmer part of the cell, staring out the cell window across the open span to the huge window that revealed outside. The sun had already set, and the first stars were popping out in the darkening horizon. When I started counting heads out loud, he glanced my way, nodded and half grinned. I finished my count, gave him a head tilt hello, and moved down to cell 31. I finished that count and was about to step through the cell block gate when it occurred to me to go back to 32. I stepped back to the cell window area, which was about three feet away from the cell doorway. Kane was still sitting there, but he turned towards me when I reappeared.

"Hey Woods, c'mere a second, would you?" I said, and he stood up and came to the barred window. He was much closer to me than before, and I scanned his face. No black eye. Not even a hint of a bruise. What the Hell was that about?

"How's the hand?' I asked, and he subconsciously flinched. He appeared to be about to either put it behind him or shove it in his pocket, but he recognized that I was aware of his intentions and just stood still. His shoulders dropped slightly for a fraction of a second, then he shrugged.

"It's ok I guess." Was all he said.

"Let me see it, would you?"

Again, fleeting drop of the shoulders, and he stared down for a few seconds before raising his right hand. He held it up next his face, which was still angled slightly downward, and met my eyes from the tops of his. They still seemed bright, not quite the glowing I remembered, or had I imagined that part last night in the infirmary? I moved my eyes from his to the hand.

The knuckles had only thin, cat claw looking scratches on them now; no redness and not the gaping splits from twenty-four hours ago. I returned my eyes to his, examining every fleck of yellow gold in them, seeking answers to questions I didn't dare ask out loud. I didn't know what to say never mind what to do, so I slowly nodded, never taking my eyes from his.

If I didn't know better, I'd swear there was a hint of relief in his, blended with an unspoken plea for me not to ask anything more. I stepped back from the cell window and exited Block 3, keying my radio to call in my count. The night wrapped up quietly; no major brawls, no infirmary trips, and no hospital runs. I got out of work a mere hour and a half later than scheduled and was pleased to even consider a night with more than three hours sleep. I could get used to this lockdown mode. We should have done it long ago, and I imagined for a blissful moment alternating daily lock downs. What a sweet rest that would be! I shook my head to clear the closest thing I'd felt to happiness in some time. No, the ACLU would sue the shit out of us for locking down for the sake of locking down. Still, it was a pleasant fantasy for a minute.

CHAPTER FIVE

The following day I got called in three hours early, so instead of starting at three in the afternoon my boots hit the catwalk at noon. Trayed up lunches were being dispersed to those in lockdown, and the catwalk level of Block 3 was first up. Opening the gate, the inmate trustees began bringing them down to each cell. I stood outside of the cell block gate, as each cell had an individual control to open the door. Since the doors to the cells were barred type doors, they hadn't been fitted with food port openings so each individual cell had to be opened, food given out, and then closed. Once all five cells were fed, it was up to the officer to enter the cell block and manually ensure the cell doors had locked. Inmates were famous for jamming a little piece of wood, cloth, wadded up paper or anything else they could imagine in an attempt to prevent the latch from securing completely.

If unchecked; those cell doors become revolving doors, and the inmates would pop the doors open at will to wander the tier, free to do whatever they see fit and then they can return to their cells and lock themselves in. This can lead to the mystery of who beat inmate so and so to death in his cell when everybody was locked in other cells becoming a reality. I check every cell door, more than once. I was performing just this task on cell 32 when Kane stepped into the doorway opening. He looked at me, the half grin on his face, then jutted his chin towards the window outside. I glanced over my shoulder at the sun, which was already turning Lawrence into a sauna.

"What's up?" I asked.

"I should be walking out the door into that." He said. His eyes squinted, as if he physically felt pain at that thought and winced. "Twenty-six and a half days right about now."

I stood there silent; no words would ever suffice. What the Hell could I say? Yeah, he got caught up in one major brawl, but I can't honestly say I was sorry for who he tangled with and how much damage he had inflicted on Martinez. I was a little envious truth be told, Kane got to *DO* what I would have enjoyed doing, if only for that moment. Then again, I got to leave at the end of the tour. Sort of anyway.

"Check my birds tomorrow, would you Jimmy?" he asked, and stepped back into the cell.

Something was off about him today, but I couldn't put my finger on it. He seemed restless, more than I'd ever seen him display before. Maybe it was a bit of regret at having lost his good time and having to sit for three and a half more days. Maybe he was tired of being cooped up in that cell with four other guys. Lockdown is bad enough when the cell is only holding the intended number of inmates, it can't be easy with two more crammed in there.

Maybe he just wanted to go home and have an omelet. But I know for a fact, that up until that afternoon? I'd never seen him pace in the cell. And the longer into my shift it got, the more agitated his pacing became. What the shit? Did somebody bring in cocaine or something? His cell mates weren't wired up, so I ruled that unlikely. By the time I did my final count just before eleven PM, he seemed ready to explode in there. I looked at him quizzically, silently asking are you going to be ok? Kane just flashed that toothy grin of his, waved his now completely healed hand at me, and wished me a good night.

#

The phone jolted me awake, and no big surprise, it was Lawrence jail calling and asking me to come in for the day shift. Great! Once again, no day off. I scrambled out of the shower, donned the last clean uniform I had and headed in for another long day. Shit, the lockdown was going to be lifted this afternoon, and we'd once again be dealing with the full population moving about the place. More than the full population, the count had reached 302 inmates last night. Fucking insanity. I swilled down coffee and chain smoked the entire drive to work, dreading the day. I stepped on the guard floor at 7:05 AM knowing there was a pretty good chance they'd ask me to work a double, and it would probably be after midnight before I left again. Here we go again boys and girls; back to the clusterfuck.

#

The cells of Block 1 and 2 were already open, as was the guard level and flats of Block 4. Inmates wandered about, yelling in English and several dialects of Spanish, and it was already muggy inside the granite walls. We got them fed without incident; even the inmates sensed the approaching heat of the day and had resigned themselves to sweating and misery. I could only hope half of them would try to sleep through the heat, reducing the encounters with each other and the possibility of an eruption of personalities. The catwalk of Block 4 got breakfast trays first, and after they were fed I entered the tier and checked the doors were in fact secured. Martinez stood in the doorway of cell 43, his face still bruised and swollen. His eyes were more open today, and he glared at me as I yanked the sliding door several times to be positive it had latched. Once I had, I met his gaze.

Eyes so dark the pupils disappeared into the irises, and they glittered with hatred. Hatred for the world, hatred for the officers, and especially hatred for me, a female 'guard'. After securing the final two cells on the tier, I walked past his cell on my way out, glancing in at him. His eyes burned with fury, and he nodded rapidly, as if he had decided on a course of revenge. I made a mental note of it, slammed the cell block gate shut, and met the trustees outside of the catwalk of Block 3. They entered the tier, distributed the trays, and returned to the kitchen below to resume their duties while I went in to check these doors as well.

Kane was standing right up against the cell door, and I motioned for him to take a step back so I could try to slide the door back a few times to ensure it had locked. I'd been around long enough to know you don't grab on to the bars of a cell door when an inmate is standing directly at it. It's too easy for them to reach through the bars and grab you and then you're trapped; either to be stabbed, have them slam your head against the bars, grab the keys, or all three. I had no desire to wind up hurt or handcuffed with my own cuffs inside of a cell, so I stood back and motioned again. He didn't move. Now this? Was another new behavior. He had never once given me anything remotely close to a problem, and while my first reaction was annoyance; I looked in his eyes and saw anything but belligerence. There was absolute terror in them, each gold and yellow fleck was filled with fear; the paralyzing fear you see in a trapped animal's eyes. It took me by surprise, and I have no doubt my expression betrayed my shock at the sight.

"Jimmy!" he whispered, so harshly he almost hissed it. Okay, now I was even more surprised. Whatever the fuck was going on was way beyond normal fear, and it more than troubled me. He motioned for me to come closer, and I glanced behind him in the cell. The other four inmates were sprawled out on their bunks having already inhaled their breakfasts; getting ready to ride out another sweltering day locked in a tiny cage inside of a larger cage. Deciding this was no set up I took a half step closer, still reasonably far enough to have half a chance at dodging if Kane decided to try and grab me. His eyes never moved from mine, and he lowered his head far enough to rest the bridge of his nose on the cross bar supports. Ok, nobody about to try to snatch you does that. That's the fastest way to get your own face smashed in against the bars. Jesus, did he know that? Did he do that in silent reassurance that he was not about to try to harm me?

Looking at him again, yes. Yes, he did. I took a quarter step closer and he nodded; non-verbally thanking me for my trusting him. Jesus Christ, this was important to him life and death important, and if Kane was rattled this much by it? I'd damn sure better pay attention.

"Jimmy, you were supposed to be off today. What the *fuck* are you doing here?"

My knee jerk reaction was to go off on him. What the Christ did he mean what am I doing here? Have you *NOT* looked around this place? He'd been here a full four weeks! 150 plus inmates over capacity; officers so exhausted they are more the dead who don't know they've died and therefore don't lie down, and just keep going. *Another* day of over 100 degrees' heat index, *AND* Blocks 3 and 4 are getting let out today. And who the fuck is this guy to be asking me anything in the first place? Are you kidding me? One look at his face and into his eyes, and my temper extinguished. This man was petrified; almost to the point of insanity.

A dark curtain of dread fell over me. I didn't know why, but I knew something bad was going to go down and Kane Woods was tied into it. The thought of that made the curtain feel heavier, and his intense urgency darkened it more.

"You have to get out of here. One shift Jimmy. That's it. No double today." He said. He spoke quietly, so that only I would hear his words, but with such conviction behind them he almost snarled them to me. I opened my mouth to say something and he raised an index finger to stop me, like one would a child. Had he not had me freaked out already? I'd have let three months of blood-soaked uniforms, shitty sleep and not enough of it; and absolute mental exhaustion loose on him full force. Instead, I closed my mouth.

"I am not kidding. This is deadly serious. You cannot work a double today. You need to leave, you *HAVE* to leave, at three this afternoon. You *HAVE* to." His speech had slipped from insistence to pleading and was circling dangerously towards begging. He glanced down the tier, and then right back to my eyes. I had never seen such desperation before, nor have I since, then I saw in that moment. He hung his head down, stared at the floor, then looked back up at me. I swear to God, I thought he was about to cry. The next few seconds proved my thinking correct. He looked up to the ceiling, drew a long, ragged breath, and looked back at me one more time.

"You cannot be here tonight."

In the three and a half years of working behind these walls; I had been in a lot of scary situations; more of them than I care to think about. I had seen things that still give me nightmares, and sometimes to this day make me nauseous; but I'd only ever been scared twice. Both times; it was meeting the gaze of a through and through, pure, cold blooded murderer. It had made my spine go artic, and it served as a reminder of exactly the types of inmates I dealt with. Looking at Kane? His movements and seeing his utter terror; frightened me more than the previous two encounters combined. For the *second* time in a month I found myself standing flat footed directly in front this man, except this time it wasn't over chickens. The hair on the back of my neck was on end, and I shuddered as an icy chill travelled through me. It was already almost ninety degrees on the catwalk, and I had goosebumps. I swallowed, trying to force some saliva to form in my mouth as it had turned into a desert. It was then, that he reached the healed right hand out through the bars and took my hand in it.

"Diana, please. Please, you cannot be here tonight. I can't stop it. It has already started. I am begging you; do *not* work a double. I cannot take it if you do. I am losing my fucking mind just seeing you here now. Promise me, Jesus Christ! *Promise me*, you will leave at three. Promise me Diana! Swear it, on whatever it is you hold most sacred, but do it. And leave. I will get on my knees and beg, I don't care. You absolutely cannot work a double. I cannot handle the thought of you being here tonight. Please! Promise me."

In the thirty-three years I had walked the planet? I had never experienced such pure intense emotion from another human being, no matter that it was fear radiating from him. There was no shadow to hide behind. This was cruelly honest and it had to be faced, as terrifying as it was. Before I realized it; I had nodded my head and sworn that I would not work a double shift.

Kane released my hand as I watched relief wash over him like a bucket of cool water. He hung his head back, exhaled, and thanked me. Bewildered, I remembered to check the other three cell doors. Only a moment of time had expired, but I felt like I'd travelled through the entire galaxy over decades, and the weariness of the previous three months settled in on my frame.

I don't really remember much of the remainder of the morning; I had gone mentally numb. The one thing that stuck with me was the gnawing of fear I felt around the perimeter of my thoughts, and I avoided conversation with inmates and officers alike.

#

It was shortly after one PM when the order came to pop loose Block 3 and the catwalk of 4. I reluctantly obeyed the call over the radio and released the cell doors of Block 4 first. Martinez strode down to the end of the tier, pressing against the gate; his eyes were burning black coals of anger.

"You know what's gonna happen, right?" he snarled through the bars. I glanced his way, my face resuming the mask of *go fuck yourself* that I had worn so many times before in this job. If I had a penny for every empty venom filled threat or hint of a threat I'd heard, I'd have been retired in Bora Bora two years ago.

"Yeah, yeah, that's right! You know, yeah, you know." He continued, bouncing on his toes like he was actually going to do something. Whatever, you hate women, based on your record of raping and brutally beating them. I'm not 120 pounds, I'm not walking alone in some dark hallway, and I know you're here. Keep banging your gums scumbag, I've got bigger worries today. And that worry, was about to be sprung from the catwalk of Block 3.

I released those doors next, and as expected every inmate poured out of the cramped cells. The catwalk tier wasn't very wide, less than four feet, but after two days in the same square footage with four or five men to a cell? Anything was bigger and welcome. Some of the inmates simply walked down two doors to enter a buddy's cell which I found amusing; get out of one matchbox cell just too go right back into another, but I guess it was just the change of scenery. Kane was the last to emerge, and he stared right at me and mouthed, *GO*. The air around me wasn't hot anymore, my blood temperature had seemed to have dropped, and I shook off another chill as I walked towards Block 2 to see what the waving inmate wanted. Turned out, he needed toilet paper.

Chapter Six

It was 2:45 that afternoon when the accident happened. I still can't believe it did, but it was one of those freak things that requires the stars and planets align *just so* for it to happen. Lockdown for afternoon count had gone smoothly and it was just about shift change. Through some miracle, the second shift had enough officers that I could honor my promise and not pull a double shift. The door from the inside of the jail into the control room was a monstrous, four inches thick, iron door designed to withstand any fire, riot or bullet. As the second shift emerged out on the guard floor to relieve us, those of us who had worked the first shift headed into the control room. I had just lit a cigarette and was about four strides away when I dropped my lighter. I stopped to pick it up and continued towards the door. A half second difference either way, and it never would have happened. The officer ahead of me; my buddy Scotty, didn't realize I was coming and swung the door shut behind him. I reached out with my left hand to catch it but I missed its edge. My hand slid into the control room at the exact moment the massive door was slamming shut. It caught me on the wrist between the door's edge and the wall, and everybody in the control room heard the crack of bone. I heard it the loudest, because I also felt it, and I ripped my hand back.

"*FUCK*!" I roared, clutching my wrist and bending over in pain. Scotty wheeled around horrified.

"Oh my God Jimmy! Fuck! Fuck! Oh my God, how bad?" he yelled, coming back out of the control room. I clenched my wrist as tight as possible, squeezing my eyes shut as if not seeing it would make it hurt less. My attempt was unsuccessful; it throbbed faster than my own heartbeat, and was stronger. I opened my eyes and looked at my wrist with dread. It was already swollen, there was some blood, and it had never been at that angle before nor had it ever been intended to be at that angle.

"It's fucking broken, I can tell you that much." I rasped through my teeth.

"Fuck." Scotty said when he saw it.

"Ya think?" I asked, and I couldn't help it. I started to giggle in my agony.

"You're driving me to the hospital Scotty. Right fucking now. And we're going Code 3. I want lights and sirens."

"Yeah, yeah Jimmy, of course. I'll get the keys to the cruiser." he stammered.

I stood up, exhaled hard, and looked behind me back into the jail. The second shift guys were looking at my wrist, their faces grimaced in sympathy. They knew that it had to hurt. A silhouette standing behind the catwalk gate to Block 3 caught my eye. Kane. How the Hell was he out of his cell? I know I checked those doors. His form relaxed when he saw it was my wrist, and that I was injured but not under attack, and he slipped back into the gloom of the cell block. Well Kane, looks like I'm not working a double today for sure now! I'm not working any shifts for a while it seems. Good thing I had banked all that extra time; I was going to need it.

Scotty returned, jingling the keys. While this was not a life-threatening emergency anybody will tell you, it's fun to use the lights and siren. I was going to be sidelined for a while. I was going to have some fun with the cruiser.

"Don't stop for a single light, Scotty. I'll kill you if you do."

#

An emergency room, in the smallest of places, takes a long time. In a city like Lawrence, it's a quagmire of gunshot victims, car accidents, stabbings, overdoses and normal stuff like heart attacks and imminent births. Obviously, those patients get priority over a broken wrist, uniform or not. We sat in the ER of Lawrence General Hospital for hours before I was even examined. Another hour and a half waiting for an X-ray, plus another hour for them to be read. Tack on more time for the orthopedic guy to show up and set the wrist, and we had spent seven and a half hours in the hospital. Scotty felt awful and after my relentless teasing for an hour; I finally let him off the hook. I assured him it was the freakiest accident I'd ever heard of, but at least I had about three months in the bank for shifts owed me. He felt a little less guilty, but he really lightened up when I laughed and said I'd finally be getting some well-earned rest, and maybe even some sunshine while he would be pulling more doubles than he had already been.

"Besides Scotty, I'm a righty. I can still open a beer, light a cigarette, and if need be pull a trigger. I can even tie my shoes. The fingers still work." I said, holding up my left hand and wiggling the fingers now half encased in a plaster cast. He shook his head, smiled and agreed, but insisted on buying the first 12 pack.

"Better make it a full case. I don't have to work tomorrow."

It was almost 11 PM when we got back into the marked cruiser to head back to the jail. No need for Code 3 heading back to the damn place; so we just drove regular through the city, making the twelve-block drive in less than twenty minutes. I got out of the cruiser and started up the stairs to turn in the doctor's reports to the OIC for the shift and write yet another incident report, this one covering the timeline of my now broken wrist.

The smell was first.

It was wrong; not the normal Lawrence jail perfume of sweat and misery. It reeked of iron; a metallic tang in the air that hung so thick it had a taste. Curious as to the source, I turned down the left hallway leading to the gate to the control room. I stopped dead in the hall, frozen where I stood. The iron barred gate was open; it had been blown or ripped off the hinges. My heart, which had stopped; started again, pounding in my chest. I could hear my blood rushing in my ears. That's when I looked at the floor.

A dark, syrupy substance coated the floor. It was still somewhat wet, but it looked sticky.

I knew what it was; I just couldn't fathom the volume of what it was.

Blood.

More blood than I have ever seen in the world; covering the floor, the walls and spattered across the ceiling and starting to congeal. My entire body was shaking. My brain retreated into a blinding white light; it knew what surrounded me, it simply couldn't process that it was indeed a reality. How was there so much of it? How? Horror swallowed me when I remembered the head count at 2:45 PM that afternoon. 305 inmates. My knees buckled momentarily, and I used my good wrist to steady myself against the wall. Scotty came up behind me just then, I had heard his boots coming but I couldn't speak. I heard his footsteps stop exactly as mine had, and I turned to see a reflection of the horror and shock I was feeling.

"Jimmy?" he slowly said, "Is that?"

"Blood." I finished for him.

"What the fuck?"

"Scotty, you have a radio, right?" He nodded. "Get on band one. We need the Sheriff, the Staties, and the Feds here. Like yesterday. Get on it, Emergency Code 1. Now."

He nodded, and somehow found his voice long enough to make the radio call.

Lawrence Jail. Disaster of epic proportions to say the least. The sirens screamed towards us almost immediately. We could hear them getting closer, and we both slumped into the wooden bench that visitors used to sit and wait for their visit time. I lit a cigarette, and Scotty, never a smoker, took it from my hand. We sat in silence beside each other, smoking, and waiting for help to arrive. Too bad we hadn't gotten the beer yet. If ever there was a time for a drink? It was then.

#

It was nearly two hours later when the State police, FBI and of course our own department had secured a command center and documented the entry to the control room thoroughly enough where we could enter the actual jail. Stepping into the vestibule of the control room, behind the door that had broken my wrist the afternoon before; I looked to the right. The cell assignment chart was shellacked with blood; below it on the desk was an arm. A human arm, just lying there as if that was where it belonged. The floor beside the key cabinet was littered with several other limbs; a sneakered foot, a shredded torso, a hand, another arm but only from the elbow down. I scanned the room, unable to feel emotion or form a thought. It was overwhelming and unbelievable in its scope. I stepped forward again and entered the jail.

Nothing could prepare anyone for this. It was carnage; complete, utter, unbearable carnage. Bodies were ripped apart; a quick survey of the guard level revealed only two intact bodies and they both wore blue uniform shirts. Their throats were gone, gaping holes where a windpipe should have been. Theirs was a quick death it seemed. Brutal, but quick compared to the dismemberment spread around them. The open floor of the guard level was littered with appendages and broken bodies, an insurmountable pile of death from the gates of Block 1 to Block 4.

Instinctively, I looked up to the catwalk; my domain. The same view greeted me. It was a warehouse of mannequin parts, various legs and arms strewn about waiting to be reassembled into posing figures displaying the upcoming fashions for the season. Only these weren't mannequin parts. Every single one had come from a once intact human body. The cell block gates were all thrown open, both on the catwalk and the guard level. I noticed a set of keys still dangling from the catwalk gate of Block 1, blood across the brass keys. An inmate, or what was left of one, was crumpled below them. Trying to free his fellow inmates or get inside and save himself; I would never know.

I didn't want to know. I turned slowly in a circle, taking in the wreckage of humans that surrounded me, and my vision settled on the catwalk gate to Block 4. I was moving across the floor before I knew it, climbing the stairs towards that iron door that had been ripped off the ancient hinges that up until tonight had withstood any assault.

Stopping at the entrance to the tier, I stepped over what might have been two or four inmates, I couldn't begin to try to piece together what part went to what, and strode down to cell 43; the last known residence of one Hector Martinez.

I recognized him because of a tattoo he had on his left forearm. The coiled cobra was still visible. The rest of him was unidentifiable. He had attempted to hide in the corner of the cell and was obviously; located. His body was sprawled across the tiny metal cell desk, and he had been ripped open from throat to gut. He had also been eviscerated, and based on his bloody finger marks on the wall; he was still alive when it happened. My brain sparked up enough to form one thought. Couldn't have happened to a nicer guy. I stepped back out of the cell and exited Block 4. I was stepping over pieces of inmates like I was hopping stones across a creek, and I entered the catwalk of Block 3 passing right by cell 31 and headed directly into cell 32.

Here too, I discovered another massacre. There was hardly anything recognizable as having once been a whole, living human being. Parts were strewn from one side of the cell to another, and the same littered the tier and even the outer catwalk. I felt a deep stab of sadness as I thought of Kane. He had known, and he had warned me. Tears stung my eyes, and I furiously wiped them away before continuing my survey of the jail.

There was no noise. No sounds travelled within the walls, save for the occasional retching of an investigator. I realized that I hadn't thrown up. I had not even gagged yet. I had to be in shock. This was too much for me not to be. I staggered down the stairs, glancing into the flats of the cellblocks as I passed them. Piles of destroyed humans sprinkled randomly amongst scattered parts of others. It was overwhelming.

I made my way outside and into the fresh air, inhaling deeply; even the stink of the city was sweet and clean compared to that metallic smell of blood inside the jail. I closed my eyes and just tried to remember to breathe. After some time, it must have worked, because for the first time in five hours? My wrist started to hurt. I sat on the granite steps outside of the jail, staring at the swollen silver orb that hung amongst the stars and at last puked over the side rail. At least I was still human. I lit another cigarette and waited to be interviewed by the FBI and State police.

#

The sun was high and far past the noontime sky when I was finally permitted to leave. I was ordered not to speak to another soul about what I had seen, as was Scotty. The Feds had taken control of the situation and would be disseminating all statements. I could not have cared less. The entire place had been searched top to bottom and there was not one survivor. No one to tell what happened, no one to argue with whatever cover story they came up with, and that was going to be a doozie for sure.

How exactly, do you explain the slaughter of three hundred and five inmates and seven officers? Had Scotty or I stayed, it would have been nine officers. How did it even happen? Who could have pulled this off? And why? I managed to make the drive home to my apartment and arrived safely in my living room. I popped open the pain pills, swallowing two of them with three beers, back to back. I stripped off my uniform, vowing to set it on fire, and crawled into my bed. I yanked the phone cord out of the wall as I pulled the blanket over me. I had been up for the longest thirty-six hours of my life, and I blissfully surrendered to the 'may cause drowsiness' side effects of the pills and finally? *Slept.*

CHAPTER SEVEN

Daylight greeted me when I opened my eyes again, and I realized two things were pressing. One, I had to pee with a vengeance. Two? My wrist hurt; I must have slept on it wrong because those two pain pills should have had me all set for at least 12 hours. It was throbbing and I took another pill before brushing my teeth. I felt amazingly good; rested for a change, and I guessed that a night of solid sleep had done wonders for my body. I almost smiled before the reality of what had happened crashed down upon me. I melted, a puddle of a woman, sobbing on the floor of my kitchen. I stayed there for twenty minutes. The wails subsided into hiccup cries, and then dwindled into whimpers.

I pulled myself together, regained my feet and my composure, and washed my face. Okay, that at least was out of me. The fact that it happened told me that I could still feel, even if what I felt was the raw pain of overwhelming loss. My humanity had been validated, and that was never a bad thing. I managed to get dressed, and even tie my sneakers. That victory gave me cause to grin; I'd have to tell Scotty. But first, I hadn't checked the mail in days, so I headed downstairs to the mailbox.

One of my neighbors got the daily newspaper, and his was sitting on the doorstep of the entryway where the mailboxes were. I picked it up, and my eyes fell on the date. Tuesday. What? I checked again to be sure. Tuesday July 10, 1990. No way. I had gotten home Sunday evening. Waking up rested but having to pee that badly and my wrist throbbing, made sense now. I had slept for over thirty-six hours. Jesus, did I sleep or did I go into a coma? The latter was a possibility, considering the enormity of what had happened. Maybe I just shut down.

I discarded the mail; it was all junk anyway, and made the short, six-house walk down the street to my favorite hangout. I slid into the stool at the end of the bar and ordered a beer. Might as well, not going to work today thanks to the wrist. I gulped the first few ounces down, delighting in the coldness of it, and let the remainder of it slide smoothly down my throat. I put the empty bottle down on the bar, motioned for another, and glanced up at the TV behind the bar. Footage of Lawrence Jail, fully engulfed in flames, filled the screen. The footage was at night; the sky was aglow from the height of the fire. The caption below read "Boiler Explosion at Jail-No Survivors. I stopped breathing and my head swam, and not from the beer. So, that was the cover story. Un-fucking-believable. Fucking Feds.

I cancelled the second beer, left cash on the bar, and hurried home. Plugging in the phone as the door shut behind me, I turned on the handset and waited for the dial tone. It was there, and I immediately pounded in Scotty's number. He picked up before the third ring, and I just gushed it all out.

"Scotty, did you see this shit? A fucking boiler explosion? Are you kidding me?"

"Jimmy, slow down. Listen, you need to call in to the Sheriff, he wants to meet up with you. They've been calling you for over a day, as have I. I figured you'd unplugged the phone, but they were coming to your house today if you didn't call in. Do it. Now. And don't say another word." And he hung up.

I was speechless. Oh shit, here we go. I hung up, and then dialed the Sheriff's office. The secretary answered on the second ring.

"Essex County Sheriff's Office, how may I direct your call?"

"Yeah, this is Officer Jameson, I was told to..."

"Hold on Officer Jameson, the Sheriff has been awaiting your call." And I was immediately transferred.

"Officer Jameson, we're so glad you called! We've been trying to reach you."

"Yes sir, I heard that. I had unplugged the phone."

"We figured that. Hey, we need you to come in to the office here in Salem, talk about some things. I'm sure you understand."

"Yes sir, I do. I can get there in say, 45 minutes?"

"That'd be great; we'll be expecting you Officer Jameson. See you then." Once again, the phone clicked with a hang up, and I sat there on my bed blinking in disbelief. A furnace explosion? '*WE*' need to talk about some things? Who was '*WE*' exactly? Shit. I brushed my teeth again to get rid of the beer smell, grabbed my keys and drove down to Salem. This was not going to be a good day.

Chapter Eight

I was led into a conference room upon my arrival at the Administration offices and found myself sitting alone for several minutes. The door to my left opened and in stepped the Sheriff and two other men in suits I pegged as Feds. They each had several folders in their hands, and they sat down three abreast across the table from me.

"Good of you to come so quickly, Officer Jameson." The Sheriff began, and added, "How's the wrist?"

"Broken sir, but you knew that already."

"Yes, well, I hope it's not too painful. Which brings me to my next point." He opened a folder and slid a county check across the table to me. "That's a complete pay out of all the time you had banked from Lawrence jail. We figured you'd need to have that during your recovery."

I glanced down at the amount. There was too much money here. Far too much money, and one too many commas before the decimal point. That comma was not preceded by a number one either; it was preceded by a number five. The Sheriff had handed me a check for over half a million dollars. My eyebrow arched, and I looked up at him.

"We've been told that the injury to your wrist is permanent. The damage is so extensive see, that you'll never be able to work in the capacity you did before the injury. The Department felt, in the interest of fairness, that you should be compensated for the loss of your career with the Essex County Sheriff's Department. We hope you find that number to be a fair one." He stood up, nodded, and headed towards the door.

"Okay then Officer Jameson; the County business is finished here. We wish you a speedy recovery and a good future in whatever path you choose. Thank you for your dedication to the Department, and best of luck." He vanished before the door even fully closed, leaving me in the room with these two vipers. I felt a grin cross my face. Yes, indeed. Sheriff was an elected position, and I had just witness political slickness up close and personal. I turned my attention to the men still in the room with me.

They opened their folders and sifted through papers and some 8 by 10 photos. I didn't have to look very hard to recognize jumbled limbs and knew what they had in front of them. They had the actual evidence, and then they had the cover story. It was their job to ensure that the cover story was the only one the public ever heard, and they were measuring me up to determine the best way to approach me to make that happen.

"Officer Jameson," Brown suit began, and I raised my hand to stop him.

"Miss Jameson. If, you please. As you heard, my injury has forced my retirement." They glanced between them, and Brown suit nodded and started again.

"*Miss* Jameson, as you know, there was a terrible accident at Lawrence Jail this past night. The furnace exploded, and there were no survivors. Of course, the Federal Arson investigation is still ongoing, so we cannot comment any further on that until it's complete. We're sure you understand the sensitive nature of this."

"Oh yes. I fully grasp the sensitive nature of an explosion and fire. It's an all-consuming force, leaves hardly any idea of what happened due to its destructive nature."

"Precisely." Brown suit continued. "The investigation could take months, and even then, we may never fully know the exact cause."

I sat up taller in my chair and stared him directly in his right eye. It only took five seconds before he shifted in his seat and glanced over to Blue suit for support.

"I'm quite sure," I said in a low, steady voice, "that no matter the outcome of the investigation? The seven officers surviving family members will be swiftly and generously compensated for the loss of their loved ones while on duty."

"Of course." Blue suit chimed in, "It's already begun."

"Good." I said, "It would be a shame if things didn't go smoothly for them, and the ashes started getting picked through."

They exchanged glances, nodded, and then turned back to me.

"It seems we all understand what's important here Miss Jameson." Blue suit said, and he opened his folder again. He slid a federal check across the table to me. This one didn't start with a five, but a three isn't a bad number either.

"We hope this will help you in your search for a new career path Miss Jameson." They both stood up, and just like the Sheriff before them, disappeared before the door shut behind them. I was left sitting alone in the conference room, unemployed due to "debilitating injury", with two checks totaling over $875,000.00. What the Hell just happened here?

I slid the checks into my pocket and left the Administration Offices for the first and final time. I sat in my car, shaking my head in disbelief, and started the Mustang up. The radio blared a McDonald's commercial. I was forever forgetting to turn the radio back down after I parked, and the breakfast jingle bombarded me at volume 40.

"*Nothing I mean nothing! Can beat an Egg McMuffin, in the mooorning*!" I tuned the dial down as fast as I could, and a wave of sickness came over me.

Eggs. Kane's chickens. Shit. I threw the car in gear and headed for Route One as quickly as traffic would let me. I knew I was going to miss those lights and sirens, but never more than I did right now.

#

It had been five days since I had driven down the hodgepodge of pavement of the 'road' Kane's house sat beside. I pulled in and quickly climbed out of the car, sweeping the yard in search of the birds. Finally, I spotted some movement by the tiger lilies. There they were. One glance assured me the ten were still there, and I walked over to check the waterer. It was full, right to the brim with clean fresh water. I released the breath I hadn't realized I'd been holding in relief. They were ok; thank God for that.

After everything that had happened that week? I don't think I could have withstood another loss, even if it was just a motley bunch of hens. I stood up, and looked around the place, enjoying its peaceful existence. An empty sadness found me again; I felt it as strongly as I had standing in the ruins of cell 32; and felt the burning in my eyes again. Not willing to crumble and shatter for a second time today, I sniffed and walked down towards the paths that led through the woods and down to the river.

I followed their graceful curves into the woods, and sat down beside the water. I watched skim spiders make their way across the surface, oblivious to the dangers of perch lurking just below them. It must be wonderful to be so blind to all the terrible that can happen, and just scoot across the top of the still spots in the river. I let the sun warm me, and it was only when my wrist started to ache that I rose to my feet. I headed back the way I came, glancing up at the canopy of leaves overhead and the birds that flitted beneath them. I bumped my foot against a root as I approached the house, and when I looked down to regain my balance; my heart began pounding.

An enormous paw print was there in the soft earth. I had seen it before; the one belonging to some giant dog, but I had never seen one so close to the yard. Kane's absence this past month must have emboldened the creature, and I immediately worried for the fat hens wandering the lawn. I picked up my pace and headed directly towards the yard. They were still there, but the fact that I had come across two more prints even closer to Kane's house caused me concern. I was going to have to find a chicken fostering agency after all. I didn't feel right about leaving them to fend for themselves with some huge dog circling the place and no one to watch over them.

It was the least I could do. Their protector had watched out for me not three days ago. I had to return the favor to these crazy chickens he enjoyed so much and worried about enough to ask me to check on them, thus starting our odd friendship.

I stopped my walking at that thought. Yes, somehow, despite the opposing roles assigned to us, Kane had become my *friend*. Until an hour ago? I'd have never allowed it, but until an hour ago? I was Officer Jameson. Now, I was simply Jimmy. Diana even. And, I had lost my friend. The one who begged me to leave, to be sure I was safely away, when whatever was about to happen, unfolded. He knew it was coming, and though I still don't know what exactly *DID* come? I knew what it left behind, and I felt gratitude he had tried so desperately to protect me from it. Yes, that was a friend. Through the regret of never being able to tell him that? I managed a small smile, because I at least knew I that I had had one.

I stepped fully back into the yard and spotted Kane's workshop. I imagined the girls could be corralled in there safely enough until I found them a new home. All I'd have to do was break the lock open and replace it with something else to keep the door shut. And if there's one thing I was good at; it was keeping doors secure.

I approached the workshop and when I rounded the corner; I saw the lock was gone. Rage swallowed me, and I gagged back a stream of profanity. Who popped the lock? And Jesus what had they stolen? I wouldn't even know; I had never been in there but the thought of it had me gritting my teeth in fury. I spun around to see if there was any trace of who might have dared, and my gaze fell upon a human frame not thirty feet away.

He was leaning up against the hood of my Mustang. I soaked the image in; his dark shaggy hair, arms folded across his chest, and the biggest smile of ridiculously white teeth I thought I'd never see again. My hand immediately went to my mouth and I'm sure I wobbled from the surprise, relief and joy at seeing him there. He stood up and covered the distance in long strides. He had to; I was paralyzed.

Kane.

The shards of gold in his eyes were even more visible in the brightness of the sun. Kane was standing there, breathing and alive, right in front of me. I didn't dare to believe it. Surely, I had suffered some psychological break-down and this was a retreat into pure fantasy. *No way* was this possible. I saw that cell. I saw that entire jail; furnace explosion be damned. I had waded through it.

"Diana? Are you okay?" he asked, still smiling.

I couldn't speak. I couldn't move. I couldn't do anything but slowly reach my hand out towards his chest, fearful that this was indeed a hallucination.

He took it in his own, like he had done on the catwalk that morning, begging me to leave at three. I felt the warmth of his skin and that touch; that simple *touch*, made it real. I threw myself up against him with enough force to knock him off balance and wrapped my arms around him fiercer than I had ever hugged another human being. Kane laughed; a good hearty laugh, returning the hug as he regained his footing. I was laughing through tears and babbling incoherent sentences, unable to finish one without starting two more and all the while clinging to him afraid that if I let go? He'd disappear in a wisp of smoke that never was. Kane managed to loosen my grip enough to pull back and take my face into his hands.

"Easy! Easy Jimmy, slow down." He said softly, looking directly into my eyes. The corners of his eyes still wrinkled with his own smile but he was also concerned for me. I'm sure I was the vision of a woman who had slipped under the watery surface of reality, and he was gently trying to bring me back topside again before I was lost forever.

"It's okay now. It's okay. Just slow down a bit. Easy now. You ok?"

I nodded my head that I was. He moved as though to let go of my face, then stopped. He stepped in closer, and gently kissed me. Then he stepped back, let go and grinned at me. He seemed almost embarrassed, shoving his hands into the front pockets of his jeans. I blinked several times. I think that was all I was capable of.

"Yeah, sorry about that. I have wanted to do that for about a month now, and I figured I'd better take the shot at it while I had the chance. Didn't know if I would get another one. Had to do it."

"A month?" I finally managed to say. At least it was something halfway sane sounding.

"Little longer actually. I have wanted to do that since you explained the unofficial, 'How to Stay Out of the Shit', rules. You had me from there. I just wasn't exactly in a position to act on it before today. I never expected you to come pulling up my driveway. Not in a million years. Had to do it, in case it never happens again."

"Kane, *how* are you here? *Alive*? Here? *Nobody* got out of there." I asked, and he grinned and raked his fingers through his hair before meeting my gaze.

"You are going to need some beer to hear that story, and *I* am going need some to tell it. I have never told anybody this so probably? More than two. How is the wrist? I heard that snap. Door got you, did it? C'mon, I have got some on ice, and you look like you wouldn't mind sitting down for a minute. Can I get you anything besides a cold one?"

I followed him up the walkway to the house and sat in the chair he motioned to. He handed me a longneck and stood a few feet in front of me. The beer was beautifully cold, but I couldn't swallow more than one swig before the blitzkrieg of questions in my mind settled in the expression on my face, and Kane saw it when it happened. He sighed, stared at the ground and then looked up at me.

"I am going to have to start talking right now, aren't I?"

"You gotta give me something here, Kane, I'm going under. Throw me a rope."

"All right. But first," he whispered, and stepped over to where I was sitting. He crouched down in front of me, put one hand on my face and kissed me again, this one a little longer and not as gentle as the first.

"I don't know what you are going to do or how you are going to react once I start talking. I needed some courage." He glanced at the ground, then back up at me, and just sat down on the flagstones in front of me.

"Obviously, someone did get out three nights ago. I did. And I am *thanking God* right now, that you were not there when it happened. Nothing has ever frightened me so much in my life as you did! Showing up that morning doing count! I thought I was going to go insane. And Jimmy? If you had not been leaving at three when you got hurt, and you had stayed for a double? I would have hurt you myself to get you out by sunset."

"*What*? You'd have hurt me yourself? What kind of a fucking lunatic are you?" He never took his eyes from mine but nodded that yes, he would have.

"Why? For the love of Christ and all things Holy! Why would you do something like that?"

"Because before sunset, I could have controlled how badly I hurt you. I cannot say the same for after dark."

I shook my head in disbelief. *SO* glad I was happy he had survived. I'm having a beer with a psychotic.

"What in *the* fuck are you talking about?" I half snarled, half hissed.

He picked up some gravel from the edge of the grass and tossed it. I watched a battle wage within him; all through his eyes. He was silent for several minutes, wrestling with whatever it was he was trying to say, or *not* say. I didn't even know at this point. Out of desperation I took a long swallow from my beer, and despite the five million questions swirling in my head, I waited. He pulled his gaze from the tree line and chickens, drew in a breath, and looked directly at me.

"What happened at Lawrence?" he began, and I leaned forward ensuring I was going to hear every word, although the weight of dread was starting to settle on me. I wasn't sure I wanted to hear this, but it was too late to stop. In for a penny. On for the ride now.

"What happened up there, Jimmy? *I* did that."

Forces from all directions slammed into me at once. Shock, disbelief, surety that Kane was insane, fury, and even pain; I was in the center of that train wreck and I didn't know which direction to run. The reality was that I was paralyzed by what he had just said; I couldn't have so much as flinched but inside I was screaming. Thoughts were flying faster than I could recognize what one was before three more had sped by and replaced it. One finally emerged from the cyclone and it was, that what Kane had just said? Was utterly impossible. There was simply no possibility that one man could have done all *THAT*. Protests and blatant accusations of mental illness formed on my tongue, but one hard look into his eyes and they all dissolved. Kane wasn't kidding, nor was he delusional. He had done it. Kane, was somehow responsible for that slaughter.

"How?" I finally managed to croak out. He clambered to his feet and paced the walkway, head down, as he glared at the ground.

"It's been happening for as long as I can remember." he spat, never raising his head. "I don't even know what it is actually called. Myths? Legends? Sure, they have a name for it and so does Hollywood, but I'm not sure anybody fully has a handle on it. There is fiction and fantasy, but all I can tell you is what I know to be the facts as *I* know them, because it happens to *me*. Every 29 days it happens, and there is *not one Goddamn thing* I can do to stop it. I can feel the pull get stronger each week, until finally? Whatever it is, *INSIDE* of me, is pulled out so completely? I don't know."

His pacing had brought him close enough to me where I could reach him, and I put my hand on his forearm. He stopped, slowly raising his head, and glanced at me. I squeezed his arm a little tighter and his expression morphed from frustration and anger to agonizing guilt.

"I.....*change*."

The words were excruciating for him to say out loud, and his body language an atlas for me to find my way to him. He was desperate in his loneliness. Its intensity blazed across his features, and he searched for somewhere to belong. He had confessed his darkest sin; left no defenses intact, and now stood waiting to be damned for it.

Flashes of the past month began to emerge from my memory and tumble into a primitive history. He arrived wrapped in a blanket, as he had been found sleeping naked in a park. Mangled fingernails. *I can only do twenty-seven days*. Teeth that seemed larger as the month went on. *I have excellent hearing*. Amber eyes that shifted to gold, and they reflected light enough to glow. Restless movements the days before the full moon. *I can't stop it. It has already started*.

"Get out before sunset." I whispered and looked up at him. He was still standing in one spot, but I could feel him trembling beneath my hand that still held his arm.

"You meant, get out before moonrise. The rise of the next full moon."

Kane dropped to his knees on the walkway, still shaking but now more with relief than anything else. He had carried this for over forty years, completely alone. He released whatever breath he had been holding, and his spine and shoulders dropped, finally free of the weight he had carried on them for so many years. He slumped forward resting his forehead on the ground, the exhaustion of his struggle overtaking him. He seemed resigned to whatever happened next. There was no fight left in him, and he had made peace with it.

So many forces had collided upon me just minutes before, but now the tempest was still. I slid down to the ground and positioned myself directly across from him. His head still touched the ground, but we both knew he was aware of my movement. He startled when I ran my fingers through his hair, and he slowly sat up. My hand traveled down his temple, across his cheekbone and down his jaw, and slid down his neck to his collarbone. His breathing was rapid; I could feel him trembling once again as his hope fought his fear.

"Why are you shaking?" I asked softly.

"It was always the forbidden dream."

"What was?"

"To be touched; like this. I never thought it would happen. Not in a way that mattered, anyway." he said, dropping his eyes for a moment, before meeting mine again. A beginning of a smile stole across his face and he whispered,

"And especially not by the Goddess of the Moon herself."

The smile was infectious, and soon it was chased by gentle chuckling from Kane.

"Well," I said, "Who says you can't teach an old dog new tricks?"

Chuckling turned into a genuine laugh that swallowed us both for some time. As it subsided, he ran his forefinger down the length of my nose, leaning in until the tip of his nose touched mine.

"Wolf." he said, voice feigning sternness, and then kissed me for the third time.

#

The sun was sliding west when we stood up from the walkway we had sat on for most of the day. It had been hours filled with laughter, some meaningful conversations, and times where no spoken word could convey the intimacy. Stretching his full height, he yawned and shook his head.

"You tired?" I asked.

"A bit. Always am the first few days after She's Full." He said, pointing up towards the sky. "And this last one was more than exhausting. It is almost twenty miles from Lawrence to Rowley."

"Well, I should let you get some sleep then." I said and began checking my pockets with my one good hand.

"What are you looking for?" he asked.

"Car keys. You need some rack time."

"Whoa, whoa, whoa," Kane started, raising both hands up as if he was being robbed. "Why would you think of leaving?"

My hand stopped half in my pocket, and I looked at him, my head cocked in the question of what do you mean, why?

"Um, this is *YOUR* house. *YOU* need sleep. I will go."

He straightened his arms to reach my shoulders and pulled me into his chest. He was taller than me but not by much, just enough so he could look slightly down to my eyes.

"Are you nuts?" he asked, "Go? Do you seriously think that after I travelled all night on four legs through the woods to get back here and was lucky enough to have you pull in the driveway, and everything this afternoon, that I would *ever* want you to *go*? *EVER*?"

"Well Jesus Kane, I don't know! You never said anything, so..."

"Well I am *NOT* going to say anything now either, but you are definitely going know whether or not I ever want you to leave here."

After finishing that sentence, he wrapped his arms completely around me and kissed me in such a way that I knew my answer immediately. When he felt he had *NOT* said enough, he drew back and pressed his forehead to mine.

"Have I made myself clear enough, Diana?"

"Jeez, I'm not sure, still a bit confused as to...."

I never got to finish the sentence; Kane was *NOT* saying anything again.

#

"Yeah, I think I've got it now." I gasped after catching my breath. "But what, exactly, is this going to look like? How's this going to play out?"

"I don't know how it's all going to play out, but I know how I want to start every day from here forward."

"How's that?"

"Waking up next to you, asking you how you want your eggs."

"So, what? You're asking me to move in here?" I said.

"I'll drop to my knees and beg if I have to." he said, winking as his grin widened.

"That won't be necessary, Woods. I've learned to trust your intentions. But in twenty-five days, what happens? I mean; you have to do your *thing*. What do I do? Lock myself inside? Or just spend a night away? What's the plan for that?"

His eyebrows folded until they met above the bridge of his nose as he considered it.

"I don't know. I never had to think about it before." he murmured. He sat down in the chair, grabbed us both another beer and motioned for me to join him. I perched on his thigh, and he leaned his head into my shoulder.

"This is an unexpected happiness for me, Diana. I told you, I was sunk at the 'How to Stay Out of the Shit' rules with you. And while I may have wished it? I never in a lifetime imagined this becoming a reality." He gulped half a beer and continued.

"I think spending a night away is the best idea for us to start with. You know I can control it right up until sunset. That is how I knew I could figure out some way of getting you out, if you had stayed for a double. I am sorry, but I'm not sorry about your wrist. That guaranteed you could not be there. By the way; the bones broke clean. Keep the cast on and it should heal good as new."

"How do YOU know they broke clean? What, did you see the X rays?"

"I told you today. I heard it break."

"From *inside* the catwalk of Three? Over all that clanging and shift change noise?" I asked, and Kane nodded.

"I heard the lighter drop. Your footsteps stopped, then continued, and then the snap. Then? Your colorful language. That's when I opened the cell door. So I could be sure you were not being attacked. Once I knew? I went back in and shut the door."

"I checked that door. It was latched."

"It was. But Diana; you saw what I can do. Six hours before moonrise? Do you think I had a problem with that latch? It is only iron. And I told you, I have excellent hearing. Just do me one favor, would you?"

"What's that?" I asked.

"No silver jewelry please. It stings quite a bit. "

August 1990

CHAPTER NINE

You never fully appreciate how much shit you've accumulated in your life until you go to put it all in boxes to move to a new place. I had lived in my second-floor apartment for several years; and while I considered myself to be a pretty low maintenance woman? Watching Kane carry boxes down the stairs to his truck time and time again as I packed even more made me seriously re-evaluate what low maintenance meant. God love him he never once complained. He just climbed down the stairs with what I considered to be a LOT of heavy boxes, only to return to the top of the stairs and repeat the act all over again. His pace never slowed. Jesus, he wasn't even breathing heavy. August in Newburyport is not as brutal as Middleton. At least Newburyport had the river or ocean breeze to lift the stifling humidity; but it was sure not late autumn in Boston. It was hot.

Kane had a pick up, but due to his profession as a custom cabinet maker he also owned a good-sized cube truck he used for delivery of his finished works. I had already donated or sold most of my furniture so the boxes contained kitchen stuff, personal effects and clothes.

I thought the pickup would have sufficed along with my Mustang and when I said as much? Kane had simply grinned, shook his head and gently suggested the cube truck would make it a one vehicle trip. Realizing he had already made more than a dozen trips up and down the flight of stairs and scanning around me to see what was still left to go, I had to confess the man was right. Damn him. I scowled at the thought as his footsteps entered the tiny loft apartment that I had called home.

"What is that look about?" he asked. His brow was creased with concern. "The wrist okay? I told you to let me pack the heavier stuff. It is only just past three weeks now."

"No, the wrist is fine. Really."

"Then what is it, Jimmy?" he asked. I mustered all the indignation I could find. How dare he be correct in the volume of crap I had! I turned to face him and say something smart ass as is my nature, but when I met his eyes it was gone as fast as shadows from a dream upon waking. The corners of my mouth began to curl into a smile no matter how stubborn I was trying to be. His golden flecked eyes were focused on my wrist; narrowed with genuine concern. He was next to me before I knew it, holding my left hand as he examined the cast encasing my wrist. He traced the part of the cast that crossed my palm with his fingertip. The light gentleness of his touch turned my skin to fire and sent chills through me at the exact same moment. Kane looked up and met my eyes. His had an odd light about them. A different sort of underlying glow than I had seen back at the jail. Fire and chills again for me. Threefold.

"I uh, well, uh. Well? I really don't know." I managed to croak out of my throat. Stellar example of grace under pressure there Jimmy! Not! He looked, and I mean *LOOKED*, deeply at me. His eyes never left mine. If I didn't know better? I'd swear he was trying to read my mind. The intensity of his gaze was nothing I had ever experienced before, and Kane hadn't even arched an eyebrow at me.

"Diana?"

His voice was barely above a whisper but it carried clearly through the scant space between where we stood. He never shifted his eyes away, nor did his body move in any way that I noticed. And noticing the slightest changes or movements was what had kept me alive thus far. No, Kane never moved. Whatever was going to follow his questioning mention of my name was going to be profound for him to say. I waited for him to finish the inquiry.

"Diana? Are you having second thoughts about moving in with me?"

I blinked. And again, and at least four more times as his question sank in. What? Wait, what? Where in the *Hell* had that come from? Are you kidding me? Did he actually just ask that?

"What?" I finally blurted out. His face said it had been an agonizing amount of time, at least for him, before I had spoken. I clamored to even remotely recognize where *that* crazy assed question came from. I couldn't even begin to find a compass for his thought pattern, never mind try to trace the steps to how it had formed. After *EVERYTHING*? All the unbelievable reality of what had happened? The enormity of what he had told me about who, and more importantly? *WHAT* he was? And in the following weeks; did I cut and run? Freak out? Check myself into a psych ward? Change my name and move to Tibet? Nope. In fact, I opted to *NOT* renew my lease and started packing. Where in the *Christ* would he ever get an idea so dead ass wrong? Really? What?

The wrinkles at the corner of his eyes told me he was smiling, and I realized the fury of questions in my mind I had apparently also been sputtering out of my mouth. Out loud, and just as broken in speech as my thoughts had been. Kane's shoulders relaxed visibly; his eyes brightened and he stood up to his full height while pulling me into him with his left arm curling around me. His soft laughter rumbled from his chest and into my ears as he held me to him; wrapping both arms around me and kissing my forehead. I melted into his frame for a moment, savoring the feel of him holding me as he finished his amusement. A flash of anger pulsed through me and I pushed away from him to face him.

"Okay I'm glad this was entertaining for you. But what the actual fuck Woods? How would you even *GO* in that direction to begin with? Never mind how you wound up thinking I was having second thoughts?"

His face still wore the memory of that smile but his tone was serious when he answered. Kane's eyes revealed more about his true thoughts and feelings than he knew, but I had noticed. I paid attention. And through that, I was learning about him.

"Jimmy. I walk through the doorway and see you. You are clearly disturbed about something. You are leaving a place that has been your home for years. To move in with *ME*. Let's be honest here, okay? I come with some... *complications* to say the least. It makes perfect sense to me that you may be doubting your choice and even wanting to change your mind. I would not blame you if you turned right now and ran as fast and as far as you could. It would kill me. But I wouldn't fault you in the least. Roles reversed? I don't know if I could do it. Or if I would even want to."

"That's because you're a *guy*. You're not me. In case you haven't noticed? I don't scare easily."

"Oh, I have more than noticed that about you. You are fearless, Miss Jameson. And yes, I'm a guy. Except every twenty-nine days, after moonrise."

Kane's breath caught a little after his last sentence. He subconsciously flinched, hung his head for a brief second and raised it back to look at me. His glare was intense. It was a command as well, and there would be no arguing it.

"And it is on that twenty-ninth day, just before dusk; that you need to *FEAR*. Deathly afraid, Diana. That moment? It is not the time for courage nor loyalty. Nothing remotely close to it. That, my Love? That is the time for you to run in terror. Not only for you, but if you have even the slightest of feelings for me? You need to run in terror for my sake as well."

Kane's words were frightening. Even if I had not known only too well the weight of them. I was there July seventh. I remember every detail of the annihilation he had left behind at Lawrence. Well, sort of him. The man standing before me was not the horror that emerges under a full moon; but it was an integral part of him. It had contributed to the formation of the man that I was so drawn to that I was moving in with him. He was two entities; yet only one was aware that the other inhabited the same soul. If that twenty-ninth-day entity even had a soul. Twenty-ninth night seemed more fitting, and that was how I classified it in my mind.

"Stop." he whispered. He was leaning forward, gripping the breakfast bar countertop, his head hung but watching me from the corners of his eyes.

He looked wounded. Badly wounded.

The golden flecks of his eyes were filled with anguish, and stop I did. Thoughts stopped. Feelings stopped. I went into pure observational mode. Every nuance of Kane screamed information. All I had to do was absorb it all and process it later.

"Jesus, don't stop completely Diana. Breathe."

I hadn't realized I had held that breath until he said it, and I immediately inhaled. It tasted sweet. Crisp even. In August. In Newburyport. He drew in a breath himself and stood up fully before he spoke.

"It is a *LOT*. I know. More than a lot. I cannot imagine how much for you. I've had my entire life to accept what I am. Both parts. Both, are *WHAT* I am. There is no separation. I can't change it, believe me if I could? I would have done so a lifetime ago. This is not like being born a red head. That's easy. That can be changed. You can dye your hair or even shave your head. Me? The Moon? What happens? There's no amount of dye that can alter that. No fix. No change. And there is, no end."

I was nodding that I understood. And I did; it was just a vast amount to take in all at once. If you are told by a surgeon that the lump they removed from you is cancer? Well, you've at least got options. Further surgery, chemotherapy, radiation or to simply do nothing. Those are all *choices*. Not the most pleasant of choices, but options nonetheless. Kane had none. No treatments. No cure. No remission. And from what I was beginning to understand; no way out. Perhaps even, no end. He remained standing by the breakfast bar, a mere three steps from me, and when I searched his gold and amber streaked eyes? I never saw a man so far away and utterly alone.

The density of it broke the last of my stubborn 'Damn him for being right' posturing, and erased the 'where the Hell did that question come from'. It almost broke my heart. I was across the distance before I knew it, grabbed the belt loops of his jeans and pulled him to me. I kissed him deeply, pouring as much of myself into it as I could. It was a promise. No, Kane. You're not alone in this world. Not anymore.

It was a long promise. When he finally believed it? He inhaled a ragged breath, resting his forehead on mine. His hand stroked down my cheek and neck. Fire and chills again. The crooked grin found his mouth as he glanced around the apartment.

"Is this the last of it?" he asked. I nodded it was.

"Okay then; let me load it. And Jimmy? Let's go home." The word never sounded better.

#

The drive to Rowley from Newburyport is a relatively short one and we rode together in silence. It wasn't an awkward silence; Kane and I had an ease of being with each other that didn't require constant talking, but when we spoke it was an honest and open conversation.

Today was mostly that comfort yet there was an underlying edge to it. While we had spent nearly half of each day together for weeks, I had not spent the night at his house nor he at my apartment. His unexpected stay in Lawrence had him a little behind on a few orders he had to fulfill; and that allowed me time to sort through my things, pack, and unload the furniture and whatnot I wasn't bringing with me.

Today, *HIS* house was about to become *OUR* house. It was a cozy two-bedroom home. Kane had given me the nickel tour that first day, but it occurred to me that other than my taking a few steps into his bedroom almost three weeks ago? I had not entered it. And tonight? Unless I decided to go full on prude and take the second bedroom? I'd be sleeping in it. Well now. Isn't *that* a kick in the ass?

The excitement of this was also tinged with trepidation, at least for me. I had never lived with anyone. Not since I left New Jersey and moved to New England almost twelve years earlier, and it was my father's house I had moved out of back then. This was a whole new world for me, and from what Kane had told me? For him as well. Two loners about to move in together. That's a challenge in the best of situations, but given our extraordinary circumstances? Challenging was a gross understatement. In five days, the moon would be full again. Great. I'm moving in and won't be more than half unpacked before I have to 'go out of town' for a night. I snorted a laugh at the thought.

"Ok, now what?" he asked as he turned on the 'road' he lived on.

"I'm sorry. It's not funny, but it *is.*"

"What is?"

"You do realize that I am *just* moving in here and have to leave for a night after four days, right? I mean, I won't even be fully unpacked, never mind know where the spare towels are before I have to 'go' for the night. Kinda weird, don't you think?"

Kane nodded as he thought about it and agreed it was a bit unconventional. He cut his eyes towards me, that crooked grin finding his features. God his teeth were white. And getting bigger now that I looked. Yep, four nights and then it would happen. His eyes were bright, but this was not the same glow from back at Lawrence. This illumination was a return from earlier at my apartment. There was something behind it; something primal swirled beneath the surface. I felt the same heat of my skin and chill simultaneously. I searched for the precise word but couldn't find it. What was it I knew I was seeing but couldn't name? Kane answered that question in his next sentence.

"Maybe we could make good use of the next four *nights*, then."

Hunger.

That was the word. There were many more I could have used but they are not as 'gentile'. Hunger. The thought of the next four nights rushed through me, and I realized that Kane wasn't the only one who had not dined in a while. Excitement surged through me. My God stop it woman! You're not sixteen in the back seat of some boy's Chevy. You're thirty-three! Obviously, I was no vestal virgin locked away in an ivory tower. There had been men in my life, as I'm sure there had been women in Kane's. There wasn't a toll booth on my bedroom door nor a parade marching through it; but yes, I had known some men. So why was I suddenly more than a little nervous? Kane reached across the bench seat of the truck, resting his hand on my thigh just above my knee, and squeezed gently.

"Relax. There is no rush for anything here, Diana. It will all fall into place exactly when it is supposed to. No pressure for a damn thing. I'm looking forward to waking up to the smell of your hair on the pillows."

Wow. Christ, can he actually read my mind? He sure as Hell knew precisely what I was feeling and what to say. Okay. Let's see if he *CAN* read every thought. This me being off balance shit was getting old. Time for a little turnabout. Devil's Advocate if you will. He turned the truck to enter the driveway.

"Oh, okay Kane. That's good to know. I mean, now that I know you don't want to..." I let the words trail off without completion.

The truck slammed to a stop in his, well, *OUR* driveway. He snapped his head around to face me so quickly I thought he might break his neck. Kane shoved the gear into park hard enough it was almost violent; his eyes never moving from mine. He opened his mouth slightly, shut it, and then repeated the actions. He broke his gaze and turned to stare out the windshield at absolutely nothing. Flabbergasted, he raked his fingers through his dark hair, scratched the base of his neck, and followed that by dragging his hand down his eyes and nose. He exhaled sharply, returned his hands to the steering wheel, and slowly turned to face me again. His eyes were ablaze with the intensity of what he was feeling.

"If you think for *one second* that I don't want to? You are sorely mistaken. And my apologies if that has been the case for you. I have been doing everything I can to keep what I *WANT* under control. It has been exhausting. And Diana? I don't tire easily. Part of what I am. I don't want you to feel any obligation, or that I have a set of expectations. I certainly do not. I have been alone most of my life. The occasional companionship? Sure. But nothing...*NOTHING* like what I feel about you. I am not going to push or pressure you in any way. Because when it happens? I want it to be because *YOU* want to and that you're giving it freely. Not because I manipulated you into something."

Well, I guess it *WAS* Kane's turn to be off balance after all. Good! He had me back on my heels most of the day. I felt the grin spread across my face. No matter how hard I tried to smother it; it would not extinguish. I suppose I should have felt at least a pang of guilt, but I did not. The re-leveling of the playing field was something we both needed. It affirmed the equality between us and that this was a *CHOICE*, for both of us. Nobody was making anybody *DO* anything. Each of us was acting of our own volition. Each making our own decisions. My grin morphed into a full smile, and Kane's quizzical look broadened it further.

"Thank you for letting me know where you stand, Kane. I think I am starting to understand how you feel. About me anyway."

"Starting?!?" he sputtered.

"Yes. I am beginning to see where you are coming from, and I appreciate that insight. Thank you for letting me in enough where I can start to see it." He dragged his hand down his face again, shaking his head back and forth in disbelief.

"Jesus. Just Jesus. How can you not know?"

"Know what?" I asked. "I only know what you tell me. I learn by what you show me. But if you don't tell me? I don't know. I'm no mind reader and my crystal ball is broken so yeah; I don't know a damn thing until you tell it to me. Or I learn it as you show me, but that takes a little longer because I first have to figure out *HOW* you show something before I can learn it."

"Fine!" he snapped, slamming his hands on the steering wheel. Oh yes, he was more than off balance. He was flustered. Frustrated even.

He glanced over at me one more time and threw his truck door open. He was out of the seat before I knew it. He didn't even bother to slam it shut. He left it wide open as he strode around the front of the vehicle and arrived at the passenger side door. He yanked it open hard enough to relay he was intent on what he was doing but was no threat to me. He stood at the far end of the now open door, right hand still gripping the handle.

"Get out of the truck."

He flinched, realizing it sounded more like an order than he had intended. He hung his head, staring at the ground for a moment, and I watched his shoulders drop slightly. Kane inhaled deeply, raised his head and faced me, hand still holding the door handle.

"Jimmy, would you please step out of the truck? Please."

His voice was quieter and his body language told me he had regained at least some of his composure. Although he was still in an agitated state it was not nearly what it had been five seconds ago. I unfastened my seat belt and his posture softened a bit more. My feet hit the ground but I remained in the exact spot where they struck the Earth. Kane dropped his head and kept it down for some time. He inhaled again, exhaled, and took another deep breath in.

He never raised his head, but extended his left hand towards me, palm up. I looked at it for several seconds, and then back at him. His head was still down. He kept it hung until the fingers of my right hand slid across his palm. He grasped my hand and released the breath he had been holding. He raised his head and gently pulled me towards him. I expected him to hug me tightly or even kiss me, but he retreated backwards a few paces leading me away from the truck and into the grass. When he stopped, I made another step forward. He raised his right hand to stop my advancement and let go of the hand he had been holding. I stood where I was. He raised his head again, staring up at the bright blue of the early afternoon and appeared to be gathering his thoughts. He blinked several times, sighed and lowered his face from the sun to my height.

"Miss Diana Jameson." he began, and I felt my heart stop momentarily before it pounded back to rhythm. Oh Lord, what was he about to say? The urge to run tugged at the corners of my mind, but his golden mottled eyes riveted my feet. The 'flight' part of my world had just exited stage left. There would be no fleeing here. This was not just a penny; I was in for the full pound from here on out. Whatever he was about to say? It was genuine. Oh, Christ save me; there would be no un-hearing it, and never a forgetting it. I subconsciously tapped into the Irish in me and felt my spine stiffen. My Jameson heritage kicked in full strength. Ok, bring it. Hit me with your best shot kid.

"Diana." His voice was softer now, almost a purr. It was something I heard as well as felt in my body.

"Jimmy." he whispered.

"Yes, Kane?" True to form, he smiled at my use of his first name, his current smile as big as the one in the infirmary the first time he heard me say it. Maybe even a bigger smile today.

"I am in love with you. Head over heels. Hopelessly in love with you."

I have no idea what expression was on my face after those words registered in my mind. Bring it? Hit me with your best shot kid? What the fuck was I thinking? I've got no problem taking a shot; but *DAMN* this one came out of left field somewhere! I never saw it coming! I scrambled mentally to regain my footing. He's in love with me? How did that happen? When?

A wave of calm washed across my thoughts. Its arrival was so unexpected it should have sent me even further into my 'what the shit' freak out mode. Instead, the cyclones of my thoughts were brushed away and a soothing peacefulness enveloped me. My heart had shut off my brain, for the first time in my life. Kane was in love with me. Well thank you Jesus because it sure had been awful being in love all by myself. I didn't even realize it until that exact moment in time. That fact, is what had me sideways for the past several weeks. I was in love with the man. *WOW*. It struck me like a two by four upside my head. It suddenly all made sense.

I was in love with Kane Woods.

He stood before me in the sun, not even two steps away, and I realized he was completely vulnerable. More exposed right now than the afternoon he sat in the booking room wearing only a blanket. Oh my God! How long had I been standing there silent? Jesus the poor guy. He had laid his throat bare for me to cut it if I chose, and my failure to say anything must have been agony. Oh, fuck tell him! I searched for the words and found my own echoing in my head. *I only know what you tell me. I learn by what you show me.* Goddammit Diana! Don't speak; *SHOW* him.

I was across the paces between us before either of us knew it, and without a word I stretched my fingers through his hair. Hand in a cast be damned, I pulled his face to mine and kissed him hard and with all of my being that I could muster. There would be no holding back this time. Defenses were smashed; the fortifications lay in ruins around us. I don't know how long we were like that or if either of us ever came up for air. It was the burning fusion of two separate people becoming one. My hands were scaling his back, across his shoulders, down his arms, wrapping around his waist and pulling him against me.

His also travelled my frame, down my shoulder blades, his fingertips tracing my spine. My hips responded to his touch, pressing against him forcefully. My body desperately tried to say the words that in that moment I could not; our tongues danced alongside each other's; each kiss surpassing the last. My intact hand managed to get under his T shirt and the tensing of his stomach at my touch made me want to feel more.

Even my injured hand had made its way under his shirt, and I was raising my hands pulling it over his head with neither of us having a sense it was even happening. He broke from the kiss long enough to allow the shirt to clear his shoulders and head. The glow of his eyes earlier today paled now. Kane's eyes were an iridescent inferno. His arms, now clear of the T-shirt, pulled me against him possessively. His skin was hot under my fingers. His hands wandered from my face, down my throat and as his left arm wrapped around the small of my back his right hand explored my shoulders. He left the kiss to taste my collarbone. His lips and tongue on my skin made my breath catch in my throat. His hand brushed the side of my breast and I moaned softly. I ached for more. His hands had made their way under my shirt and his fingertips traced my skin. My back arched. His fingers slid under my bra and brushed across my nipples. His touch sent fire through me and made them stand at attention, pleading for more. Kane did not disappoint them.

Whimpers of pleasure emerged from me, and his breathing grew more ragged each time they did. He was straining to stay in control, and I could feel him straining against his Levi's as well. My hands travelled across the tight denim and he groaned before feverously resuming his exploration of my now freed breasts. Hands and lips and tongue were catapulting me into a frenzied state. It was broad daylight and I didn't care in the least. I was consumed by him. I couldn't take any more of it but would surely die if he stopped now. The feel of him against my skin drove me to the brink of madness. Yes. Don't stop. Oh my God please I can't take any more. Don't stop. There were no complete thoughts anywhere in my mind. It was all purely sensory now.

Instinct.

Primal.

Hunger.

My fingers were at his belt, and even with my cast I got the buckle free. Kane suddenly drew back, his breath somewhere between gasping and panting. His eyes were pure gold now and they were not just bright; they were illuminated. They were glowing. Even in the full blaze of the sunlight they were reflective. It was stunning to see, and I realized he had his hands holding on to mine, which were still on his buckle.

"Be sure, Diana. The hold you have on me? This close to a Full? I don't think I could stop if you do that. Even if I wanted to. Which I most certainly do not. But please, Love. Be absolutely sure this is when you want me to change that to *Lover*. Because *I will not stop*."

My eyes never left his as my fingers undid the top button of his jeans. The golden hue of his eyes got darker. Richer. Kane released his fingers from mine, ran them through my hair and grabbed a handful at the back of my head. His mouth swallowed mine, and the power radiating from each muscle in his body was intoxicating. His right hand swept behind me, lifting my feet from the ground as he lowered me to the grass. The weight of him against me was addicting. Each second he was caressing me, lips and tongue and gentle brushes of teeth against my skin, was an agonizing ecstasy I didn't want to end. My fingers clawed at him; his spine a furrow between muscular planes. His hands were rough but belied the tenderness of his touch, and when they travelled down my body the regions they weren't on craved them. My back arched, raising my hips against him. I had his jeans open and I reached in them, grasping what I desperately wanted inside of me. He groaned loudly. His body tensed at my touch, and the tenderness of his diminished. He was on me, his form covering mine, and my jeans had not only been opened but were removed. My legs bent to wrap him against me, and I pulled him free of his restrictive garment, shifting my hips to guide him. Kane needed no direction.

He thrust inside me. As his hips touched down against mine a white fire scorched my mind. Every cell in my body was engulfed in the flames of orgasm. Muscles locked and shudder after shudder of searing pleasure surged through me. Each movement he made sent pulses through the core of me. I had no rational thoughts. Pure raw instinct consumed me.

His jaw was against my neck, teeth skimming my throat as my moans of pleasure escalated into a scream of rapture. I was blind in it, paralyzed with each physical wave that crashed upon me. My limbs felt as though they would tear themselves away from the intensity of it. Kane had my body ripping itself apart in massive orgasms that never seemed to end. I gasped for air in between them only to be greeted by another; it's intensity stronger than the last, rendering me unable to breathe until it subsided. I felt the coiling in his spine and stomach as he grew closer to joining me, his tension growing with every movement. His breathing was faster and his groans had a growling edge to them. His lips left my neck and returned to mine, his tongue plunging as deeply into me as the rest of him was. The kiss lasted a lifetime, and yet ended too soon.

His back muscles felt tight enough to snap beneath my fingers, and he buried his face in my neck and released himself. His body convulsed just as mine did. He roared as the breath was forced from his lungs. The two of us were locked together; each body feeding off the others pleasure until finally absolute muscle exhaustion swept through me and I could do nothing more than simply tremble beneath him.

Useless arms lay across his back as I searched for oxygen. Kane bent his knee to allow him to raise up and look down on me. His eyes were that deep gold still, but the iridescent light had softened. His breathing was rapid but far slower than mine, and he waited for me to be able to fully inhale once again. The half grin found its way back to his face as I began to recover. He chuckled softly and though I was nowhere near being able to move, I managed to speak.

"What?" I gasped.

"We are on the front lawn."

Shit. He was right. The sun was much farther west now, but it still illuminated the sky. Oh my God. My expression must have mirrored my thoughts because his chuckling continued.

"It's okay. I have no neighbors. Nobody comes back this far."

"Yeah. My luck? Today will be the day."

"We are fine. I would have heard anybody drawing close." He said, and then jerked his head to the left. "Although we *MAY* have traumatized them a bit."

I turned my head to see what he was talking about. Twenty feet away; ten chickens stood huddled together. Their necks were fully stretched up, and several had their beaks open as they stared at us.

"We may not see any eggs for a few days." Kane said, the chuckle growing into a full laugh, "But if it goes more than a week, we may have to barbeque one to get the others back to work."

#

Kane was unloading the boxes from the truck. How he found the energy I'll never know. I was doing good to be standing upright after our fun in the sun, and here he was back and forth from the truck to the house. He had brought in the miscellaneous kitchen crap and bathroom stuff to the corresponding rooms, and the heavier garments such as winter coats were placed in front of the hall closet. On his fourth trip back inside from the driveway, he held several boxes. They were marked jeans, T shirts, socks. He stood at the edge of the living room, glanced down at the boxes and then back at me. His bedroom was to the right of where he stood. The second bedroom was to his left. He was silently asking me which room he wanted me to have him put the boxes in.

"Well Kane? That's really up to you. I will understand either way."

There was no crooked grin this time. A full smile spread across his face and his golden eyes danced. He turned to the right and disappeared into what had just become *our* bedroom. I felt a similar smile on my face. He emerged from the bedroom still wearing his, and it grew even broader when he saw mine. He changed the direction of his pace, turning away from the still open front door and crossed to where I 'stood'. It was more of a leaning against the kitchen counter for support than a standing, but it was the best I could manage after the marathon my body had just been through. His eyes had a glow again, but it wasn't the hunger light in them. In fact, I had never seen this particular light in them at all.

I guess I was starting to understand the *how* he showed things, and also learning from it. Kane's eyes were his *HOW*. Granted, being four days from a Full moon they were obviously going to get a shimmer to them; I had witnessed that back at the jail. However; each mood, or feeling he was experiencing came through in varying degrees of brightness and gold. Just over three weeks, and I had already begun to read him. This glow was different though. It was a new one, and it made me curious as to what it was revealing to me.

I have never been the kind of woman to ask a man what he was thinking. I'd always felt if somebody wanted me to know something; they'd tell me in their own good time and when they were ready. At least, on a personal level.

Professionally? Whole different animal. I had a gift for interrogations. I could sniff out a way to get whatever information it was that I sought by what I called 'simply paying attention'. There are some people you can approach directly, some you have to dance with a bit, and some you just have to be prepared to do whatever it takes to get that information from them and count the cost to your soul later. I had no desire whatsoever to 'extract' information from Kane. Hell, why would I? I was in love with him.

No, I would never 'interrogate'. This was free will and choice from the beginning. No way was I going to be the one to change that. Still, the glow intrigued me. He had crossed the span of the living room and had wrapped his arms around me before his feet had stopped, pulling me into him and holding me there.

"Thank you." he murmured into my ear. One hand had slid up to the back of my head and he pressed it into his chest. I could hear his heart beating, steady and strong. He held me like that for quite some time, and I was content to stay right there for the rest of eternity. Oh yes. I was home.

"For what?" I asked, still pressed against him. The scent of him was so....*Male*. It's funny, despite thrashing through a quagmire of male inmates? I never recognized any of them even having a gender. They were inmates. My charge was to keep them behind bars and as intact as I could manage. The end. I had never once thought of any of them as men. Even Kane had fallen into that category during his stay although I did at least allow myself to consider him as a human being towards the end. The sheer maleness of him now was overwhelming. Or perhaps, it was that I was no longer Officer Jameson. I was now? Simply a woman responding to the man she loved; all roles and masks long forgotten.

"Thank you, for moving in here. I still can't believe you did considering all of it. I am amazed by you."

I've had a lot of people say many things to me in my life, but 'I am amazed by you' was never one of them. My father had once said that something I had done at the age of fourteen was *amazingly* stupid, and he was right at the time. But never had anyone said they were amazed *by me*. It felt strangely good to hear those words spoken aloud, and I snuggled a little deeper into him. His arms tightened around me and genuine affection flowed between us.

"Well how could I *NOT* move in, Kane?"

I felt the rumble of laughter coming from his chest; it was becoming an intimate feeling and I liked it immensely. I had pegged it that first time we met in the booking room; his humor was familiar.

"Oh, I am fairly certain I could list so many reasons they would have to be put into volumes. Let's see. You booked me into *jail*. And I was wearing a blanket. Nothing more. You're a *cop*. Now that is not exactly the kind of first impression a man hopes to make. Then what else? Oh yes! I was willing to deliberately injure you so that you would not be there when, a-ha! Yes! There it is! The best reason *ever* not to move in. So that you would not be there when I *changed*. Have I forgotten to mention anything? I'm just touching the highlights here, but I am more than certain they are enough."

I found myself joining his laughter though mine was softer. The man had a point. Several actually. Still? It was funny. In a gallows humor sort of way. Right up my alley.

I drew back from him and looked into his eyes. The laughter was still there, as was the yet unnamed glow. Again, it had me more than curious. He seemed to sense it from me and his face slowly softened as the focus became more on me, on us, than on the strange events that had brought us to this moment. His eyes narrowed slightly as he peered into mine.

"What is it you want to say, Diana?"

For once, I didn't have to search for the words. They had been lurking behind my teeth the whole time.

"Your eyes."

He nodded silently, waiting for me to continue.

"The light. The iridescence. The reflectiveness. Part of it has to do with the moon I know, and in general just...well, *you*. But right now? There's a different sort of glow in them. I haven't seen it before. I'd like to know the 'why' of it. But to quote your own words, Kane? I have no expectations. I'm not going to push or pressure you either. You'll tell me what you want me to know when you're ready to."

He grinned at me; his teeth whiter still. I couldn't help it. I thought it was kind of cool, now that I understood why they got larger and whiter. Yes, he was capable of atrocity that no one would believe, but in spite that? Still cool. Clearly; there was something wrong with me.

"Fair enough. Do you mind if I ask you a question?"

"Not at all. Shoot."

"Why *did* you agree to move in here? With me? And be okay with your jeans, T shirts and socks being in the same bedroom as *my* jeans, T shirts and socks?"

It occurred to me I had not yet spoken the words. I had done my best to show him, and I'd like to think I had succeeded; but just like me Kane had to understand *how* I showed him before he could learn from it. And just like me, he didn't *know* something unless I told him. I couldn't believe I hadn't said it yet. Duh.

"Because I am in love with you, Mr. Kane Woods. No holds barred, *in love*." The glow I had seen before grew even brighter, but it was without the reflective edge. His smile was enormous and he traced my cheek with the back of his fingers.

"The reason you have never seen this particular 'glow' as you put it, Diana?"

I nodded but remained quiet.

"It is because you have never seen me *happy* before today. And I am willing to bet my eyes got a lot brighter after you spoke. I have never been this happy in my life."

He kissed me softly, as if worried he might injure me. Its intimacy was powerful; a contrast to the kiss itself.

"I am afraid." He spoke quietly, and though the words were an admission of fear, he smiled again. "Almost blindingly afraid of this. How much I love you. The fact that you say you love me. And I wouldn't change a single thing about it. Which is frightening as well. I have never loved anyone, Diana. And I have never had anyone tell me they were in love with me. It is a terrifying joy I find myself in. I'm not quite sure what to do with all of it. But I know one thing. I am thankful to my core for it."

"Well? If you want the truth, Kane? I've never spoken those words to anyone before either. So, there. Guess this is a whole new world for both of us."

"Seems we are the least innocent of innocents here, Lover." he said; that purr I heard as well as felt returning to his voice. It drew me to him; it both excited me and made me feel completely safe at the same time.

"I can't think of anybody I'd rather discover this new way of life with." I said. The golden stripes in Kane's eyes grew bigger and again, richer in color. He pulled me against him, his arms surrounding me and threatening to swallow me into him. I was drowning in his maleness. Not a bad way to go.

#

It only took another fifteen minutes before Kane had the truck completely empty. I had regained enough stamina to start opening some of the kitchen boxes and my head was inside of one when I heard his footsteps stop. The silence lingered for more than what it should have, and that concern drew me to an upright position again. He stood still in the living room, holding a single box. I cocked my head in a silent question of 'What?' and he lifted the box ever so slightly to draw my eyes to what was written on it.

ECSD.

Those four letters never carried as much enormity as they did right now. That box became the elephant in the room, and Kane was quite aware of the massive size of the beast he held in a 14 by 14 cardboard cube as he stood silent. His eyes locked mine. He revealed no emotion, no preference for what he thought I should do with what he carried. He waited patiently for me to determine what to do with it. I sucked in the biggest breath I could and held it. I wasn't even sure what to do with it.

Bury it. Set it on fire. Throw it into the river.

Flashes of emotion sparked inside of me. Anger. Sadness. A bit of amusement at the warped humor I had shared with my fellow officers who wore those same four letters on their collars just as I had. Seven of whom were now dead. And they had been killed by the man standing on the carpet who held that box in his hands. The same man who held my heart. I felt my knees give out ever so slightly at that realization. If Kane noticed, he never conveyed it. If he had? And had afforded me that escape? It was a mercy on his part, and a big one at that. What the fuck indeed was I going to do with that box? The basement. There was a basement. Perfect. My eyes flicked to the door which led down to it. Kane followed my glance to the door, but he didn't move.

"Breathe."

His voice was gentle, and barely above a whisper. Once again, he had to point out that I had stopped. He was getting good at reminding me. I was getting worse at remembering to. Not a habit I wished to continue for either of us. I exhaled. My eyes again found their way to the basement door.

"No, Diana."

His tone was quiet, but firm. I found myself looking at him. The gold had softened, but there was no mistaking the adamancy behind his expression. If that box was going down into the basement? Kane would not be the one who carried it there. I felt my right eyebrow arching. Oh no you did *NOT* just say that! His shoulders dropped slightly but his stance did not waver. My ancestry once again gripped my spine, and the heat of an Irish temper began to intensify. I remember inmates telling me that they knew they were in trouble the greener my eyes got. I'm sure they resembled the Emerald City of Oz right about now. No apologies were to be found anywhere near me; for the simple reason that I was not remotely sorry. Our eyes met once again, and for the first time since I had met him? Kane looked away.

He never spoke a word. He silently turned to the left and walked into the second bedroom, the Pandora's Box he held still in his grasp. I didn't hear the closet open so I could only presume he hadn't stashed it in there. He stepped back out into the entryway, gently closing the bedroom door behind him, and closed the front door to the house as well. His back was to me and he let out a sigh, scratched his head and finally turned to face me again. The silence between us was different this time. Kane looked at me, his eyes still awash in gold but not quite as rich, and I stamped that color into my mind.

I would have to 'learn' that particular 'showing' but I was not open to that lesson right at the moment, and he knew it. He shifted his weight from one leg to another, seemingly unsure of where to go in his own home.

This, was a new world, and neither of us had a map. Not even a compass. I remembered the box I had been emptying before he came in and bent at the waist to resume digging through it. I was rummaging through useless items trying to busy my mind, and after a few moments; it was working. I felt my temper satiate, and I began sorting through coffee mugs.

As anyone in law enforcement will tell you? A coffee *CUP* is useless. Crazy long hours and incredible stress compiled with the general weirdness you encounter? A 'cup' of coffee will only piss you off. A *MUG*, usually at least 4 ounces larger, *may* prevent a homicide. I was digging out my largest one when I heard the fridge door open, and shortly afterwards, shut.

The *PFFT* of a beer cap being snapped open is an unmistakable sound. I heard it but being stubborn in my lingering Irishness; I kept my head in the box. It was when I heard it the second time, that I felt the Jameson grip release slightly from me. The gentle tap on the side of the box ceased my sorting and I rose up just enough that my vision cleared the box's edge. Kane had extended a long neck to me; the fog still wafting from the rim of the bottle. Well shit. He may not have known exactly what to say or do, but he was offering an olive branch. I may be an asshole, but I am not a douche bag, and there *IS* a difference. I stood up fully and accepted his peace offering.

He also had one, and we took the first swallows without looking at each other. The coldness felt wonderful in my throat, even though I was not the one hauling boxes in the house. Kane would not allow it thanks to my injury; but the day was still plenty warm. After the crisp taste ended my thirst, I glanced over at him. He was watching me from the corner of his eyes, and when he saw me look his way? He tried to pretend he wasn't. The complete and utter awkwardness on his part trying to pull that move off made me snort a laugh. Oh smooth one there, Kane! Subtle as a train wreck. Success rate zero, thanks for playing. Here's a crock pot as your parting gift. I found myself giggling.

"That bad, huh?" he asked, a smile spreading across his face.

"Miserable failure." I replied, feeling myself returning the smile. "Like, New York Jets kind of failure."

"Ouch." He said and winced dramatically. My giggle matured into a full laugh, and apparently it was contagious because he soon joined me in it. When we had fully embraced it, enjoyed it, and the laughs subsided? I found myself tracing the back of his hand with my fingers.

"So? Looks like we've survived our first fight." I said.

"Disagreement. And yes, we did." And he clinked his bottle against mine. He raised the beer, and I returned the gesture.

"*Slainte.*" He said. His use of the word caught me by surprise, but I raised my beer a little higher, nodded, and enjoyed another taste.

#

Unpacking is a tedious business. However, unpacking in a place that someone else is already inhabiting, and trying to figure out where to put *your* stuff in the midst of *their* stuff? Makes it a bit more difficult. Kane had been kind enough to clear space prior to today in the bathroom, kitchen and hall closet for me to put things away, and I did appreciate that. When the last of my 'girlie' things had been stowed in the vanity, I moved to tackle my clothes. I walked into the bedroom and found him rummaging through the closet. It ran the length of the room so space would not be an issue unless I had moved in with a clothes horse. Somehow, he didn't strike me as a slave to fashion. He had his back to me and was shifting hangers closer together.

"Which side do you want? The left? Or the right?" he asked, examining the contents of the closet. As I suspected, he was a pretty simple guy. Jeans, T shirts, some long sleeve shirts for the cooler months; yes, there was ample closet space. I had almost an identical wardrobe. There would probably be left over space in it when everything was put away.

"Side of what?" I asked, a smirk crossing my face as the mischief rose within me, "The closet? Or the bed?"

Kane stopped relocating his clothes. He turned his head slightly left so that he could see my expression, and he allowed a smile to overtake him. His eyes got a familiar glow to them, and despite my still recovering from the afternoon? I enjoyed the flash of heat I felt as his eyes travelled my body. The deep rich gold of them carried an almost physical touch on my skin.

"Be careful, Diana." He said, his voice again having the purr quality to it I felt as well as heard. Another wave of heat raced through me. "I don't tire easily, and She's close to Full. And as you know; I will not stop."

"Threaten me with a good time." I retorted.

I was on my back across the bed before I knew it. I never saw him move. Kane was covering me, kissing me deeply and gearing up for round two. Questions of how that happened began to bubble in my mind but were deflected as his hands wandered down my body. Again, rational thought succumbed to my physical reaction to Kane's touch. His mouth began to travel my neck, and my hips rose against him.

"I won't have the energy to finish unpacking, Kane." I murmured. His hands had journeyed down me and had opened my jeans. That was the last coherent thought I had before I was once again screaming his name.

#

The shuddering aftershocks of pleasure had begun to subside as I lay curled against him in the bed. *OUR* bed. The thought of that made me smile despite my exhaustion. Kane's arms were wrapped around me, and his fingertips lightly traced my arm. My head rested against his chest. His breathing had returned to its normal pace far faster than mine, and its steadiness was soothing. My eyes were closing, and I allowed the peacefulness to swallow me. Yes. I was home. I don't know how long I slept, but it was dark outside when my eyes opened again.

The first thing I noticed was Kane's absence from the room. The sheet and a light blanket were covering my shoulder, and I smiled. He had tucked me in before leaving the bed. Oh, he was a charmer. Gentleman even. I stretched and felt my legs complain. Well, he had warned me. I was going to need to eat my Wheaties to keep up it seemed, and I laughed to myself. I rolled over to climb out of our bed, and glanced towards the closet. The boxes containing my clothes were gone and the doors had been shut. I staggered over to the side closest to me and peered in. Everything of mine was hung up.

"I figured I would finish it up for you."

He was leaning against the door frame wearing that crooked half grin I was beginning to find irresistible. Gentleman indeed. Kane was revealing himself to be one of the most considerate human beings I had ever encountered. His eyes were alight, with the happy gleam this time, and I returned his grin.

"I got the left side."

"Made sense." Kane answered and shrugged his shoulders. "Seems we have naturally sorted out the sides of things. You fell asleep on the right side of the bed. The left side of the closet is closest for you. I can move it if you want."

"It's perfect. Thank you."

His half grin disappeared into a full smile and I again found myself marveling at his teeth. I reached for my clothes, and he feigned sadness.

"Well that's unfortunate." He said as I slid one leg into my jeans. "I was enjoying the view."

I laughed despite the true effort it was taking to make my legs move. Once I was dressed again, I 'walked' across the room to where he stood and wrapped my arm around his waist. It was motivated by both affection and a genuine need for support. He sensed its nature and pulled me to him, laughing gently.

"I know. You warned me." I said.

"I would apologize," he began, still holding me against him and also upright, "but I would be lying. I am not sorry in the slightest."

"Neither am I. But I would appreciate some help in getting out to the porch. I could really use a cigarette."

"You're welcome."

I laughed in spite of myself. I couldn't even pretend to protest. He had more than earned that confidence. My inability to walk was testimony to it. Kane hugged me tight for a moment, lifting my feet from the floor. Rather than release me he simply carried me to the porch. I lit the Marlboro Light and drew it in deeply, savoring the taste of it. Kane had ducked inside after he had placed me in the chair and he returned now with two cold beers. He handed me one and sat down beside me. An ice-cold beer and a fresh smoke following incredible sex? The only thing better was the company I now kept, and I told him as much. Even in the dark I could see his smile. His teeth were almost as bright as his eyes.

"Kane," I said as I realized exactly how dark it was, "You don't have a porch light. Or any outdoor lighting now that I look at it." He quickly scanned the yard.

"You're right. We don't have any. I shall remedy that tomorrow."

The fact that he said 'we' did not elude me, and I liked the sound of it. I would have commented on it, but I was more confounded over the lack of lighting.

"How have you lived here with no outside lights? It's pretty dark out here. You're lucky you haven't broken your neck."

"I know my way around."

Something in his voice and the way he answered me caught my attention. It was too casual. Cop instinct kicked in and I was questioning him before I knew it.

"What....*exactly*....do you mean by you know your way around?" He glanced down at his beer before answering.

"It's not just my hearing that's excellent."

"So, what? You can see in the dark?"

Kane took a long drink of his beer before answering me.

"I don't know that you could call it 'seeing'. I perceive things differently than you or anybody else for that matter. But I have lived here my entire life, so I know my way around is also the truth."

I finished my cigarette and crushed it out. This was something to think about. It never occurred to me all of the 'side-effects' Kane had from this. And what do we even call 'this'? Condition? Affliction? I needed some clarification, on a lot of things.

"I don't want to sound cop or anything here Kane, but I've got a lot of questions."

"So? Ask them." He said, his grin brightening his face.

"First, what do we even call *it*?"

"I don't know. I have never had anyone ask." He said, his smile was now full and he laughed softly. "But I like that you said *we*."

"Of course it's *WE*. I didn't think I had to explain that."

"You don't. I just like the sound of it."

I smiled back at him, but kept my focus on the question.

"What do we call it?" I asked again.

"*Werewolf* does sound like a B movie, but I suppose it is the general idea. What would *you* like to call it, Diana?"

"I think? If you describe it to me, *WE* can come up with a fitting title."

"That is an excellent idea." He said, his smile growing. "I like your approach."

"Cop." I said, and shrugged at him.

"Just the facts, ma'am."

We shared a moment of laughter at his retort. When it had subsided, Kane got us two more beers. I was thankful for that; my legs were still not quite up to par. I lit another cigarette and settled in to listen.

"As you already know, I have excellent hearing. I can hear your heartbeat from across the bedroom."

I startled at that bit of information. It was surprising, to say the least.

"It's ok, Jimmy. I can hear everybody's. Always could; as far back as I can remember."

"Holy shit! The noise you deal with constantly must be deafening!"

"I have had a long time to learn to filter it. As I've said, as far back as I can remember. I guess you could say I have developed mental barricades. Shields, if you will."

Kane stopped and smiled at me. Jesus those teeth were a marvel to behold! And even better to feel on my skin, he certainly knew how to use them. Heat surged through me and I shoved that thought out of my mind. His smile got wider and he chuckled.

"I do not know what exactly you just thought about," he began, leaning slightly forward in the chair, "but your heartbeat changed. It stopped for half a second and then sped up."

What the fuck? Oh shit, this was unreal. He *HEARS* that?

"And your skin got warmer too."

"Wait a minute. How would you know that? You're not touching me."

"I saw it."

"You *WHAT*?"

"I saw it. You got brighter for a second."

"Brighter?"

"Yes. Right now? You're an orange yellow. But just for that second there; you flashed to red."

No fucking way. *NO WAY* was he saying this shit. Yet he was. I raced to comprehend what he was telling me as more questions flooded in.

"I don't know if it is truly infrared vision, Love. I don't know how *you* see. It's a mixture of heat signatures and extreme colors. I 'see' facets of colors others do not. My green has hundreds more shades than what you see. At least? That is how my father explained it to me when I was young."

Father. Wow. It had never occurred to me that Kane had parents once. What the Hell was I thinking? Of course, he did. He didn't hatch.

"Your Father. Was he? Like, you?"

"No. Neither was my mother. They have been gone a long time. But my father had considerable knowledge about, well, whatever we decide to call what I am."

"So, they knew?" Duh Diana! Of course, they had to know! They'd have been pretty shitty parents if they didn't notice their son changing every full moon! God I was an idiot. I mentally smacked my forehead. Kane was chuckling again, and I wondered what color I was to him now.

"Yes Lover; they knew. I realize you have not actually been down in the basement, but that is where they stayed on a Full once I got bigger. As a small child they could manage me, but as I grew it became more difficult. My father built them a fortress of sorts down there. Going out of town wasn't quite practical for them. For you? For us? It is. I can afford to send you somewhere nice once a month."

The laughter erupted from me with such force Kane startled. *He* can afford to send *me*? Oh God that was good! I bent in half in the chair as it rang out of me. I looked up at him and laughed even harder. He wore the 'what the fuck' expression for a change, and his head was cocked to one side as he watched me howling. He was trying to be patient and wait for me to stop, but that only increased my amusement and I hit the point of near hysteria. The kind of all-consuming laughter that renders you unable to breathe or make a sound as it encompasses you.

"Well Jesus, Jimmy! I cannot expect you to pay for it! You are not only injured but unemployed. That just would not be right."

I was waving my hands helplessly in the air as I tried to stop laughing. Kane was scowling, a mix of confusion and uncertainty painted his eyes and I tried desperately to rein myself back under control.

I snorted in the attempt, which only reignited the laughing on my part, and despite his utter loss at what was so funny Kane slipped into joining me. He shook his head back and forth as he did, his disbelief at not only me but himself oozing out of him.

It took several minutes for me to calm myself enough to even make a sound, and when I found my voice again it was higher pitched than normal. I hoped it didn't hurt his ears too much but I couldn't quite manage my usual tone just yet.

"Oh Jesus, Kane! I'm sorry. That was fucking funnier than you know!" I gasped.

"I can see that; though I have no idea why."

"Oh God, that was great!" I managed after a minute, the octave of my voice dropping a bit closer to normal. If the higher pitch had hurt his ears, he never showed it. God, I loved him! He squinted slightly, clearly still confused, and again I wondered what colors he was seeing me in. I forced myself to focus on him. It wasn't fair to leave him so bewildered.

"You don't need to send me somewhere nice when *it* happens."

"Well I am not sending you to a roach motel, Diana."

"No, no, no," I said, fighting another round of giggles as best I could, "I mean you don't need to be the one to afford it."

He cocked his head again. He was lost, and that was my fault, because I hadn't told him about what had happened in Salem on July tenth.

"Kane? I have a considerable 'retirement' package from Essex County. And the Federal government chipped in a bit too."

"Oh good! So they didn't leave you high and dry. I have been wondering about that."

"Don't you worry. I won't be sleeping in a no-tell motel on the side of Route 3 in New Hampshire. I'll check in to..."

"*DON'T*!" he barked, and my sentence remained incomplete. He held his hand up as if stopping traffic.

"I am sorry, Diana. I did not mean to snap at you. But do *not* tell me where you're going. Please."

Well this was another new discovery! It was my turn to angle my head in an unspoken question. There was more I needed to know it seemed. I nodded slightly indicating my agreement to not tell him, and also to encourage him to tell me why. Kane inhaled an enormous breath and released it slowly.

"When it happens," he began, his voice softer than before. It still had a slight purr feel and sound to it, but it was more subdued. He hung his head and stared at his feet. "When it happens, I have no idea what I do. No memory at all when it is done. Nothing."

I leaned towards him, sliding my fingers through his. He smiled slightly and squeezed my hand in his; a silent thanks. He raised his head to the stars and exhaled sharply before speaking again.

"Still? There appears to be some residue of my mind present when I change. It has to be something powerful. My father was the one who noticed it. I was maybe? Twenty? I don't fully know what I did, but he pointed out that things that evoke a strong response from me seem to linger even when I am? Well? Not *quite* me."

"Like what?"

"As I said, I don't fully know. But my father would not have spoken lightly of such a thing; which is why I have always remembered it."

The pieces were falling into place. Kane loved me. He was *in* love with me, and we were, well? A *WE*. An *US*. Clearly, at least for Kane; I was one of those powerful things.

Something he felt strongly about. The weight of that responsibility settled on my shoulders. I couldn't imagine what he would do to protect me. Maybe I didn't want to imagine it. The clash of Block 3 and the catwalk of Block 4 pierced my mind. Jesus Christ! He tried to kill Martinez right there on the guard level. And he hadn't even changed yet. Scotty's voice echoed in my memory.

Woods fucked him up.

The slaughter Scotty and I had returned to last month. Cell 43 exploded in my vision. Bloody finger marks on the wall as Martinez was eviscerated alive. My mouth was suddenly dry and I was slightly nauseous. More than slightly.

"Diana, what is it?" Kane whispered, and I heard a tinge of fear in his voice. One look in his eyes and I knew I was not mistaken. His eyes were pleading for an answer and afraid to hear it.

"What did I do?"

I felt an iron resolve grip me. Oh no. *NO WAY* was he ever going to hear this from me. Kane may be protective of me, but that was *not* a one-way street. I loved him fiercely. If he learned of what he did while *changed;* it would destroy him. Not on my watch.

I have always had a ridiculously strong sense of duty and instinct to protect. It runs deep in my family; a lot of cops and other 'sheep dog' type professions for over a century in my bloodline, and from both parental sides. If I was willing to risk life and limb for strangers? There was *no way*, no fucking way in the universe I wasn't going to protect the man I loved. Not happening.

"Nothing." I said softly, and gently squeezed his hand. He opened his mouth as if to argue, and I raised my right index finger from the cast before he spoke.

"Don't."

It was spoken softly, but a command at the same time. Kane remained silent. We sat that way for a minute or two; staring out into the now dark yard. I watched the flashes of fire flies as they broke the night, and the crickets performed a sound track to their display.

He was still holding my hand, and Kane raised it to his lips and kissed it. A gentle smile found him after and he looked at me, his golden eyes held a warmth in them.

"Ready for some sleep?" he asked, the purr still soft but present in his voice.

"Yeah, I could go to bed." I answered.

"C'mon then."

He stood up, and gently assisted my rising to my feet. My legs had found some of their structure again, and I was able to stand on my own. We entered the house together, and Kane shut the door behind us. I turned towards the bedroom and he fell into step behind me. His footsteps were a comforting sound. I rounded to my side of the bed; smiling at that thought and he noticed it. The warmth in his gaze had not diminished, and the happy gleam was bright again. I hoped my greens reflected it as well. I shrugged off my clothes and slid into bed beside him, enjoying the feel of his skin beneath my hand as he pulled me against him. A feeling of complete tranquility blanketed me, and felt each rise and fall of his chest beneath my head. I could hear his heartbeat as well though I needed my ear pressed against him to do it, and I wondered what color I was emitting at the moment.

"*Enhancement*." I said quietly.

"What?" he asked.

"What we call '*it*'. It's your *Enhancement*." He kissed me gently and laughed softly.

"I like it."

Those words were the last I heard. The rhythm of his breathing and the steady beat of his heart ushered me to sleep, and I gladly surrendered to it.

CHAPTER TEN

Waking up with an arm wrapped around you after a very long time of waking up alone is a pleasant experience. The fact that it was Kane's arm holding me against him graduated the feeling from pleasant to wonderful. Somewhere in the night I had rolled onto my left side and he was curled around me, his right arm across my waist. I sighed and snuggled against him, savoring his warmth. He groaned softly; that noise you make when you are content and appreciative of a good night of sleep, and he pulled me tighter to him. I felt incredible, as if I hadn't slept in weeks and had finally rested; and while it had energized me I was happy to just lie still beside him. He buried his face against my neck and inhaled deeply. Another content groan came from behind me.

"I have been waiting a lifetime for that." He murmured and gently kissed my neck.

"What's that?" I asked.

"Drinking in the scent of you before I even open my eyes. There is simply? No possibility of it *not* being a good morning." He said, and inhaled against me once again.

"Is your sense of smell also *Enhanced*?" I asked. Kane laughed softly; his nose still buried behind my ear.

"Yes, it is. Which makes the perfume of you even sweeter."

"Charmer." I teased him, and he drew me against him more, still chuckling. After a moment he relaxed his arm enough and I rolled over to face him. His eyes were still closed but his lips wore a small grin, and I gently kissed him.

"Good morning, Kane."

The grin was gone, replaced by one of his enormous smiles that revealed his large white teeth. Yep! Still cool.

Lethal; but cool. There was definitely something wrong with me. He opened his eyes; the amber hue all but gone. They were gold and aglow.

"Indeed it is." His voice drenched with the purr I could feel resonate somewhere inside of me, and he wrapped both arms around me. I didn't think it was possible, but his smile grew bigger as he raised his head from the pillow.

"How do you like your eggs, Miss Jameson?"

#

The house, *our* house, was very well constructed. I had noticed that the first time Kane had shown me around, but as I unpacked various items in different rooms, it afforded me the opportunity to fully appreciate the craftsmanship of it.

The kitchen cabinets were incredible, as I had expected given that was the trade Kane was in. But as I opened each door stashing mugs and various other items, I noticed there were no nails, no staples, nothing visible that held the doors together. It was stunning the level of skill he possessed in constructing them, and I began to understand why he had developed a regular clientele of high-end contractors who ranged from Maine to Connecticut. The more I moved about the place; the more I marveled at his talent. Kane Woods was not just a master; he was an artisan.

Once the kitchen was unpacked, I opened the few boxes in the living room. The centerpiece of this room was an enormous stone hearth fireplace. I loved it the moment I saw it back in July, and I found myself looking forward to the first chill of fall and a warm fire offsetting it. I ran my hand down the stones admiring the precision in which they were embedded in the mortar. Again, undeniable craftsmanship was present in its construction. It was flanked on each side with floor to ceiling bookcases, and Kane had amassed an impressive library. I scanned the titles; his taste ranged from the classics to King, and I was surprised to see some poetry tucked into the shelves as well. A gentleman and a scholar it seemed. My attention dawdled on the books for a bit, and then returned to the stonework.

"My father and I built it together."

I hadn't heard him come in, and I jumped slightly at the sound of a voice behind me. After years of hyper vigilance pertaining to my surroundings; it was unsettling that I found him surprising me more than once. You're losing your edge Jimmy. That'll get you hurt or killed. I smiled slightly when I realized I didn't exactly have to worry about that sort of thing anymore. I was retired. That thought made me giggle inside despite the twinge of sadness I felt. At age 33, I was retired and financially stable. No need to get an actual job. Jesus I was going to have to find a hobby; I'd go crazy with nothing to do all day. I turned to face Kane. He was wearing his crooked grin as he leaned against the doorframe, arms folded across his chest. This was probably my favorite pose of his. It was reminiscent of the way he appeared that day I discovered he was alive, and learned about all of what he was. His eyes met mine for a moment, and then returned to the fireplace.

"I was fairly young when we did it. There had been a smaller one there prior, but he had decided it needed to be enlarged. Bigger fire for the winter months."

"What was his name?" I asked, and Kane started a bit, then chuckled softly.

"Angus."

"That's a good name." I said. "It's strong."

"So was Da." A shadow of sadness touched his voice, and darkened his eyes as well. Kane's vocabulary intrigued me; he sometimes slipped into what I would call the Queen's English. His use of Slainte was one, and now referring to his father as Da. My last name reeked of Irish descent, but it was becoming obvious Kane had some genetic ties to the Emerald Isle as well. His eyes regained their former gleam, and he smiled.

"My mother's name was Maureen Delany, before she married Angus Woods, and I am their only child."

"How long have they been gone?"

"Feels like a century." He said with a sigh.

"I'm sorry."

He shrugged, meeting my eyes once again, his gentle smile conveying his appreciation. I watched it as it grew bigger, and an impish light danced in his eyes.

"While they surely would have adored you, Diana? If either one, or both were still alive? We would not have woken up in bed together here. Grown man for a son or not; they were both from Ireland, and Catholic." He said with a wink.

Well that explained his use of language from time to time. Not quite the London or Oxford version of the Queen's English, but far more formal than my Tri-State area vernacular that was for sure. I smiled back at him and crossed the room, sliding my arms around his hips.

"It would have been a tragedy to have missed out on that." I said, and looked up into his eyes. "You might have had to have come for a sleep over in Newburyport."

"If I had? After the first morning?" he said, his smile returning, "I'd have moved to Newburyport. I don't ever want to wake up without you next to me again."

"Technically, I don't think you will." I said.

"Technically?" he repeated back to me, his eyebrows bent in a question.

"Well, sad for me," I began, tracing his jaw with my fingertip, "I have to wake up without you beside me the morning after a full moon. I'm going to assume you don't exactly sleep during that night?"

"I can't really say for sure. The entire night is a void for me. The final thing I remember is feeling as though my ribs are being forcibly spread apart to allow my... *Enhancement*, to escape. The next thing I remember is feeling is like I've regained consciousness on the floor after a three-day bachelor party. It takes a few seconds for me to get my bearings."

"Jesus, Kane." I whispered, "Does it hurt?"

"When it starts, yes it does. But I only feel it for a few seconds before I'm gone. And when I come back, I am sore. Every muscle is stiff and even my joints ache. But that only lasts for a few minutes. I mend rather quickly, if you recall." He said, and raised his right hand up.

Oh yes, I remembered the wide split knuckles that were barely scratches the next morning. A favorable side effect from his *Enhancement*. Too bad he couldn't share it. I was ready to get this cast off.

#

The following three days were filled with me settling in and getting used to where things were. The spare towels were kept in the linen closet in the bathroom, and Kane snickered when I announced I had located them. There was a lot of that; the laughter found us easily and the affection between us was as natural as breathing. The simplest of daily activities had a joy to them. Just passing by each other as I moved to pour a mug of coffee led to a smile, the touch of a hand on my shoulder, a quick kiss on the neck. The physical contact affirmed our happiness in being with each other. Kane had left earlier this morning to drop off an order he had completed, and though he was only gone for three hours? I found myself missing his company. It was the first time since I had moved in we were more than 200 yards away from each other. I was in the kitchen when I heard the truck tires crunch on the gravel driveway, and I realized I was *glad* he was home. He stepped through the door some thirty feet away as I was reaching into the refrigerator to get us a beer. It was August after all, and unloading solidly built cabinetry would give anybody a taste for a cold one; even someone with Kane's tireless energy.

He was beside me before I shut the appliance door. He startled me so much I dropped the beer. Kane caught both longneck bottles midair in his left hand while pulling me against him with his right. He held me firm and kissed me. It was a powerful kiss, strong enough to make my knees buckle slightly and my thighs ignite. I was breathless when he released me from it.

"I missed you, Lover." He purred the words more than spoke them, and I felt them vibrate within me more than I heard them. It left a fuzzy sensation in my mind, and it took me more than a few seconds to recover from both the kiss and the purr. The realization of how quickly he had just moved sliced through my mental fog, and I slapped his shoulder with my right hand.

"Jesus Christ Kane! You scared the shit out of me!" What the fuck?"

"What?" he exclaimed, honestly confused as to what had frightened me, which baffled me even more.

"How in the name of Christ and all things Holy did you get from the front door to the kitchen in less than half a second?" I exclaimed, the edges of my voice ragged with the fear he had just sent through me. He looked back towards the door, and then turned back to me. His eyes still held the confusion.

"That's over thirty feet Kane!" I said, pointing to the door.

"Oh." He said.

"Oh? Oh? That's the best you've got? Fucking Oh?"

He was starting to smile, and it wasn't the half grin. It was more apologetic. He looked sheepish. The irony of that did not escape me; a Wolf with a sheepish grin.

"I apologize for startling you."

"Startle? You scared the Bajeezus out of me."

"Yeah," he began, "I may have forgotten to mention that."

"What? The lightning speed?"

"Not lightning; but yes I can move quickly. I am sorry Diana, I sincerely am. I just missed you while I was gone today, and when I came in and saw you? My heart leapt. I was so happy and excited to see you. I couldn't get to you fast enough."

"Oh you certainly got to me fast enough! You're lucky I didn't take a heart attack." I was still slightly shaken, but my stance had softened. Yes, he had scared ten years off my life, but he only did it because he missed me. All right, fine; etch that on my headstone. I found a smile tugging at the corners of my mouth, and Kane saw it. He returned it with his crooked half grin. Damn it! That was my Achilles' heel with him, and I was beginning to suspect he knew it. Just when you're ready to strangle the man, he does that and I'm Jell-O. Shit. He pulled me against him again and kissed me. It wasn't as hard this time but it had the desired effect, and I'm sure he felt my resolve to do him bodily harm exit my body. He finally let me up for air, and the grin returned. I raised an eyebrow at him. He raised his left hand and shook it gently. I heard glass clink.

"At least I saved the beers." He said, and I slapped his shoulder again and took one from him.

#

It was odd to be packing an overnight bag when I had just that very afternoon finished *unpacking*. I had thrown a change of clothes into the small duffel bag, and was rummaging in the bathroom for my extra toothbrush and the like. Kane lingered in the doorframe; this time he leaned against it with his left arm over his head as he watched my movements.

"I am sorry." He said softly. I stopped and met his eyes. They were completely gold now, but his remorse did shine through. I reached and took his hand and he tugged me towards him, wrapping me in one of his enveloping hugs. I allowed myself to melt into him, indulging in the feel of every sinewy muscle as he held me against him.

"Jesus. I've waited a very long lifetime for a woman such as you Diana. It's not quite fair that four days later you have to…"

Kane let the sentence go unfinished. I squeezed him a little tighter, and he returned the gesture.

"Errrrgh." A half yell, half groan was all he vocalized. My response would have parroted him, so I remained silent. He relaxed his arms and afforded me the opportunity to step back and look at him.

"I hate that you have to go." He whispered, and even in that hushed tone; I felt his purr resonate through me. It was a frequency seemingly dialed in specifically for me to feel, and it was sniper caliber in its accuracy. The fact that I *FELT* his words as much as I heard them should have been disturbing. Instead I found comfort in it. Oh yes, I was indeed; *HOME*.

"I do too." I said, and he winced at my words. I reached up and ran my finger along his jaw. Kane closed his eyes at my touch, and I felt his stomach quiver at it. His physical reaction to my hand on his face released a wave through me. It was my turn to feel *hunger*. I was thankful his eyes were closed. God only knows what colors he'd have been seeing me in.

"We do have tonight though." I said softly, my fingers now tracing the side of his neck. His breath caught momentarily, I wasn't sure if it was my words or my touch; but I felt his arms begin to coil around me and the front pockets of his jeans suddenly had less room in them for car keys or random coins.

Heat surged across my skin, and I traced the path my fingers had crossed on his throat with my tongue. A low rumble escaped him as I continued my tasting. His fingers pressed harder against my shoulders, and my teeth skated along this neck. His breathing took on a ragged edge, and its uneven measures excited me. Oh yes, Mr.

Woods. I do believe it is *my* turn now. He moved his hands down my back to pull me closer and I seized his fingers in mine, removing his arms from around me and stopping his effort to take control.

A woman can reach much farther behind her than a man is able to, and Kane allowed me remove my body from his embrace. I interlaced my fingers with his and slowly stepped towards him, my tongue still on his skin, forcing his retreat into the kitchen. Well, he permitted it; there was never going to be a forcing of Kane to do anything, and most certainly not the evening before a full moon. Judging by the rasping in his breath; it wasn't going to be difficult to convince him to allow me to continue.

I backed him across the room until he was against the cabinets that supported the long counter. When he could go no farther, I pressed my body against his and released his hands. He moved them to pull me to him, and I grasped his wrists and brought them to rest on the three-inch-thick span of butcher block countertop instead, and then let go.

He left them where I had placed them, and I grinned. He couldn't see that of course; I had my face against his neck, alternating tongue and teeth. He groaned long and low but remained where I had placed him. Once again, I was sliding his shirt up over his head, and when he had freed his arms; he grabbed the edge of the counter again. Thank you, Kane. Let me *SHOW* you exactly how much I appreciate that.

I slid lower on him, a gentle bite where his neck and shoulder met, and his breathing grew harder and louder. My tongue traced further down his chest while I softly dragged my fingers across his stomach. Kisses interchanged with grazing teeth and flicks of tongue across his torso were having a powerful effect on him. He was panting and his groans weren't quite as low as they had been before. I ran my hands up his chest as I lowered myself to my knees, my tongue skimming across his stomach. His knuckles were white as he gripped the counter; every muscle in his arms clearly defined as he struggled to keep them there. I slowly brought my hands back down him, and then let them travel down the length of his legs before raking my spread fingers across the denim to return them to his waist. My fingers were at the button of his jeans and I opened them, slipping them down a bit. My teeth found the inside of his hip, and I lingered there for a bit before sliding the Levis lower still.

"Oh my God, Diana." He groaned, "I can't take much more of this."

He gasped loudly when my lips found the inside of his knee and he lurched like he had just been electrocuted. I held his leg still with my left hand and began to work my way up. My right hand slid up his thigh opposite of where I was currently teasing him with teeth now. He was straining to remain where I placed him. The effort it was taking was apparent in his desperate breathing and moaning.

My right hand moved closer to where my tongue, lips and teeth were heading and they were converging together. When they finally met, I grabbed Kane's hips. He cried out in pleasure as I ran my tongue down the length of him. His hips pushed against my hands as I teased him further, and his panting alternated with gasps. Finally he roared, and I heard the countertop crack in his grip as his entire body convulsed. His muscles remained locked for several moments, and then he shuddered and relaxed slowly. He was breathless; his head hung back as if he had just howled at the moon, and his thighs began to tremble. I regained my full height and kissed his chest. He groaned softly and wrapped his arms around me, leaning on me as he kissed the top of my head.

"I don't smoke." He gasped into my ear, "but you may need to help me to the porch. I think I just might start."

"You're welcome." I said, and laughed softly.

#

Kane decided that he would not start smoking, but he gladly accepted one of the two beers I brought out on the porch.

"You need me to open that for you?" I asked teasingly. He looked up and smiled.

"I may."

I laughed and sat down in the chair beside him. He may have decided against smoking but I hadn't, and I lit one up. I watched as the blue gray smoke curled from the burning end. I knew it was not good for my health, but I knew it was good for everyone *else's.* I smoked to prevent myself from landing a life sentence for real; one that would not be afforded an installment plan. The truth of the matter was that I loved smoking. I genuinely enjoyed the taste of a cigarette. We each took a long swallow of our beers, and I smiled at him. His eyes were slightly closed, but the gold light emitting from them was undeniable.

"What is that smile about?" he asked.

"Guess I'm just happy Kane. Cold beer in one hand, cigarette in the other, and you right beside me. Can't ask for much better out of life, except maybe some great pizza." I answered him, smiling even broader. He returned it with one of his own.

"I know where we can get delicious pizza. Allow me a few days, obviously tomorrow is not an option, and my *Enhancement* takes a bit out of me the following day, but once I am fully back? I would love to take you."

"They serve beer, right? I mean, I don't want to go to Hell and eating pizza without beer is a sure-fire way to land in the express elevator heading down."

"I would never allow it. Of course, they serve beer." he said, and he grinned. The way he said it, I almost believed him. If there was a way to prevent any harm from happening to me? Kane Woods would find a way.

It was a double-edged sword with him. The extent he would go to in his protection of me was limitless, and it gave me a sense of safety I had never experienced before. I loved him for it.

It also was a responsibility. There is nothing he wouldn't do, and he had his *Enhancement* side effects to enable him to. There was not a doubt in my entire being that he would kill to protect me, and I had witnessed what he was capable of with my own eyes. True, he wasn't *exactly* himself when he committed that violence, but if it ever came to me being in danger? I knew in my bones he would be just as ruthlessly lethal, even in his two-legged form. Martinez on the guard floor of Lawrence jail was only a scuffle to Kane. Yes, it was a comforting yet terrifying knowledge to be in possession of. I realized my beer was empty.

"I'm grabbing another one. You ready?" I asked.

"I'll get us the next round, Lover." his voice again a physical sensation as well as a sound. His eyes were fully open again and seemed lit from within they shone so brightly. He rose to his feet and took the empty bottle from my hand.

"Huh." I said.

"What's wrong?"

"Must not have been that good."

"What wasn't?" he asked, and I shifted right to get another cigarette. I felt the smile starting across my lips, and knew there was no way to conceal it. I had to turn away before he noticed.

"You're standing on your own again."

"You cannot be serious Diana! The night before She's Full, and you had to hold me upright in the kitchen. *NEVER*... in my *LIFE*... have I *EVER* been that weak. Certainly not inside of the eighteen-hours-before-moonrise window I can guarantee that!"

I had turned away to hide my smile, but there was no concealing the shaking of my shoulders as the laughter rose within me. I swiveled back around towards him again, and his expression was still one of utter disbelief. It was precious, and my giggles found their way to sound. Once Kane recognized that I was teasing him; it changed. His signature grin appeared, revealing his blindingly white teeth, and he shook his head slowly back and forth. He laughed softly, and then spoke.

"Not that good?" he began, the purr present once again, "I suppose not. I have intended to replace that countertop for some time now; though I installed that one less than six months ago. Not that good. Indeed."

He leaned down and kissed me, then nuzzled his nose to my ear.

"You may be the death of me yet, Miss Jameson." The purr was stronger, and I felt it resonate in my body while he went in for the beers.

He returned quickly, as I now knew he was capable of doing and handed me an open one. He kissed me again before sitting in the chair beside mine. He glanced at his chair, then over at mine, and then looked at me.

"Jimmy, we need a porch swing. I don't like this separate chair nonsense."

"Well then. I guess now I have something to do tomorrow night."

"What would that be?" Kane asked.

"Porch swing shopping. You want a free standing one or one that hangs from the eave?"

"A hanging one would be ideal. Thank you for doing that for us."

I liked that he said *us*. The words 'us' and 'we' warmed me. When I realized it, I wondered what colors I was emitting. I considered asking him, but decided against it. However he 'learned' my *how*, was fine with me. For me? I read his eyes. Maybe he just checked my 'brightness'. I finished my beer and stretched.

"You ready for bed?" I asked him.

"Indeed I am." Something in his tone struck me and I cut my eyes sideways at him. His were almost neon in the brightness of the gold. His grin held an edge to it, and my skin flushed when I recognized what lurked behind it.

"I cannot be with you tomorrow night." he said, and it wasn't a purr anymore. It was a humming that found its way into the marrow of my bones. "So please, permit me to indulge of you before you must go."

Jesus. Maybe it was Kane that was going to be the death of me. I didn't have *Enhancement* to aid in my recovery. So be it. There are far worse ways to check out.

"It'd be my pleasure." I rasped.

He smiled, revealing blazing teeth.

"I certainly hope it will be. Several times; if I am as successful as you were."

I was heading 'out of town' tomorrow. Seems I was going to be leaving Rowley walking like John Wayne wished he could. I was a lucky woman.

Chapter Eleven

I was stirring back from the delight of true, restful sleep. Kane was draped across me, his right arm across my shoulders and tucked under my chin; holding me against him, and his right leg over my waist and thigh. The entwining of him into me brought a smile to my lips before my eyes had even fluttered. He wasn't snoring, but his nose was just under my ear and the steady pace of his breathing made me wish I would never have to leave this spot. Lord, if I'm going to die today? Make it at this moment. Throughout eternity, I would be okay with that. I'm not sure where I'm spending the afterlife, but this feeling would be more than enough to get me through a trip downstairs. If I went up instead? Pretty sure this is where I would be. I inhaled and savored the smell of his skin. Male. 100%. It was my turn to purr, and he stirred at the sound. His arm pulled me closer and he took a deeper breath.

"Mmmmmh."

I responded in kind.

"My need for this is consuming." He murmured; voice still thick with sleep.

"For what?" I whispered. My vocal cords weren't fully awake yet either.

"For you. Beside me. When I wake up. And when I fall asleep. And every moment in between those two events."

"Jesus." I said as I snuggled closer to him, "I am so in love with you."

His arm pulled me tight against him. His presence was all I would ever need. Kane filled empty places in me I never knew I had until he occupied them. It's a funny thing to go through life and you are A-OK, and then somebody waltzes in and it's only after that you realize what you had been lacking. And you never knew you were missing anything until that moment. Kane? Was the part I had been missing, while I was unaware I wasn't intact.

He didn't 'complete' me...I was already whole. But he *Enhanced* me. I laughed softly at the pun.

"How would you like your eggs today, Diana?" he purred.

#

"I hate this." He spat as I dropped my small duffel bag through the passenger window of my Mustang. He was kicking gravel in the driveway and clearly past being simply restless. The only reason he wasn't pacing was because he was no longer confined to the cramped quarters of cell 32. He was circling the driveway and lawn; unable to stay still for more than five seconds but lingering near me. His shoulders were tense, his jaw clenched, and he continued moving because he simply *could not stay still*. I honestly felt pity for him. He had not asked for this, nor had he done anything to merit it. He was born with it. And the *Enhancement* wasn't something that could be discussed in open conversation with any Joe Blow from down the block. Kane had weathered these years with it completely alone after his parents were gone. Pity was not strong enough. My heart broke for him.

"Kane." I said, and despite the Pull of the moon, his ceaseless movements stopped. He smiled, a full smile as always when I used his name when he wasn't expecting me to. It was enormous today. Maybe it was simply the larger white teeth of a full moon. Whatever it was? It was dazzling. I crossed the few steps that lay between us and wrapped my arms around him.

"It's one night." I said, pulling him closer to me. He released a long sigh.

"I know Diana. I know. But to have finally found *YOU*? And now you have to go; because of what I am. Yes, I hate this."

"But I love you." I said, holding his golden eyes with my greens. The brilliant light in them shifted, softened even, and he dropped his head.

"Jesus." He whispered.

"What?" I inquired my voice low but above his whisper.

"That makes it all worthwhile. All of this long road. It finally means something."

We lingered a bit in the driveway, starting several conversations that were not of any urgency; mostly because the truth of it was I didn't want to go any more than Kane wanted me to leave. My logical mind said it's not even an eighteen-hour period we faced. It was just past 4:30 in the afternoon, and I could return safely at sunrise. Barely fifteen hours. So why was I discussing the Red Sox with Kane? I hate baseball. Cold facts lay bare? Neither of us wanted to separate. I reflected back on the last full moon and how he had been desperate to get me away, and decided it was my turn this month. I wouldn't make him do it again. I pulled him close and kissed him. His arms encircled me and I wanted to linger forever, but after a minute I summoned the 'duty' in my genetics and drew back from him.

"I've got to go." I said quietly, and Kane nodded.

"Be safe, Jimmy. You must be, for my sake. I love you too much to be able to survive without you."

I kissed him quickly and walked to the driver's side door of my car. He beat me to it and opened the door for me. I smiled and traced his jaw with my fingers.

"Do *NOT* tell me where you are going." He said. His gaze held an iron to it. I grinned.

"Babe, you already know where I'm going." I said, and his forehead creased in a silent question. I kissed him again quickly and climbed in the vehicle.

"I'm shopping for a porch swing."

#

Maneuvering the Mustang down the patchwork of pavement was one of the hardest things I had ever done in my life. I've worn uniforms soaked in blood that didn't belong to me on more than one occasion. On other occasions, I've worn uniforms wet with blood that *DID* belong to me. I've dealt with fires, both figuratively and literally. I've been threatened countless times, and had people try to kill me more than once, with weapons or their bare hands. I've buried those I loved, and those I worked with. I had been forced into 'retirement' from a calling so deep in my DNA the words *job* or *career* are comical. Driving down that 'road' to leave for the night because I *HAD* to? Trumped all of those experiences ten times over. Still, I did it. When I reached the end; I sat at the T intersection and looked both left and right.

I had no idea where I was going. I could not have told Kane where I was spending the night because I didn't even know. I made no reservations anywhere. I don't know if that was a subconscious action on my part or not. The point was; I had no plan. I remained at the end of the road for some time. I lit a cigarette and inhaled its toxicity deeply. It tasted great. After I had smoked half of it, I took a deep breath in. Pick a direction Jimmy. I put my left blinker on, but turned right. Just in case Kane could see that far. It was a color after all.

I made my way to 95 and headed south. Perhaps a night in Boston. That would be fun; wandering through Fanueil Hall was always a treat. People watching was a favorite pass time of mine, and no better place than the outdoor bar of the Salty Dog in summer. I was exiting 95 on to Route 1 when the thought slapped me. Building 19 in Peabody! If there was ever a place to find a porch swing? That was it! I laughed out loud. Jesus, I was actually going to shop for a porch swing. Who knew?

#

It was dimly daylight when my eyes opened. I had spent the night at the Holiday Inn in Peabody, just off Route 1. There was a pool there and Bickford's Pancake House was right next door if I craved food, but I had gone to the room early and fallen asleep faster than I knew. Kane had worn me out more than I realized. I smiled at the memories of how I had gotten so tired.

Kane! It was dawn! I could go home! I launched myself from the bed and shoved my legs into a pair of jeans. I was still zipping them up as I entered the bathroom. I raked my fingers through my spiky blonde hair and snatched up my toothbrush. Quick strip of Colgate and I was scrubbing them clean. I washed my face, hit my armpits with deodorant and threw a T shirt on over my bra. I was going home by Jesus! I took two steps back into the bedroom, and stopped.

Home.

Until that minute? At the end of the day, I simply went to where I lived. Going *HOME* was a completely new thought pattern for me, and it stopped me dead in my tracks. Home. I inhaled deeply, and my breath had a jagged edge. Home. Why was this so foreign to me? Yeah it was a solid house; cozy even. But it wasn't the first place I had ever laid my head down in and written a check for electricity for. So why was I so fired up about getting back there? I took a few more steps before the realization slapped me right between the eyes.

Home, was not about the structure. Home? That was wherever Kane was. I laughed out loud in the empty room. Jeez, there were times I was pretty slow on the uptake! Home is where the heart is. That cheesy cliché actually had truth behind it. Oh, fuck me, this was so stupidly good I laughed aloud again. I was still laughing as

I tugged the laces of my sneakers and tied them. Cheesy cliché or not; I was going *HOME*.

Heading north on Route 1 early in the morning is not what anyone would call rush hour traffic. Southbound? Absolutely; everybody is heading *IN* to Boston not coming *OUT* of it. I was on the road with a few semi-trucks and cars, moving quickly at 70 in a 55. Still, I felt like it was a snail's pace. Shit! I knew I was going to miss those lights and sirens! I considered buying a used cruiser at the next police auction. Why not? I still had my mirrored 'Hey You' cop glasses. 'Hey You' glasses are another trade term describing the sunglasses every self-respecting cop wears. The mirrored lenses make it impossible for anyone to see your eyes, and that is unsettling. The informal name given to these sunglasses stems from the dread every person feels when a cop wearing them points directly at you and barks 'Hey You!', and then beckons you to them by curling their index finger several times.

I was turning left on to our street before I knew it. A mustang is not exactly a vehicle known for its ground clearance and on a normal day I would have taken a bit more care driving on the broken trail that led to our house; but this was not a normal day. I zipped into the driveway and sprung out of the car. My feet traversed the ground just shy of a run, and I reached the door. As I was about to fling it open, I stopped. What was I going to walk in to?

Was he even home yet? The sun had crested the horizon well over two hours ago. Surely it had to be safe. *HE*, had to be safe. But what was I going to encounter? An exhausted Kane, curled up on the floor? I heard his words echo in my head. *When I come back, I'm sore. Every muscle is stiff and even my joints ache.* Jesus Christ what must *THAT* be like? And the ribs *forced apart* so the *Enhancement* can escape? What the shit! God, what did he do to deserve that? I glared up at the sky, a fury igniting within me. For the first time ever? I was pissed off at God. Completely pissed off.

His name is *KANE.*

Not *CAIN*.

What the fuck, God?

While I had been raised somewhat Catholic; it never truly took with me. I had too many questions, and they too little answers except for saying that's why they call it Faith. I had accepted that explanation, and while I was no longer a Catholic? I had my belief in God and Jesus and the Holy Spirit. The Trinity. I liked the Holy Spirit the best of the three personas of One Being. The Holy Spirit was responsible for creativity, laughter and inspiration. Basically, the Holy Spirit? Was the ruling facet of Chaos.

Chaos was something I could relate to; and the Holy Spirit had a pretty good sense of humor to boot. Yep, my favorite of the Trio. Even when shit goes sideways and upside down? The Holy Spirit was the one who said, Oooh! What a delightful mess we have here! Fantastic! Let's check it out! Maybe the Holy Spirit was a cop. I laughed at the thought, because it actually made sense. God was the Judge. Jesus was the Defense Attorney working to save you. The Holy Spirit? Well, the Holy Spirit was there when the shit went down, but never judged. The Holy Spirit experiences the shit *WITH* you, and even on the darkest of scenes? Appreciates the random things that not only got you to that point but happen *while* you are there; and finds the same laughter you do in how truly wonderfully fucked it all is. Yep. The Holy Spirit is definitely a Cop, and one I'd ride partner with any day.

My hand was on the doorknob, and I turned it and opened the door. I stepped inside, not quite sure what to expect. The smell of coffee reached me and I smiled.

There is not a cop on Earth that doesn't appreciate good coffee, and Kane did make one Hell of a pot. If the coffee was on, he must be ok. I released the breath I had been holding and smiled again. Nice job Jimmy! Didn't even need to be reminded this time! Well done! A nose in my hair and lips brushing my neck occurred without warning.

"Good morning Diana. I missed you." He breathed in my ear, kissing my neck again. He wrapped both arms around my waist and drew me against him. I didn't even jump when he seized me, though I had no idea where he came from nor how fast. It was *Kane*. That fact alone made me safe. I relaxed into his form, enjoying the feel of his body against me. After a long moment, I nudged loose enough to turn to face him. Kane looked tired; more so than he had the day I discovered him leaning against my car when I thought he was dead. Then again, that was three days after a Full moon. This morning was not even four hours past moon set. He had to be exhausted.

"Are you okay?" I asked him, peering deeply into his eyes. The dapples of gold were present, but their metallic sheen didn't overpower all of the amber today.

"I am now." He replied, and the gold glinted brighter momentarily.

"Kane, I'm serious. Are you all right?" I said, and he smiled.

"I love the way you speak my name." he answered, and his voice had resumed its physical resonation in my being. I must remember to ask about that, but now was not the time. The man was wrung out. My hands found his jaw line, and I followed the angle of it with my fingers. He closed his eyes and sighed.

"Yes, I am all right. Just tired. It takes a day as I've already mentioned."

"You still stiff and sore?"

"Not so much as earlier, but thank you for asking. Mostly I would enjoy some sleep, in our bed. There's coffee Love, I know I may be tired but you probably are not. Let me pour you some." He moved to go to the kitchen and my hands grasped his shoulders. Kane stopped, and gave me a questioning stare.

"Let's go to bed." I said. He slowly remembered his grin, and as it appeared I found myself wanting nothing more than to be lying beside him.

"It would be my delightful pleasure." He whispered, and a yawn overtook him. He seemed embarrassed by it, and that made me smile. I took his hand and led him to our bedroom. Kane followed without protest. Oh yes, he was exhausted all right; I hadn't even made a sexual innuendo and he was on my heels heading for the bed.

I slid under the sheet at the same time he climbed into it, and we found each other as if we had been sleeping beside each other for decades. The ease of all should have concerned me; I was not used to something feeling this natural that didn't involve violence to survive. Then again, that was a lifetime ago. It was something Deputy Sheriff Jameson was used to. She was no longer present, though her influence was still felt and probably would be for the rest of my life.

Kane moved to wrap me to him, but instead? I inched up a bit farther on the pillows and pulled him to me. His body language suggested surprise when I did it, but he almost immediately loosened and rested his head against my right breast and shoulder. I stroked my fingers through his hair and his weary body relaxed upon me. Each pass through his mane resulted in his unwinding further, and he was inches from sleep when he whispered.

"I love you. More than anything I have ever known."

What I felt was not just the vibration of his voice. It was my heart leaving my possession and finding its way into his hands. Hell, or high water? I loved him, and I could now truthfully say I was heartless. I had given mine away. Free will; no pressure, no manipulation. I gave it. Kane had more than earned it. I felt his breathing and presumed he was asleep. That was a good thing, because I was following suit. The coffee would work hot or cold. It was August. Iced coffee suited me just fine.

September 1990

CHAPTER TWELVE

August is a funny month, no matter where in the nation you reside. The excitement of summer has long passed, and you find yourself just waiting out the heat; anticipating Labor Day and the hope of a morning where the crisp taste of Fall has found the air. The shining moment of the month for me was the removal of that goddamn plaster cast from my left wrist. Kane was not wrong; the bones had broken clean and even the doctor was impressed with the way it had mended.

Kane and I had settled in to living together quite nicely. There are always speed bumps and pot holes in any new relationship; even more when it evolves to sharing a home but there were far more checks in the plus column than the minus. Any hiccups between us were addressed quickly and more often than not with humor. The ease we each felt in being honest with each other was astounding given the short time we had been, well a *WE*, but it smacked of understanding and mutual respect. No matter the issue, be it who left the coffee maker on or the cap off the toothpaste, it was so completely trivial in the scheme of how much we deeply cared for each other it became the buzz of a fly in the back drop of a picnic. It was a slight annoyance; but nothing important enough to disrupt our enjoyment of the sunshine. For me it was surreal. I was sitting at the kitchen table across from Kane, sipping my second mug of coffee when I remembered something he had said the day I discovered him alive and leaning on my car.

It was always the forbidden dream.

I had never thought of anything being forbidden, so long as you are willing to accept the consequences of your actions. If you live 'right' or you live 'wrong'; either way eventually the check comes due and you have to reach in your pocket and pay what you owe. Then again, I wasn't the one who was *Enhanced*. I had the luxury of 'normal'. That word, floating through my thoughts made me spit the coffee across the table, and Kane jumped in surprise.

"Are you all right?" He was on his feet and around the table, concern clearly painted in his expression. An iota of sorrow approached me but was deflected. His genuine caring was endearing, but it still struck me as funny that 'normal'? Now referred to *ME*. Jesus, Mary and Joseph; how do I begin to explain *THIS*? I waved him off, silently assuring him I was more than fine, and started to giggle. He returned to his seat across from me.

"I'm sorry Kane. Sometimes, I just think funny shit. I crack myself up."

"I have noticed, and I adore your humor. Please share the joke."

"You know I love you, right?" I asked, and a generous smile spread across him. He nodded, and waited for me to continue.

"Well handsome, I never once in my life thought I would be the 'normal' one in a relationship."

"Oh, you are nowhere *NEAR* normal, Jimmy."

"I know! Right?" I exclaimed, "That's why it was so funny. It's so fucked up its perfect."

Kane considered that for a moment, and then began to laugh quietly.

"Given it all? You are in fact correct; in every aspect of what you've said. That is actually funny."

"Told you." I replied, and I laughed a little more. "I am the funniest person I know."

"The way you look at things, and how your mind works, is stunning sometimes." he said, and my laughter quieted. It did not go without notice by Kane.

"Oh, no. No, no, no Lover." He said, and the undercurrent of vibration his voice carried found my core once again. He was around the table before I knew it, and kissed me gently. The gold splashes embedded in the amber of his eyes were bathed in warmth, and he pulled the lethal half grin from his arsenal. He crouched down in front of me.

"That perspective is very much a part of why I love you like I do. Normal would *NEVER* be a word I would use in describing you. You are exceptional."

"Uh, thanks I guess?" I felt my eyebrow arching. Kane grasped my hands, kissed the backs of them, and then gazed up at me.

"No." he whispered, "Thank you."

"It has been my pleasure." I said softly, and ran my fingers through his hair. It was incredibly thick yet surprisingly soft. I let my fingers trace the ends that curled at his collar, and he let his head fall back while I touched him. When he returned his eyes to mine, the gold flecks had multiplied and almost obscured the amber. There was still a week left in August and another four days in September before the moon grew fat, and I was surprised to see the color shift this early. We were barely past mid-month, and his eyes looked as though the full moon was tomorrow.

"Speaking of pleasure…." He began, and I felt my color flash to red. Kane smiled, and his eyes caught a playful light. I had no doubt he saw the color change. His grin spread, confirming my suspicions.

"Tempting, and oh yes later," he said, and ran his hands up my arms, "But I am a man of my word." I peered at him, questioning in silence.

"I believe, I promised you pizza."

Pizza is like winning the lottery where I come from. If you get a great one? It's as close as any poor schmuck like me is going to get to hitting the winning six numbers. Should you have the misfortune of getting a shitty pizza? Well it's still *PIZZA* for Christ's sake; so instead of a million dollars you get 5 bucks. Not what you hoped for but still a win. I glanced at the clock. It was 9:15 in the morning.

"Where are we getting pizza this early?" I inquired.

"By the time we get there? The bricks will be hot. Trust me."

"I do; without a second thought." I said, and he startled for a fraction of time. Then he smiled, a full consuming smile, and even this far out from the next full his teeth were large. He kissed my hands quickly once more and then rose to his full height.

"Miss Jameson. Please permit me to enjoy your excellent company over a pitcher of beer and slices direct from Heaven."

"How can I refuse?" I teased him.

"If I am a fortunate man? You will not."

"Well then you might want to stop at 7-11 for a Megabucks, because I'm in."

#

We were in Kane's pick up and cruising down Route 1 South, when I realized he had passed through Danvers, Peabody and Saugus while still in the left lane. All three towns had great pizza joints, and I turned in the seat to face him.

"Exactly *where* are we headed?" I asked. He patted my thigh and grinned. He let his right hand remain on my knee, and after six weeks of being in a cast? I seized the opportunity to slide my now freed left hand fingers through his. His grin spread into a smile.

"I thought we would try a tasting tour."

"We're not in the Napa Valley, Kane."

"No, but we are in a region loaded with authentic Italian family recipes that have been passed down from generation to generation. Why not go on a taste tour of Italy? Minus the jet lag."

I returned his smile. The man was a genius! A pizza and beer tour of Boston was the most brilliant thing I had ever heard of! It was even better than trying to 'Drink the Ave'.

Drinking the Ave was a local thing. It referred to trying to have a shot and a beer in every bar on Dorchester Avenue, conveniently located in Dorchester; a *very* Irish section of Boston second only to Southie. There are many bars on Dorchester Avenue, and after three attempts the farthest I ever got was seven. All three times I ended up puking at the end of the night, and re-evaluating my choices the following day. Those three times? My day after face was as green as my eyes. Pizza and beer were a far better plan, and I loved it.

"I'm in the truck with goddamn Einstein." I said, a giggle finding my voice. "This is the best idea I have ever heard!"

"Jimmy, I wasn't born last night. Even if you had not mentioned pizza? I have heard how you say *CAUWFEE*. I have excellent hearing, remember? You are a New York gal. Pizza and New York go hand in hand. I'm just glad you are not a Yankees fan, although I am not sure about this whole *Mets* business."

"*OH MY GOD*! They *STILL* had *ALL* of game Seven to win it! *STOP* with the Buckner defense, would ya?"

We both laughed at that. The 1986 World Series was still a touchy subject in Boston, and when I was feeling particularly cocky? I would don my Mets cap and strut through town. The local rabid Red Sox fans would snarl, but I just smiled and pointed at the orange NY on the cap and say '86. They would grumble into their beers, and a few nasty looks or comments were sent my way, but it was part of the fun. Boston and New York were rivals for eternity, and both towns knew it. That was what made it so enjoyable. Depending on the sport and the season the team was having, the verbal jabs were either thrown out or taken. Good fun, in an asshole East coast sort of way; which was how we all were brought up. Don't dish it out if you can't take it. I looked out the window and saw the exit sign for Malden.

"Kane? Why didn't you hit Oak Grove? Take the T in, since we're having beer with the pizza and all? I mean neither of us needs a Deewy."

Deewy is local slang for a DUI. The T is the commuter rail that goes in and out of Boston. Depending on what town it goes to and the schedule; the T lines are color coded. Oak Grove was the most northern part of the orange line, ending in Melrose. The purple line went as far as Salem, but it was not as regular of a train. The green line was strictly in Boston and was more a trolley system as it travelled surface streets. The blue line and red line also intercrossed, as they are also part of the 'T' aka transit system. It was hodgepodge compared to New York City, but the streets of Boston were just and random and confusing. New York City is laid out like a grid with the exceptions of Tribeca and Soho. Boston is laid out like somebody threw spaghetti against the wall and decided to design the streets by what stuck to the sheetrock. Its maddening chaos was part of its charm. After all, it's *BOSTON*. It doesn't have to make sense.

"I am not worried about a Deewy."

"Oh, so what? You're Teflon from the law? I don't think so Fido or we never would have met."

"Fido?!?" Kane sputtered, and followed it with a laugh. It was a good hearty laugh, and I found myself infected by it and joined him. I was as caught off guard as much as he was by what I had said. Jesus Jimmy; the shit that comes out of your mouth.

"Oh my God Kane, I'm sorry. I don't even know where that came from."

"Doesn't matter Lover! That was excellent!" He said, his eyes still dancing with laughter. Thank Christ the man has a sense of humor. A warm flush of affection for him swept through me.

I was sunk when it came to Kane; I was absolutely in love with him. The fact that he could laugh at himself was just another nail in my coffin. I am the type of person incapable of doing anything half assed. I undertake everything 150%, and it seemed that being in love was just like the rest of my life. I put everything I had into it. I honestly just don't know any other way of doing things. I may not do things perfectly, but I give it my all.

I've found that so long as you do that? You don't regret much. You can be disappointed that some things didn't go as you had hoped, but at least you didn't have to endure the sting of 'if I had only tried a little harder' as well. If you lay all your cards out on the table, you may not win every hand, but at least you can walk away with your head held high, knowing you didn't hold anything back. Most people are a bit intimidated by this approach, but I'd rather scare a few than have the nagging in the back of my mind that I didn't give it my very best shot. Kane reached across the bench seat and rested his hand on my thigh.

"It is certainly never boring around you Diana." He said, and the purr was present again. I loved the way I felt his words. It was an intimacy I had never known before, and it brought me a sense of peace. Hard to believe I was using that word as well in reference to myself. Not too many weeks ago? That was a foreign concept. I found myself enjoying it immensely.

"No shit, right?" I asked and giggled a little, "Sometimes even I am surprised at what I friggen say."

"Part of your countless charms."

"Oh, who's the charmer now?" I retorted. Kane flashed his crooked half grin, the yellow flecks a little brighter in his eyes in that moment. Oh yes, I was sunk. The Titanic was found faster and far shallower than I would be, and that's if they ever found me. If I was lucky? They wouldn't. I was perfectly happy to stay this deep involving Kane.

"So where are you taking us?"

"The North End of course."

"And exactly where do you plan on finding a parking spot?"

The North End of Boston is narrow streets, even by Boston standards. There are some parts that are brick, and the brick was laid over the cobblestone that dated back to colonial times.

Originally designed for a horse and buggy; through the centuries they had become not only two-way traffic; but also had on street parking. On street parking in the North End involved some minor use of the sidewalk as well, but it was a given and nobody got upset. It is what it is, and everybody just accepted that there would be a Cadillac with two tires six inches up on the sidewalk. It was a hysterical nightmare in winter when snow banks got factored in. As I said; it's Boston. It doesn't have to make sense.

"While I did not stop at a 7-11, you agreed to join me today. I'm feeling fortunate." He said and winked at me; the grin again melting me. We had crossed the Tobin bridge, toll paid, and I had barely noticed it.

"I would join you in Hell." I said, and he looked across the truck at me. I smiled and continued. "It wouldn't even take pizza and beer. Although that is definitely all the more reason to go."

"Join me in *Hell*." Kane mused.

"Absolutely. Wherever you go? I will be there, for as long as you want me to."

"Thank you." he whispered, and it was the softest I had ever heard him speak. He looked slightly off balance, almost like he never expected me to say that. I could practically see the mental wheels that were turning in his head, and for as much as I wanted to ask? I held back. Kane seemed to be working something out and it was clearly important, so I gave him the space. He piloted the truck down the streets and I listened to the radio.

"Ha!" he said, and chuckled. I looked across at him, and he pointed out the windshield. I followed the direction his finger led, and I'll be damned if a truck wasn't pulling out onto the street, leaving us a primo parking spot. Son of a bitch. Seems he had a horse shoe up his ass today considering the great luck he was having. He really needed to buy a lottery ticket.

"Did you eat Lucky Charms this morning?" I teased, and he continued to laugh softly as he parked the truck. He killed it and took the keys out of the ignition and opened his door. I put my hand on my door handle and he stopped.

"Diana, we both know I can get around the truck fast enough before you open it but I would prefer not to draw attention. Please, allow me get your door for you."

I took my hand off the door handle and smiled. Kane returned it, and climbed out of the pick-up. He appeared at my door in a normal amount of time and opened it, extending his hand to assist my exit from the vehicle. I accepted it and slid out of the seat.

"Thank you." we said simultaneously, and laughed together.

"It was indeed my pleasure. You will never open a door again while I am present." He said, and his tone told me he was serious. Gentleman and scholar; wrapped up in that smoking body and lit with golden eyes and big toothed grins. Maybe I should be buying a lottery ticket. Then again, maybe I had already won. It sure felt that way. Kane kissed me quickly and ushered me to the sidewalk, his hand at the small of my back, guiding me safely away from oncoming cars. Once we were off the street and on the concrete pedestrian pathway, he stopped and kissed me again; this one a little longer and with more behind it. When we stopped, I'm positive I was redder in his view. I caught my breath and smiled. He took my hand in his, interlacing his fingers between mine and smiled.

"I'm hungry." He said, and smiled even bigger. His eyes caught a light that smelled of the very best sort of trouble.

"But first? Pizza." He finished, and if there was any orange left in me, it was gone. He tugged gently at my hand and led me down the street.

#

Our short walk led us to Fanueil Hall. Fanueil Hall is the most wonderful place for anyone with an appetite. Every food you can imagine from all over the globe is prepared here. It is a flea market of food. Once upon a time, it was a warehouse where loads of goods from the bellies of wooden ships were stored and sold. Names such as Ames Plow still remained dating back to when Boston was still a British colony. Yes, Boston is *THAT* old. Remember, the sister jail to Lawrence was Salem jail; as in Salem witch trials. Massachusetts is old, by 'New World' standards. The main floor of Fanueil Hall is a few steps up from street level, but there are downstairs establishments as well. In one of these sub ground lairs; Pizzeria Regina is located. It was originally founded in the North End of Boston, but the Fanueil Hall site was simply amazing. You go down a flight of stairs, and turn left and there you're in. The smell of pizza lures you in from the street level, and it is not uncommon on summer weekends to find a line of hungry patrons not only on the stairs but wrapped around the railing and stretching down the way. It is *THAT* good.

Kane and I entered and the familiar brick walls reminded me of New York, and also how long it had been since I had been here. My God, was I actually returning to human life? It felt like an eternity since I had enjoyed so much as a day of uncoiling. Today, I was more than that. I was relaxed, and to be honest? I was happy. Kane had followed me down the stairwell and the cop in me picked up on where he placed himself.

He had my back, and that was what had relaxed me. The fact that it was Kane? That was what made me happy. The tables in the room and the booths that lined the right side of the place were unoccupied at the moment; it was a Wednesday morning after all. The long bar ran down the left; its dark wood worn from years of patrons yet still warmly inviting. Kane looked at me and glanced across the place, an unspoken 'where do you want to sit?' It occurred to me that this was our first time going out somewhere together. I veered left without hesitation. I'm a belly up to the bar kind of girl. He smiled broadly as he sat in the barstool to my right.

"Love it. I knew you were exactly my type of woman."

A woman with blonde hair pulled back into a ponytail appeared from the back area. She wiped her hands on a towel, and an enormous smile erupted on her face when she saw us hunkered down at the bar. The way she crossed the place, which I had always loved because it felt like you were eating in a New York alley except there were no rats or muggers, told me I already liked her. This was going to be a fun time; not a doubt in my mind. She was just shy of my height, and a curvy build that somehow embodied her personality though I had only her smile and stride to base it on. When she opened her mouth, I grinned. The cop in my bloodline is rarely off, and today it was spot on.

"Hey guys! Welcome! I see you've seated yourselves. That's awesome; the hostess called out the bitch." She said, smiling the entire time. I laughed, truly enjoying her candor. Oh yes, this one was *way* okay. Kane joined my enjoyment with a chuckle of his own.

"I'm Ann. I'm the bartender slash pizza pimp here today." And she extended her hand across the bar to shake mine. I was still laughing as I accepted it. She had a firm grip; not the wimpy girlie one I had run across too many times with women, but she wasn't trying to arm wrestle me either. It was honest, or what I would call? Stand-up. Yep, I liked Ann from the start.

"Ann? I'm Kane, and this lovely lady beside me is Jimmy." My gentleman said, as I was still giggling a bit too much to answer straight off. Ann released my hand

and shook his just as firmly. She wrinkled her nose a bit and looked to me.

"Jimmy. I *LIKE* that. Very cool. You *must* tell me how that came to be."

"My last name is Jameson." I said, having stopped laughing long enough to be able to talk like a person.

"Oh." She said, and glanced Kane's way and then back at me. "And what's his last name?"

"Woods." Kane said, and Ann glanced at him before returning her bright blue eyes to mine.

"Funny how he thought I was talking to *him*." She said, and smiled even bigger. Oh yes; I *REALLY* liked her. Kane blinked for a moment, and then smiled. He was following the flow. Absolute ball busting was happening here. God love him; he was okay with it.

"Well, we only met last night. I wasn't sure she would remember when we woke up this morning." He said, and cut his eyes at me. Ann wrinkled her nose even more and grinned.

"How fun!"

Kane managed to keep a straight face for a total of two seconds before laughing. There was no way for me to stop from joining him, and Ann followed suit. When we had quieted a bit, she looked at us both and placed her hands on the bar.

"Listen you two. That was great and all, and I love a good bullshit story for a laugh, but I was never going to buy it. No way are two people so in love with each other just grabbing pizza after a one nighter. Beer?"

"Yes. A pitcher of whatever is coldest." Kane said. Ann turned to pour it, and he looked at me.

"Is it that obvious how I feel for you?"

"Oh, most definitely." was the response Ann threw over her shoulder as she tilted the pitcher now filling with beer. "And how Miss Jimmy feels about you."

Kane and I exchanged glances. It was my turn to wear a sheepish smile. Bartenders are funny. They have seen it all, almost as much as cops. And while they will tell you directly what they see; they hold a confidence as well as any priest or attorney. Probably better. If you ever hide a body? A bartender you've never met before is probably the safest person to tell; at least any bartender worth their salt. Ann had more salt than Lot's wife. She was awesome.

Kane's smile was not subtle. If I didn't know better? I'd say the man was beaming. His eyes were completely gold, and bright. His teeth were blazing white, and they seemed bigger than they should have for this week. He leaned over and kissed me. It was a short kiss, for us, but there was no denying the intent behind it. There was the hungry edge; sure, but also happiness. I found myself swept up in my own as well. Jesus, so *THIS* is what it's about? I love it. Ann placed the pitcher in front of Kane and pulled two glasses from the freezer under the bar. She put those in front of him as well, and then glanced at me.

"I assume the gentleman will be pouring? If not, I'll be happy to." Kane waved her off and smiled.

"My only regret is that there are not *three* glasses on this bar. It would be my pleasure to pour." Ann did her nose wrinkle again, looked right at me and stuck her tongue out under her teeth.

"Oh yes Miss Jimmy; this Kane fellow is gold."

"I know." I said, and from the corner of my eye I saw Kane sit up a little taller. Even at a sideways glance, I noticed his smile. It was big. Ann looked from me to Kane.

"Oh my God!" she exclaimed. "He *IS* gold! Those eyes!"

Kane startled and his automatic reaction was to look away. Ann was not having any part of that. I knew I liked her.

"Oh *NO*!" she barked, and Kane returned his eyes to her. She studied them a moment, then looked my way and peered at mine. I took a swallow from my beer as she did, and Kane followed suit.

"Your kids are going to have the most gorgeous eyes!"

I'm not sure which one of us choked harder on our beer, me or Kane, but we both were sputtering. Ann laughed, and acted as if nothing had happened.

"What kind of pie? You strike me as a purist Jimmy, so cheese for your half. Tall, handsome and *golden* seems to be more the carnivore type. Not a bad trait in a man. Pepperoni at the very least." She said and winked at me. I was still recovering from her 'kids' comment, so I nodded. She looked at Kane. He had regained himself a bit more than I had, but was still flustered.

"Pepperoni would be perfect. Thank you, Ann."

"Got it. Be right back." She said, and sashayed across the place to turn in the order. Her absence afforded me time to compose myself, and once I had I snuck a sideways glance at Kane. He was smiling again.

"She's not wrong you know." He said, and his smile grew bigger. "They would have amazing eyes, especially if they got your green."

Children had never *in my life* crossed my mind. Yet here I was; the topic laid bare on the bar, and there was no tactful way to skirt it. Kids. Wow! When the fuck did *THAT* option come up? Oh wait, that's right. While out having a beer waiting to eat pizza. Perfect, in a twisted way. It truly was. I had to smile.

"Kane, I never once even thought about it."

"Nor have I, before you. Or even before dear Ann mentioned it. There would be risks of course, as you are more than aware. The *Enhancement* and all. But if there was ever anyone that I would chance it with? It is you, Diana." He ran his hand down my back from my shoulder, letting it come to rest on my leg. His simple touch conveyed so much; it spoke entire conversations in silence and was so crystal clear in its meaning. I leaned into him and he breathed into my hair. Spiky as it was; he never once sneezed although I had on occasion caught him rubbing his nose. I'm sure it tickled at the very least.

"I know you have taken precautions.' Kane began, and I smiled. He had seen the birth control pills in the top drawer of the bathroom vanity. It didn't take *Enhanced* senses to spot that nor to see that there was one less every day. I wasn't out running the roads before I had met Kane but hey; better to be safe. Besides, it shortened my periods by three days every month. It was a win-win in my book.

"Diana? If you ever want to change that, let me know."

"Jesus Kane, I can't even fathom that. Until two minutes ago, I never remotely thought about it. Doesn't it freak you out in the tiniest bit?"

"Oh, it more than rattles me considering what I am. I don't know the how, or the why, of how it happened. There are a lot of legends and myths. It may stem back to where my mother was from. It might have something to do with my birthday; I don't know. It may be something I can pass on, and I would *NEVER* want to burden a child with that."

I considered his words, and let them sink in. I had questions no doubt about that, but they were too hefty to address at the moment, and there were too many to ask. I never wanted to interrogate Kane; not in a million years. I was too good at it and truthfully? I didn't want to exercise my talents in that department on him. I loved him too much. Hell, the fact that I loved him was enough to silence me. I sipped my beer. Just as I made my peace with my refusing to ask questions, an enormous one rose in my mind. Try as I might, I could not silence it; it practically screamed.

"What do you mean; your birthday?"

He stopped breathing for a moment, and then hung his head. This was not a good sign. I glanced to my right; Ann was wiping down tables that no one had sat at. Yes, I liked her even more now. She was making herself 'busy' to afford us space to talk. She knew she had opened a can of worms with the mention of children, and part of me was glad that she had. I returned my attention to Kane. His head was still down but he had at least inhaled again. After a long pause; he raised his head and spoke again in a whisper.

"I *may* have misled you in the booking room."

My eyebrow was arched before I knew it. I held his gaze with my eyes. Kane looked away from me, for only the second time since I first met him. Uh-oh. This was major. I waited for him to speak. Once he realized I was not letting this one go? He sighed, and his shoulders did their tell-tale drop. He had resigned himself to the fact that he was going to have to tell me something. I ran my fingers up his thigh in an effort to convey that whatever he said was going to be okay without having to use my voice. He smirked, and then relaxed. Apparently? He understood exactly what I had not said.

"I wasn't born on July 15th."

"Okay. What day *WERE* you born?"

"December 25th. Christmas Day." He said softly. I almost started to laugh. So *THAT* was the big secret? Really? You were a Christmas gift? Something in his body language told me to shut up before I ever spoke, and I listened to that wisdom. He remained quiet for several minutes, and my mind retraced every conversation we had ever had. Kane's eyes told me a *LOT*, but so did his silence. He had never lied to me, but he had omitted some of the 'whole truth' that Lady Justice was so keen on. Then again? That was back in Lawrence, and our respective roles and circumstances had been very different than they were today.

He sat there, head still hung and remained mute. I allowed the jumble of pieces in my mind to form their own questions. It was simple. It was also *VERY* complicated. I don't think Kane had it in him to be able to lie to me. The real question was; did I want to ask something he *WOULD* answer honestly? The air was colder somehow. At least that what I told myself, trying to explain the chill I seemed to have found. No half assed bullshit was happening today. I was inn for the whole pound now. I decided to ask.

"Was the birth *year* accurate? 1948?" I asked. Kane raised his head and faced me. A soft smile crossed his lips before he let out a breath.

"No." he said, and attempted a grin. He didn't manage success on that one, and he knew it.

"Jimmy? I am a *bit* older than forty-two."

"Exactly *how* much of a *bit* are we talking here, Kane?" I asked, and he glanced around the room. It was still empty; even Ann had gone into the back area with her busy work.

"What is your actual birth date?"

"Promise not to leave me for a younger man?"

"Never gonna happen. *When* were you born?"

"December 25th." he paused for a second, then continued. "1863."

My mind was spinning. I tried to attach myself to one thought out of the million that were whirling around but it wasn't working. 1863? What the fuck? How? Not possible. He was over a hundred years old! How in the shit was I supposed to believe that? My mouth was opening and closing but no words were coming out. Too many questions were blasting through me at once to find the words to ask just one at a time.

"So you're...." I began, but never finished.

"I'm one hundred and twenty-seven years old." Kane said quietly, and drained the contents of his glass. He poured another and topped mine off but never looked at me. Instead? He found something fascinating on the floor and stared down at it.

By some miracle my thoughts cleared immediately. A hundred and twenty-seven years old! My God! My heart had ached for how lonely he had been for forty-two years! It absolutely shattered for him now. All those ridiculous amounts of years; spent completely alone. *How long have your parents been gone? Feels like a century.* Jesus, it probably *WAS*! All that time; carrying the secret of what he was and not being able to tell a soul. The enormity of his isolation was practically drowning me. I stood up, slid my face under his gaze and kissed him deeply.

His arms wrapped around me and pulled me into him. When he finally released me his eyes were *glowing*. It was a minute before I managed to regain my breath. When I had, movement to my left caught my attention. Ann had returned to behind the bar.

"And *THAT* is exactly how those gorgeous eyed children are going to happen." She said, her smile was infectious and mischievous all at once. I couldn't have stopped myself if I tried. I returned the expression. She winked and glanced at Kane.

"Oh *YES*!" she cheered, and returned her attention to me. "His eyes are not just gold now; they are on *FIRE*! Oh Miss Jimmy! He sure does love you. And yours? Would put Ireland Herself to shame."

Ann clapped her hands together in a rapid repetition. She actually did a little tap dance behind the bar. Next thing I knew? She had thrust both hands over her head in the victory stance and let out a whoop. No doubt about it; she was my kind of crazy and I more than liked her now. She was a rock star. Kane and I exchanged glances, each of us grinning as we watched Ann rapture in whatever it was she was celebrating. Her zeal was incredible, and she had zero problems expressing her joy at, well? *US*. When she finally stopped? Both Kane and I were laughing.

"Hungry?" she asked, and we both nodded as our laughter ebbed.

"Well; I already know you're *HUNGRY*," she said and wrinkled her nose again, a giggle escaping her. "That just oozes from you both. But your pizza should be about done." She said, and scooted across the restaurant to go get it.

"I like Ann immensely." Kane said, and ran his fingers through my hair over my ears.

"Kane? I don't like most people; but she is awesome."

"Agreed." He said, and kissed my neck. His lips on my skin flushed me. Ann was right, we were *HUNGRY*. But as Kane had said earlier that morning; the pizza was first. Something told me I was going to need the carbs. Ann returned with our pie. It wasn't just a pizza. It truly was a work of art, and an absolute masterpiece of thin crust and cheese. I knew it was more than hot; it was steaming, and still it took every bit of self-control I had not to snatch a slice and devour it.

Ann had classified me as a purist and she was correct; but I was also a pizza junkie. Before Kane? There were three things I truly loved; smoking, beer and pizza. Now there were four, and the man to my right topped the list by miles. Who knew?

"Enjoy, lovers." She quipped as she rounded the bar. A group of four had entered, and she was soon hustling from table to table taking orders and pouring drinks as more people came in. Kane and I enjoyed our slices, which had cooled enough to be handled and eaten but still allowed the cheese to stretch as I bit into it.

The original plan was a taste tour of the finest pizza Boston could create but when I looked at the aluminum circle our first sampling had sat on; it was empty. I had eaten *HALF* a damn pizza and we had finished the second pitcher of beer. I looked over at Kane, and he was smiling brightly. His eyes had slipped back more towards amber as we were dining, but the flecks of gold were still visible although not glowing at present.

"What?" I asked, and his smile grew larger.

"Where else would you like to try?"

"You've got to be shitting me." I said, and nodded towards the empty pizza pan.

"Yes, it was amazing, Lover," Kane purred, "But don't you want to try some other places? To be sure we find the best Boston has to offer?"

I have never been the kind of woman to get 'mushy' or say sentimental things. I've always been more of a cut to the chase; that's exactly where the dog died and let's get about the business of the moment we find ourselves in. Then again, I had never before felt anything close to what I felt for Kane. It was uncharted territory for me that was for sure, and I was excited to be blazing this new trail. I absolutely loved him, and I was *in love* with him. There were no reasons at all to hold back on anything. Vulnerability was entirely new for me and though I had never experienced it before; it was Kane that had wriggled through my defenses. I was surprisingly comfortable in speaking of my feelings to him.

"I have *already* found the best that Boston has to offer. Or anywhere else for that matter." I said, and looked directly into his eyes. They flooded gold; an iridescence lit them from within. His gaze never wavered, and mine remained with his. I watched each change of the illumination in them; they drifted brighter for a second, and then softened in color but not intensity. A metallic edge, followed by a warmth that washed across his entire body; then a return to shimmering. Kane had an enormous smile I already knew that, but the one he wore right now was simply huge. The creases at the corners of his eyes as he wore it thrilled me. Seeing him happy, *THIS* happy? Was wonderful. I could have burst into song. He raised my hand to his lips and kissed it.

"In all my years... that is the best thing anyone has ever said to me."

"You'd better get used to it, Woods. I'll be saying them for the rest of mine."

"May they be many." He whispered, and kissed my hand again. A movement to my left again caught my eye, and I broke from the intimacy of Kane to see what it was. Ann was standing opposite of our barstools. I had no idea how long she was there for. Her hands were rolled into fists and she had them pressed to her mouth. Tears glistened in her eyes, and I immediately shifted into the familiar protective sheep dog persona that was the essence of me.

"Ann? What is it? Honey? What's wrong?" I asked, my attention now fully on her. Whoever had upset our new friend was going to answer to me at the very least. Given what Kane was? I was by far the safer option. Ann shook her head gently.

"Not one thing is wrong." She said softly, taking her hands down from her face. "That was the most beautiful thing I have ever seen or heard." Kane and I exchanged glances. I was confused. He was smiling.

"For me as well." He said, and nodded at our bartender. Ann reached across the bar, and grasped my hand in her right and Kane's in her left. I was surprised by her actions but not alarmed. I suddenly became aware of how many people had filled the restaurant, and was shocked that I had not noticed the din that comes with a full lunchtime crowd. My God what the Hell? When did *THEY* show up? And how had I missed it? Ann squeezed both of our hands in hers.

"There are not many times that the moon and stars align just right." She began, her words spoken quickly but not rushed. Kane shifted slightly at her mention of the moon but he said nothing. Ann truly meant what she was saying, and its importance to her did not elude me. I paid attention as she continued.

"I sense things sometimes about people. I knew the moment I saw the both of you, that whatever brought you two together? Was one of those times. Miss Jimmy? Kane? Yours, will be a love story spoken about for centuries."

As soon as she had finished her words, she released our hands and darted across the brick walled restaurant. Seems somebody else's pizza was ready. Kane and I sat silently, just looking at each other. I was off balance a bit; I had never had anyone express such thoughts before. Kane appeared to be more sure-footed on this one. I watched as his crooked half grin found him again, and I felt my eyebrows draw together as I tried to piece together what had just occurred. Ultimately, I looked to him. His expression told me he was far more comfortable with what had just happened.

"Sometimes? There are old souls residing within a young person's body, Jimmy. We just met one."

"So; you've seen this before?"

"I've encountered some, yes. It happens from time to time."

"What in the fuck did I get into with you, Kane?"

"Evidently? A love story for the ages." He said, and a full smile replaced the grin.

There are times in life to fight against the current; to swim upstream. No one knew that better than me. It wasn't exactly my sweet nature that had me as the first woman in the cell blocks of Essex County. There are times to hunt down the facts of the situation and to ask the how's and why's and expect evidence to back them up. This was neither of those moments.

This was the time to simply accept what had been presented, and *NOT* ask a single question. Like a riptide; I simply allowed it to take me as far as it wanted knowing in my bones that I would eventually end up in a safe place. My God! It seemed I had finally grasped what the word *FAITH* meant.

"I should go pay our tab." Kane said as he rose to his feet. While the hostess had called out sick? The cashier was on the clock, and one scan of the room told me she was needed. The place was packed, and even on a Wednesday a line was lingering on the stairs. Jesus Christ. How had I missed the arrival of so many people? Thank God I was 'retired'. My awareness of what was happening around me had more than dimmed; it was sloughing off of me like last year's winter coat. I'd be dead if this ever happened in Lawrence. Lawrence. It felt like a lifetime ago that I had been *THAT* person. Hyper vigilant Officer Jameson was indeed gone.

She may as well have been there when the 'boiler exploded'. I shook my head slightly and reached for my glass. There were a few swallows left in it and I didn't want to speed up my arrival in Hell by leaving them abandoned.

"Miss Jimmy." Ann's voice reached me from across the bar. I turned towards her, and she motioned her hand in a gerbil wheel movement indicating I should continue with the beer. I obliged but I was tuned into her completely. The blue of her eyes was even more sparkling now, and she spoke quietly to me.

"There is something about the two of you together. Yet there is also something about the two of you as individuals. I can't put my finger on it. Promise me you will come back to see me. Bring the golden boy of course some times, but swear that you will come by yourself at least once. I'm off Mondays and Tuesdays. I'm here the rest of the week until 3 PM."

I finished my beer and nodded my agreement as I placed the glass back on the bar. Ann wrinkled her nose at me again, her smile as infectious as before, and I returned it. There was no way I could not honor her request. Maybe the stars and moon had aligned for a second time, only this time it brought me a new friend. I chortled at the thought. Ann glanced my way once again, and slid past me closest to the bar's edge as she could.

"Yes, it did." She said and winked. Then she waded into the full noon hour masses.

"Seems there is no tab for us." Kane whispered. His closeness to me and the feel of his breath behind my ear sent a swell of heat through me. I closed my eyes and basked in it, not caring that there was probably not a hint of orange left in me. Once it had subsided; I opened them and found Ann. She waved from across the room and when I shrugged and pointed to the cashier, she flicked her hand in a dismissive shooing motion. If there's one thing I know; its people. Once certain people have made up their mind about something you're better off smashing your forehead into the Empire State building than trying to change their minds.

Ann was one of those people; and this was one of those moments. I nodded that I understood, and turned to look up at Kane. He smiled at me, looked across the room to Ann and jerked his chin upwards in the accepted 'hey what's up thank you'. She flashed a quick smile, winked at me, and returned her attention to the man ordering his lunch. I rose from my stool; it wasn't fair to occupy prime lunch hour real estate when we were finished and slid my arm around Kane's waist. His left arm swooped around me and gently hugged, and he reached into his back pocket for his wallet with his right. Also needing his left hand to open it was advantageous; at least for me. It meant he had to pull me in closer against him and I wasn't one to complain about that. He slid a twenty under our empty pitcher. I knew he had class.

Kane had become something I needed to be near. Until that moment I had never needed a thing in my life; at least not anything I was aware of. The ease of how I swallowed this new realization should have surprised me. It did not. It was as natural as breathing. There was no separation anymore, at least not from where I stood. I no longer knew where I stopped and Kane started. The borders were blended like pastel chalk drawings; no clear lines and all the more beautiful for their absence. What the shit had happened to me? I looked up at him and his golden eyes met mine. Yep. *THAT* was what had happened; right fucking there. Stick a fork in me. I was done.

Chapter Thirteen

Kane was a man of his word. The pizza was amazing, and the 'pleasure' he had promised 'later' was far more than that. I had indeed needed those carbs, and then some. The man wore me out and he might just be the death of me, but at least I'd be going with a smile. I wouldn't be able to walk, but I'd be smiling. He was curled up against me, and the rise and fall of his chest hinted he was sleeping. Good, at least I had given partially as well as I got. I stifled a yawn and considered resuming my nap. It was either dusk or dawn judging by the amount of shadowy daylight. I couldn't be sure how long we had been asleep. Kane excelled at exhausting me and sleeping for 12 hours after would not be out of the question.

"It is sunrise, Lover." He murmured into my neck. Jesus, what? Is he reading my mind in his sleep now?

"Did I wake you?" I asked him, ignoring the musings I always got when he pulled out one of his *Enhancement* quirks. Kane was so accustomed to living with them that it never occurred to him that it might freak me out a little. I was getting acclimated to them, but it was still a relatively new thing for me. Some of his 'quirks' took a little more getting used to than others.

"I've been awake for some time now."

"I thought you were sleeping. Your breathing was so steady."

"I was enjoying you sleeping beside me. It is the best feeling I've ever known."

When a man says something like that to you, you feel good. When the man you're in love with says it; you are enthralled. Nothing can make you soar higher than being in love and having it returned just as fully and just as freely. I reached behind me and ran my fingers through his hair. Kane pulled me closer against him and kissed my neck. I could have stayed right there for the rest of my time on Earth and been just fine with it.

"Lord," Kane whispered, "If I am to die today make it right now in this very moment." I ran my fingers down his arm and slipped his hand in mine.

"That's my line Woods."

"I know, but it sums this up perfectly."

"Agreed. But you're probably not going to die today. You've managed to avoid that for over a century."

"Teasing me about my age, Jimmy?" he said, nuzzling my ear. I had no doubt I was shifting redder by the second.

"*GOD NO*! I just slept for over twelve hours after your pleasure fest yesterday. I am the *LAST* person to give you shit about years. Thank Christ you're this old! You'd have killed me if you were younger."

"Actually," he spoke softly but I again felt it rumble within me, "The older I get? The stronger I get. It works the opposite for me."

"I'm going to need a wheelchair by the time I'm thirty-five." I groaned. Kane chuckled and again kissed my neck.

"*CAUWFEE*?" he taunted.

"Sure! And later I'll go put gas in my *KAH*."

He laughed, and I enjoyed the sound of it in the early morning. Seeing him smile, the sound of his voice, feeling him against me; all of it put me in a place of happiness and peace. It wasn't rainbows and unicorns. There were no illusions of fairy dust and eternal bliss. It was however; genuine. I'll take something real over the fantasy world any day of the week. Especially the strength of the bond that Kane and I shared. That doesn't come rolling down the Pike every day. Maybe we were embarking on a love story for the ages after all.

#

We had finished the last of the coffee lounging together on the porch swing. It had proved to be a good investment. Kane had gone into the workshop to continue his progress on an order. While he was capable of moving at incredible speed, when working? He took his time. He was meticulous in his craft and the end results showed it; which is why he was booked through November with orders. I finished my cigarette and carried my mug into the kitchen.

The mail was laying on the *SECOND* countertop Kane had installed that year, and I grinned as I recalled why it was the second. I may not get stronger with age but this youngster had her moments. I washed the mug and the pot, and went into our bedroom to get some clothes. A pair of jeans and a T shirt had become my new uniform, and it suited me fine. At least my feet were in sneakers now.

It was still early morning, so I opened the window in the bathroom and turned on the shower. The house was over one hundred years old, and before exhaust fans, a window in the tub area was the only way to allow the steam to escape. The August heat hadn't yet smothered the day so I took advantage of the chance to shower with a breeze. I stepped into the falling water, enjoying its warmth across my face. I scrubbed the shampoo into lather and let it run down my back. Random thoughts of what errands I was going to run today were laying themselves out into an atlas.

Which place I was going to go first, how many stops in total, and charting my course to make it all in one smooth circular trip rather than crossing the county numerous times. Obviously, the food store was the final stop unless I wanted to haul an ice chest around in the Mustang all day. I tilted my head back to rinse the suds from my hair' pleased with the route I had planned.

I heard something crash down in the tub. It was too big to be the shampoo bottle, and it was moving. There was a scratching sound of something sharp on the metal beneath my feet. I swiped my hands across my eyes to clear any soap before I opened them and looked down. There, at the bottom of the tub, was a black and white striped chicken. A barred rock Kane had said. Her feathers were fluffed out making her appear twice her normal size, at least momentarily. As the water splashed all over her as well as me; her feathers got too wet to stand out, and they gradually plastered themselves to her body. I had always heard the expression, mad as a wet hen. I thought it was just one of those things people say that had no actual meaning to it. Meeting her beady eyes, I realized exactly how wrong I had been. She was beyond furious. The bird was livid.

Chickens are vocal creatures. I had heard them countless times 'talking' to each other. Sometimes it was a muttering to themselves; other times they seemed to speak in varying clucks and occasionally they would argue amongst themselves with squawks. The sound that she emitted at the bottom of the tub was a growl. An actual growl, like I would have expected from an unfriendly dog. I had never in my life heard such a noise from a bird, never mind one that was at my feet while I was in the shower. Her rage at how utterly soaked she was coupled with her current location came to focus on me.

Tingles of fear spread down my spine. Oh fuck, this was not good. She started flapping her wings, which were now too water logged to grant her flight. This sent her even farther into a fit. Before I knew it she was pecking at my toes and jumping at my legs, her talons seeking to rip me apart. My feet were moving as quickly as I could make them to avoid bloodshed. I was hopping around the tub trying to avoid her assault. I initially started pleading with her to stop but then her beak struck home on my pinky toe.

"Oh, *FUCK NO* you didn't you *BITCH*!" I yelled, and my voice echoed from the tile and iron tub. Miss zebra stripe pissy pants decided to intensify her attack, striking at me three more times. I dodged each one, and she glared up at me.

"Okay fucker!" I barked, "It's *ON* now!"

She moved towards my left foot. I wiggled my toes to bait her and she lunged. As she did, I kicked her with my right foot. She bounced off the tile wall and slid into the shower curtain liner. She scrambled to regain her footing and somehow her head got stuck between the liner and the side of the tub. She was slipping and flopping as she tried to get loose, the whole time her eyes glittering with hatred, and it was focused on me.

"How you like me now, *BITCH*?" I said, and gave her the finger. "Fuck with *ME*? I'll *FRY* your ass!"

The shower curtain flung open. I jumped at the violence of its disappearance. Kane was standing there; right arm extended and holding the curtain. His eyes were gold and lit, but it was a cold light emanating from them. His muscles were tight, ready to spring into action. He looked positively lethal. He absorbed the scene before him, and the light that was cold melted into a comforting glow. His entire body began to shake yet he made no sound. He released the curtain and wrapped his hands around his stomach, bending slightly as he did so. He finally inhaled, and once he did a roar of laughter erupted from him.

I stood there blinking in disbelief, then turned and looked at myself. I was bare ass naked, standing in the bathtub, my elbow locked and arm fully extended as I gave psycho chicken the bird. The shower was still running, and water was splashing all over the floor. Barred rock had gotten her head free when Kane had ripped the curtain open but she wisely stayed put. I turned back to see that Kane had now dropped to his knees on the bathmat and was leaning sideways. He again was making no sound; his laughter was strangling him. He finally gave up and rolled onto his side on the floor. He was still looking at me. I turned the shower off and raked my fingers through my hair, trying to regain some dignity.

A wail came from the floor as another spasm of hysterics came from him. I cut my eyes to my feathered combatant, silently threatening her, and I stepped out of the tub.

"Oh my God!" was all Kane could manage before grabbing his sides and rolling again, his voice lost in another consuming laugh. I grabbed the towel from the hook and began to dry myself off.

"You're in a puddle." I said.

"I know." He managed to half whimper before succumbing to the humor again.

I tried my best to behave snobbishly indignant which was never a natural role for me, but one look down at him destroyed my ruse. His gray T shirt and faded jeans were splotched with wet spots from the floor. His face was wet from both the overspray of the shower and the tears he was wiping from his eyes as he tried to calm his laughter. I felt the smile occupying my face and the rise of a giggle within me. Kane reached out and ran his hand down my calf. When he looked up at me my breath caught for a second at the hue his eyes held. They were molten gold, like you could pour them into any form and have a masterpiece. I finally let a bit of that giggle out as I exhaled.

"I can only imagine what that looked like."

"No. No, you can't." he said, his voice still carrying the music of humor. "That was the funniest thing I have ever seen, and I have seen a lot, Love."

"Shut up." I said, the smile I wore growing bigger. Kane leaned over and kissed my leg.

I extended him a hand, which he accepted, and I jerked him to his feet. He wrapped his arms around me and pressed me to him.

"You bring me joy Miss Jameson, in so many ways. I cannot remember the last time I truly laughed. I thank you for it."

"Wasn't my idea. Talk to Rodan over there." Kane chuckled and hugged me tighter, and I permitted myself to laugh with him.

"You're getting her out." I said, and he laughed again.

Chapter Fourteen

Labor Day weekend was in bloom, and Kane was more energetic in all aspects of his life. His work was still incredible, but he was finishing quicker. His appetite was also larger, and for more than just rare T bones. The past three days I had been his favorite meal, and there was still tomorrow night before I had to 'go to camp'. He was restless again, and while no longer confined to a cell? He was pacing the living room. After watching him cross into the kitchen for the fiftieth time; I had had enough.

"Jesus, sit still would you?" My words had a slight edge to them, but his constant movement for the past days had me frazzled. He glanced at me and his golden eyes filled with angst.

"I am sorry, Diana. It's the upcoming Full."

"Babe, I know that. You just seem far more agitated than last month."

"I am. Some are more powerful than others. I cannot help it." This new revelation from him once again made my heart break for him. Until then I had no idea there were varying degrees of Pull from the moon, or that Kane felt them all too much.

"I'm sorry, I didn't know." I said softly, and crossed over to where he stood. My poor Kane; the man I was in love with, was powerless over what was happening. He was a victim to the silver rays as much as the tide was, and he could control it no more than the oceans. I grasped his hand in mine, brought it to my lips and kissed it. He looked at me and the golden light and hue again shifted. He appeared wounded, or sad, or even both. I kept his hand in mine and pressed it to my chest. His shoulders softened, and he attempted to smile. Even his brilliant teeth seemed to carry a burden.

"September is a strong one. It is the Harvest Moon, and the closest to the autumn equinox. The amount of moonlight that reaches the Earth is increased. It makes me more restless than a regular Full and it affects me earlier in the days before. Diana, it is only Sunday and I feel like my skin is crawling. That is how desperately it wants to come out."

"Jesus." I whispered. "Is September the worst?"

"No."

"Fuck I'm so sorry, Kane." I muttered, again kissing the back of his hand. His response was somewhere between a groan of pain and a whimper. I had never before heard him make such a sound. It was agony for me to hear it, but I would not look into his eyes.

There was nothing I could do about whatever my color scheme may be revealing to him, but if he saw my eyes he would know how truly awful I felt for him and the man was in enough distress. Kane's protective streak when it came to me surpassed even my own sheep dog instinct. Perhaps it was because he had never protected anyone *BUT* me, maybe it was how strongly he felt for me; but whatever the reason I was not going to add to his misery by broadcasting how much this upset me too. That would just be insult to injury. Not on my watch. I kissed his palm this time, and released his hand and turned to the fridge. I avoided his gaze.

"Beer?" I quipped as I reached inside the door.

"Please." His voice carried and edge of pain on it which shattered my insides. I had turned to meet his eyes before I even realized it. When he gazed at me, a soft smile curved on his face.

"Thank you." he whispered.

"For what? A beer?"

"No. For finally looking at me. It's frighteningly lonely for me when you don't."

"Oh God Kane..." I began, but he cut me off.

"I know. What I am is not what one would call 'pretty'. It is monstrous. I know this. But when you avoid me because of it Diana? It is a living Hell, and it makes me long for death."

My fingers had lost their strength, and for the second time since I had changed my address; I dropped two long neck bottles. Kane snatched them out of the air mid fall in one hand for the second time as well. He hung his head as he studied them, as if he was having a final exam on the contents of a Coors Light label that evening. He cracked them both open and handed me one. He downed half of his as he walked into the living room.

He never looked at me; he had his back to me completely, and he finished the remainder of the bottle. His breathing was deeper than usual and as I watched his shoulders and spine, I could see it was not the normal rise and fall of his rib cage. It was uneven, jagged, as if he needed to cough to clear his lungs. Except Kane wasn't sick.

I know he heard me come near him, no way he couldn't, and I pressed up against his back. My hands slid around his waist and I hugged him to me, and then ran them up his chest and around his shoulders. I pulled him tightly to me and kissed him just below his collar.

"Oh no. Not at all, Kane. You are *WAY* off base on this one." His shoulder flinched ever so slightly and I could feel him turning his head to speak to me.

"Then why did you just do everything in your power to avoid so much as *looking* in my direction?"

"Oh my God," I began, muttering into his spine between his shoulder blades, "Jesus, no; I wasn't avoiding you. You are my world, Kane Woods. My fucking *WORLD.*" His breathing increased its pace as I spoke and his rib cage took on a more ragged effort than it already had. He leaned his head backwards and exhaled.

"Then what is it?" he asked softly.

"I didn't want you to see that how much this is hurting you? It hurts me just as much. Maybe more."

Kane was a sturdily built man. His body was not enormous or huge; he was slimmer than a weight lifter but the strength he carried did not require such bulk. Each muscle was lean and well defined, and stronger than the casual eye would notice. He had both power and endurance deep within every fiber of him. His movements were balanced to the point of graceful. He was very much, wolf like, even though he spent 99% of his life on two legs. Wolves will trail prey such as elk or caribou for over twenty miles a day for several days, and still have the reserve strength at the end of that distance to make the kill. I had never once seen Kane neither slip nor lose his balance. When my words reached his ears, he staggered slightly. His skeletal system buckled and I feared for a second he might drop to his knees. I dug my fingers into his shoulders, gripping him tighter, preparing to hold him up if he did.

"Arrrrgh!" he released to the ceiling and his entire form went rigid under my hands. He dropped his head down and leaned it to his right, kissing my hand that was still curled around that shoulder. He repeated it on his left as well, and then let out a long sigh.

"If you will allow it, I would like to turn around and look at you." The reverberation I felt in my core when he spoke was enchanting. I released my grip on him and he was immediately gazing down on me. He cocked his head slightly as that crooked grin of his stole across his features and ran away with my heart.

"So…"' he began, and squinted slightly as he peered into my eyes, "You avoided looking at me, to prevent me from seeing that you hurt in this as well. Am I correct?"

I nodded.

Kane squinted a little more before he continued.

"Why?"

"Because I love you; ya dolt." If anyone no longer living in Dublin was going to understand the meaning behind the word dolt; it was this son of Irish immigrants. He chuckled, and I knew I had chosen well; both in my vocabulary and the man I was speaking to. I smiled up at him.

"Jimmy, I will never understand you."

"Good!" I exclaimed and he chuckled again, hugging me tightly to him. I inhaled deeply, drawing every bit of his presence into me. He kissed my head and squeezed me tighter.

"I do however; understand what motivates you. You are *quite* protective of me."

"Sheep dog." I said, and kissed his chest through his T shirt. He ran his fingers through my porcupine spikes of blonde and began to laugh gently.

"Sheep dog protecting the Wolf." He marveled.

"The same Wolf who would kill for the sheep dog." I answered. Kane sighed, and released me so I could look up at him.

"You know I would. On two legs or four."

"Yes, I do. Which is why I didn't want you to see how much *you* hurting, pains me. You would lay waste to anything that tried to hurt me, right?"

"Hellfire pales compared to it."

"And *that* is why I didn't want to let you know. You feel bad enough already. You think I want you trying to protect me, from *YOU*? Jesus! Talk about a recipe for self-loathing! Next thing I know you'd be asking me to leave so that you don't hurt *ME* by me seeing *YOU* hurting." Kane's breath caught, and I looked at him. A small curl at the corner of his mouth spoke the words he never said.

"My God, you've thought about it haven't you?"

"Only now, and scarcely for a moment."

"You son of a bitch!" I snapped, and punched him in his shoulder. He may be *Enhanced* but I was pissed. Resilient as he was, Kane rubbed the spot where my knuckles had struck.

"Ow." He said. I unleashed on him.

"I'll give you fucking Ow! And don't even act wounded; you'll be healed before I can punch you again. Which I should! Even *THINK* about asking me to leave to 'spare me'? Fuck you! Want me to leave because you don't want to be together? Fine! But leave to 'protect' me? What kind of bullshit is that? Kiss my Irish ass, Rover! I don't need goddamn Lancelot riding up."

Kane was listening to every word I was saying but that damn crooked grin was perched on his lips. It kicked my temper into overdrive and I was the one to pace the kitchen this time as I continued my rant. Italians are known for talking with their hands as well as their mouths. Angry Irish people are worse, and I was more than simply angry.

"And don't you try that half grin charm shit with *ME*; it ain't working right now! Goddamn have me move in here as an equal, and now you're going all Sir fucking Galahad? I don't think so! I'll put a fucking shock collar on your ass you just watch me! Full moon be damned I'll juice you enough where you look like Peter Frampton."

Kane was standing about ten feet from me. He was doing his best to appear to be listening and understanding of my onslaught, but the dance of his eyes told me he was more amused than anything else. Now my temper was being stoked with feeling like I was being patted on the head like a child, and the blaze of shamrocks caught my eyes, my spine and my tongue.

"Don't you look at me like *THAT*! You are *NOT* my father and I am *NOT* five; don't sit there like you're waiting for me to get over some tantrum. I am *PISSED*, and *YOU* earned every word of this. What the shit! So help me Kane, if you even think..."

I never finished the sentence. He had traversed the space between us in less time than a blink, and I was silenced by his mouth covering mine and his tongue smothering my next words. He kissed me long, hard and deeply. The rage that had initially bubbled to the surface when he started the kiss slowly cooled and soon faded into the shadows.

Sure; he was trying to shut me up, and he was succeeding. The insult I had felt when he confessed that he had thought of asking me to leave soon melted away too, and I was paying more attention to what he was saying without speaking a word. His kiss carried a hunger of course; it was less than two days from the full moon. This one was stronger for him as well, but there was something else accompanying it. The kiss was rather distracting; they all were, and it took me more than a minute to pinpoint what else it carried. When I did, it struck me like a bolt from the sky.

His kiss carried an apology, one he hadn't the words for. Once I recognized its taste; I quenched any embers of anger and accepted his remorse. Kane sensed the moment I did and he pulled me to him. His body softened momentarily, a silent thank you, and then I felt every corner of his essence ignite. I wrapped my right leg around his, and he grasped my thigh and pulled it higher towards his waist. He kissed harder than before, and my back was arching. He was leaning further in and I felt like I was about to be dipped, but this was not the tango. It was definitely heading in the direction of what it would take two to do though, and I was not going to be the one to stop it.

His mouth broke from mine and I felt his tongue on my throat. He gently slid his enormous teeth down my neck and I disappeared into the abyss of zero coherent thought. I only knew physical sensations. His hand was on my left thigh and he pulled that higher to his waist, and I wrapped both legs around him as he held me aloft. He had no effort in carrying me and though I am one hundred and fifty pounds; he did so with one arm.

He moved across the tiles and I felt the long countertop beneath me. The intensity of him was pressing against me and laying me back across it. His hands were across the skin of my stomach while his tongue traced my collarbone. I was on fire. Kane crawled up on the counter on top of me.

"You may be replacing this again." I panted as I felt his fingers open my jeans.

"I will rip this kitchen apart Diana, but I will have you." He growled before burying his face into my neck once again. I raked my fingers down his back as his weight covered me. He had my jeans unzipped with his left hand and his right was under my shirt. I pressed up against him and moaned. Kane snarled and tore both my T shirt and bra off of me. The shredded fabric was cast aside and he resumed his mouths journey on my skin. He was grasping at the last threads of any form of self-control, and his near abandonment of rational thought or any sense of reason was both frightening and thrilling. He was consumed by animal instinct, and in so brought me to the edge of madness. He *WAS* going to have me; right there on the kitchen counter, and there would be no stopping him. I was submerged in pleasure as his hands and tongue delighted me. I grabbed a handful of his hair and pulled his head back and kissed him.

When I stopped; his eyes were incredibly gold and burning from within. There was a shadow of logic left in him. I ran my fingers down his chest and that final trace disappeared like a wisp of smoke in a hurricane. The gold darkened and burned from a fire I'd never seen before. There was no further discussion, and he resumed his consumption of me. I was gasping, screaming, and thrashing beneath him in seconds. He was relentless in his appetite, and my body seized in throbbing orgasms again and again. He was everywhere against my skin and my sanity vanished as his body entered mine. Searing white heat engulfed my being and I was lost to the raw instincts that had overtaken the both of us. Our frenzy continued, and his muscles tightened in pace with mine. I screamed out his name as we finished together.

Kane rested his forehead against my shoulder as he regained his breath. I struggled to find any oxygen at all in the room. My throat was burning from both the search for air and numerous occasions he had brought me to climax. My entire body was trembling beneath him and if the house caught fire right then I would be powerless to escape the flames. I was still panting when he raised his head and chuckled softly.

"Seems the counter survived." He said, and kissed me gently.

"I don't know how. I'm not sure I did."

#

I was slumped in the porch swing trying to recover as Kane brought us out another drink. I was useless. He had to carry me out there, and even now I had only barely gotten enough breath back to smoke. The stupidity of that made me laugh, and he smiled down at me.

"What is so funny?"

"The fact that it took me twenty minutes to catch my breath, and as soon as I did? I lit a cigarette. Just think about the logic in that."

"There is none." He said, and handed me an ice-cold bottle. I snorted a laugh.

"You're absolutely right." I said, and took another drag from the cigarette. I leaned against him as he sat beside me, his arm protectively wrapped around my shoulder. The feeling of safety once again filled me, and it brought to memory something he had said in the living room.

"Kane, can I ask you something?"

"Of course ,Love. Anything."

"Earlier, you said that you would kill to protect me", I began, and he nodded in agreement. "But then you said on two legs or four. How could you on four? You told me you have no idea of what you do when you're changed."

Kane sighed and stared out into the yard. The chickens milled about lazily and my nemesis eyed me but kept her distance. I glared at her and she slowly waddled away. I looked back to Kane, and he was clearly thinking my question over. He stayed that way for a few minutes and then nodded his head slightly. He turned back to face me. His eyes were so golden they reflected even in the sunlight. I dismissed my awe of them and focused on what he was about to say.

"My Da made mention of the Residual that stays with me when I have changed. Do you remember me telling you about that?"

"Of course. He said it had to be something you felt strongly about."

"Yes. Diana, *you* are the thing I feel the strongest about in all of my life. There is no way you would not be more than just a tint."

"So you wouldn't hurt me?"

"As me? Never. But changed? I would kill you just as I would any other creature I cross paths with. That is why you *must* leave every month."

"Then how would you kill to protect me on four legs? Doesn't make much sense if you'd kill me just as easily." I said, and lit another cigarette. The knowledge that I would be ripped apart by Kane in his 'other' form was more than a little disturbing. It was terrifying, and it shook me to the marrow.

"That is why I insist you not tell me where you are going. It would put you in danger of me." He said softly, and hung his head. He looked lost and completely alone. His eyes squinted slightly at the painful truth of what he had just said. He hated it, as did I; but hating something does not make it any less fact. That was the hand we were dealt. Railing against it wasn't going to change a shade of it, and we both knew it. I had accepted it and yeah it sucked to have to go and be completely covert about my destination, but rather than whine about the injustice of it all we had invested our efforts into working within the reality we had. Kane couldn't stop what happened and what he became any more than I could stop the moon from growing fat. If either of us could? Of course we would have, but that is not the way the world works. So? Size up the situation and try to find a suitable solution. That is exactly what we did.

"Danger of you. You're gonna have to give me a little more on that."

"I will *never* allow any harm to befall you."

"I know that. Still need a bit more Kane."

"If I know where you are going it may remain with me when I change. It pertains to you. More than likely it would. It is only natural that if it did? Even in my 'changed' form I would seek to protect you. Therefore, I would try to be near you. That cannot happen. *Ever*. The risk of me finding you, while *Wolf?* Is too terrible to imagine."

His eyes were still averted from me, but he reeked of pain and I didn't need any *Enhancement* to smell it. A small whimper escaped my throat as he drew in a ragged breath. He turned at my sound and his eyes swirled in golden agony. It destroyed me. Kane hated himself or at least this part of him. The depth of love he felt for me was killing him because of what he was. For a fleeting second; I thought of leaving him to spare him this. Who's Lancelot now, Jimmy? I scolded myself at my own hypocrisy.

"You thought about it too, just now. But only for a moment." He said.

"Please don't punch me. You're a lot stronger than I am and I don't heal as fast." Kane slowly smiled and took my hand in his.

"Never." He whispered, and kissed the back of my hand. A small laugh formed in me, and I freed it.

"Jesus. Ain't we a pair, Raggedy Man?"

"Indeed."

"I'll take it." I said, and the crooked grin captured his mouth once more.

"I'll take it any day of the week." I finished, and smiled as his eyes flooded with warmth. Any day of the week, any week of the year. I'd take this fucked up life with Kane Woods.

October 1990

CHAPTER FIFTEEN

The sun had crested as I climbed into the Mustang that morning of September fifth. Kane had been almost relentless in his hunger and truthfully; a night of reprieve was needed though my stubborn pride had some difficulty choking that realization down. I woke refreshed at pre-dawn and once again found myself excited to go *HOME*. Ridiculous that I missed Kane so incredibly over and eighteen-hour span yet there I was; pedal to the metal, missing the code three paraphernalia and anxious to see him.

I had gone to the north this time and spent the night in Maine, which is maybe an hour drive from Rowley. I had seriously considered Boston, as I would have loved to have talked with Ann but somewhere in my mind I heard a whisper that it was too obvious. I had never kept myself 'predictable'; I wasn't about to start now. A blind observer would have seen the friendship that Ann and I had forged immediately; and Kane was neither blind nor stupid. No, Fanuiel Hall was lit up like a runway. Maine was invisible, and that's exactly where I went. My tires crunched on the gravel driveway just past six A.M.

I opened the door to our home and immediately knew something was off. Not 'wrong' per se, but *off*. There was no welcoming aroma of coffee to greet me. This immediately raised my antennae. This was *NOT* what I had come home to twenty-nine days ago. Something may not have been *wrong*, but all was not quiet on the Western Front. I assumed Officer Jimmy, and was surprised at the ease I found in resuming that mantle. Old habits do indeed die hard; though I thought only an aftertaste of her still remained.

"Hey, Love." I heard from behind me. The voice was undeniably Kane's, but I had never heard such tiredness in his tone before. I stopped, half expecting the feel of his kiss on my neck and his arms around my waist but after a second of it not occurring? I turned around.

He was sitting on the floor, his knees bent and his elbows rested on them while his back leaned against the footrest part of the couch. He attempted to smile, and the effort that took revealed more than any words he could say ever would. I rushed to him and knelt in front of him.

"Oh, Jesus Babe; you look awful. You okay?" I asked and ran my hands across his face into his hair. He leaned his head left and rested his head in my right hand. He again attempted a smile, and the best he achieved was a closed mouth grin as his head relied more on my hand for support. His eyes were closed, and I took a good long hard look at him. He was ragged; as if he had just gone three weeks without sleep and then had decided to run a marathon.

"Sorry there's not a pot on, Diana..." he murmured, as if talking in his sleep. My heart hurt for him. Literally hurt. It had stopped when I saw him on the floor, and once it started again? It beat with a sorrow I had never known before. I wrapped him in a hug as massive as I could manage, and felt him soften into my shoulder. I was holding him against me and stroking his hair, and with each pass of my hand he seemed to crumble a bit further. I had known Kane Woods for several months now but I had never once seen him so drained; not even after snapping a counter top. It shattered me, and at the same time I felt a fury ignite once again between me and God. How fucking *DARE* You! This is Kane; *K-A-N-E*....not *CAIN*. *BIG* fucking difference there, Pal! What the *FUCK*, and *WHY*? And *WHO* do You think You are anyway? Yeah, sure okay, You're *GOD*; but let me tell You something buddy! You're *WAY* wrong on this one. And where's the Defense Attorney Jesus? What? He out on a union break? What is *THIS* shit?

I have no idea what color signature Kane would have seen if his eyes were open, but I know what I was seeing. I was seeing red; and it was not multi- faceted. It was the red of beautifully pure anger. I inhaled as smoothly as I could, and while I know Kane heard and felt it's 'not as smooth as usual'; the man was too exhausted to do more than softly kiss my shoulder. I disconnected from my raging at the Almighty to focus on the here and now; the in the moment situation I was in where I could actually *DO* something. Oh yes; God and I were going to have *MORE* than a talk, but right now I had this completely wiped out man in my arms. Yeah, fuck You God for that as well; and yeah, You'll answer for that but You are *NOT* my priority. Kane sighed softly, and God and His entire Divine Court vanished from my thoughts.

"C'mon Kane", I began, and even in his current state he found the reserves to manage a momentary smile when I spoke his name, "Let me help you to bed."

The smile slipped to a grin, and he nodded. I took his hands in mine and yanked him to his feet. It was the first time it ever required a true physical effort to bring him upright, and I felt my eyebrows meet over my nose with my concern. Jesus. *September is powerful* he had said. *Is it the worst?* I had asked. *No*.

FUCK! How much was he going to have to endure? I shot my eyes skyward; reminding God that He and I had unfinished business, and wrapped my arm around Kane. He leaned on me more than I had ever experienced before. He stifled a yawn, and followed my lead as I guided him to the bedroom. I backed him against the bed like one would a drunk person, and he slid off me on sat on the edge as if he had indeed gone on a three-day bender. I took a step back, and he grabbed on to my hand.

"Thank you." he whispered, and looked up at me. His eyes were mostly open, but the weariness he was fighting revealed itself in the heavy appearance of his eyelids. I felt my own half grin assume its post on my lips, and cocked my head slightly.

"Of course. Do you want me to leave you to sleep?"

He mustered enough energy to shake his head slowly and release a small chuckle.

"No." was all he managed. I climbed across him in less than a second, and pulled his exhausted frame down on the bed beside me. He easily slid into his head resting on my shoulder, his arm across my waist,as I ran my fingers through his hair. His breathing slowed and grew deeper, and while it wasn't loud? Kane started to snore softly. I kissed the top of his head as I did his arm squeezed me a tad tighter. Even in his completely exhausted slumber; he was protective of me and lovingly affectionate. And while I didn't think it was possible; I fell even more in love with him as he slept.

#

It had taken Kane almost an entire day to fully recover. While he was up and about after a three-hour power nap, he hadn't hit his usual full stride for almost twenty-four more hours. Jesus he wasn't kidding; the Harvest Moon had done a number on him.

Is September the worst?

No.

That conversation bounced around my head for most of that day, and I wasn't all that happy with it. I glanced skyward more than once as I watched this wonderful man regain himself and nodded; reminding God that there was going to be a reckoning. I was having some difficulty with forgiveness. The injustice of what Kane had endured for over a century and that he still was going through was like a splinter under your fingernail. Yeah, you can carry on about your day but it still was irritating and it was painful. I had never hurt for another person as much as I did for Kane. If I became obsessive about it, I would go crazy. So I stopped myself from dwelling too much on it; but it still skittered across my mind from time to time.

The morning of September sixth I opened my eyes to not only the wonderful aroma of coffee but a steaming mug of it being extended to me in the hand of and even hotter man. His eyes had gone more amber as we slept, but the gold flecks that speckled them were full of a soft light. Kane was back, and he was happy. I smiled before I even stretched, and he returned one just as big.

"Good morning, Lover." He said, and I felt every syllable in the marrow of my bones. Oh yes, he was back. I felt my smile grow.

"Yes, it is." I replied as I accepted the goblet of resuscitation from him. Kane winked and gently shook his head.

"My apologies for not having this life-giving nectar ready for you yesterday."

"You are forgiven." I said as I sipped the wonderful brew. Kane did make one *HELL* of a pot of coffee. Between that and that crooked half grin of his, I don't think I could ever truly remain mad at the man. Diver down! Diver down!

"And what, pray tell? Is your agenda for this day my Lady?" My eyebrow was moving before I knew it. I am a sheep dog; protector of those whom I call my flock and no one was more important than Kane Woods, but really dude? I've had one sip of coffee, and haven't even brushed my teeth or had a cigarette yet. Like I planned my day in the last ten seconds. Cut me some slack. Kane seemed to sense my mood, and he raised both hands in the 'I surrender' motion.

"Again, my apologies. I realize you have not had your initial requirements of stimulants yet."

"And those would be?" I asked, and enjoyed some more of my personally delivered coffee. Kane smiled and ran his fingers through my hair.

"You need coffee, fluoride and nicotine before you are even *remotely* civil. In that order."

"Fuck you."

"I rest my case."

We both laughed at that, because he was right and I wasn't worried about it and neither was he. It was an even exchange. I was a bear before my daily minimal three, and once every twenty-nine days he morphed into a murderous creature. In the very strangest of ways, it worked. No sense in raging against the unchangeable; just figure out how it's going to work best and run with it. Somehow? We had managed to do just that. I leaned forward and kissed his knee. He stroked the back of my head and a small laugh came from him. I looked up into his amber eyes and saw a hint of rascal light in them. My eyes narrowed and the eyebrow again moved of its own volition. Whatever spectrum I was emanating to his vision I will never know, but his smile spread farther.

"It is rather perfect that your cycle coincides with my recovery, Miss Jameson."

Jesus Christ. He was talking about my period. Are you fucking kidding me? I haven't even had a full cup of coffee never mind brushed the sleep off my teeth, and let's not even discuss the lack of nicotine for over ten hours. And *this* is where you want to go right now, Kane? And yeah, so what? I started yesterday while you were sleeping. He leaned backwards and held his hands up, surrendering once more.

"Whoa, whoa, whoa! Wow! No. *Not* what I meant." He quickly sputtered. I have no idea what color he was seeing me in but it made him nervous. I realized my features had gone a bit harsh. I don't know if I succeeded, but I tried to soften them a bit. Kane lowered his hands and shook his head.

"Jesus; it is true. Women are *not* kind every twenty-eight to thirty days."

"Kiss my ass Cujo; you're no love child every twenty-nine yourself."

"Fair enough." He said in a serious tone. It lasted all of two seconds before we were both starting to chuckle. I was engulfed in full laughter before I knew it. The whole thing was so gloriously fucked up it made perfect sense.

Welcome Home Jimmy! Once we had stopped laughing, he ran his hand down my arm from my shoulder and took my hand in his.

"What I meant is that it is great timing. You have your female issues to attend to, and I am still getting my strength back. By the time your womanly time is over? I am back to one hundred percent."

"And?" I said, and there was a tinge of 'what the fuck' in my tone that did not escape his keen ears. I raised the mug again and drank as I waited for his response.

"Jimmy? I am an old man, and the day after the Full? I am worn. I would not want to have you disappointed in my lack of vigor."

Coffee splattered across Kane's T shirt and throat, and it had erupted from my mouth. He blinked in surprise as he wiped his neck; watching me the entire time to be sure I wasn't choking to death. In a sense I almost was. Lack of vigor? Are you shitting me? Oh, this was too much. I regained enough composure to swallow the drops of coffee still on my tongue and laughed.

"Oh, Jesus you're fucking kidding, right?" I managed to say before laughing again.

"No. No I am not."

One look into his eyes told me he was serious, and he was concerned. I worked to absorb that, and sort through the ninety things I wanted to say all at once. I reached out and ran my left hand up his thigh. God even through soft denim the strength of him emanated under my fingers. I gathered myself and spoke.

"Kane? On your *deathbed* you would cripple me." He cut his eyes at me, as if wanting to believe my words but holding on to some misguided doubt. And it *WAS* misguided. Jesus I could barely find my breath half the times we were 'intimate', and this guy was questioning if he was up to par? Holy shit!

"If either of us needs to be worried about being 'disappointing'; you're looking at her." I said, and watched as an expression of honest confusion set up residence on him. He shook his head slightly and glanced over at me, then repeated the motion. Finally, he looked straight at me, and bewilderment filled his eyes.

"What are you talking about, Diana? There is no way you could ever not be..."

I pressed my finger to his lips stopping his speech. He glanced down at it and almost crossed his eyes, then returned his focus to me.

"Then it's settled. We both rock each other's world." His lips moved under my fingertip, and that damn grin emerged. I kept it there and continued.

"It is because it's you, Kane. I'm not capable of holding a thing back. You'll never have anything less than all I can give you and it's not just the sex I'm referring to. You'll have all of me, always. I simply can't, *NOT*, give you that. It's impossible." He pursed his lips under my finger and kissed it. The warmth in his eyes was a comfort I never knew I ever wanted, and now that I had it? I would not survive losing it. I removed my finger from his lips and he smiled, leaning into my hand as I ran it down his cheek and jaw. He waited for my hand to leave his skin, and then stood up.

"Finish your *CAUWFEE*, and brush your teeth. I will meet you on the porch swing with your cigarettes and you can complete the 'Jimmy's Holy Trinity' that is required for you to rejoin the living."

"Be there in a heartbeat."

"I know. I can hear it." Shit I had forgotten about that as we spoke. I felt mine resume at a quicker pace; it had briefly stopped when he said that.

"And what exactly is it telling you right now, Wolfman Jack?"

"That perhaps I am not as much of an old man as I had thought."

"Oh no you are not even close, Woods."

"I am glad we are on equal ground then." Kane said and winked as he circled the bed towards the door.

"Equal? I'm playing catch up it seems like to me."

"I believe you have forgotten about a countertop that I had to replace, young Lady. And I will bring them on the porch for you." he said, and held up my lighter. His smile was big and mine matched it.

Yes, indeed. It was a good morning.

#

My *Holy Trinity* requirements to *rejoin the living* as Kane had so eloquently called it were met a half hour ago, yet we both lingered on the swing enjoying the quiet presence of each other. Just being together was enough for me, and it seemed to be so for Kane as well. I watched a butterfly bob and weave over the tiger lilies and rested my head against his shoulder. He leaned his head over on to mine and sighed.

"Still tired?" I asked.

"No. I am almost completely back to normal." He said, and I snorted.

"Normal is not a word you can use about any of this, Kane." He chuckled a bit in agreement.

"I am sorry for that, Diana." He said softly. "What I wouldn't give to change it."

I raised my head from his shoulder and turned to look directly at him. The scattered flecks of gold were filled with a sadness I couldn't bear.

"Why would you want to change it?" I asked incredulously. His brow furrowed with confusion.

"Why?" he asked me. I nodded and he continued. "Jimmy, none of this is fair to you. I am this thing..."

"You're *Enhanced*, Kane. That's it. *Enhanced*. Not a *thing* and I will *NOT* tolerate you referring to yourself as such again." I snarled. *THING*? Oh Hell no! Kane Woods was the finest man I had ever known and one of the gentlest souls I had ever encountered. *Nobody* was going to get away with speaking badly about him; not even

Kane himself. No way. That was just bullshit. Kane gently shook his head back and forth as a smile crept across his lips.

"Once again; I am amazed by you, Miss Jameson." He said softly.

"Why? What did I do?"

He sat beside me on the swing and was staring at me. His expression was one of confusion and astonishment. He opened his mouth to speak, closed it, and continued to stare at me. The half grin returned but he still said nothing, and maybe it was the cramps, but I started to get slightly annoyed. He looked like he knew an inside joke and I was left out of the humor. Well what the shit was this about? I was crossing from slightly annoyed into irritated.

"What did you do?" he whispered. Okay, he at least spoke; and I slid back into slightly annoyed.

"Yeah. What?"

"Jimmy, I am what I am. And not *only* do you deal with my...my *Enhancement* with grace and compassion, but you refuse to allow me to hate myself for it. What did you do? Indeed."

"Well duh, Kane! It's not like you volunteered for the fucking job. I don't understand why you'd want to change any of what's between us. I am completely happy. *Completely*. I thought you were too, but it seems that maybe you're not as much as I had thought. And I'm sorry for not realizing you weren't, and I don't know what we need to do to change that for you but..."

A crushing kiss ended my sentence. Powerful arms wrapped around me and pulled me tightly to him. The speed at which he could move was still astounding. The longer he kissed me the deeper my surprise grew. When he finally released me, I was both breathless and confused. I looked at Kane. His eyes were gold and glowing and he wore an enormous smile. I blinked several times, both to regain my rational thought; a good solid kiss from Kane always had a way of rattling that, and also because I was truly lost as to the *WHY* of what had just happened. Kane continued to smile, and it was accompanied by a soft laughter from him. That sent me further into confusion. He seemed to sense it, and took my hands in his and peered deeply into my eyes.

"Diana, there is no possibility of you being happier than I am with what we have together. I can scarcely breathe when you are not around."

"Then why would you want to change anything? I'm lost here, Kane."

He smiled as always at the sound of his name, and raised my hands to his lips. He kissed them gently and returned his eyes to mine. The gold flecks were soft but warmly lit, and the amber in them was bathed in the same glow.

"I would change what I am, if I could. You deserve a more normal life. A life that does not require overnight trips to secret locations; one where the discussion of possible children does not involve speaking of the risk of passing along this *Enhancement*. And especially one where you do not have to fear the man who loves you on the night of a Full."

He hung his head after speaking those last words, and his shoulders dropped slightly. It had become his signature body language of anguish, as much as his half grin was his signature of happiness and humor. I hated the first. I shot a quick glance skyward before returning my attention to Kane. Oh yes, God.... there *WILL* be a reckoning. I leaned forward and rested my face on the back of his head. He startled a bit at the contact, and released a long breath. It had a raggedness to it, and it screamed the pain he felt without making a sound.

"Don't you dare do it Woods; don't you dare." I hissed, and kissed the back of his head. His shoulders sank lower and he took in a deep breath before he spoke. When he did, it was a whisper.

"Do what?"

"Blame yourself. Feel guilty. Tear yourself apart for the lack of 'normal'. Don't you *fucking* dare. I'll kill you myself if you try."

He laughed sharply but kept his head down. That drove me into a further fury with the Man Upstairs. Seeing Kane suffer drove me to the brink of insane rage. Watching this wonderfully kind, affectionate and admirable man in pain made me rabid.

There was a sound consuming the morning quiet. I had never heard it before and I certainly did not recognize it. It was barely human in its savagery and it came from the deepest darkness of a soul. My ears detected it and latched on to it as my mind scrambled to determine what it was. Kane's head snapped up and he stood up, staring at me with his mouth hanging open. Somehow, I was standing as well, facing up at the blue sky though I didn't remember rising. Kane just stood there; eyes wide in shock. I was stunned when I determined what the sound was, and where it was coming from.

It was me.

I was roaring at God.

CHAPTER SIXTEEN

Kane was sitting on the walkway beside me. He stayed close enough so I knew he was there, but just far enough away to allow me my space. I don't know precisely how long I had been sitting on the concrete in silence; but it was long enough that my butt was getting uncomfortable and the three singed cigarette filters beside me told me it had been at least a half an hour. I lit the fourth and drew deeply on it. Kane remained beside me and while he didn't speak; I could see him glance my way several times a minute. I closed my eyes and released the cloud of glorious nicotine laced toxicity from my lungs. It burned my throat slightly, and I'm not entirely sure if it was from the rapid succession of cigarettes or the sound that had erupted from me.

Though it was maybe 10:30 in the morning, I wanted a beer. I looked over at Kane. It happened to be at one of those times he was glancing my way and our eyes met and held. I managed a half grin or at least the effort of one and he returned my attempt with a huge and bright, full-on smile.

"There she is." He said softly, and placed his hand on mine. Even at the low volume his words resonated within me. I felt his speech as much as I heard it. The warmth of his skin brought me comfort. Peace even. Shit. Whatever may come, that was the one thing I knew I could count on. Kane was my refuge. I finished the last drags of my cigarette and field stripped it as I had the prior three.

"I'm sorry." I began, staring at the spider vein cracks on the side walk as I searched for the words to convey my feelings. "I don't even know what to say or where to begin."

His nose was nuzzling against my ear before I knew it. I never saw him move but I was getting used to that; for so much as anyone could I guess. His arms encircled my waist and he gently drew me into him.

"Sssh. None of that. There are no apologies needed here, Diana. Not anymore."

He kissed my ear lightly and whispered, "For either of us."

The monumental force that lay behind those words crashed down upon me. Well Thank Christ! Kane was finally through ripping himself to pieces over what he was and how it affected me and the 'normal' life he felt I deserved but would never have with him. I shot a quick look up. Well God? You at least got that part right! I'll give You that. But only that; for now. We still have shit to deal with, but I'll thank You for that one mercy for Kane. *K-A-N-E* You sonofabitch, but we'll cross that bridge when we come to it. For now? Thank You.

I had melted into Kane without even realizing it. The amount of lost actions I had done this morning was staggering, and I had barely been awake for three hours. Jesus, where has Officer Jameson gone to? Hopefully someplace safe because this kind of shit would have gotten her killed. I chuckled at the thought.

"I don't know what it is you're thinking, but I am glad to hear that sound come from you again, Lover."

I snuggled further into Kane's chest, allowing his essence to drown me. A soft laugh grumbled from within him and I let myself get swept away in it. He hugged me to him and inhaled deeply before letting a groan of happy frustration escape him.

"Do you want to get up?" I asked, and he laughed.

"Yes, *PLEASE*. This walkway is a bit tough after a while."

"Well you could have gotten up before now Kane, you're not the one in a fight with God." I said, and looked up at him. His eyes deepened but remained as full of warmth as before.

"I am in any fight you find yourself in, even if it is with the Almighty Himself. So long as you are in it, my Goddess of the Moon? So am I. You will face nothing alone so long as I breathe." He kissed me gently and I felt my color change. I was glad his eyes were closed at least for the moment.

"But, since the battle seems to have slipped into a truce for now; shall we get off this stone? I am old and it bothers my hips." He said with a quick wink and flashed me a toothy grin. I giggled and wrapped my arms around his waist. I hugged him quickly, then slid his hands into mine and jerked him to his feet.

"C'mon, you decrepit bastard before we need to get you a walker."

"Ugh. There is no need for such hostility, Miss Jameson. And my parents were married." He said, and the light in his eyes changed. It was brighter in the gold flecks but deeper in the amber. I had never seen this combination before, and it intrigued me. The word *scoundrel* flashed through my mind though for the life of me I couldn't say why. Kane was up to something; there was a devilry in that rich glow, but I sensed it was nothing he was going to share any time soon. I cocked my head slightly; the eyebrow had already resumed its arc, but he simply smiled and quickly kissed me.

"I believe I asked you earlier this morning what your plans for the day were. Now that you have had ample coffee and cigarettes and your teeth are brushed? I will ask it again."

"Jesus Kane, I don't know. I didn't have any. I was waiting to see how you were today. You worried me yesterday. You were so tired. I've never seen you like that before so I figured I'd play it by ear and see how you were."

"Well my Love; I thank you for that but as you can see I am far better today."

"Even with the hips?" I teased. His grin broadened and his eyes shifted into full mischief illumination.

"Yes. Even with my hips. They will need some time to bounce back. As I also said this morning; it is a fortunate thing indeed that your cycle falls on my recovery time. By the time you are ready? I will be as well." He smiled at me, and I have no doubt that even in my current cramping state I shifted far redder from orange than I'd care to know.

"We might need that walker yet handsome, but for me." Kane laughed and kissed me again.

"I will be as gentle as I can.", he began, and his eyes got that dancing trouble glow again. "But as you know; the closer She gets to Full, the less I can stop myself. And being with *you* Diana? I am doing well to control myself any day of the month."

"There are worse ways to become an invalid." I said, and he smiled.

"Perhaps. But I have digressed. If I may say something? Without you getting angry?"

I cocked my head questioningly. Kane simply raised both eyebrows in a silent explanation of his question. I stopped and thought about all that had occurred this morning. He had seen me crampy, bitchy and witnessed me unleash on God. Okay, it was more than a fair question for him to ask. I laughed at myself in spite of it all. Shit, he was a wonder. And not a fool that's for sure! He had made his *point* to the bear, without *poking* the bear. Crafty sonofabitch. I loved him the more for it. I shrugged my shoulders, my silent acceptance that he was correct, and nodded for him to continue.

"Labor Day weekend is over. No tourists. And Jimmy? Forgive me, but you look like you could use a drink. Not a beer; we have those. A *drink*." I burst into a loud but honest fit of laughter. Jesus Christ he was right! Mary and Joseph, thank you! Once again the genius of Kane Woods emerged, and perfectly timed too.

"Oh Lord, *YES*!" I exclaimed, and continued to laugh. Kane had visibly relaxed, which made me laugh even harder. He was truly nervous about saying that to me. Ha! What was my hundred- and fifty-pound-self going to do to *him*? Yeah, I may rant and rave and threaten shock collars but in the end we both knew nothing was going to happen to him at my hand that Kane didn't *ALLOW* to happen. With his height and build? He'd have been challenging to take down without any *Enhancement*. With it? I was as lethal as a gnat and we both knew it. God love him all the more for his patience with my shit talking! Jesus, he was a keeper for sure. Kane watched my laughter with a big toothy smile. He seemed a little unsure of what I found *that* funny but he went along with it nonetheless; no questions asked. Wise man indeed.

"Please, allow me to take you to the best worst bar on Plum Island." Kane said with a bow, and extended his right hand to me. I slipped my fingers into his and curtsied. He snickered and took my hand, kissing it gently before smiling brilliantly at me.

"You didn't know I knew how to do that, did you?" I asked, and he smiled broadened even more.

"No, I did not. But you never do cease to amaze me, Miss Jameson. I discover more reasons to adore you every day."

His words stopped me mid-stride. The genuine feelings he had for me were unfathomable, and yet I felt zero doubt of his sincerity. Amaze. Adore. Love. Scarcely breathe when you're not here. These are words every woman prays to hear once in her life; and I was being showered with them daily by a man I loved beyond even my own comprehension. It would almost seem too good to be true, like some bullshit story, but one look into Kane's golden flecked eyes quieted any doubt I ever had. This was no joke. This was as serious as a heart attack. I had always heard that fact was stranger than fiction. Seems it is.

"Kane Woods." I said softly, and he stopped beside me. The smile was there briefly, after all I had said his name, but he sensed something deeper was following my addressing him. He stepped closer to me and looked intently into my eyes.

"I don't know why, but I feel your voice sometimes. Actually, *FEEL* it; like a rumbling vibration of some radio station that only I seem to be able to tune into. It's happened a lot, but when it happened at Pizzeria Regina and Ann didn't seem to be affected by it? It has made me wonder. It reaches into the marrow of my bones and feels like I'm standing too closely to iron church bells when they ring. I don't know how I *FEEL* it, but I do. And I know I will not survive if I never feel your voice again. So, there you have it."

Kane's eyes never moved from mine, but a myriad of storms went through the gold and amber in seconds. I don't pretend to know what lay behind them all, but when he kissed my hand and met my eyes again? His had the shine of tears in them. I immediately moved towards him but he shook his head no so I stayed put. He pulled in a deep but uneven breath, and spoke softly. I felt his words as he spoke them.

"I have prayed you would not feel it, and I have hoped beyond hope that you would. Until today that is; because I know what it meant if you felt my voice and that was Damnation for you because of what I am. We have addressed that now, and there are no more apologies from either of us. You have chosen me despite it all. I will not make you defend your choice of me, nor will I attack your choice of me; which is in essence? What I do every time I hate what I am. I am not sure I am worthy, but I am happy beyond any dreams I ever had." He paused, took another deep breath, and peered intently into my eyes.

"My Da knew some things about what I am. He didn't speak of it often, but when he did? I paid attention. The Residual was one part he mentioned. The feeling of my words? The vibration inside of you?"

Kane's voice was strained with the emotions he was struggling with, and I again moved towards him. He held his hand up to stop me, so I remained where I was. He had afforded me my space in my fight with God. Of course I would return the favor no matter how badly I wanted to hold him and reassure him it was all okay; no matter what it was.

"Only the true, life-long mate of a Wolf, feels his voice within her."

The clashing of his guilt over this *Damnation* as he called it and his joy that I felt his voice was painted in neon colors on a black wall. Jesus he was far too good of a man *NOT* to feel awful that I was destined to be his soul mate because of the Wolf, and he wrestled with that even as he stood before me promising not to argue my choice. That was the duty side of him; the part that had carried this burden for far too long and lonely. A century of resigning himself to a solitary existence because of what he became for twelve hours every twenty-nine days, had left him utterly alone for the entirety of the other days and hours of every month. My heart both shattered and sang for him. I resisted the urge to allow the shattering part to resume my fight with God at present, and focused on the sing part of what Kane had said.

Kane could move quickly; that was an established fact. However, this catwalk queen was no slouch herself and I knew I had succeeded when I felt him startle under my touch. I had crossed the two feet between us in less than a blink and kissed him faster than he could react. His rigid shoulders relaxed after a moment of my tongue conveying what no words could ever say, and he gradually abandoned the moral high ground he had taken watch from. His fingers travelled between my shoulder blades and down towards my waist as my hands ran through his thick mane and down his throat. When I had silently assured him that the only person who had a problem with me feeling his voice was *him*, I allowed him up for air. His breathing was faster and deeper, but a beautiful toothy smile found its way home to his lips.

"I should be sorry." He muttered as he leaned his forehead down to mine, "But I am not."

"Good. Then that makes two of us who aren't sorry."

"Jesus. Just Jesus. And may I be forgiven for the happiness I have knowing you *feel* my voice. I should burn eternally for it because I know what it means for you. If I eventually do? I will have the memory of this joy to get me through those fires. I would not change a second of it to save me."

"Stop it. Nobody is burning. Nobody has been forced to do a damn thing. As you said; it is my choice. I have chosen you, just like you have chosen me. Sorry for your luck here Woods, but you're stuck with me now. And you will be until the day you tell me to go."

"I would beg for death before I utter that. The result would be the same. I cannot be without you Diana. It is a fact I resigned myself to the first morning I woke up with you beside me. It is simply? Not possible. I need you. Always."

"Even before *my* Holy Trinity?"

"Even then." Kane said, and started to laugh.

"Well thank God, you're lightening up a bit! Jesus, who looks like they need a drink now? You know, for a man who just found out the woman he *says* he loves is some sort or destined soul mate for him? You got awful serious there. What the shit is that about? All I did was get in a fight with God. You get the answer to your prayers or so you say and act like you're walking to the gallows. No wonder I look like I could use a drink! I can! So step it up Sparky, and take me to the best worst bar on Plum Island!"

"As you wish M'lady. Your chariot awaits." Kane said, bending in a deep bow and flourishing his hand towards the pick-up. I laughed brightly and Kane followed suit. Wow, it had been one *HELL* of a morning! We both had been through the wringer. Somehow, a Captain and Seven wasn't such a bad idea, no matter it wasn't noon yet. We had covered a week's worth of emotions in three hours. Yep, it was beer thirty for sure. I climbed into the truck and Kane closed the door behind me. Nine chickens looked up and seemed almost happy we were laughing again. One glared at me. I gave her the finger and laughed. Nope. Not even you can screw up today, you bitch. Kiss my ass. Kane slid into the seat beside me.

"I love you." he said, and my smile had to be enormous. Kane cocked his head slightly and asked, "What?"

"I know you do. I felt your words." His eyes lit with the warmth of happiness, and this time there was no tinge of guilt to dim them. Kane had made his peace with it.

"And you know I love you, Mister Woods."

"Yes, I do."

"Oh?" I asked, "How are you so sure?"

"Two ways. You feel my voice. And I hear your heartbeat, Jimmy. Since the moment I met you; it has never once held a lie. Reserves? Yes. But never a true lie. So, if you say it? It is truth."

"Well, isn't keeping a Christmas present secret going to be challenging from now on?" I said, and Kane chuckled and kissed my shoulder.

"I promise not to ask."

"Shut up and buy me a drink."

"My pleasure." He said, and started the truck.

Chapter Seventeen

It's not a far drive to Plum Island from Rowley; north to Route 1 through Newburyport then down to Water Street and travel along the river to the island itself. We made the trip in good time because as Kane had said; the tourists had gone home and resumed their normal lives of getting the kids back in school and returning to work. Traffic at eleven in the morning on a Thursday heading *TO* the beach is not exactly gridlock. Kane was parking the truck in front of a one-story shingled building before noon.

"Jimmy? Allow me to introduce you to the Beachcomber."

"I look forward to it."

"Don't be too sure." Kane said and laughed.

"Now I'm *really* looking forward to it. I love a good dive."

"I thought you might, Love; I had a feeling after you chose to sit at the bar in Boston."

"Belly up, handsome. That's me."

"Just when I thought I could not love you more than I do; you say something like that."

"Come on Woods, you and I have both had one *HELL* of a morning. And Lookie here! It's noon." I said pointing to the clock on the dashboard. "We're not even heathens."

"I thought it was five o'clock that made it acceptable."

"I'm from New York. We move faster than you New England Puritans. We've got shit to do."

"You are beautiful."

"You know a girl could die of thirst." I said and started to laugh. Kane joined me in it, got out of the pickup and crossed to open my door. I was finding that I liked that. Who said chivalry was dead? We crossed the mixture of sand, crushed shells and plain old dirt that comprised the parking lot and Kane held open the screen door that led into the bar. I stepped in. It was far darker inside than the parking lot, and I immediately liked it. Yep; dive bar all the way. I glanced back at him. He was smiling broadly.

"You are a genius." I said, and leaned back to kiss him quickly. He smiled even brighter and winked.

"I thought you might appreciate an establishment such as this. I know my girl."

"Yes, you do. In more ways than I knew," I said, and Kane's smile expanded. I couldn't help myself; the Devil grabbed my soul for a second and my smile curved guiltily before I continued,

"And in ways I *very much* know as well."

He was still outside in the sun when I said that, and for a moment I thought maybe the *Enhancement* might have become contagious because I saw him change color. Wait, what? Was it the lifelong soul mate thing where I could catch it?

When it clicked in my head what was happening, I burst out laughing. Kane was blushing! Oh, this was awesome!

"What?' he mumbled and glanced at the ground before returning his eyes to mine.

"You are precious. That was adorable."

"Yeah, thanks. Adorable. Precious. Wonderful words to bolster the ego." He said, but the half grin was on him. I kissed him quickly again and jerked my head towards the bar.

"Get in here. First round is on me now."

"It should be after that embarrassment." He said, but the grin told me that all was well. We made our way to the empty bar and slid on to two high backed barstools at the far corner. Old habits I guess; but this perch let me see both the door and the windows, and there were no doors behind me. A stocky bartender smiled and made his way down to us.

"Welcome to the Beachcomber. You missed all the Labor Day festivities."

"Precisely why we are here today." Kane said as a smile returned to him.

"My kinda people." the bartender quipped, and extended his hand to Kane.

"I'm Colin. What can I get for you two today?"

"Kane." he said and shook Colin's hand, "And this delightful lady is Jimmy."

"Cool name." Colin said and he shook my hand as well.

"Last name is Jameson." I said.

"Way cool now. Being Irish, I appreciate both the name and the whiskey."

"That actually sounds good, Colin." Kane said, and winked at me.

"Two please. Unless you prefer something else, Love?"

"Jameson would be perfect."

"All right then. Neat?"

"Chilled but neat, and in a rocks glass if it's not too much trouble." I answered. Colin nodded and looked to Kane.

"The lady has both taste and style." Kane said, "Two that way, if you would."

"Yes, she does." Colin said, nodded again, and prepared our drinks. Kane used that time to lean in and whisper in my ear.

"No wonder you feel my words, Diana. I've enjoyed Jameson that way for many years now. Destiny indeed, it would seem."

I smiled as he lightly kissed my ear. Oh yes, this was going to be a good day for sure. This whole 'retirement' thing wasn't so bad after all. Noon on a Thursday in an empty beach bar, with a hearty pour of Jameson in my right hand and Kane's knee under my left. Yeah, today did not suck. I sipped my glass and smiled when I realized Kane was too. Yes, the man had class. Only a slob shoots down a fine Irish whisky. He smacked his lips and smiled.

"I have not had a Jameson in a long time. Not since Drinking the Ave." he announced, and admired the rich color of the whiskey that still remained in the glass.

"Wait. What?" I asked.

"Jimmy, surely you have heard of 'Drinking the Ave'."

"Well shit yes I have, Kane." I began, and true to form the smile appeared at the sound of his name. Colin had returned to our part of the bar, and he was as curious as I was about Kane's mention of it.

"But did you actually *DO* it?" I asked.

"Yes. Why?" Kane asked.

"My fine sir; let me again shake your hand." Colin said, and Kane squinted. He looked perplexed, but brought his hand up and shook Colin's. Colin and I looked at each other, and that's when I realized my mouth was half open in amazement. I shut it as casually as I could, but our barkeep saw it and laughed.

"I agree one hundred percent, Jimmy."

Kane switched his glances of confusion back and forth from me and Colin several times, and I started to laugh. He truly had no idea what he had just said. Precious and adorable; all over again.

"What is it that I am missing?" Kane asked, and Colin and I both laughed. Kane was beyond confused now. He was baffled.

"I have never met anyone who has completed the task. Well done!" Colin said, and Kane cocked his head, puzzled. He stared at him for several seconds, and then looked over to me. I nodded my head in agreement with Colin.

"Me either." I said, and smiled gently. Kane was honestly surprised by our reactions.

"I've tried it three times. I've never got farther than seven, and I was sick for two days after." Colin jerked his head up in surprise.

"Seven! Well done Jimmy, I'm easily fifty pounds heavier and that's as far as I've ever gotten as well."

"I'm a professional. Don't try this at home without the proper safety equipment and a spotter." I replied, and we both burst into laughter. Kane just blinked, his gaze again alternating from me to Colin and back to me.

"Kane," I said softly once the hysterics had subsided, "It's quite a feat to 'Drink the Ave'. It's like the Holy Grail of alcohol. And you did it."

"Yes. Twice. It is not that hard."

Colin and I slid our eyes to each other. His mouth was hanging open as much as mine was, and I'm fairly certain my eyes were just as wide as his. I shook my head incredulously, and Colin just stared at me, then returned his attention to a befuddled Kane.

"Didn't learn from the first time there, Kane? Had to go back again?" he asked, and I sipped my drink.

"Go back?" Kane asked him, and his eyebrows were dangerously close to meeting in the middle. Oh, my poor gentleman was astonished at our marvel of him. He really had no idea.

"Yeah, you know. Go back and do it again." Colin said, his right hand flipping as if to set the timeline. I wondered if he thought Kane had some mental impairment and wasn't quite keeping up. I of course knew better but I could see where Colin might be coming from; he didn't know us from Adam. Kane just looked blankly at him.

"Why would I go back?"

"Well, you said you did it twice." Colin said, and I found myself leaning in closer. A realization was creeping up on me, and it was truly one I was struggling to believe. I knew Kane, oh yes, I knew him. I had seen him do unbelievable things. But what was beginning to dawn on me was more shocking than even the speed he could move at and the fact that he heard my heartbeat or saw me in colors. I squeezed Kane's knee gently. He looked at me, still utterly lost; and placed his hand on top of mine on his leg.

"Babe?" I said softly, and his eyes warmed even in his uncertainty. "You *DID* do this on two separate trips, right?" In the peripheral of my vision I saw Colin's head snap in my direction, and then slowly swivel back towards Kane.

"Why would I make two trips? It is not what one would call scenic, in Dorchester."

"Whoa. Wait. What?" Colin sputtered, and Kane glanced his way. Our curly haired bartender was an observant man, and while I understood his calling bullshit on Kane's story as he now understood it? The way he locked eyes with him and the stance he took afterwards told me he did not doubt what Kane was saying.

"You Drank the Ave? Twice? In one day?" he asked, and while I could see that Colin didn't believe the words coming out of his own mouth; he completely believed Kane. A bartender as I've said is like a cop. They *KNOW* people. The set of Colin's shoulders resonated that he did in fact believe Kane, because he had already 'read' him and sensed that Kane was neither a liar nor braggart. As mind blowing as this was? Colin knew it to be true.

"Well, yes." was Kane's simple reply. Colin's reaction was nowhere near as subdued.

"Holy *SHIT*!" he exclaimed, and started laughing as he emerged from behind the bar and dropped to his knees. He bent at the waist, arms extended over his head, and bowed to Kane repeatedly.

"I am not worthy!" was all he kept repeating, and I howled with laughter. I considered joining him down there, but Kane's expression of shock and surprise at the two of us kept me next to him. I leaned in and kissed him, my attempt to reassure him that all was well. It took a little persuading, not that I minded a long kiss with Kane, but finally I felt his shoulders relax.

Damn. Wolf is legendary enough. Drink the Ave? Twice? In one day? Mt. Olympus had nothing on Mister Kane Woods.

"Jesus Christ." I muttered, and Kane looked at me. He was earnest in his confusion, and he shrugged.

"No wonder you weren't worried about a Deewy." I finished. That lethal half grin, while tinged with confusion, found him again.

I was in love with both a myth and a legend. My life was now complete.

#

We had finished our Jameson's and ordered two more while conversation flowed easily between Kane, Colin and me. Kane and Colin seemed to have found the sort of instant connection that Ann and I shared, and I enjoyed seeing Kane have an honest conversation with guy. He needed a buddy, and while neither of them realized it as fully as I did? That is exactly what they were becoming. I smiled into my glass and finished the last of my drink.

"Another Jameson?" Colin asked, and I shook my head.

"I'm not nearly as fortified as my boyfriend is Colin, I need to slow down." and out of the corner of my eye I saw Kane sit up taller in the stool. His smile, which was always bright, positively glowed. I turned and looked at him; my head cocked in a silent 'What?' He said nothing but the smile grew bigger, something I didn't think was possible.

"What'll it be then guys?" Colin asked.

"I'll take a Coors Light." I replied.

"For me as well." Kane said, still smiling.

"Two silver bullets coming up!" Colin said as he turned and reached for the bottles. Kane stiffened at his words. His smile had faltered for the briefest of seconds, but returned when he saw I was grinning. Silver bullets. That was actually funny, though Colin had no idea why and had missed Kane's physical reaction to it. Jesus Jimmy, you're more than just a little warped. You may need some sort of professional help.

"What are you smiling so big about?" I asked Kane, and he leaned in closer. The golden flecks in the amber were warmly lit, and the shimmer had returned to them.

"Boyfriend." He said, and kissed me quickly.

"Well, yeah. What the Hell else am I supposed to call you?"

"You are not wrong, Diana but you have never used that word before now."

"Was I out of line?" I asked, and his smile slipped into that half grin that would absolutely be the death of me.

"No. It pleases me to hear you say it." He said, and each word he spoke rumbled through my bones. Destined soul mate, oh yes, I apparently was. Still, that was awkward to say in public and would be difficult to explain. Boyfriend would have to suffice. Colin had returned with the beers.

"My *girlfriend* and I thank you Colin." Kane said, and winked at me. The devilment in those flecks of gold danced, and I felt my smile spread. Kane was right. It was *GOOD* to hear that said out loud. It was like staking a claim, and I realized I *LIKED* that he named me as *HIS*. I raised my beer to him, and enjoyed its coldness as it slid down my throat. Kane followed suit, and put his hand on my thigh. So much for the coldness; Lord knows what colors I was now.

Just the slightest of touches from him set my pants on fire, and the light in his eyes told me he saw every bit of it. Two more days until my 'womanly time' was done. I was not entirely sure I was going to be able to hold out that long. Could be time to consider water sports. Might be nice to be 'attacked' in the shower by something that didn't have feathers. A new light flooded Kane's eyes, and I didn't need any moon driven super powers to know what lay behind it. Great minds think alike, and of course the whole destined lifelong soul mate thing probably didn't hurt.

"Summer may be over guys," Colin began, and grinned at Kane, "But it sure just got really hot in here. I'll leave you to it. I'm over there watching TV if you need me."

Kane's eyes followed Colin's back as he walked to the far end of the large bar. "I like him." He said, and returned his attention to me.

"I do to. He's gonna be a good buddy to you."

"Buddy?" Kane asked, cocking his head slightly left.

"Oh yeah, you two are going to be pals. I can see it already. A poker night maybe, and when I piss you off or we get in an argument? That stocky sonofabitch right there is going to be who you come and talk to."

"Buddy." Kane whispered, and peeled the label off the bottle. The magnitude of what he was experiencing slammed me right between the eyes. He had never had a buddy. My heart broke in two, and then tripled in size with joy. No, Kane had never had anybody besides his parents. Until now. Jesus he was going to be off balance for a bit. A century spent alone, and now he has a buddy and a girlfriend. He may as well have just landed on Saturn. I laughed at the thought. He looked up and the half grin was there, swelling my heart even more.

"Welcome to your *LIFE*, Mr. Woods. It's about goddamn time you start to *LIVE*."

"I blame *you,* Miss Jameson.", he said, and smiled broadly. "You and your 'How to Stay Out of the Shit' unofficial rules."

"I accept complete and full responsibility." I said, sitting up straight in my stool as though I was in front of Internal Affairs. Kane chuckled and ran his hand up my arm, gently squeezing my shoulder.

"And you're welcome. You more than deserve it." I finished. For the second time today, Kane blushed. I laughed and before I could say a word, he held up his index finger in a warning '*DON'T* you even say it.' gesture. I howled with laughter and eventually it rubbed off on Kane, his soft chuckle reinforcing my happiness for him. Precious and adorable, yes sir right there! Colin glanced our way, a smile almost big enough to be in on our humor.

"Yes, Colin my lad; we will be in need of two more!" I said loudly, and he was in front of us before I had stopped laughing; three ice cold longnecks in one hand. He handed us each one and raised the third in his right hand.

"To winter made friends in a beach bar." He said, and we three clinked the bottles.

"They are the ones that stay." Kane replied, and Colin laughed in agreement.

"I thought bartenders weren't supposed to drink while they're working." I said after enjoying our toast.

"What're they gonna do? Fire me? It's *winter*." Colin said, and I shrugged my shoulders. The man had a point.

"Agreed." Kane said, and the two men nodded at each other. Oh yes. Buddies. I was happy, and also screwed. I'd be losing my monopoly of Kane's time. It was a small sting to bear, knowing that Kane would have someone to talk to that also stood when he peed. We raised the bottles once more, and Kane and Colin finished them simultaneously.

"Besides," Colin said, winked quick at me and grinned at Kane, "I own the place."

Kane loosed a good solid laugh and extended his hand to Colin. Colin grasped it and shook it firmly.

"I knew I liked you, Colin."

"And I you Kane, though I will never go out drinking with you." he replied, and the two laughed again.

It was the perfect way to end the summer. For all of us it seemed.

CHAPTER EIGHTEEN

After the most delightful afternoon of doing absolutely nothing of substance but everything of worth; Kane escorted me to the passenger side of his pick up and quickly slid behind the wheel. Jesus he was a sight to behold. Eyes lit up with happiness, half grin resuming its normal perch on his face, and the smell of sea air blended in perfectly. I inhaled the salinity and closed my eyes, savoring the perfume of the Atlantic.

"It *IS* something, isn't it?" Kane said softly as he grasped my hand. I squeezed his back gently, and felt the like response. So little a gesture that spoke so much.

"If it registers this much with me? I can only imagine how strong it is for you."

Silence filled the cab of the pickup. At first, I simply assumed through my closed eyes that Kane was enjoying the heady scent of the ocean, sand and all that embodied the beach. After a moment; old habits do indeed die hard and my 'cop' ears detected a different sort of breathing coming from my left. My eyelids snapped open and I immediately scanned everywhere. Perceiving no imminent threat, I allowed them to settle on Kane.

He had propped his left elbow on the window of the driver's door, and rested his head in that hand. The fingers of his right hand were still interlaced with mine, and he gently squeezed his fingers against mine to let me know he was still 'here'. His eyes wandered across the far horizon to the white crests that edged the small waves finding their way to the shore, and then back to that straight line of gray blue only the Atlantic can possess. He stared that way for a long bit, a sad half smile finding its way to him, and eventually he shook his head.

"What is it, Kane?" I whispered, and his smile at my use of his name flashed again.

"I don't know, Diana. I simply do not know."

Five million questions came roiling to the surface, and I struggled to sort through them and give them an order of importance. Damn if it wasn't a tornado! Where to begin? I slid my eyes over Kane. His gaze had never left the eastern horizon of the Atlantic, and while his were fingers laced with mine? I don't think I ever saw him quite so far away before now. I squeezed his hand.

"You okay?" I asked. He released a small sigh that bordered a laugh.

"I am now, Love. I am now."

"I am too, *boyfriend*. Take me home please."

"With pleasure, my Lady Love." He replied, an enormous smile sweeping across him. I was powerless to stop myself from responding with the same.

"It's 1990. Pretty sure I'm just the girlfriend, Kane."

A short choke from his throat made me pivot and fully direct my attention to him. I wasn't entirely sure what was going on, but Kane did not make odd noises lightly. I paid attention.

"You will never be *just* the girlfriend." he said, and every syllable struck my spine with a silent reverberation only I could feel. Like fighter jets breaking Mach one, they thundered within me and I smiled because of it. Destined soul mate wasn't that terrible now was it?

#

The following week had proven me correct. Kane had gone down to the Beachcomber for a beer by himself several times, and a friendship was being forged. He had invited me of course, but I feigned tiredness and encouraged him to go on and get himself a beer. He came home maybe two hours later, and it was wonderful to see him cross the threshold smiling. He was genuinely happy. Thank Christ. If there was anyone on the planet who deserved it? I was looking at him. Kane had spent enough time in the lonely Hell of isolation. I shot a quick glance up, nodded my thanks to God, and smiled.

His arms were around me before my heart had even beat. He moved exceptionally fast, even for him. He seemed faster somehow; I couldn't believe that was even possible but here he was. His lips brushed mine, and the gentleness of it caught me off guard. He stopped after that intimate kiss, and looked at me. His eyes had also changed too early in the month, and an echo of his words and an earlier conversation found footing once again my mind.

The Harvest moon is a strong one.

Is it the worst?

No.

"Kane?" and the appreciative smile returned to him.

"Hmm?"

"It's not even mid-September. And you're already showing the Pull of October's Full, which is damn near three weeks away. What's up?"

His shoulders slumped for half a second, but he quickly regained himself. God love him; he had promised to stop hating this part of him and at least he was trying to honor his word. While I noticed it, I remained silent of my observation and waited for his reply. He raked the fingers of his right hand through his hair and pulled me to him with his left.

"October is always the worst."

The tone his voice carried, and the depth of which I felt each syllable resonate within me, conveyed far more significance of *WHAT* he was saying than the short sentence he spoke. I pressed my nose into his shoulder and inhaled. The maleness of him was not lost to the female of me, but this was not about ying and yang. There was more to come. He remained silent longer than I expected and when I looked up at him, he was staring aimlessly out the window trying to figure out what to say and how to say it.

"Tell me what Angus told you of it then." I said softly. Kane snapped his head back to look at me, and the clarity of his eyes was matched only by his surprise.

"I never expected to ever hear you speak his name." he whispered, and an appreciative albeit surprised grin appeared.

"I'm not a predictable woman. Aside from my morning Trinity."

"Indeed, you are not. Bless you for it."

"So? Tell me."

Kane loosed me from him and stepped back half a step. He did this when he was going to say something of magnitude, and often he moved about as he spoke. This was no exception, in fact he almost paced. Until the morning after the Full of October? It was going to be rough.

"October is the Blood Moon. Many people assume a Blood Moon is any Full that catches a red hue no matter the month. Maybe to them it is. To *ME*? No. There is but one Blood Moon in a year, and it is the Full of October. And this year I am fortunate; it comes early. The closer to Halloween it comes, the fiercer it is. The *ONLY* Full worse than the Blood, is a Blue Moon. Two in one month. Jesus Diana; that is about as bad as it can get."

"So, why is this one the worst? The October Blood Moon?"

Kane stopped his pacing on a dime. He stood stock still, and his shoulders once again slumped for the briefest moment in time before his spine stiffened with resolve. He had promised me, and Dammit he was going to follow through no matter how much it was killing him. I can only imagine how many things he stopped himself from saying. Guinevere had Lancelot as her champion. I had Kane. He had given his word, and a century of recoiling at himself had to be quite an obstacle to overcome. He was determined, and in just over one week? He had struggled but in fact had stopped shredding his soul. Remarkable progress truthfully; even for a man who could cross thirty feet in half a blink. I had an enormous respect for him, and my subconscious tipped my hat to him. Well done Mr. Woods. It's not an easy task, but you are succeeding. Kane lowered his head and stared at nothing on the floor for five seconds, then raised his eyes to mine.

"The Blood Moon is the moon of Wolf origin."

"But you were born in December, Kane."

A fleeting smile covered him before he glanced at the ground. It lasted half a second before he once again found the resolve not to hate himself. I had seen a lot of brave acts, heroism even, on ECSD. What I was seeing before me now was raw and pure courage.

"I mentioned that this *Enhancement* as you titled it may have had many reasons for coming to being. Do you remember?"

"Yes, of course. Your actual birthday. Christmas Day, and it was a full moon that year. Something about where your mother may have been from. A whole lot of 'not really sure there's too many possible factors' kinda thing."

"Yes. My mother. The area she was from in Ireland was a pagan village. You have heard of Saint Patrick; I presume?"

I scoffed at him. What an insult! Really? Last name Jameson? Nope! Never heard of the fucker. Please tell me all about it. Enlighten my ignorant ass. My thoughts must have revealed themselves in both my expression and stance, because Kane had raised his hands in the 'I surrender' gesture again and I wasn't even cramping.

"I apologize, Diana. That was ridiculous for me to say." I nodded my forgiveness, and he continued.

"Saint Patrick rid Ireland of the snakes is the legend. Snakes are serpents. Serpents are the symbol of Satan, or honestly anything not of the Trinity; and I am not speaking to your coffee, tooth brushing and cigarettes. The *ACTUAL* Trinity."

Kane looked directly into my eyes as he was speaking, but truthfully I could have been blindfolded and seen the intensity of what he was saying. No, not seen it. I *knew* it, because I felt every word within me; more than my own heartbeat.

"What village?" I asked, and Kane stopped his pacing.

"Osriage."

"I've never heard of that."

"It is now Killkenny."

"No shit?"

"No Jimmy; no shit. But there is more." I nodded that he should continue, and reprimanded myself for interrupting him. This, whatever *this* was; it was major. Shut up and let him speak. He smiled softly at me, a silent assurance that all was right between us, and then his features hardened as he steeled himself to continue.

"Osriage had many pagan clans and Chieftains. Not all subscribed to the teachings of Saint Patrick. Some were convinced; others were tortured into submission, and some were just too stubborn to be beaten into fealty to the Pope."

"There are whispered myths that the ones who would not submit to Rome were cursed by Saint Patrick himself. Entire clans, families and bloodlines were damned by a man acting of God's instruction and apparently with His authority. It was at this time, that the first mentions of the Wolves of Ireland emerge."

My head spun at this knowledge, but in the end? I knew it to be fact as Kane knew it. My family had ties to Ireland. Kane's parents *CAME* from Ireland and there is an enormous difference. The pulses of his voice that travelled my bones told me there was no lie in what he was saying.

"So, what does this have to do with the Blood Moon of October?"

"There are two versions of it." Kane began, and he inhaled deeply. He set his shoulders the same way he had when I had discovered him in the infirmary after the melee with Blocks 3 and 4 and his attempt to kill Martinez. He was determined to finish the telling of his tale, and I was not about to stop him.

"The first version is that Saint Patrick arrived in Ireland on the full moon of October; and thus any curses he lay down fell back to that moment his toes touched Irish soil. The second is that he had come earlier, but once the pagan hold out clans could not be converted or beaten into conversion? He cursed them all at once, and it was in October. This tied the damnation of those he cursed with Wolf to the October Full; and under it they changed for the very first time spilling the blood of both man and beast. That was when it became known as the Blood Moon. Either way? It is the moon of Wolf origin. It's Pull on me begins immediately as the Harvest Moon wanes."

"Jesus Christ, Kane. What the fuck? And *HOW* do you have no fight with God? It was His damn foot soldier that started all this shit!"

Kane was against me before I had finished the words, his hands gently rubbing the lengths of my arms. He wore a soft smile of warmth, and the gentleness of his fingers helped quash what may have very well been the start of Jimmy vs. God; the sequel. I felt myself calming, and my spine was not quite so ramrod stiff as it had been moments before. Okay, okay; fine. I won't fire the first rocket, but I still could grumble about who started it. He watched me succumb to the acceptance of it, and as I softened his smile grew bigger. *Fine*! If Kane wasn't going to start hating himself again because of it; who was I to get righteous and angry at the why. Well shit. If there was ever a reason to forgive God? It lay in the bright white smile I was watching grow across the face of the man I loved.

Touché God. You win.

#

By the fourth full week of September; Kane could barely sit still. Even sitting at the kitchen table over supper, his leg bounced up and down. He ate enough food for three lumberjacks and I found the grocery cart looking more and more like I was feeding a family of five. He slept no more than two hours at a time, and even then? He was restless. I on the other hand, found myself waking later and later each morning. Might have had something to do with the increase in his *other* appetite. I wasn't complaining exactly, but the thought of buying a horse to justify the way I was walking did cross my mind more than once. This particular Thursday morning found me opening my eyes past ten-thirty. Damn good thing I was 'retired'. The increase in his energy level did serve one good purpose. His work was ahead of schedule, and it was breathtaking. If I survived the next six days we could relax. The Blood Moon was the worst he said. Based on what the Harvest had done to him? I was betting he'd take more than twenty-four hours to recover. It was going to take me a week.

I limped to the porch for the third stage of my becoming civil, and heard a saw running in the shop. I smiled at the sound. There was something comforting about him being 'right there', but not joined to my hip. He was a perfectionist in his work, and he took great pride in his craft. Though he'd never admit it; creating cabinetry and custom orders made him happy. It fulfilled something within him; perhaps it made him feel like he had accomplished something. I winced at a twinge in my hips as I sat down and chuckled. Oh yes Mr. Woods, you have definitely accomplished something. You've about crippled your girlfriend. Not a bad way to end up in a wheelchair.

The saw shut off and I heard the shop door swing open. Kane emerged from the corner of the building and strode over to the mailbox. He wasn't doing Wolf speed, but he was moving at a pretty good pace for his 'normal human walk'. He pulled several letters from the metal receptacle and shook the sawdust from his hair as he sorted through them. The man was adorable when covered in the residue of his work and I giggled. Jesus Jimmy, don't use that word; he'll be all out of sorts. He looked up at the sound of my laugh and smiled broadly. Even at fifty feet I could see how large his teeth had gotten and they were dazzling white in the sunlight. His eyes were almost completely golden now, and they shone in the day. He crossed the yard quickly and stepped on to the porch, and even three steps away I could feel the energy radiating out of him. Oh boy, six more days. It was going to be rough that's for sure. Thank you God!

"First or second?" he asked, jerking his head towards the coffee mug on the table beside me.

"Fourth."

"Good. Then you are amongst the living."

"Don't be too sure about that. You've practically killed me and we still have six more days to go."

"And nights." He said, his eyes glowing even more with hunger. Oh God, I was going to die. I groaned softly and he smiled. It softened after a moment, and the light in his eyes shifted and gently warmed.

"I am sorry, Diana."

"No apologies, Kane. Remember?" The consistency of him smiling when I spoke his name was flawless. He had never failed to do so. He looked down for half a second and then met my gaze again. He nodded and the half grin appeared.

"I honestly cannot help it. I have been through the days leading to the Blood Moon many times, and not all of them I spent alone. Nobody that ever mattered in any fashion of the word; but still. Jimmy? Diana? I cannot get enough of you. No sooner have we finished making love and caught our breath, I am starving for you again. I don't understand why, but I do."

Making love. That was the first time he had said those words, at least out loud and to me. The vibration I felt within my ribcage as he said them was different than when he spoke the other words he had just spoken. It was softer, yet more powerful. Me being me? I had nine thousand wise ass things to say but the change in how I *felt* those two words silenced me. I reached out and took his hand in mine and he gently squeezed my fingers. Lifelong, destined soul mate indeed. I snickered at my use of the word, even though it was only in my thoughts. Kane was rubbing off on me. He looked at me quizzically, but I said nothing and pulled him closer to me.

"Jesus Christ, I love you Kane Woods."

It was the biggest smile I had ever seen him wear the entire time I'd known him.

CHAPTER NINETEEN

By a miracle of God or perhaps simply by the Grace of it; I managed to survive and wake up relatively mobile on the morning of October fourth. Kane had maybe slept an hour the night before which meant that I slept maybe an hour and a half; my added thirty minutes through what I'm sure was an exhausting exercise in self-control for him. I was tired and sore, and smiling brightly. He had said he felt starved for more of me. Well, the man had absolutely devoured me all night long, and I'm sure I looked rough but I was grinning ear to ear. I made my way to the porch swing as he was halfway up the walk returning from the mail box. The way he checked the mail daily cracked me up. He was like a kid who had a pen pal and was anxiously awaiting a letter. I was doing good to check the mail once a week in Newburyport. Guess I wasn't that excited to open the gas bill.

"Seems you have a certified letter at the Post Office Lover," he began, holding up the pale green slip the mailman had left in the box, "And good morning."

"A certified letter? For me? Here?" I asked, and I felt my eyebrow arching. It truly was an unconscious reaction on my part. I had better not take up poker. I had a tell.

"Diana Jameson. Last I checked that is your name." Kane said, and his eyes slipped back into the deeper brighter gold light I had seen the morning I roared at God. There was no amber left this morning; it was twelve hours before the Blood Moon would savage him, but the same word floated across my mind.

Scoundrel.

I don't know what it was, but he was up to something. I thought to question, but he was already tapping his toe on the sidewalk and his finger on the letter notification. I let it go for the moment, tucked the questions into my mental file drawer of 'To Be Handled Later' and took the small card from his hand.

"I can pick it up on my way out this afternoon." I said, and Kane flinched as though I had struck him. He inhaled sharply, but true to his word fought the urge to apologize and hate himself. Or at least the Wolf part of him. He attempted a grin, which was more a smirk than a success, and I grabbed his front belt loop and pulled him closer. The smirk disappeared and a full, blinding toothy smile replaced it. I swatted him on the butt and laughed.

"Better yet? Let's both go. Right now. I always miss you when I'm gone, so I'll spend every moment I can today with you, White Fang." He laughed at the reference, and though I could plainly see he was not thrilled about my having to enter the Wolf Protection Program this evening; he was trying his best to honor his promise.

"You are a Lady indeed, Diana."

"Yeah, right." I said, and kissed him quickly. "With exceptionally colorful language."

"I do so admire a vast vocabulary." Kane said with a chuckle.

"Just call me Noah Webster."

"Precisely."

"That's me. Ever the fucking Lady."

Even in his distress, Kane laughed solidly at that. I'll mark that a win. We walked to the truck holding hands. It was pathetically perfect. I again contemplated seeking professional help, but what can a shrink do to make gloriously fucked up yet happy sound sane? Not a damn thing. Cool. I'll stay in the screwed column. It was a lot more fulfilling.

#

Half a block to the left of our road was the Post Office. Kane had so much pent up energy he practically danced up the two steps into the place, and despite how sore my hips and shaky my legs were? I found myself infected by his electricity and managed to locate a little spring to my stride. He may in fact be contagious. Lord knows he had become more than an addiction for me; he was now a requirement for me to live. He was everything I never knew I wanted, and everything I now knew that I needed. Life's a funny thing.

The sound of a southern accent surprised me. It's not very often you hear the slow drawl of Georgia in Massachusetts, and even then? It's usually at a tourist location such as Bunker Hill or the U.S.S. Constitution. To hear it in Rowley, in October, was a rare event. I stopped in my tracks. Officer Jameson had stepped forward, and I smiled at how quickly she could emerge. Almost as fast as Kane could move. Kane. I realized he too had frozen, and I could see him out of the corner of my right eye. He was rigid, and if I didn't know better; I'd have said he was bristling. An icy finger ran down my spine, and I wasn't sure if it was cop instinct or Kane's body language, but something was off. Way off.

"Yes ma'am, thank you. I appreciate the help you've afforded me."

"Of course, Mr. Galiver, and welcome to Rowley."

"Thank you, I'm sure I will like it here."

I focused on the man who was speaking. He was older, probably mid-fifties, and stood just shy of six feet tall. Solidly built shoulders, broad across the chest and his once dark hair was now shoulder length and streaked with gray. His eyes were a pale blue, and he had what looked like a three-day stubble along a mushy jaw line. He turned to leave the counter and saw both Kane and I standing there. I made an effort to soften my stance, though I remained bladed with my right leg slightly back. I hoped this passed as me simply moving to let him by, but something about the set of his chest said he was familiar with 'cop' stance. He smiled at us. It was a forced smile. It was too big and lacked sincerity. I focused solely on him, even Kane disappeared from my tunnel vision, and I absorbed every detail and nuance of the man who was walking towards us.

"Good morning. Sir. Ma'am." He said as he passed by me and exited the door to my left. I nodded once as he went past me. Yankee politeness on my part.

My head turned as I followed him walking out the door and getting into his truck. A faded red Ford, early eighties model based by the grill. The silver bumper was scraped and had a dent under the passenger side headlight. Touches of rust on the fenders over the wheel wells. Unremarkable, if it was a farm truck. But this was Rowley, and while there were small farm areas; the truck sat no softer within me than the driver did. He fired the engine, looked over his right shoulder as he backed out of his parking spot, and never once glanced back as he pulled away. It was casual. It was smooth. And it screamed of wrongness. I stocked every detail of him and the truck in my 'cop' file drawer.

"Can I help you?" the woman behind the counter asked. I didn't move, I was still staring out the glass of the Post Office door. BFL 317. Georgia tags, Ha! I was right about the accent. The plate would soon be turned in for a local one, but the numbers were already branded and at the top of the 'cop' file in my mind. BFL 317. That, I would remember.

"Can I help you?" once again travelled to my ears, but it was only when Kane gently squeezed my fingers in his that the words registered. Wow, how long was I gone? Jesus, I really was born into this wasn't I? I looked over to him and he half grinned at me. That brought me mostly back, but a whiff of Officer Jameson lingered on the wind.

"I'm sorry, yes. I have a letter to pick up." I said, and slipped into normal life conversation. At least I hoped that was the appearance I presented. She may have taken a half step back, but Officer Jameson was back on duty. I signed for and collected the letter, shoving it in the left back pocket of my jeans.

I never even looked at who had sent it. I smiled at the Postal employee and thanked her, flashed Kane a grin and turned towards the door.

He nodded at me and led me to it, opening the door as always. Even submerged in cop mode; his graciousness and genuine gentleman nature did not escape me, and I pecked his cheek as I left the Post Office. He opened the truck door for me and I climbed in, and he was soon sitting beside me. His hands were on the steering wheel but he made no move to start the truck. It took me longer than it should have to realize that; and to notice he was staring out the windshield once again at nothing. I looked over at him, and his eyes blazed metallic light.

There were hundreds of edges of thoughts flashing through it, and while I understood this was the Blood Moon, I was fairly certain that there should not have been that many. After five minutes of us sitting wordless in the truck, Kane finally cranked the ignition. He backed out and we rode the half block to our road quietly.

"He was wrong."

Kane had broken the silence first, and while I had grown accustomed to feeling his words and the tone he spoke in; neither happened right now. There was no soothing rumble in my bones. His voice was icy, and he practically snarled the phrase. While it scared me, I felt a shower of relief that I wasn't the only one who sensed it. Lifelong mate in more ways than one. He really would have made a great cop. Or maybe I would have made a fabulous Wolf. Maybe there wasn't that much of a difference; aside from the whole twelve hours of bloodlust and carnage. And maybe? Just maybe, those twelve hours are what we mortal cops secretly desire in our deepest of hearts dreams. I slid my fingers across his thigh but said nothing.

"Jimmy? I know you sensed it. I saw you."

"What color?" I asked, and I wasn't joking.

"Blue. Completely blue. And dark, not warm like the Caribbean. Midnight blue."

"Is that bad?" I asked, and he inhaled deeply.

"Darker blue than I ever saw in Lawrence."

"Shit." I whispered, and for the first time since we stepped into the Post office, Kane grinned.

"Yeah, tell me about it."

"Well, my Wolf of Ireland; what did you sense? I may not see you in colors, but you were on full alert. I wasn't alone in that instinct." A full moon toothy smile spread across his face and I couldn't stop myself from donning one just as big.

"Wolf of Ireland. For some reason? When *you* say it? It takes the sting out of it."

"Probably because it is said with love. But don't dodge the question. What did you sense? Was it his colors?"

"No. His scent."

"What did you smell, Kane?" and his smile kept him batting a thousand. It was brief, but there nonetheless. Even ten hours before the Blood Moon, whatever he smelled was enough to darken the shimmer of his eyes. That icy finger on my spine became a hand, and it gripped it tightly.

"Decay."

"I'm gonna need a little more, Love of my life." The dimming of the gold vanished, and Kane smiled brighter than I had ever seen. Ever. The magnitude of what I meant to him had never escaped me, but it slammed home with a vengeance right now. It was quite a thing to realize that someone else is your whole world. It is another thing entirely when you realize that *YOU* are the center of someone else's universe. It is wonderful, but also initially a little overwhelming. Kane and I had both reached that moment together, just now in the cab of a pickup truck. Well? Stranger things have happened, and in a lot of stranger places.

"Decay. Not the natural smell of rotting vegetation becoming good soil. Not even the inevitable smell of Death. He reeked of sepsis. An infection that only grows more toxic. The kind that spreads and destroys the healthy tissue surrounding it until it is cut out. It makes me want to snort bleach."

"Snort bleach?!?" I exclaimed, and burst out laughing. "Damn! I knew you had the soul of a poet, but that was the most *COP* thing I have ever heard you say!" Kane shot me a sideways glance and grinned.

"Seems you are a bad influence, Miss Jameson."

"It's a gift. You're welcome."

"God, I love you." he said, and his smile was almost blinding.

#

My eyes snapped open and I glanced at the clock. 4:47 AM. I had checked in just before 6 PM the night before, and had a quick bite in my room and was surely asleep by 7. I stretched, feeling each muscle come to life, and practically leapt out of the bed. I had stayed local this time; only going two towns south and grabbed a room on the Peabody/Topsfield line. Something told me to stay as close as possible and to get home as quickly as was safe for me. Kane was going to need me. I knew it in my bones as surely as I felt his words vibrate within them. I slid into jeans and slung on a bra, brushing my teeth before the mini coffee pot had finished. I may have broken the exact order of my Trinity, but I would genuflect just the same.

I didn't even bother to pour the coffee into a cup; it was a micro pot after all. My mug at home was probably of equal volume, if not bigger. I swigged it straight out of the carafe as I continued getting dressed. I had finished it by the time I needed to tie the laces of my sneakers, and a Marlboro Light was half smoked and hanging from the corner of my mouth. Class act I was not that morning, but appearances were the absolute farthest from my mind. Kane was going to be in rough shape was the sense I had, and there was no way on God's green Earth I was going to wait one second longer than necessary to be there to help. I glanced up at the ceiling, nodded and actually winked. Yep. God? We're okay. Just let him be safe and home.

While my mustang had no lights or siren, I was doing what most New Englanders would describe as 'hauling ass'. I actually arrived at the turn to our road before the sun had kissed the horizon, and I found myself impatiently waiting in the idling car. I lit another cigarette and began to roll the window down. Something made me stop; and it made me afraid. The echo of what Kane had said to me when he was helping me move from my apartment.

That is not the time for courage nor loyalty. That is the time for you to run in terror. The time for you to FEAR.

I slipped the transmission into reverse, and headlights still off; I crept the car backwards from the road to our home. I backed all the way up until I was in the parking spots of the Post Office, and then cracked the driver window to release some of the smoke.

As soon as I did it, I knew I had fucked up. My scent would be everywhere and this place would hold 'Residual' for Kane. I shoved the Mustang into drive and gravel flew as I pinned the gas pedal down. Thank God for Code 3 driving, because I had that car fishtailing inside of two seconds as I headed back towards the highway. I never looked in my rear-view mirror. Truthfully; I was afraid to. It was a quarter of a mile before I dared turn on the fog lights, and I didn't turn the headlights on until I had reached interstate 95. While I logically explained to myself this was smart and I did well; I was simultaneously kicking my own ass. Not even a quarter of a mile? Against the speeds Kane was capable of moving at? Jesus fucking

Christ Jimmy! How blonde *ARE* you exactly? I'm not sure what scared me more. Kane finding me in Wolf form and killing me, or what I knew he would endure if that scenario ever played out. Yes, it would be awful to be shredded by the man I loved, but it would be the worst possible Hell for an eternal Kane to know he had done it. Wake the fuck up Jimmy! If you live to see the dawn? Drop to your knees and be thankful; for both of our sakes.

#

I had 'hauled ass' to a diner in Peabody on Route one. Remarkably enough the silver sided old school joint had a liquor license; and I had not one but two Irish coffees to calm myself. I watched the sun break over the tree line, and still remained until it had fully appeared above the horizon. When it was fully visible, I paid my check at the register and handed my waitress a five-dollar tip. She smiled and winked at me, and then leaned forward and rested her hand on mine.

"Honey? I don't know what it is you just went through, but I'm glad we could be here for ya."

Sometimes the most amazing acts of true humanity come from perfect strangers. My cynical late fifties waitress had just committed one; and I smiled as I watched her stout form approach a table of truckers and immediately begin giving them shit. I found myself smiling and honestly laughing. I dropped another ten in her tip jar and left without a word.

I drove like a sane person back towards home. The sunlight dappled the street that passed the Post Office, and I spotted my sinewy tire treads in the gravel. I shook my head in amazement of my own stupidity and had managed a smile when something caught my eye. It was just on the corner of the sidewalk where I had been idling.

A small pile of something broken lay there, and I slid the Mustang into park. I stepped out, still focused on the oddly shaped form. It was colors that didn't belong here on the street. A dark maroon circle surrounded a striped pile of angles that were wrong. I glanced down and my entire body went subzero. The largest paw print I had ever seen was pressed into the soft silt of the parking spot. I had seen it's like before; in the woods behind Kane's house. Our home now. My eyes flashed to the 'pile'. Darkness crept in and grasped my heart.

I *felt* what I was seeing before I *knew* what I was seeing. My eyes stung with tears as forced myself to cover the steps required to kneel down and pick her up. I gently lifted her broken and lifeless form from the street and hugged her to me as I cried. Psycho zebra bitch Rodan. You should have hidden in the shower.

#

I had planned on burying my foe in the woods behind our house before I 'officially' parked my car in the drive; but as I approached our home the sight of the front door left wide open had me yanking the wheel left. My tires skidded in the gravel and I was out of the seat before the engine fully died. Kane could move quickly there was no doubt of that, but I covered the yard in four running strides that would rival a gazelle. I burst through the door and scanned the living room. Nothing. I crossed to the bedroom; again no Kane. I was growing frantic in my fear for him, and I dashed back out into the entryway. I quickly turned and my eyes swept the yard. Nothing out of the ordinary, save for there now only nine chickens wandering the edge of the grass. They seemed remarkably calm, and I surmised they were not present when Kane had killed the tenth. I scowled at the thought.

No. *KANE* did not kill her. The *Wolf* had. There *WAS* a difference.

After visually sweeping the yard and living room one last time; I accepted that he was not there. I walked over to the kitchen to put on some coffee. The two Irish ones I had enjoyed while returning from the brink of terror inspired madness had worn off, and I longed for another warming mug. I rounded the long breakfast bar to grab the filters when another 'pile' caught my eye. This one did not contain broken angles and stripes. It was naked and on its side, curled in a fetal position and filthy. Rust colored swaths were bandaged with fresher maroon; and I knew only too well every streak was blood and that every varying hue told the age of the kills he had made. By the mosaic painted across him? I surmised it had been a busy and lethal night. I dropped to my knees beside him and lifted his head from the floor.

"Kane? Kane! You all right, babe?" I muttered into his ear as I held his head in my lap. I ran my fingers through his disheveled mane and leaned protectively over him. He had a mixture of mud, sweat and what I assumed was blood in his hair; and the corners of his mouth showed the same rust and maroon graffiti. His eyes fluttered but remained closed, and a whimper came from him. I had never seen anyone so utterly wrung out, and I had just survived Lawrence. It made me look like an amateur. Or it made Kane look like he had gone through a wood chipper. Once I realized he was alive but not about to open his eyes any time soon, I slid out from under him.

I snatched a pillow and light blanket from our bed and returned to the kitchen. I got the pillow under his head and draped the blanket over him. Once again? I find myself looking at Kane wearing only a blanket. I smirked at the thought. Been a wild three months, that was for sure. I grabbed some of the spare towels and a large bowl of warm water and soap. The least I could do was clean him up a bit. No need for him to see exactly how busy he had been.

I spent the next fifteen minutes doing my best at wiping off the traces of God knows what carnage from him. He stirred from time to time as I did so, and occasionally he made some noises that sounded more like a groan or a purr than a crushed moaning. I took that as a job well done. By the time I had gotten his face, hands, arms and chest reasonably clean; he had uncoiled from the ball I had found him in and began to resume a more human stature. His eyes fluttered a bit, and I had managed to get most of the varying shades of death off of his body before he opened them.

"Hey, Love." He murmured as if stirred from a deep sleep. Maybe more like waking from a coma. Even through barely open lids, the golden sheen of his eyes was breathtaking. I nuzzled his neck and kissed his throat. Jesus, Thank You. Kane wasn't remotely back, but he had at least spoken. I'll take that; hands down, no questions asked. He was breathing, and he knew who I was. Check off another box in the Win column.

"How you feeling, Kane?" I asked, and Damn if he didn't find the reserves to smile. It was brief, a simple flash in the pan, but it meant absolutely everything to me right then. How he responded to my saying his name was warming to the core of me; though I didn't know why he loved it so. Maybe a hundred years of no one saying it had something to do with it. I didn't know and honestly? I didn't care. He was coming around, and that was all I needed. He would recover. Obviously he had weathered over a hundred Blood Moons and was still here kicking. But when I looked down at him; I wasn't so sure I could. It sucked the breath from me to see him this way, and I kissed his neck once more.

"Hmmmm." was all he purred softly, and I was thrilled to feel even that in my skeleton.

Yep, Kane would be all right. I didn't realize exactly how frightened I had been until I felt him echo within me again. I had said it correctly the first time. I would not survive *not* feeling his voice in me. I ran my fingers through his moderately cleaned up hair, and inhaled the scent of him. Destined lifelong mate. No doubt about it. Seems cop wasn't the only thing I had been born to do.

We lay on the floor for over an hour, and I had Kane wrapped in my arms as he slept. He would occasionally twitch or even startle; but overall? He rested well. Apparently somewhere I too had drifted off to sleep, because when I felt him stir beneath me the sun was farther west than I would have imagined. I had draped my right arm and leg across him, and had slept more than half covering him. I opened my eyes and looked up to see a fully awake set of golden glowing eyes watching me. The half grin was there, and for the briefest of moments I was thankful we were already down on the floor. That grin? Those eyes? On *that* man? I'd have wound up on the floor one way or another.

#

Once Kane had regained enough strength to stand up and move on his own; he headed for the shower. I gathered the bloody and mud smeared towels and threw them into the washing machine and cleaned up the kitchen. He was still scrubbing clean when I finished, and I took the opportunity to grab a shovel to bury my feathered combatant. I removed her mangled body from my hatchback and quickly walked down the path into the woods. I didn't go too far. Somehow; I felt she should be close to the house. I chose a sunny spot under a dogwood tree and dug the small grave. The Earth was soft and it didn't take long. I gently placed her in the bottom and placed a tiger lily bloom on top of her.

"Rest well, Rodan. Believe it or not? I will miss you." I said, and covered her with the soil I had just dug up.

I was stepping through the front door when Kane emerged from our bedroom. He had dressed in a faded pair of Levis and a blue T shirt. He was nowhere near his normal self; but he looked a thousand times better than when I had found him five hours earlier on the kitchen floor. He smiled when I came in and I looked at him. I attempted a smile but apparently? I didn't pull it off because he stood stock still and his eyes shifted into a deeper gold. The smile vanished from him and his shoulders slumped.

"What is it, Diana?" He whispered.

"Nothing Kane, I'm just tired." He flinched as if I had slapped him, and for the very first time? He didn't smile when I said his name.

"Love? That is the first time your heartbeat has ever sounded so close to a lie."

I hung my head and raked my right hand through my spikes. Jesus! He knew I was holding something back.

"Please don't ask Kane, or I will tell you." He smiled at that mention, because no matter the harshness of the words; they were the truth. Exhausted as he was, he was wrapping his arms around me before I knew it. He pulled me into his chest and I inhaled the richness of him. Soap and deodorant were far better accessories to his natural smell than the blood and gore from this morning, and I buried my nose into him. I encircled his waist with my arms and we stood there holding on to each other in silence for several minutes.

He would know soon enough he was missing a hen. Please Kane don't ask; don't make me tell you out loud. He stroked the back of my head and thankfully stayed quiet. Seemed my Peace Treaty with God was paying off. It was the smallest of mercies and monumental at the same time.

The remainder of the day we spent lazing about; Kane was slowly gathering his strength and I was getting over the shock of what he had done. I know the hen's body was not there when I had first stopped that morning. I had screwed up and come home too soon, and screwed up again when I cracked the window. It was like sending up a beacon to where I was. Why Kane had singled her out I can only imagine. It had to be the Residual he was talking about. Somewhere deep within the Wolf, he remembered the shower fight. Or maybe not the actual event but the impression or feeling of she was something that had put me in danger. The smallest of dangers of course but still.

Maybe it wasn't so much that I was in danger but that he had thought I was, and that made him fear for me. After an hour of turning it over and over in my mind; I decided it was probably a blend of all three. I had finally put it to rest when a thought jolted me so badly I actually flinched. My entire body felt cold, and I started to shake as if I had just fallen through the ice of Erskine Lake in January. Kane saw it and was immediately crouching down in front of me as I sat in the porch swing.

"What? What is it, Diana? Jesus Christ you look terrified. What? Tell me, please tell me." His eyes were flooded with loving concern, and fear drifted on the edges of the gold. A few small specks of amber were beginning to return to them, and even in my frightened state I admired how beautiful they truly were.

"Kane?" I began, and he smiled despite his worry, "Please, if it's not too much trouble? I'd love a drink."

"Of course, Love. I would crawl if need be. But first; are you okay?"

"Yes, I will be." I said, and he began to rise to his feet. I grasped his hand once he stood, and he stopped and faced me. His eyes were lit from within at the intensity of what he was feeling for me, and I smiled softly. This seemed to reassure him a little, but the fear clung to the gold just the same.

"When you get back?" I began, and he nodded, "Please, don't ask me okay? Just be with me. But don't ask."

He nodded again, and I let go of his hand. He disappeared into the house and I exhaled the ragged breath I had been holding.

Kane had killed the chicken. And he was there, at the Post Office parking lot after I had sped out of there. The entire incident had taken less than 30 seconds to unfold. He had killed her *and* gotten that far in that short of a time. The realization of the swiftness was not what scared me. The terror was when I realized he had *NOT* shown up there to give me a present. He was full *Wolf* then.

He would have killed me.

That thought was horrifying enough; but the knowledge that he would then forever have to *live* with what he had done to me for the rest of his life? A life that had already spanned over a century and seemly would continue. Jimmy you have *GOT* to be smarter! This was a dangerously close call; for the both of us.

That is not the time for courage nor loyalty. That is the time for you to run in terror. The time for you to FEAR.

Pay attention Jimmy; pay attention! Kane knew himself better than anybody! He had been dealing with this for one hundred and twenty-seven years! Kane returned to the porch with two glasses half full of Jameson and a frosty long neck.

"I wasn't sure which one you may want." He said softly, the half grin melting the icy grip of fear that had been strangling me.

"Both." I said, and he smiled.

"I thought as much." He replied, and I felt the vibration within me. It helped knock more of the coldness off me, and I accepted the Jameson first. Kane put the beer on the table beside me and slid into the swing on my right. He draped his arm around my shoulders and I leaned into him and sipped the whiskey. It was warm on my tongue and as it travelled down my throat the last whispers of cold disappeared. We sat there quietly together, enjoying the evening air and our libations. When my glass was almost empty; I looked over to him. He met my eyes and the warmth of his affection for me washed through the gold.

"Kane," I began, and he smiled. Funny, that's what I was about to ask him. "Why do you always smile when I say your name?" He chuckled and the corners of his eyes creased as his smile grew bigger.

"Two reasons, Lover. One? The first time you ever said it with meaning; you were yelling at me in the infirmary. That is an amusing memory. I have never seen anyone so frustrated *for* me and *about* me since my Mum died. It felt good to know that you cared. I never imagined it would grow to this, but in the moment? It was the first time in almost eighty years I did not feel completely alone. So that's one."

"And the second?"

"Ah yes, the second. That is as surprising to me as anything I have ever encountered." He said, and then paused. He scanned the yard with his eyes before looking back to me. When he did, the depth of his gaze was immeasurable. Every fleck of amber and streak of gold was ablaze and even in the waning daylight they radiated light.

"Because ever since we first made love, right out there on the lawn? I can *feel* you say my name. I feel it hum inside of me. My Da knew some things, but he most certainly did not know that. It is the only word you say that I physically feel. And I *like* it."

I nodded my head as I considered that. He felt my voice when I said his name. That was more than interesting. It was fascinating. I felt my smile emerge and grow huge. All traces of fear were gone, replaced by a wave of peaceful comfort.

"Guess that lifelong mate thing goes both ways, huh?"

"It is my very good fortune that it seems to." Kane said, and he gently kissed me.

"My very good fortune indeed."

November 1990

CHAPTER TWENTY

The Blood Moon had wreaked havoc on Kane more than I realized. It was almost three days before he fully hit his stride again. Wow. I thought back to when I had slept for the entire day after my wrist and the brutality of Lawrence Jail. And I was not *Enhanced*; my recovery was not as quick as Kane's. Had it been me? It would have taken me a week, maybe longer. Jesus. October was no joke, that's for sure.

"Hey, I'm going to the store. You want anything?" I asked as I poked my head in the shop door. Kane was leaning over another masterpiece he was creating, but when I spoke he stood up to his full height.

"I think I will come with you."

"Really? Wow. Okay. Let me know when you're ready." He quickly examined his hands and forearms. No stain or varnish was on them. He glanced down at his clothes and knocked some sawdust off his jeans. One more inspection of himself and he nodded his head in approval.

"I'm ready now."

"Okay then, let's get this show on the road. Truck?"

"You drive."

"Whoa. Really? Kane, have you fallen ill?" He smiled at the feel of his name and laughed softly.

"No, Love. I just think maybe you should keep some of your treasured independence. Besides, I know you can drive. Code Three and all that."

"All right then, let's go." I said, and jingled the keys in my hand.

We made the short drive to the grocery store in less than twenty minutes. I parked the Mustang and Kane was opening my door inside of thirty seconds. I found myself enjoying his company at the store. Running errands was something I had been doing alone since I had moved in. While it didn't bother me, having him with me was a nice treat. He grabbed the wheeled basket and pushed it along beside me. I don't know why it struck me as some sort of special occasion but it did. Obviously, this was not Kane's first trip to the grocery store; he had managed to stay alive for quite some time before my arrival. Still, he looked; well? Cute. I smiled and he slid his eyes towards me.

"Do *not* call me adorable."

"I was not even thinking of that word."

"Good. Please keep it that way. I'm a guy, remember?"

"I was thinking, *cute*."

He stopped and put his face in his right hand, gently shaking his head from side to side. I found myself giggling and he buried his face deeper in his hand. When he raised it, most of the blushing had gone. It could almost pass for a slight sunburn. *Almost*. He had the crooked grin, and while he still was embarrassed; his eyes told me he was happy.

"*Why* do you do this to me?"

"Because it's the truth. You look cute walking in a grocery store pushing a basket."

"Ugh." He moaned, and ran his fingers down his face.

"Hey now. You're the one who wanted to come."

"I know. I figured I had better."

"Better? Why? There's no imminent danger lurking in the aisles of Shaw's."

"No, there is not. But there is a very real threat of you returning home once again without any junk food. I am going through Twinkie withdrawals."

I burst into laughter, and he stared at me. He was actually serious! That made me laugh harder. He stood there watching me laugh, and while he was not angry; he was in fact *not kidding* about the junk food.

"Oh God Kane, why didn't you just say something? I would have grabbed something for you."

"I couldn't risk it, Diana. It is too dangerous. I have not seen an Oreo in weeks."

"Oh, you are…." I began, and he held up his index finger in a warning *'Don't'*. I left the sentence unfinished, and he nodded a silent thanks.

"Okay then, aisle seven it is."

We walked across the front of the store, and Kane was moving at a brisk pace. He rounded the corner into the chips and snacks aisle and stopped. He closed his eyes and inhaled deeply, raising his arms as if calling the sun to rise.

"Ahhhhh." He said as he exhaled.

"Jesus Christ, Kane. I had no idea you were such a shit food addict."

He turned and smiled at me, and while I'd like to think it was the feel of his name? I wasn't so sure this time. He may have been drunk from the scent of Doritos. He grinned and shrugged his shoulders.

"I'm a guy."

#

Fifty-seven dollars and eighty-four cents later; we exited the store. No actual *food* was purchased. Kane was grinning ear to ear as he quickly crossed the parking lot with the loaded basket. I popped the hatchback and he loaded the twelve bags of crap into the compartment. When the final bag was dropped in, I went to shut it. He grabbed the metal frame with his left hand and seized a bag of Fritos and pork rinds out of the top bag with his right. He smiled, let go of the hatch and snagged a can of Dr. Pepper with his left. I raised my eyebrows in a silent question of 'You done?' He nodded vigorously, and I shut the trunk. He looked at his full hands and then at me.

"It's okay Kane; I can open my own door today" I said, but he moved to my side of the car.

He placed the two bags in his teeth and opened the door for me anyway. Once I was seated, he shut it; snatched the bags from his mouth and jogged, *truly jogged* around the car. He had barely gotten his ass in the seat before he cracked the can open and swigged half of it down. He tore the pork rinds open like a man who had not eaten in days and shoved a handful into his mouth. He still had one leg outside of the car, and he chewed quickly before swallowing them down. He ripped the Fritos open and just poured them directly into his mouth from the corner of the bag. His eyes closed as he gnawed on them, and a look of rapture canvassed his face. When he had swallowed the Fritos as well; he finished off the remaining soda. He leaned his head back against the seat and sighed. A soft smile appeared, and he closed his eyes again. He opened them after a moment, and glanced across the car at me.

"*Much* better." He purred, and the absolute satisfaction he felt came through in his voice. I shook my head and smiled.

"Jesus Christ." I muttered, and started the car.

#

The red light on the answering machine was blinking frantically when we walked into the house. I hit play as I crossed the kitchen, and we listened as the three messages played. All of them were pertaining to Kane's business, and all three were large orders and increases in the existing orders. Kane looked at me and shook his head.

"Looks like you're going to need some help there, handsome." I said, and he raked his fingers through his dark hair.

"It would seem to be the case."

"I can help you, but I'm no woodworker. You are beyond a craftsman. You are an artist. I see that idea leading to a lot of fights."

"Diana, I would never..." he began, but I cut him off.

"You would not mean to, Kane," I began, and he smiled, "But you will never accept less than perfection leaving that shop. I don't want business to spill over into personal. I love what we have, and I won't risk it because I don't know how to varnish."

Kane smiled at me and nodded his head. I was right and he knew it.

"Guess I need to put an ad in the paper." He said, and reached for the phone book.

"I have a better idea." I said, and he looked up at me, head cocked slightly in a silent question. I smiled and continued.

"Go ahead and place the ad if you want. It won't run until Sunday anyway. But I think I can get you help by tomorrow afternoon. If you're willing to trust me, that is."

Kane dropped the phone book on the counter and was across the room in half a heartbeat. He wrapped his arms around me and held my eyes with his. The few golden flecks were warm, and gentleness filled the amber.

"Diana, I trust you with all that I am." He said, and I felt the truth behind his words in every cell of my body.

"Okay then, give me first crack at it. I hope I don't disappoint you."

"Impossible. Even if you do not bring me help, you will never be able to disappoint me. The fact that you are even *trying* is more than I ever dared ask for." He said, and kissed me gently. Even a gentle kiss from Kane sent a rush through my skin, and his arms around me wasn't the worst feeling I've ever known. Jesus I was in love with him, and yet somehow managed to fall deeper every day. I don't know how far down this rabbit hole could go, but I wasn't complaining and I was enjoying the ride.

#

It was almost three-thirty in the afternoon when my Mustang turned into the gravel of our driveway. Kane had risen early that morning and had not emerged from the shop all day. He was going to be busy dawn to dusk every day from now through Thanksgiving; even with help. I glanced over at the kid sitting in the passenger seat to my right. His jet-black hair was cut short, and his dark eyes had a kindness behind them. I liked him the moment we met. Officer Jameson approved of his character.

"You ready for your interview?" I asked, and he glanced over at me.

"I guess. I've never had one before; I just turned sixteen last week."

"Well no time like the present. Come on, he doesn't bite." I said,and realized I had in fact, just lied. Well, *Kane* doesn't bite. It was only a half lie. And the young man to my right was nervous enough; no need to add to it just yet. I opened the door to the shop and found Kane crouched down examining the surface of a beautiful cabinet door. His back was to me but we both knew he heard me before I ever reached for the door knob.

"I brought help."

Kane stopped whatever he was doing, stood up and faced me. I stepped to the side and his eyes rested on a five-foot seven teenager. He looked him up and down, and then looked at me.

"Kane, this is..." I began, but I never got to finish. The 'kid' stepped into the shop, walked over to Kane and extended his hand.

"I'm Alejandro. Miss Jimmy said you needed some help. I'm here to do just that."

This may have been his first interview, but his confidence made me grin. Officer Jameson had done well it seemed, and my grin became a full smile. Kane shook his hand and focused completely on the young man standing before him. I knew the *Enhancement* gave Kane quite an unfair advantage when it came to sizing people up; and the fact that he shook Alejandro's hand as firmly as he did and *was* sizing him up told me he was willing to learn more about this kid.

"Alejandro; it is nice to meet you. My name is Kane. Welcome to my shop."

"Thank you. It's wicked in here! You have *EVERYTHING*."

Kane smiled and glanced around.

"Yeah, I guess I do. I have had some *time* to collect things." He said, and winked at me. Oh yes, more time than you could imagine Alejandro, but I wasn't going to freak the kid out.

"What do you know about wood working?"

I slid backwards out of the shop while the two of them discussed various tools, machines, finishes and Lord knows what else. Like I said; I'm no wood worker. I had built a thing or two in shop class, but nothing came close to what Kane was creating. I went back to house, grabbed a beer and plopped down on the porch swing to enjoy it along with a cigarette. It wasn't long after that until Kane emerged from the shop and crossed the yard over to me.

"*Where* did you find Alejandro?" he asked.

"Why? Was he not a good choice?"

"He is a perfect choice, Lover. He knows a lot already and seems eager to learn."

"I went to the high school and asked the wood shop teachers who was their best and brightest. It was unanimous about Alejandro. So? I asked to meet him. They may know lumber but I know people, and after one look and a short conversation; I knew he was a good kid and I offered him an interview."

"The high school. I never would have thought of it. You amaze me yet again, Miss Jameson." He said, and his eyes were bright with happiness.

"You're welcome. Where is Alejandro, anyway?"

"Sweeping up under the saw. He *is* on the clock after all."

"You hired him! Outstanding!"

"Of course. As I said; you made the perfect choice."

I slipped my fingers between Kane's and pulled his hand to my lips. I kissed it gently and then looked up at him.

"Yes, I did." I said quietly. Kane's eyes flooded with light, and he grinned at me.

"Be careful, my Wolf of Ireland; you're blushing again."

"Yes. We cannot have our *employee* seeing me 'precious' and 'adorable.'"

"Why not?" I asked, and Kane shifted his weight from one leg to the other.

"Because as you are so fond of pointing out Jimmy? I'm a guy." He said, and I burst into laughter. Once it subsided; I pulled him closer to me. He remained standing and I wrapped an arm around his hips and rested my face on his stomach.

"Alejandro's father died six years ago. It might not hurt for him to learn that you can be precious and adorable, and still be a guy. Especially to learn it from a man of your caliber, Kane. He needs a good man to learn from, and not just about working with wood."

Kane put his hand on my spiky hair and hugged my head to him.

"Jesus, Jimmy," he began, and I didn't have to see his eyes to know they were flooded with a light that could shatter midnight, "Perfect choice indeed."

"Yeah. Somebody might think I know what I'm doing sometimes, huh?" It was Kane's turn to laugh now, and I danced inside at the honesty of it. He was happy. About Damn time! A century alone, and now he had an apprentice, and a buddy in Colin. Oh yeah; and a girlfriend. I glanced up at the sky and nodded slightly. Okay God, you got this right. You *finally* got it right. I'll hold to the cease fire.

CHAPTER TWENTY-ONE

A week later I woke after eight in the morning, and although it was a Saturday; Kane was slammed with orders and had already gone to the shop. I heard machinery whirring as I made my way to fulfill the first part of my Trinity. As always; he had made an excellent pot of coffee and I savored its smooth taste. I carried the mug with me into the bathroom to complete the fluoride part of my morning, and once done refilled the mug and grabbed the half-gone pack of Marlboro Lights. I was on the porch swing becoming 'remotely civil' when I heard laughter from the shop. It wasn't Kane's laugh which meant Alejandro was here, and the fact that he was? And *he* was laughing? It made me smile. Not bad; not even through the second mug or the first cigarette and I grinned. Perfect choice. For both of them it seemed.

It was still cool this early, so I decided to open the windows of the house. Yep, today was a good day already, and it wasn't even nine. I entered our bedroom and opened those windows, then made my way through the living room and kitchen. I poured another mug and was headed back outside when it occurred to me the second bedroom had been shut tight for some time now. I turned and opened the door to it. I stepped inside and put my coffee on the dresser to the right and opened both windows. When I turned to go back out of the room, my eye found what I had forgotten was in there. Maybe I had deliberately forgotten it was in there and had avoided ever opening the door since the day I moved in. On the edge of the bed rested a box. The elephant box. The letters scrawled across it seemed larger than I remembered writing them.

ECSD.

My breath caught in my throat at the sight of it, and my heart stopped. I stared at it for what felt like eons, and I forced myself to breathe. Slow deep breaths Jimmy, and steady your heartbeat. He might be able to hear it even out in the shop. Easy girl; nice and easy. There you go. Inhale. Exhale. Slow and even. Bring that pulse down. You're okay. It's just a box, and it's taped shut. Nothing says you have to open it or even touch it. You can grab your coffee and go. Matter of fact, that's a great idea. Another coffee and a cigarette; then decide.

I walked calmly across the room, snagged the handle of the mug in my left fingers, and made my way back into the kitchen. I poured the fourth and went back outside. I had intentionally left the second bedroom door open. It was almost symbolic. The door was open and the box was there, but nothing dictated I dabble with either. It was my choice.

Smoking is a terrible addiction, and I knew it. I was fully aware I should quit. It would kill me in the end I'm sure, and all nonsmokers say it stinks, so I can only imagine how pungent it must be for Kane's powerful nose. The problem was that I loved smoking. I truly enjoyed it, and the one I lit just then was sweeter than most. ECSD. I had not expected to be greeted by those letters this morning. I drew deeply from the cancer stick and felt its scrape across the back of my throat. Today? I'll take the rasp. I finished the coffee and cigarette in silent contemplation.

In the end, I knew I was going to go back in that bedroom. I know myself, and I know I don't do half assed. I had been presented with my past; the past that had led to this current life and an actual future. It had been almost three months. Time to bring the monsters out of the shadows and face them in the light of day. Today was a perfect time to do it. Kane was busy with work and teaching Alejandro, so whatever I felt or experienced? He would be none the wiser. He had finally stopped hating the *other* part of him, and I was not going to be the one to return that to him. I knew him well enough that if he saw any flicker of pain in me stemming from that box and what might be in it; he would want to tear his own heart from his chest.

No. Today was the perfect time to exorcise my demons. I would have to eventually, or they would linger about as Kane and I tried to build a future and that was something I would not abide. I smiled when I realized I wasn't just protective of him; I was protective of *US*. Rip open the bandage, let whatever blood and tears flow that must, and let it begin to heal. A scar is better than a wound that festered. Sure, it hurts a lot initially, but it's never going to heal if you don't draw out the poison.

I thought of snapping the cap off a longneck, but accepted that this was going to require a bit more anesthesia than a Coors Light. Kane had brought a bottle of my namesake home yesterday. I retrieved it from the refrigerator and poured a few fingers worth into a rocks glass. I smelled the whiskey deeply but didn't bring it to my lips; not yet. There would be time for that, and the time would be when I finally opened the box and reached into it. I carried the glass into the second bedroom and sat down on the edge of the bed across from it. It was the final item Kane had brought into this house. Our home. And it was the only one that had not been dealt with.

It was several long moments that I watched the cube. I don't know if I expected it to coil up and strike at me like an angry cobra, but after it failed to move, I placed the glass on the night stand and reached across the bed. My fingers grasped the cardboard, and I slid it over to where I sat. Two quick wrist movements and the steak knife had sliced the tape wide. All I had to do was open it. I drew in a deep breath, and unfolded the flaps of my history.

Peering inside; it wasn't as frightening as I had anticipated. The tools of my former trade were a far cry from what would ever be labeled as feminine, but they were just that. *Tools*. A set of Smith and Wesson nickel handcuffs, still tucked in the basket weave leather belt case. I removed them from their cocoon, and the weight felt familiar in my hand. The next item I pulled was a uniform shirt. The collar brass was still perched on the lapels, though it wasn't true brass it was silver. The faintest of the Lawrence Jail 'perfume' still clung to the shirt, even though it had been laundered. Some things can't be washed away no matter the amount of water and soap. I closed my eyes and let the smell bring me back. Only in revisiting it would I ever be free of it.

In my mind, I heard Kane's voice say one word. *Residual*. His Residual was what remained with him while Wolf. Jesus, would I ever lose *this* residual? Sometimes I thought I already had; only to be reminded at odd moments that while Officer Jameson was no longer her presence remained beneath the surface. She showed up from time to time, and while I had been 'retired' for not even a quarter of a year; I had a sense she would never fully leave me. I felt a smile creep across my face.

Well? I guess that would be okay. Officer Jameson was a good ally to be able to call on. She had managed to keep me alive this long. She may not be front and center anymore, but knowing she would always be within earshot brought me some comfort in a twisted yet peaceful way. I sipped from the glass, the warmth of the fine whiskey tingling on my lips. Just shy of ten-thirty in the morning. Today? I was a heathen.

The other contents of the box were not as profound. Some paperwork, reports and the like, my pocket notebook with the cover almost shredded, my personal set of keys including the longer handcuff key. Black leather pat down gloves. I held each item in my hand and allowed it to tell me its story. I didn't rush the tale, but I didn't wallow in it once it was complete. I gradually placed each belonging on the bedspread around me. Before the hour was through, I was encircled by things that were faced one at a time, acknowledged, and then softly released. I reached in again and felt cold metal against my fingers. Even in the darkest of nights I would have been familiar with this, and my fingers resumed their post on the Pachmayr grips of my revolver. Again, a Smith and Wesson; but this brushed nickel was a .357.

Every gun is loaded, whether there are bullets in it or not. It's the 'unloaded' guns that accidentally kill people. This was my weapon, and I know me. It was not only 'loaded', but it was in fact, *loaded*.

Six Winchester silver tip hollow points slept in their chambers, content to remain dreaming but ready to wake and do their job if need be. I held the gun as easily as I was breathing. It occurred to me that I was indeed breathing easily, and that realization both surprised and comforted me.

Sorting through in order to let go; had not been as bad as I had anticipated. I glanced to my drink. Only half gone. I was doing better than I thought. I returned the Smith to its holster, and gently tapped the box. Something slid within it. I scanned the bed taking inventory, wondering what final item was still inside. There was nothing I could think of, so I pulled the box to me and tilted it at an angle to look inside.

The final item was my badge. The six-pointed star was face down, so the heavy pin back was what I grasped as I lifted it out. The box was empty. No major breakdown on my part, and nothing had been omitted. The star felt heavy in my hand, but not as heavy as it had felt when I had worn it over my heart. Interesting. Maybe Officer Jameson could now take a well-earned rest and enjoy the peace she had deserved. Lord willing? She would never need to be recalled to duty. I laughed softly at the thought. God knows she had more than earned it. I flipped the badge over to look at the front.

The dark rust colored spatters across the State Seal of Massachusetts sucked the air from my lungs. Only a slob shoots Jameson whiskey, but I instantly became Oscar Madison and emptied the contents of the short glass. I felt the burn as it travelled my esophagus, and knew that I had lost my clarity of vision. I could still sense the daylight but couldn't actually see; it was all distorted and blurry. Wet streams ran down my cheeks, and it occurred to me the tears were pouring faster than I comprehended their arrival. Those spatters were not mine, yet I felt as though I had been sliced open by a hundred blades.

Blood. God only knew, who's. I was instantly back in the sickening wreckage of body parts Scotty and I had returned to in early July. It was as if I had travelled back in time to the worst images I had ever seen; the horror movie that was not fiction and one I could never speak of, not even to Kane. It would kill him to know he had the starring role.

I folded in half at the waist and my forehead touched the bed. I don't know if I breathed at all, it was the metallic smell and sheer slaughter that filled my senses. I don't know how long I stayed like that. It may have been seconds or hours. I may have actually fallen asleep or passed out but when my eyes fluttered open; there was a fairly good-sized wet circle on the bedspread beneath my face. The badge was still clenched in my right hand. I drew in a breath which was more ragged than I had expected. I wiped my face with my left, and managed to find my feet. My throat was dry and raw and while I had not glanced at the clock; I didn't care what time it was. I had hit heathen earlier that morning; I think a cold beer would be okay in the overall scheme of the universe.

I got to my feet, slightly impressed at the strength my knees held, and stepped towards the door. When I reached the kitchen? Two things that were not there earlier greeted me. A hefty pour of Jameson in a rocks glass, and an opened bottle of beer. I touched them both lightly with my fingertips. They were still cold. My grip on the badge loosened in my right hand, and despite the mornings agony? I smiled.

Well fuck me, and I'll be damned. I glanced around the house but found myself alone. I slowly shook my head in disbelief because I couldn't fathom the possibility of it, yet here I was; right smack dab in the middle of it. I laughed gently out loud to myself. I had just fallen deeper in love with Mr. Kane Woods.

#

I had heard Kane's truck tires crunch the gravel when he returned from dropping Alejandro off at home. During the week the bus dropped the young apprentice at the end of our road, but on Saturday's Alejandro's mother dropped him on her way to work and Kane drove him home. Sunday was everybody's day off at Kane's insistence. Work was one thing; but *'even God rested on the seventh day'* were Kane's exact words, and having just signed my Peace Accord with the Big Guy Upstairs I respected that. I was chopping the last of the celery for the stew I was making for supper when I heard the front door open and shut. My back was to the door but I heard Kane's footsteps as he crossed the room. It was a normal human stride, which was not normal for Kane. I stopped what I was doing and turned slightly to look at him.
He hovered at the edge of the countertop; hands shoved in his front pockets, head angled slightly downward and looking at me from the tops of his eyes. He wore a questioning grin and he angled his head slightly to the left.

"How you doing, Love?" he asked, shifting his weight from one leg to the other. I realized that I had not actually laid eyes on him since the night before when I fell asleep curled up against him. I had known he was just 'right there' in the shop all day; I knew without a doubt he had seen me today and that he was also responsible for the still cold beer and whiskey after I stirred from the ECSD box episode. His eyes were warm and had not begun to shift gold and reflective, which comforted me somehow as the next Full was still more than two weeks away. Perhaps the November Full would not be as hard on him, nor as terrifying for me. God knows we could use a break. I absorbed every detail of him as he stood there, and I smiled. It was genuinely *GOOD* to see him.

"Better, now that you're home." I said, and his grin spread into a smile. He lingered where he was, but his shoulders softened slightly. Thank you for your keen eye Officer Jameson; it has given me such insight into reading Kane. I returned my attention to the cutting board and with five more short drops of the blade the celery was ready. I put the knife down beside the cutting board, wiped my hands on a towel, and turned back towards Kane. He still stood in the same spot, but his smile had softened and his eyes had grown richer in color. I walked across the kitchen to him and wrapped my hands around his neck. His hands found my waist, and for a moment I just looked into the predominantly amber depths of him.

"I wasn't quite sure what to do for you today Diana..." he began, and I pressed my fingertip to his lips. It seemed to be an effective way of stopping him from speaking; far better than a muzzle, and he once again allowed me to silence him.

"Kane? You did *perfect*." He smiled as always, but then creased his brow.

"I have never felt as lost as to what to do in my life, Diana. I could taste the pain you were in. I did not wish to intrude or crowd you. I know how you despise being pushed or cornered. I just wanted to let you know that I was there, am still here, and forever will be should you ever wish to talk about it. So..." he left the sentence unfinished but waved his hand towards the counter where he had left the beer and whiskey for me, and then shrugged his shoulders.

"It was the most thoughtful and touching thing anybody has ever done for me, Kane. Thank you. I mean it. Thank you."

He pulled me into his chest and wrapped me in a firm hug.

"I have wanted to do this since I saw you on the bed. It almost killed me to stand idly by watching you hurt like that. I felt physical pain, not being able to stop it. I would have traded places if I could have. I have never felt so helpless."

"I understand completely." I murmured into his chest, and he hugged me tighter and kissed the top of my head.

"Yes Lover, I know you do. Today was my lesson it seems." He whispered, and I coiled my arms around his waist.

"Just don't get in a fight with God, okay? I just signed the Peace Treaty." I said, and I felt his chest rumble as a genuine laugh escaped him. Once it subsided he released his hold on me enough where I could look up at him. There was a deeper light behind the amber; it was not quite as much a brightness as it was a fullness. He sighed softly, and the Woods half grin found its way home once more.

"You have brought such wonders into my life Diana Jameson, with you being the top of the list. Colin? Alejandro? Your friend Ann, even? I have been alive for a hefty amount of time, but I don't think I understood what living *was* until that morning in July when you pulled into this driveway. Seeing you here? Finally, being able to touch you? And oh Christ, to kiss you? It was then that I took my first breath. No. I have no fight with God."

"I am very glad to hear that." I said, and the light in his eyes shifted.

"How long until supper?" he asked.

"I haven't actually started cooking." I began, and his smile widened. "I just finished the prep. Why?"

The amber grew deeper, and his smile curved with a touch of what my mother would have called 'trouble'. He said nothing but gently tugged my hands as he backed up towards our bedroom. I took the first steps stiffly, but that smile and the warmth of his eyes shattered any resolve I had after the first two steps.

When we had stepped into the bedroom, Kane stopped. He ran his hands up my face and kissed me as softly as he ever had. It caught me off guard, but it had an effect. I imagined I was now far more red. I expected the intensity from him to increase the longer he kissed me, but if anything? He grew gentler. His hands moved softly and slowly down my face and neck, tiptoeing across my shoulders and down my back. It was familiar and new at the same time. There was tenderness in his touch and kisses. While he had sometimes been consumed by a hunger ignited by the moon, tonight was an entirely new experience. He moved closer and pressed against me but his touch remained delicate.

I was lowered slowly to the bed, one strong arm supporting my back as he did so, and Kane covered me with his form. Each kiss was a lighter tease than the last, yet he never pressed for more. I slid my hands under his shirt and savored the feel of his skin beneath my fingers. When I did his breath caught momentarily, but he stayed the course and kept his pace. It occurred to me he was controlling himself, and it gave me pause. This was not something I had experienced with him, and it was both surprising and delicious. He drew back from a kiss and a soft smile crossed his features. The few flecks of gold that had appeared were as warm as the sun, and the darker amber smooth in their light. This was indeed uncharted territory.

He slid his hands to my waist and lifted my T shirt up and over my head. The bra came off easily enough, and I pulled his shirt off as well. Gentle kisses followed; Kane was serving them up like a gourmet meal, each course followed by another. I ran my hand down the front of his jeans and my fingers told me he was more than ready, but he never changed the softness that he touched me with.

He had opened my jeans and unzipped them as well, his left hand sliding them off my hips. I wriggled my legs free and he undid the button of his as well. He shifted his weight and slipped out of his faded Levis, sliding his right leg between mine. Still; his lips and fingers were light against me but the weight of it was enormous. His hands travelled the length of me patiently, and while my back arched in response, he made no move to accept it. I was swimming in his touch, drowning in each light brush of his lips, and it was heavenly.

Kane slowly pulled me closer, and his body touched every inch of mine. His chest was against my breasts, and I delighted in the way he felt. I wanted him; I wanted him thirty minutes ago but this was a dreamlike pace and I was in no rush to wake. He moved me closer to him, and wrapped his right arm around my waist while stroking my neck with his left. I was consumed with desire for him and a sense of safety I had never felt before. The polar opposites of it were overwhelming. He stopped the kisses long enough that when I inhaled it was shaky yet sure footed. He ran his fingers through the hair above my ears and a crooked grin visited him once again. The embers that lit his eyes were the most comforting light I had ever seen. I opened my mouth to say so.

"Sshhhh." He whispered, and pulled my head into his shoulder. He traced his fingertip along my collarbone and I felt my skeleton collapse. I lost the structure of me, and he gently kissed my forehead. I tilted my head up towards him and another kiss, soft as the landing of a butterfly, was given to me. Kane continued this off and on until I curled against him and rested my head on his shoulder. He had me held against him, and I closed my eyes in the silence of Eden, listening to his breathing and heartbeat. Later when I awoke, and Kane still had me encircled in his arms. I glanced up and was met by a soft smile and warm eyes. I had my arm across his chest, my hand resting on his right shoulder.

"How long was I asleep?" I asked in a quiet tone.

"Two hours. Give or take."

"Wow. How long have we been in here?"

"Just shy of four."

"Are you hungry? I can get us something. Maybe actually cook that supper?" I said, and a small chuckle came from Kane.

"I am perfect right where we are. Unless you're hungry? I don't want to move."

"Me either." I replied, and he squeezed me gently.

"It's settled then." He said, and kissed me as softly as morning dew. When he finished; I dropped my head back to his chest, closed my eyes and felt the rise and fall of his ribcage as he breathed. I slept through the night wrapped in his arms.

CHAPTER TWENTY-TWO

It was the last full week in October, and Kane's eyes were still slow to shift completely golden. His appetite for me was ever present, not a bad problem to have for my part, but the physical changes the *Enhancement* took on him had not fully seized him yet. He and Alejandro had been working together six days a week and a friendship between them had developed quickly. It wasn't a father and son type of relationship, more an uncle and nephew, and I must confess hearing Kane talk about Alejandro at supper each night made me smile. Kane took pride in his craft, and I could hear similar in his voice when he spoke of the young apprentice demonstrating that same quest for perfection.

I had made a very good choice it seemed, and Kane had taken Alejandro under his wing in both the trade and in his personal life. He offered advice to the young man on a variety of subjects ranging from chemistry to dealing with his three younger sisters, but only when asked. Kane was not the type of man to intrude or force himself into anyone's life. Still, the teenager sought out his thoughts and guidance. I smiled when I realized Kane was helping shape what would grow to be a fine man in a few years. Someday? There would be a woman almost as lucky as me that found herself being loved, by grown Alejandro.

A sharp metal snapping noise emerged from the shop and it caught my attention.

"SHIT!"

Kane rarely swore, and I had never heard him yell one. I leapt off the porch swing and was crossing the fading grass when I saw him come around the building. He was stomping across the yard, and I examined him for any sign of injury. Thankfully, there was none and I released the breath I had been holding.

"Oh my God Kane, are you okay?" and even in his anger he smiled when he felt his name.

"Yeah, I'm fine. Just a broken saw blade." He said, waving his hand back towards the shop. The aggravation in his voice was thick and I didn't need to feel it to know he was pissed.

"Well you have more, right?"

"Of course, I do. The problem is that when it broke? It snapped off part of the guard. That particular part I need to get? I have to go to Boston to get it. I am going to lose the *entire* afternoon and I have no way of contacting Alejandro to tell him he will be having the day off."

"No. No, you're not." I said.

"Not what, Lover?"

"You're not going to have to lose an entire afternoon. I'm standing right here, dumbass. *I* can go to Boston, and you can continue working on something that doesn't require whatever saw broke while I'm gone. And then Alejandro can help you finish *that* while I go get the guard thingy that you need."

"You would do that?"

"Jesus Christ Kane, are you daft?" I exclaimed, and he smiled at both his name and my use of that word. "Of course, I will! Tell me what I'm getting, and where. I'm sure it will take me all afternoon with traffic, and slow getting home during rush hour so you're on your own for supper but shit yeah, I'll go get it. Idiot."

Kane's smile grew wider and his teeth were brighter but not quite blinding or huge yet. He shook his head and chuckled.

"I suppose it never occurred to me that you would go for me. I've never had anyone around to help before."

"Well, get used to it. I'm not going anywhere."

"Indeed, you are not. Not if I have a say in the matter." He said, and pulled me to him. He looked directly into my eyes, and the flecks that were present glowed warmly.

"Thank you." he said softly, and I felt a smile cross my face.

"Of course. Anytime." I said, and the golden warmth took on a sheen of hunger.

"I'm ready now." He purred, and I have no doubt I was shifting red in his vision.

"Well, okay; but you will lose me for the afternoon. How about when I get back?"

"Ugh. Fine then. I *despise* when you are responsible and make sense." He said, and that half grin found its way home. Seeing him wear it made *me* despise being responsible as well. Jesus, he could disarm me with that every time.

"Look at it this way. The part will be here. After you cripple me; you can fix the saw thingy while I recover my ability to move. Just get me to the porch with a beer and my cigarettes first."

"Jimmy, you are a genius. The way you think is magic." He said and laughed. "How could I *not* be in love with you?"

#

By the time I had gotten into Town, found the place that had the part and gotten it and sat back behind the steering wheel; it was approaching three in the afternoon. Boston traffic is a nightmare on a good day, and today was not a good day for the arteries in and out of Beantown. Boston radio stations give traffic updates every ten minutes; that's *how bad* rush hour is.

I was maneuvering through city streets when I heard there was an accident on the Tobin Bridge. Two cars and a semi-truck. Oh, fuck *THAT* noise! I'm not sitting for two hours while they clean that shit up. I hooked a left. Pizza, beer and Ann was a perfect way to wait out the rat's nest of cars that would be creeping along at inches an hour.

The planets must have aligned perfectly because I slid the Mustang into an on-street parking slot half a block from Pizzeria Regina. I fed the meter enough quarters for two hours, and knew I'd be repeating the action based on the lack of driving skills that were on display today. I crossed the bricks and was walking down the stairs in less than ten minutes. The delightful aroma of pizza enveloped me, and I realized I had not eaten yet. My stomach growled as if to drive this point home. Oh yes, this was *WAY* better than sitting in traffic. I rounded the corner to the left and stepped inside. I stopped, closed my eyes, and inhaled the deliciousness. It was beautiful.

Arms seized me and wrapped around my shoulders. I snapped my lids up and only relaxed once I saw the blonde ponytail and sparkling blue eyes of Ann. She had seen me enter and I found myself in a fierce hug full of affection. I let my muscles uncoil and my spine return to flexible as I hugged her back. It was good, genuinely *GOOD*, to see her.

"I have been waiting for you to come back! Oh, how I've missed you, Miss Jimmy! No golden boy today?" she asked as she glanced behind me.

"Nope, sorry. Just me today."

"I'm not sorry, not in the least! I mean he's great and all, and he's crazy in love with you, but I'm glad he's not here. Gives us girl time. Pitcher of whatever's coldest?" she asked, and I smiled at her quoting Kane word for word. Ann was sharp; sharper than most. I knew I liked her. I think I liked her even more now. She waved her hand towards the bar and ushered me to middle stool of three that were empty.

"I don't know about a pitcher. I gotta drive back to Rowley."

"Yes, but I am off in fifteen minutes and there is *NO WAY* I am not sitting right there and having a cheese pizza with you." she said, pointing to the empty stool to my left. She wrinkled her nose and winked. "I'm a purist too."

"A pitcher it is then, my friend!"

"Yes. Yes, I am, Miss Jimmy." The sincerity in her voice surprised me. Yet, I did not doubt a single word she said.

"Well, if you are? You have got to drop the *Miss* part. I'm just Jimmy."

"You may be *Jimmy*," she said, and her blue eyes latched mine, "but there is nothing about you that is only '*just*'." *Old soul living in a young person's body*. That was what Kane had said. If anybody would know, it would be my *older* boyfriend. I smiled at the thought, and Ann saw it.

"You just thought of something he said or did, didn't you? Kane. The golden boy."

"Yeah. Yeah, I did. How did you know?"

"A smile like that only comes from pure love. And that is what you feel for him." She said as she placed the pitcher in front of me. She grabbed a frosty glass and poured my beer. No sooner had she put it on the bar she dashed over to the kitchen and placed an order for a large cheese pie. I considered what she had just said as I swallowed the cold delight. She was right. Spot on; one hundred percent right. Pure love. There was no wiggle room here. And truthfully? I didn't want any.

It was fifteen minutes later when Ann perched in the stool beside me and grabbed the pitcher. I reached over and removed her hand from it, and wrapped my fingers around the handle.

"Oh no, my friend! You're off the clock. Allow *me*." She smiled and did her nose wrinkle. It was as much her signature as Kane's half grin or dropped shoulders. She clapped her hands together a few times and laughed.

"Thank you, *JIMMY*." She said, emphasizing my name, and I joined her in a short but honest laugh. She raised her now full glass and nodded before swallowing almost half of its contents. Damn, I *KNEW* I liked her!

"So, tell me" she began, wiping her mouth with the back of her hand, "What did your Kane say after I said that yours would be a love story spoken about for centuries?"

The respect I felt that she remembered word for word what she had said two months earlier was only tied with my respect for her wiping the beer from her mouth with the back of her hand. I was not wrong; not in the least. Ann was in fact? A rock star.

"He said that sometimes old souls live in a young person's body, and that you were one of them."

Ann burst out laughing, slapping the bar and wrinkling that perky nose of hers. "God Almighty, I knew I liked him! Yep! He is a wise man."

"So it seems."

"And he's pretty hot to boot. Lucky you, Jimmy."

"Isn't he though? And oh my God, he doesn't even know it! Makes it that much hotter! Christ you should see him when he gets embarrassed. He actually blushes! It's fucking adorable and it just makes me want to hug him and tear his jeans off and throw him down!" I said, and realized I was gushing. Wow; I just went completely chick! Girl time was in full force, and I laughed at myself. I don't think I ever really *HAD* girl time before right now. I found that I liked it. Ann threw her head back and laughed. Seemed she was enjoying the estrogen moment as well.

"Yeeessss! The hottest guys are the ones that don't know it!" Ann agreed. She downed the rest of her beer and chortled.

"It's the ones who are so surprised that anybody thinks they're worth a second look, that are the finest caliber of a man. It's like they're blind to it."

"Don't I know it!" I said, and smiled thinking of Kane's reactions to various moments when I had expressed that very same thing to him.

"Do you know he actually thought I was making a mistake by being with him?" Ann cut her eyes over to me and squinted.

"Jimmy? I thought he was an intelligent man."

"Yeah, me too. Don't worry; I set him straight."

"I have no doubt that you did!" she said through a laugh and refilled our beers. After the two of us enjoyed another hearty portion of both humor and beer; her expression changed into a more serious nature.

"Still, Jimmy. He may have had reason to feel that way."

I felt my eyebrow rise, but remained quiet. Old souls tend to have wisdom. I was as blonde as Ann, but neither of us was stupid. She was going somewhere with this, and I was not about to stop her. She stared at the streams of bubbles rising in her beer for the longest of moments. Finally she nodded, and turned to face me.

"That man loves you more than he knows what to do with it. It consumes him, and he wants to protect you from a hang nail never mind the rest of the bullshit we encounter every day. But he also knows himself. I don't know what it is exactly. But Jimmy? He carries a burden; and it is a heavy one. And even in those gold eyes of his? Whatever it is he carries? It has darkness to it. Be careful. You may know what it is or you may not. I don't know and I don't want to know. But this much I can tell you, because I know it in the depths of me. He will not survive anything happening to you. And Kane knows this as well. He will kill or die before he allows anything to happen to you. He will not survive without you. He would finally.... die."

I felt like I had just been struck between the eyes with a sledgehammer. Ann had met us once. Spent less than three hours in our company and it was not an exclusive three hours; the place had been jumping that day. She had been hustling table to table, running pizzas and beers to the entire establishment. And yet, she nailed it perfectly. All of it. Old soul? Ha! No. Hers was an ancient one, and apparently been gifted with insight that was off the scale. Darkness to Kane's burden? Finally die? I smiled as I realized exactly who, or what, I was seated beside.

Ann was a *Seer*.

#

One large cheese, another pitcher of beer, and eight more quarters shoved down the throat of the parking meter later; I climbed in the Mustang just before six in the evening. I was full, I was relaxed, and I was happy. While Ann had offered perspective to things on a level I wasn't quite sure I could fully grasp; she had also provided simple girl stuff. We had cackled at things only women do, and only women see. We shared our downfalls with men. Ann had a husband in the military, and he had been guarding the 38th parallel for over eight months now. She was excited for his return in February.

I watched her glow as she spoke of him, and wondered aloud if I did the same when speaking of Kane. She assured me I made her a mere night light when I talked about him and it was my turn to blush when she said it. She vowed never to speak of it again, and I truly believed her. It is a rare thing indeed to find a woman friend who is as girl, and as stand up, as Ann was. Maybe it wasn't just stars and planets lining up perfectly to bring Kane and me together. Maybe they also coordinated for a lunch of pizza. And for Kane? A trip to the best worst bar on Plum Island, and my visit to the high school shop teachers. Things were coming together for him, and in very good ways. Christ, it had been long enough coming for him. I smiled as a realization struck me.

They were also coming together for me as well. I glanced skyward and nodded my thanks. It had been long overdue for me as well. I was north of Saugus on Route One, still replaying the afternoon conversations with Ann. It had been fun and even though some of the things she had said were unsettling; it was also comfortable because she demanded no explanations. Ann knew what she knew.

She never questioned why or how, and not once pressed me to expound upon it. I was crossing into Rowley when the last things she said to me settled in.

"Jimmy, he will need you. He will need you in the most wretched moment of his life, and there have been many but this will be his worst. It will shatter you and it will test you. And what you do, in that moment and the days after; will determine *both* of your fates. I am here but you will not reach out to me. He will not reach out to his new friend Colin. Not until it's over; whatever it is. I already know this. I don't know what it is, but it will determine *everything*. And it will also decide if he lives, or finally dies."

Ann had said *finally dies* twice that afternoon, though I don't know how she would know Kane was already one hundred and twenty-seven years old. I don't know how she would know his '*darkness*' actually came under the bright silver light of a full moon. But she knew something, and it both made my spine chill and warmed my skin. Jesus, I had been around so many 'odd' things it was becoming comforting. Might be time to hide that .357 of mine. Bizarre, even by *MY* standards; was becoming 'normal'.

#

I stepped through the door at seven-fifteen in that evening. I heard the shower running as I entered, and though there was no actual reason to announce my arrival; I poked my head in the bathroom door.

"I'm home."

"How is Ann?" Kane asked. What the Hell?

"What are you, a mind reader or something?" A solid laugh emerged from the curtain and filled the steamy room.

"No Love, I smelled the oregano on you before you locked the front door. I may not have been a Deputy, but even *I* can put this puzzle together. A trip to Boston for a saw part, and the smell of oregano. Makes sense you would stop by to see your friend. I don't suppose you brought me a slice or two?"

"Sorry Kane; Ann joined me. We ate the whole damn thing." Jeez, I sucked as a girlfriend. Another laugh emerged as the water shut off. When he opened the curtain; he was smiling.

"I wouldn't have it any other way." He said, toweling his shaggy head of hair. "I'm glad you got to spend some time with Ann. She is good for you."

He stepped out of the tub and kissed me quickly.

"Besides Jimmy; you are a purist. What would I do with just *cheese* pizza?"

"Point taken, my carnivore boyfriend."

Kane smiled at my use of his 'title', but his eyes took on a devilish gleam. There it was again; the *scoundrel* light. Even the corners of his mouth curved differently, and I had no doubt he was up to something. I tilted my head and my eyebrow arched which only served to make his smile larger. Whatever this particular grin was about had zero to do with my use of the word *boyfriend*.

"You are dripping mischief, Kane Woods. What are you plotting?" True to history he smiled at the feel of his name, but shook his head gently and remained silent. I folded my arms across my chest and tapped my left foot, and his smile continued to spread. The amber danced and the flecks of gold reflected the light in the room. He stepped closer and wrapped an arm around my waist, lowering his head until the tip of his nose touched mine.

"You will just have to wait and see, Lover."

"It would seem so." And a touch of the Devil himself flashed through me. I unfolded my arms and ran my fingers up his still damp thighs.

"But you will not have to wait, if you don't want to."

"I have been waiting since before you left. That is already far too long. And you are overdressed."

"Perhaps I should fix that." I said, and reached to unhook my bra.

"Allow me to assist you." Kane said, and the low rumble I felt in my bones excited me even more. I knew the man could move quickly, but it was scarcely a second before he had me in the bedroom and undressed. The only thing better than when he moved that fast? Was when he took his time. And Kane took his time that night. For hours.

Chapter Twenty-Three

When I woke up on Saturday morning; two things were missing. One, Kane was not in the bed beside me. I focused my vision on the clock. Nine-thirty. Okay, that made sense; he had massive amounts of work and at this late hour I'm sure he and Alejandro had been in the shop for at least two hours. Which brought me to the second thing that was missing. The sound of machinery running. I laid still and strained my ears, but there was no saw, no sander; nothing. They must have been staining something or whatever the Hell they did. Whatever it was it was art; art that had function.

While there were two things absent; there was one that was not. The aroma of one of Kane's masterpiece pots of coffee. It smelled amazing, and if I was not mistaken? *Creamy*. I stretched and slid out from under the covers and into my jeans, bra and a long sleeve T shirt. It was the end of October after all; the mornings were cool and crisp. I yanked on a pair of socks, straightened the bed and shuffled towards the kitchen. A steaming mug was handed to me by a broadly smiling Kane before I had cleared the bedroom doorway.

"Good morning, Diana." He said, and the resonation of his words was stronger for an odd reason. I returned the smile as best I could pre half-pot of coffee, and accepted the mug. One sip and I knew what smelled so lovely. Bailey's. Bailey's, in my first mug of coffee. I savored the sweet flavor on my tongue and nodded my appreciation. Kane had perfected the ratio; it was exactly creamy without milkshake taste. The man was indeed a genius. I slipped my arm around his waist as I swallowed my second dose. Jesus, it *WAS* good. He kissed the top of my head and gave me a gentle one-armed hug before stepping back.

"Finish that, then while you complete step two? I will pour you another and meet you on the porch. I have your lighter."

I obliged, and he relieved me of the mug as he ushered me to the bathroom. For as much of my life that I had spent refusing to set predictable patterns; Kane had my morning routine down to a science. I scrubbed my teeth clean and realized that I really wanted more of that heavenly concoction he had crafted this morning. I was halfway to the front door when I seized the thought. It was Saturday, and he had pressing deadlines.

Why was he not working? And where was Alejandro? I stepped outside and was greeted by another mug of Heaven, and a smiling Wolf of Ireland. The Full was six days out and his eyes had shifted more gold over the past few days, but the way they looked at that moment? I would have thought the Full was six *minutes* out, not days. They were positively iridescent and almost fully metallic. My wondering about Alejandro took a back seat just then as I got lost in his gaze. Whatever Kane was feeling? He was feeling it a million percent, and while I had no idea what it may be? I found myself returning his brilliant smile with one of my own.

"Come, Love." he said, and waved his left hand towards the swing. "I have something to speak to you about, but I know better than to start before you are fully? Yourself."

I snorted a laugh and allowed him to guide me to the swing. I accepted the pack of cigarettes from him, removed one with my teeth and inhaled as he lit the end. Kane slid in the swing beside me, draped his left arm across the back and smiled at me as I smoked and had more coffee. When I had finished both, he arched both eyebrows up in a silent question of, did I want more. Of course I did, and I nodded as much. He snatched the mug and was gone and back again before I had crushed the last embers of the Marlboro Light. I once again accepted the mug of delightfulness from his hand. He resumed his station beside me.

"Thank you, Kane." I said, and his smile was enormous. I sipped it, and cut my eyes at him. He was bouncing his right knee, something he only did during the day of a Full and it was blatantly obvious he was excited about *something*. The man could barely keep still. This next Full was a November one; almost puny compared to the prior two months. So, what the fuck was *up* with him? He was as close to exploding as a three-year-old after a giant pixie stix. I couldn't take it anymore. I turned and faced him fully. His eyes were completely lit from within and no amber remained though there had been almost a fifty-fifty ratio when we went to bed last night. Oh yes; something was up.

"Okay, Kane." I began and watched the smile find him again. I half grinned myself. I knew what it felt like to *feel* his words, and it happened a lot more for me than for him. He only felt me speak his name. I felt his voice every time there was feeling behind his words which was more often than not. My half grin became a full smile.

"You're obviously happy and excited about something. I am human enough to now hear what it is that you are so excited about. So? Have at it."

"Happy birthday, Diana Jameson."

"Wait. What?" I asked, and his smile got brighter.

"It is October twenty seventh. Happy birthday Diana, you are officially thirty-four today! For the next two months, you are only ninety-*THREE* years younger than me." Kane said laughing, and then kissed me briskly. My mind had somehow awoken and I did the math as well as recalled the calendar. Shit! He was right! It was my birthday!

I tossed my head back and released a good and honest laugh. Jesus, I had not realized it. I hadn't forgotten per se; I mean most people are aware of the day they were born, but so much had happened and was still happening I really had lost track of the date. And my birthday? Well, it stopped being an important event after age twenty-one. Finally; of legal age to be in all the bars I had been going to for five years prior anyway. As my laughter subsided a realization crept in on me, and once it did? I had no choice but to ask. I'm *ME* after all. Cop.

"Why *THANK* you, Kane!" I exclaimed, and I was in fact genuinely appreciative. I was also happy. If there was ever a person walking the Earth that I wanted to have tell me Happy Birthday? I was looking at all six foot plus of him. Kane grasped my right hand in his and kissed it.

"It is my complete pleasure." He purred, and I felt the honesty ring in my every rib. Destined life mate for sure. Once that had subsided, I glanced over to him. He was smiles and happiness, topped off with golden glowing eyes. It *was* a happy birthday.

"How did you know? I've never told you." I asked, and I watched the *scoundrel* light intensify the sheen of his eyes. So *THAT* was it. Okay then; question resolved. He had discovered my birthday.

"No. No, you have not." Kane began, and raked his fingers though his hair as that damn crooked grin set up shop, "I snooped your license after I told you my true birthday. Sorry for that."

"I'm not!" I exclaimed through a laugh, "The cop in me is proud for it!" and his grin bloomed to a full smile.

"So, you are not angry?" he asked.

"Not in the least."

"And are you fully awake, and civil?"

"Yes. Yes, I am, thank you." I said and laughed again. He was justified in asking these questions. I could be a bear some mornings, and a grizzly at that. "Where is Alejandro?"

"I told him today was a non-working Saturday. He seemed pleased. He is taking his sisters trick or treating in Newburyport. The shops do it for the kids this weekend since Halloween falls on a Wednesday this year."

"That's awesome. He's a good kid."

"Indeed, he is. I have grown rather fond of him." Kane said, and a warm smile spread across his rugged features. He turned and met my eyes, and I was surprised to see that the *scoundrel* light still remained. They were still fully gold too, and shone with reflective intensity. Something told me their appearance had nothing to do with Alejandro.

"What are you up to?" I asked, and his eyes brightened further though I don't know how that was possible. They were coming a close second to the sun itself.

"I am glad you asked." He said and rose from the swing. He stepped a stride or two in front of me, and turned to face me once again. I knew he was going to start his pacing; it was what he did when he was about to say something important and with the Full less than a week away I knew that he had to be beginning to feel its Pull. Thankfully it was a tamer month for him. If tame could ever be used in the same sentence as transforming to Wolf that is. Perfectly fucked up. So much so it made absolute sense.

Kane stood as still as Death in front of me, and his eyes never left mine. He didn't shift his weight; he didn't tap a toe, nothing. Absolutely motionless, and his eyes never wavered. He was one hundred percent focused on me, and it was a little unsettling to be the center of that intensity coming from him. I found myself leaning forward slightly in the swing. Whatever this was about, I wanted to pay attention for as much as he was zeroed in on me.

"I have called you many things since we met.", he began, and I nodded slightly in agreement.

"I have called you Officer Jameson. I have called you Jimmy. I have been lucky enough to be able to call you Love, girlfriend, and Lover."

"And I have called you many things as well. Woods. Kane.", and his smile emerged as always when I said his name. I returned it and continued my list. "Fido. Rover.

Sparky. Cujo. Boyfriend. I'm sure a few more colorful names as well, when I'm in a rant."

"There have been several mentions of the Knights of the Round Table, from time to time." And we both grinned at Kane's mention of that.

"Yeah, I guess we each have several aliases. Yours for me are far kinder than mine it seems. I must really love you Kane, because it takes a pretty strong emotion to bring that much temper and creativity to my language." He smiled huge this time, and his teeth had gotten larger and whiter the past few days. Between the brilliance of his smile and the extreme light of his eyes I was going to need sunglasses soon.

"Your timing for saying just that is impeccable." And the *scoundrel* flooded through the gold. He stepped back over to where I was sitting and crouched down in front of me. He locked my eyes with his and held them there. I couldn't have looked away if I wanted to.

Planes could start dropping bombs all around us and I would not have noticed. I did notice his breathing had changed slightly; it had become faster. I felt my heart in my chest and realized it must be deafening for him because I could hear it myself. Something huge was about to happen, and I had no idea what it was. He shifted slightly from the crouch, his eyes holding mine the entire time, and rested a knee on the ground.

"I would like to add to my list of things I call you Diana. If you will allow it."

"What would you care to add?" I managed to croak out. My mouth had gone dry under his intense concentration on me.

"*Wife*. If you will have me." He said, and removed a box from the front pocket of his jeans. There was no doubt what the tiny velvet box contained. It held a ring. Never, not in ten of Kane's lifetimes, would I ever have seen this coming. I was dimly aware my breathing had stopped as did my heart when Kane last spoke, but the involuntary nervous system is a magnificent thing and I felt both resume on their own. I was grateful neither required me to think to make it happen, because at that moment in time I was incapable of any thought at all.

Wife. I had never entertained the idea of that word pertaining to me; not once in my entire life. Yet here I was not only having it mentioned, but I had just been asked to become one. My thoughts spun and skittered like cars on black ice, and it was dizzying the speeds they were firing. I managed to find Kane's eyes again, and the chaos was suddenly still. The brilliance of the gold silenced everything, and there was only one thing to say.

"I would be proud to call you husband, Kane."

His smile flashed for the briefest of moments before he had me in his arms. His crushing hug as he stood up and had my feet off the ground was the most exhilarating display of his speed to date. Lightning seemed slow by its standards. I laughed as he held me, and he kissed me quickly before joining me in the music of happiness. Kane gently lowered me so my feet once again felt the Earth and he kissed me again. This time, there was no blinding speed. It was a long, slow delicious kiss with every atom of his being behind it. I was breathless when it ended.

"This is not quite fair," he said, resting his forehead against mine, "It is your birthday, and I am the one who has received the gift."

"I don't know about that." I said, and my smile had to be as big as his. "You're stuck with me now. Coffee, toothpaste and cigarettes. Every morning, for the rest of your life."

"A life sentence I look forward to serving." He said, and I laughed aloud at the irony of that. Life sentence. This one was *FAR* better than the one I had been doing the past summer. And this one, would not be on the installment plan. I wanted every moment of it; back to back.

#

The afternoon of November second found me begrudgingly dropping an overnight bag into the passenger seat of my Mustang. Kane walked me to the car as always and while the Pull was strong; today he did not pace. Instead, he held me tightly against him and I nuzzled into his chest.

"Eighteen hours Kane; it's not that long." I didn't have to look up to know he smiled at the feel of his name.

"I know. November is not so bad, but even half a day without you feels like a year. And I know years." He said and chuckled softly.

"Yes, you do. Cradle-robber." His chuckle exploded into a full and heartfelt laugh, and I had no choice but to join him. Jesus Jimmy; the shit you say sometimes.

"We will have to add that to your list as well. You are quite creative, Miss Jameson."

"And you? Will have to remove that from your list soon, Kane." He drew back from me far enough so that our eyes could meet. The gold flooded with a joy I had never seen before.

"I look forward to that moment." I felt the resonation in my body as he spoke, and it warmed my soul.

"We can discuss plans when I get home and you have recovered; *Fiancé.*" I said, and his smile was as bright as his eyes. Damn those teeth! Even though I knew what they were capable of, I still liked them. While he had used them in savagery, Kane had never hurt *me* with them. In fact, he was quite gentle with them. I felt a surge of heat go through me at that thought. There *definitely* was something wrong with me.

"Really? Have I not satisfied you?" I must have flashed over to a redder color in his vision.

"Don't be ridiculous Kane; I can barely fucking walk. And shut up, I know my color shifted. I am wrung out, but you're not the only one who can't seem to get enough. Sheesh, you're my addiction okay? I'll crave more no matter the cost to my body. Worse than a goddamn junkie."

"Thank you. In cop speak that is a compliment, I believe."

"It is and you know it. Now let me go before you do cripple me, because I'll let you." I said, and Kane sighed and loosened his arms. He kissed me before he fully let go, and it took every ounce of determination I had not to undo his jeans right there in the driveway. When he had finished saying good bye, I stepped back from him. Ugh. The half grin. I was done. My hands were at his belt before I even realized it, and he was tugging my shirt over my head in seconds. There was still five hours before dark, and walking down the aisle was overrated. I could be wheeled down it just as easily.

#

"Will your fiancé be joining you this evening, Miss Jameson?" the woman behind the desk of the beachfront hotel asked as I checked in. I glanced to my left ring finger and smiled.

"Sadly, no. He has some things he must to do tonight."

"Then I'm glad you decided to spend this evening with us. The moonlight is beautiful on the waves, and tonight's a full moon. It will be breathtaking. Your room faces the beach, so you can see it from your balcony."

"Full moon. Yes, I know. Perfect time to watch the tide."

"Oh, for sure. The moon controls the tides, you know."

"Yes. It controls a lot of things." I said, and rubbed my left thumb along the bottom of my engagement ring. I accepted the key from the friendly clerk and made my way to the room. Hampton Beach is a mad house in the summer, but in the off season it was quiet and perhaps a little lonely. The quiet appealed to me, and the lonely part made me want to keep it company. I couldn't be with Kane tonight for obvious reasons, but there was no reason for two things to be lonely. Besides, the Sea Ketch made the best scallops I had ever eaten in my life and though it was winter and the off season? It was also a Friday night. There was a guitar player who had a gravelly voice and sang his lungs out. Might as well enjoy good food and music if I had to be 'away' for a night.

I had finished my wonderful meal and was sitting at the bar listening to the band when the hair on the back of my neck stood up. It was the feeling of being watched, and I had worn a uniform long enough to know that there's a damn fine reason the good Lord gave us instincts.

I had learned a long time ago never to doubt my 'gut' and I was not about to start now. I glanced into the mirror behind the bar and scanned the reflection of people behind me. The only time I sit with my back to the door is when there's a full mirror behind a bar. Another reason I liked the 'Ketch'. It had just such a mirror. The Ketch and the Old Salt were the only two places in Hampton Beach I ever went to, and for the same reason. I could appear relaxed and still see everything. I never shifted in my stool but I was looking for who, or what, was watching me. The *WHAT* part worried me. I had never mentioned the beach to Kane; so I had no reason to expect the Residual he felt to apply to this place, but still. There was always a possibility I talk in my sleep. How would I know? I grinned at the thought briefly, and resumed my survey of the room.

There were people in the place but it wasn't packed. No one seemed to be paying any particularly attention to me; well no more than was normal. I am a tall woman with spiky blonde hair. I gain some glances and the occasional 'look', both from men and women and both for the same reason. They wonder if I'm gay. Some hope I am; those are the women. The men who wonder it seem to be very interested in 'changing my mind about that'. I ran my left hand through my hair before I realized why I had done it. The ring that encircled the finger on that hand was an unspoken sentence. *I am not available*. When I grasped my motivation for my action, I smiled and looked down at it.

Kane had had it custom made and it was stunning. When he told me how long he had planned on asking me to marry him; the weeks spent designing it and then waiting for it to be crafted? The timeline was identical to the *scoundrel* I had seen in his eyes. While I had never imagined that this was what he had been 'up to'; it made perfect sense. The thought and effort he put into everything he did for me was astonishing, and the ring was the crown jewel. I was a very lucky woman. While the *Enhancement* made it challenging; the way he felt about me and for me made it miniscule. Kane was a one of a kind, and in more ways than every twenty-nine days. I have never been a woman who was hung up on the material things in life, but this ring was the most precious thing to me aside from the man who gave it to me.

The center stone was not a diamond, which is why I loved it. It was a rectangular moonstone, and a blue one at that. It was clear like a diamond, but held a silver blue sheen no dead dinosaur would ever possess. Along each side of it ran smaller flawless diamonds, and each corner had perfect emeralds. I was surprised when it was silver, and relieved when Kane explained it was in fact platinum. I didn't want to have to take it off to touch him. His choice of materials again spoke to how he felt for me and how he showed it. The moonstone was obvious and I adored the choice. The diamonds were because of tradition, and the emeralds were of course; Ireland. The fact that there were four spoke to the four corners, four seasons, four winds and four directions. All are constant, timeless forces. His decision of platinum was because it was the strongest metal he knew of, and a reflection of the strength of the love between us. I don't know who the jeweler was, but he was an artisan as much as Kane was. In the five days that I had worn it? I received easily fifty compliments on it, and I didn't go that many places.

After visually ensuring no one was staring at me too long or too hard; I unwound slightly and enjoyed the band. I still eyed the reflective glass every few minutes or so, but the hair on my neck had gone down. If it was a *WHO* that had been watching me their attention was now diverted. Clearly it wasn't a *WHAT*, or the place would have been a crime scene and I would be evidence. I ordered another beer and turned when the guitar stopped and a piano rang out the first notes of a song that I hadn't heard in quite some time. As the melody unfolded I smiled, anticipating hearing the raspy voice of the singer bring the lyrics to sound. It was perfect, both in who was singing it, and what the words would be.

"Maybe I'm amazed at the way you love me all the time....and maybe I'm afraid of the way I love you."

Paul McCartney and Wings. Ann would be proud. The stars and planets once again had to have come together in *just* the right way for this to have happened. Kane may have been fifteen miles away, but I felt him as though he was sitting right beside me with his hand resting on my thigh. He was in his altered form now, and while he was invincible on two legs and untouchable on four? I cast my eyes up in a silent prayer. Lord, keep him safe. The fates of *two* rest in Your Grace tonight. I will not survive without him.

#

The sun had fully cleared the horizon of the Atlantic by the time I was lacing up my sneakers. I had spent several hours watching the silver light dance across white crests of waves the night before once I had walked the four doors down from the Sea Ketch to my hotel. The tides were stronger under the full moon, and I spent those hours deep in thought about the pull of things and how they all were different yet the same. The moon mastered the oceans, and the man I loved. Yet its power was a slight shadow compared to the pull Kane had on me. There was nothing in existence that could touch that. It had not been very long since we had first met according to a calendar, but the forces behind it were eternal. Destiny *indeed*. I smiled as that particular word once again found residence in my thoughts. He was rubbing off on me that was for sure. Or perhaps, it was the birth of that rare occasion where one person so completely merges into another that they don't know where they stop and the other begins.

One glance at my left hand told me I was not alone in that. The sheepdog and the Wolf. Historically mortal enemies. But in our very unique case? Utterly one being; and each vital to the other's very existence and survival, for all of Time. Perfection in how fucked up it was. The very definition of a love story for the ages.

I had thanked the morning clerk for an excellent stay and trotted down the seven steps to the sidewalk with my mind singing at thoughts of seeing Kane when I got home. I had deliberately waited until full sunrise before I entertained the thought of heading home.

Last month had driven that fact home, and I would not be making *that* error in judgment again. Kane could not help what happened, but I could damn sure prevent it from becoming a tragedy. The price would be far higher for him. Sure, I'd be dead and all and that would suck, but he would have to go on carrying the knowledge that he was responsible. The Wolf part anyway, which while it was a separate entity it was still *him*. Thinking about the intricacies of the whole thing could drive somebody crazy. I brushed these thoughts aside. It was worse than a dog chasing its tail; a whole lot of wasted energy and in the end it never gets you anywhere even if you catch it.

November mornings are not crisp on the beach; they are cold. I felt a chill settle in my shoulders but after three steps I realized it was not the mercury level that had me feeling cold. The hair on the back of my neck was standing up again. Dawn had come and gone; so there was no *WHAT* watching me. It was a *WHO* and I knew it as much as I knew my name. I glanced behind me but the sidewalk was empty at this early hour. I continued my pace and rounded the corner to the off-street parking lot of the hotel where my Mustang waited for me. It was the off season but there were still a few vehicles besides mine scattered in the lot. My eyes rested on one and my blood froze.

The license plate was different; it was now a Massachusetts tag of white with green letters and numbers, but the vehicle was undoubtedly the same. Faded red paint, rust edging the wheel wells and the scraped bumper and dent under the passenger headlight. Farm truck. Even more so out of place in New Hampshire just feet from the sand than it was in Rowley. I focused on the registration. CKA 012. I again etched it to memory as I had the Georgia identification. I was concentrating on the truck so intently I didn't hear him approach until he was almost upon me.

"Well howdy, Miss! I recall seeing you in the post office the day I moved to town." I internally squirmed at the sound of the accent and voice but held my spine still. Not tipping this asshole off this time. Stay cool Officer Jameson; you know what to do. I had slipped back into that role with an ease that should have concerned me, yet I didn't give it a second thought. I deliberately turned around slowly and smiled at the man who stood four feet away. His pale blue eyes were colder than the morning. No matter how hard he tried to force warmth into his smile? I was not buying it. I hoped my 'act' was pulled off with more success than his. I consciously stood flat footed and directly in front of him. It was a chore but I managed to do so smoothly, and judging by the set of his chest and shoulders? I was a superior actress.

"Well hello! Imagine running into you on an early Saturday morning in November! I remember your accent! Not many southern gentlemen about this time of year."

"I can understand why not." He said, still faking that icy smile as he rubbed his arms in the chill. Sure, it was about forty degrees but it was a sauna compared what I felt emanating from him. Kane had used a few words when talking about the stoop shouldered man I found myself making polite conversation with. Wrong. Decay. I smiled inside my head when I realized that Kane was a far cry kinder in what he called people than I was. One word would be all I ever held for this creature I chatted with. And the word was *Evil*. Without a soul was too soft. He was *Evil*. Through and through.

After five minutes or so, a reasonable amount of time spent on meaningless talk that met the requirements of politeness; I shivered exaggeratedly and giggled like a girl.

"I am sorry, but it *is* cold." I said and motioned towards my car. "If you will excuse me?"

"I understand completely Miss; I am not used to this either." He reached out and patted my left forearm. I was thankful for the jacket; my skin was crawling already. Had he actually touched me I may have puked. His eyes came to rest on my ring, and he glanced up at me.

"Soon to be a Missus, it seems! Good for you. The taller man I saw accompanying you in town? He has interesting eyes. Congratulations to you both."

"Yes, and thank you!" I said, and took two steps backwards. I waved my hand in the air as if to shoo him to his truck.

"Get warm yourself!" I said and waved as I continued to my car. He returned the wave and walked quickly to his own truck. Once he had climbed in and started it, he rubbed his hands together in front of what I assumed were heater vents. I mimicked the action; though forty degrees was not that chilly once the sun was up. Better to have him think I was delicate.

It was frustrating to wait because I really wanted to get home to Kane, but I stayed put for a solid ten minutes after he departed before I slid the Mustang into gear. While the Evil was still present in my mind; the idea of being able to touch Kane and both hear and feel his voice made me smile. The further I drove south the happier I became, and by the time I parked in our driveway I was elated. A small tinge of dread found me as I approached the door. Today it was shut, and that dread vanished. He had shut the door. He was okay.

The savory aroma of one of Kane's masterful pots of coffee surrounded me as soon as I stepped inside. Excitement to see him filled me and I glanced around for his location. Strong arms slid around my waist and a nibble on my right ear let me know I was *very much* home. The speed he could move was astounding; and I loved it. Something was *very*, very wrong with me.

"Good morning, fiancée." He spoke, but I more felt it than heard it. I leaned my head back into him and relished in how good it felt to be back with him.

His teeth were still gently present on my ear and I reached my left hand up to run through his hair. Kane went entirely rigid and spun me around to face him. His eyes were glowing gold but they were ice. He had appeared lethal the morning of the shower fight with the now deceased Rodan. The way he looked right now made that a pathetic joke.

"Are you all right? Did he hurt you?" It was a snarling demand for information in a frighteningly quiet tone. There was no vibration inside of me save for the fear I felt at what his eyes and expression revealed. What he was capable of doing to protect me crashed down around me like nuclear weapons. My hands were on his biceps and I could feel them shaking. His entire body was shaking; and I'm not entirely sure if it was fear for my wellbeing or a boiling fury he was battling to contain. His eyes remained locked on mine and they were boring into me. I scrambled to make sense of what he was saying while staggering to recover from what I was seeing before me. Kane was the embodiment of the Apocalypse. Any harm befalling me would unleash it, and the aftermath would make Lawrence Jail seem like child's play.

"What? I'm fine Kane, I'm fine." And for the second time since I had known him; he failed to smile at my speaking his name. The arctic sheen of his eyes never softened and every sinew of his body was concrete. Jesus Christ, what was this about?

"Kane? Kane. You're scaring me. What's wrong?" I asked, and I heard the quake in my voice. Kane had as well, and it seemed to snap him out of whatever he was going through. While he had failed twice to smile; he did not make it a third. It was brief, but it was there. I felt myself exhale in relief as he flashed his blinding white teeth. Okay. It's gonna be okay.

He's back. Sort of. The feel of his name had made him smile but that smile had not yet reached his eyes. He had them locked on the wall behind me, and they were murderously icy. I gently placed my hands on his jaw and directed his face to me. His eyes fell on to mine, and the gold softened slightly. They were still far beyond predatory but at least they had stopped scaring the shit out of me. After several moments of him gradually softening, I leaned in and kissed him gently. He relaxed a hair more and that encouraged me. I continued to repeat the kisses, allowing each one to grow longer than the one prior; and each time he took another small step back to the man I loved. My last kiss resulted in his arms gently coiling around my waist, and I smiled at his touch.

#

It had taken over thirty minutes to rein him back but once he returned? I was delighted to see him. His eyes were warm again, and I grinned up at him. He half smiled, not the signature crooked grin that decimated any resolve I had; but a half smile that blended relief and a touch of shame.

"Are *YOU* all right?" I asked him, and he scoffed with a short laugh. My question seemed to have crumbled the last of his frozen blood, and he ran his fingers through my hair. That simple motion soothed me, and I felt myself uncoil. Kane felt it too, and he pulled me into one of his enveloping hugs. We lingered there a delightful moment, and I felt him exhale the final traces of whatever it was that had seized him. His form finally released, and I kissed his throat when I felt it.

"Diana, I am so sorry. Truly. I cannot apologize enough." The gentle vibration in my bones warmed me to my toes.

"We are done apologizing, remember?" I said, and he laughed softly and hugged me tighter. I nuzzled into his neck.

"Okay, you are right." It was several minutes before he released me, and when I looked up at him, he was smiling.

"What in the Hell set you off? I have never seen you look like that, and Christ Almighty I don't ever want to see that again. You scared the fuck out of me."

"For that, I *will* apologize. But for as frightened as you were, Lover? It is nothing compared to the fear I felt. *Nothing*." The gravel in his voice shook me.

"What? What was it?" I asked.

"Decay."

My knees buckled.

#

It was a long moment sitting on the couch before I could begin to think clearly. My hands wrapped around a mug of Kane's wonderful coffee that he had taken the liberty of adding Bailey's to. Its warmth comforted me, as did the kindness of the man who sat beside me with his arm wrapped around my shoulder. His fingers gently traced my arm and I realized I was blessed beyond compare. I don't know what I had done in this life or any prior to deserve this; but I would do it again a thousand times if it earned me five minutes of this. I glanced down at my engagement ring. I was to have a lifetime of it. Yep, I'd do it again a million times. In a New York minute.

"Did I actually pass out?" I asked, and Kane chuckled.

"No, Love."

"Good."

He sat quietly, allowing me to sort through my thoughts. The uncanny sense he had for allowing me space was a gift, and I appreciated it more than I could ever say. I don't know if I shifted color or if my heartbeat changed, but he picked up on my thought and wrapped his hand around my left shoulder. A gentle squeeze spoke the same unworthy words I had been unable to find. Lifelong mate. Sometimes, no words are needed. Not even a whisper.

"So, what happened; from your side of it?" I asked, and Kane cut his eyes sideways at me. He shifted on the couch, and the motion revealed how uncomfortable the morning still was for him. He took a deep breath, and then faced me fully. A scattering of amber had returned to the gold, and I was relieved. November had been a merciful Full. I silently thanked the Judge above, and nodded my appreciation to the Defense Attorney and the Cop.

"As always, I was thrilled to see you. The feel of your skin, the smell of your hair and the green of your eyes had me delirious with happiness. When you moved your arm....do you remember doing that?" I nodded that I did, and Kane grinned before he continued.

"It was faint, maybe a few cells he left on you somewhere or I would have picked up on it sooner. But when it reached me? I locked on to it. Diana? I have not been so frightened since that morning in Lawrence when they called you in to work. You said you never want to see me like that again. Love, I don't ever want to *feel* that much terror for you again in my *life*."

"Jesus, Kane." I whispered, and his smile assured me I was very much loved. I returned it and finished my coffee.

"Another?" he asked and jerked his chin at the mug.

"In a minute. I ran into Georgia in the parking lot as I was leaving this morning. We spoke briefly, and he patted my forearm as I left."

"That's what I picked up on. I knew he had to have touched you for there to be a trace."

"He touched the jacket sleeve. Not *ME*. I would not have allowed that scumbag maggot piece of shit to touch *ME*."

Kane tossed back his head and laughed heartily. I was slightly confused as to what exactly was so funny; but it was contagious in its joy and I joined him in it though not completely sure why. In the end; who cared? Kane was happy. That was more than enough for me.

"Scumbag maggot piece of shit." He echoed and smiled brightly at me.

Kane was as twisted as I was.

No wonder I had said yes.

DECEMBER 1990

Chapter Twenty-Four

It was well after dark when I heard the saw stop for the final time that evening. Kane had only taken half a day to recover from the November Full. He and Alejandro had been putting in longer hours as the deadlines approached; and their work was beyond beautiful. My fiancé and his apprentice were creating masterpieces, and I had taken to bringing them sandwiches in the afternoons.

The work was physical, and Alejandro was a sixteen-year-old kid which is synonymous with ravenous. I enjoyed it truth be told; it gave me a chance to watch them interact and also admire their progress. The cabinetry was being built in the workshop, but so was a friendship that both Kane and Alejandro needed very much. It wasn't difficult to determine which one I most liked watching occur. Kane teaching and talking with Alejandro offered glimpses into what he must have been like as a teenager with his own father. I was a bit sad I never got to meet Angus Woods. He must have been a man of the finest caliber; his son was.

It wasn't long before Kane had returned from dropping Alejandro at home, and I was making supper while listening to the news. I never 'watched' the news, but I always had it on the television as I cooked. My way of keeping up with the world. I heard him come in to the house, but my ears had focused on the reporter. An eight-year-old girl had been found murdered in New Hampshire. Her tiny body had signs of a sexual assault prior to her death. I turned to actually look at the screen, and my blood froze. The reporter was standing on Hampton Beach.

"Jimmy? Jimmy what is it?" a concerned Kane was beside me faster than a bullet and his hands were on my shoulders. I blinked and looked up at him. Amber streaks had returned to the gold that was all consuming the day before. He narrowed them slightly as he watched me. I nodded towards the TV.

"Jesus. What the fuck is wrong with people." It was rare when Kane swore, and in the time since I had first met him? This was only the second time I ever heard him use the word *fuck*. While it was one of my more popular words; he reserved it for the morning I got called into work that awful July day. Seems child rapists and killers ranked up there as well in evoking it from him. He looked back to me, and again concern found its way into the mosaic of hues.

"Diana? You are white as a ghost. What is it, Lover? What's wrong?" His words hummed in me, echoing the worry his voice carried and eyes revealed.

"I was there last night." I whispered.

"Where?" He asked, and I nodded towards the TV again. Kane glanced at it, and then snapped his head back when he realized what I was talking about.

"You stayed in Hampton Beach? Last night?"

"Yeah."

"Oh Jesus Jimmy; thank God you're all right. Sick bastards like that running about." He said softly and wrapped me in one of his protective hugs. While it warmed me somewhat, the chill in my blood kept a foothold. I had been there. Fuck. I wished I had come across the baby killing piece of shit. It wouldn't have been a child's body that had been found in the morning.

In my time on the Sheriff's Department I had once been part of a search for a young boy that had gone missing. We found him. But not in time. The image of his naked and mutilated frame haunted me still. Child rapists and killers had a special place in Hell; and a front row reserved seat in my forum of hatred. I would have ripped the guy apart, and it would not have required any *Enhancement* for me to manage it.

Kane rubbed his hands up and down my back and I tried to soften my body. I knew he worried for me, and he didn't need to carry the weight of my mental scars. Bad enough I shouldered them; no sense in both of us having that image in our heads. His would only be imagined of course, but even an imagined picture of a dead boy is horrible. He looked down at me and sighed.

"Tell me." He whispered, and peered into my eyes.

"My color or my heartbeat?"

"Both."

"Damn."

#

I was not in the habit of sharing the worst moments of my life, but I have to confess that having Kane be there to listen was incredibly soothing for me. I initially started the awful memory in cop mode; citing facts and removing the emotional impact, but the more I talked to him the more those lines blurred. By the time I had finished, he was wiping tears from my eyes and wrapping me in a gentle hug. I had never cried in front of anybody; I avoided crying altogether as best I could if I could help it. I had always viewed it as a weakness on my part and I was not going to advertise that I had chinks in my armor. I'm a sheepdog; people look to *ME* for protection. I can't have them knowing their guardian had a heart. They might doubt my ability to keep them safe if they knew I *FELT* anything. I inhaled deeply against his chest, and let the warmth of not only his arms around me but the love he felt for me begin to heal the deep wound in my soul over finding the boy too late. So, this is what therapy was all about, huh? Well thank you, Doctor Woods.

When I opened my eyes the next morning the sun was already up, and I was surprised to discover Kane was still in the bed beside me. I had slept; *truly* slept, and I felt like my batteries had been recharged. I snuggled in closer to him and he smiled though his eyes were still closed. This was a rare treat; he had been starting work before six every morning and I didn't realize how much I had missed waking up next to him until I found myself doing exactly that today.

"How did you sleep?" he murmured.

"The best I have in a *long* time."

"Glad for it. You have needed that."

"Indeed." I said, and he opened one eye and looked at me. His smile grew larger and he pulled me closer to him.

"Seems like you did too. You haven't been in the bed when I wake up for weeks."

"Today seemed like a perfect day to be lazy." He said, his fingertips lightly tracing my shoulder, "Besides, you didn't flinch in your sleep like you do most nights."

"I do that?"

"Some nights more than others. I had thought it was your resisting being completely comfortable being next to me. I understand now."

I rose up on my elbow and looked at him.

"What?!? Jesus Christ, Kane! Really? Comfortable? You? Are an idiot! An absolute fucking idiot." He smiled as he felt me say his name, and chuckled softly at my description of him and his current thought pattern.

"And you understand *WHAT* exactly? Apparently not much if you think I was subconsciously 'resisting'. Jesus! I thought you were intelligent."

"Love," he began, and pulled me back down to his chest, "Easy. I realize you have not had caffeine yet, but hear me out. I had *thought*; that is the key word here. It is past tense."

"What are you talking about?" Another gentle rumble from his chest as he laughed. As I heard and I felt it, and I slowly realized there was no malice in it. My shoulders relaxed, and apparently Kane felt it too. He pulled me closer still. Okay Jimmy, shut up and listen to what the man has to say.

"Diana, you were a completely independent woman. You lived alone, and on your own terms. Answered to no one. And in a very short amount of time, you agreed to give all that up to be here with me."

"Yeah...." I let the sentence hang and waited for Kane to continue.

"That is an adjustment. I'm a *guy*, as you so often remind me. It is expected of me to be on my own. For a woman, and a woman in your former profession? That is an enormous achievement. You were one hundred percent successful and managing perfectly. What did you need of me?"

I started to raise myself up again but Kane pulled me back into him. I did not resist too strongly; just enough to satisfy my pride. I am Irish after all.

"I had thought, again past tense, *thought*, you were holding on to that independence on some level. As I said, you didn't need me. After what you told me last night?"

"Yeah?"

"It let me understand that your twitches and startles in the middle of the night have nothing to do with me. That was simply me doubting I deserve you. Which I do not." he paused, kissed the top of my head, and stroked my spikes.

"Jesus, Diana. The things you have seen. I cannot even begin to imagine. It is a miracle you sleep at all. One I am thankful for; because if anybody deserves to rest? It is *Officer Diana Jameson*."

The magnitude of what Kane had just said slapped me harder than my mother had the day I said fuck for the first time. I was four when I did it. Seems even that young I loved the word. I was stunned to discover that he had ever doubted his worth. Jesus, are you kidding me? He was the most incredible man; Hell the most incredible *human being* I had ever encountered. I thought of Ann.

The ones that don't know it are the hottest. She was dead on point there! I marveled that he truly did not see it. How could he *NOT* see it? My *God*! I finally broke down and asked him.

"Kane?" and the smile flashed, "Have you ever *looked* in the goddamn mirror? Really looked? Jesus. Deserve *ME*? Ha! Pretty sure it's the other way around."

He rolled on to his side and met my eyes. I don't know if he ever *looked* in the mirror, but he was definitely *LOOKING* at me. Intently. It would have made me nervous except I was so in love with him even *THAT* stare was a thrill.

"Have you?" he asked.

"What? Of course, I have. No big deal; spiky hair and green eyes. And my father's nose, which I love and thankfully is still straight. Never been broken, shockingly enough."

Kane could move quickly; but he was on his hands and knees over me before I knew it. The gold and amber blazed mere inches from my greens, and I didn't recognize the emotion behind them. I had never seen it before, and it was only when I felt his words that I realized what it was.

"*GODDAMNIT, DIANA!* If that is all you see? Then you are blind!"

Anger.

Not pissed.

Anger.

I should have been afraid. Truthfully, there was a tinge of fear on the peripheral; but my stubborn heritage jumped right in and smashed it. Fucking glare at *me*? I don't think so!

"*NO!* No, you will *NOT*." He growled, still over me, "And it's not your color or heartbeat. Your eyes are brilliant green. But *YOU WILL* listen."

The way he spoke and the way it thundered through me, was deafening. His words held me as still as if I had been physically pinned down. I met his gaze and refused to blink. My last-ditch effort at revolution. It faded as I watched his eyes soften.

"You are the most incredible woman I have ever known. I did not *KNOW* a woman such as you could even exist! Your strength? The way you never fail to do what is right? No matter the personal cost; you *NEVER* fail! I have slept beside you for *months*. They have been the best months of my entire life. I know now *some* of the price you have paid; and it is dear. I *hate* that you have paid it and that you continue to do so. I would take it away from you if I could. Yes, I may wage my own war with God over this. He certainly deserves it! Every twitch you make while dreaming? It is a payment you make on a debt that you *DO NOT OWE*. It infuriates me. *Sheepdog*? No Love; you are a *champion*. I do not understand why you stay with me. I don't know why you said yes when I asked you to be my wife but you did and I am beyond grateful for that though I will *never* understand it. I will spend the rest of my days making sure that you never regret that. But I will *ALSO,* make *damn good and sure* that you *SEE* how amazing you are!"

It's not every day that somebody rebukes you because they think you are awesome. There are not many times Kane swears. It was a lot to handle. Especially before coffee. I had my Trinity in the mornings; of that there was no doubt. My 'requirements'. On this particular morning? I realized what it was that I truly required; and his eyes were lit from within but far softer than they had been. I found myself able to move again, and ran my fingers through Kane's hair. My hand had reached the back of his head, and I pulled his face down to mine and kissed him. I poured everything that was me into it, arched my back to feel him against me and wrapped my left arm around his hip. I may like coffee, toothpaste and cigarettes; but the only thing I *needed* was a man named Kane Woods. It wasn't long before Kane was 'pouring' into me; and I was happy for it.

Chapter Twenty-Five

The following two weeks were hectic for both Kane and Alejandro. They had been cranking out stunning work; and the sheer volume of it was surprising. I did what I could to assist them; but my contributions were mostly assembling sandwiches for them to devour and handling the phone calls. I almost felt guilty that my biggest pressure was planning a Thanksgiving dinner for the following week. When I had said as much to Kane, he smiled and assured me that I had spent more than enough time dealing with stress and that I had earned some time to relax. Today's big adventure for me was the grocery store for the components of that very meal. The exciting life and times of Diana Jameson.

"Kane?" I said as I stepped into the workshop. He smiled as always and stopped what he was doing and looked at me. His eyes were that beautiful amber today; only a few flecks of gold in them, but they were warm.

"I'm heading out to the store. How big of a turkey should I get?"

"The biggest one you can find." was his reply, and one glance told me he was not kidding.

"Are you serious? It's just the two of us."

"Yes I am."

"I had no idea you were a turkey junkie."

"I'm not."

"Then why on Christ's green Earth am I going to be cooking a twenty-pound turkey?"

He glanced down for the briefest of seconds, and when he looked back at me his eyes were colder and slightly sad. He sighed and I watched his shoulders drop. Uh-oh. I hated that. I'm sure I flashed a different tint because for as long as his shoulders stayed down? I felt anger in me. I glanced up; ready to start Round Two and he saw it. Kane drew himself up to his full height again, once more keeping his promise to stop railing on himself for being

Enhanced. As soon as he did? I kept the Peace with the Big Guy.

"Diana, in two days? I am going to feel the Pull of what is going to be the worst."

I knew he was speaking of the moon but I didn't understand why he was going to feel it so early. It was mid-November, and fifteen days before the next Full. I crossed over to where he stood and slid my arms around his waist. He donned that damn crooked grin of his and laughed softly. He leaned in towards me, closed his eyes and rested his forehead against mine.

"Even now; you bring me happiness." He whispered. I had no idea what I had done or what was coming next, but I was glad to be there with him.

He lingered against me for a few seconds longer. Then he stood up fully, and I peered into those gorgeous eyes once more. I waited as he figured out exactly how he was going to tell me something that did not bode well. I saw the amber set once he did, and I stepped back to let him pace. He grinned, and proceeded to do just that.

"In a normal year? I get a month 'off', and that month is December."

"Oh my God, that's great! I had no idea! Fuckin' A! No stealth mode hotel stays until after the New Year!" I knew I was smiling; Hell, I had to be because I was practically dancing a jig. One look from Kane and my joy vanished.

"It is not a normal year."

That simple six-word sentence felt as heavy and cold as the Control Room door of Lawrence did. The words boomed louder within me than when that very same door was slammed shut. Dread smothered my entire being. A crazy phrase streaked through my mind. *Something Wicked This Way Comes.* I shivered, though the workshop was warm' and waited for him to continue.

"This year, December has *two* Fulls. That makes it a Blue Moon month."

Kane's words struck deeply in me, and I flashed to his explanation of the Blood Moon. *The only Full worse than the Blood, is a Blue Moon. Two in one month. Jesus Diana, that is about as bad as it can get.* Fuck! The Blood had wreaked havoc on him. And now I had just been informed a Blue was coming up. Great!

"Well aren't we just the luckiest people ever? The first month we could have had 'off', and it's a Blue month. Fucking stellar!" I could taste the sarcasm as I spoke, and was surprised to see Kane with a full smile. I cocked my head at him.

"What?"

"I just told you December is a Blue; and you still say *we*."

"Of course I did, ya jerk." I replied, and raised my left hand. I wiggled the ring finger and Kane's eyes softened and warmed again. "I said *YES,* remember?"

"I will never understand you Diana, but I am happy for my luck that you did."

"Okay; so tell me why we get a month off in a normal year. You failed to mention that when you explained the Blood and the beginning of the Wolves of Ireland. Lay it all out."

Kane shook his head slowly, the smile still present, and then crossed back over to where I was standing. He kissed me and pulled me into him; a gesture I did not resist in the slightest.

It was a long and deeply delightful kiss and I savored every bit of it. When he finished, I'm sure I was a far redder vision to him than I had been moments before. It took me a few seconds to catch my breath. Damn I loved this man and Jesus could he set my pants on fire!

"You better start talking, Kane. And fast, or you will not be the hungriest one in this shop." His smile at the feel of his name was followed by a hearty laugh. The sound of it was music to my ears.

"All right. Though that is a *very* tempting scenario." He stepped back and began to walk back and forth. Classic Kane.

"Again, there is a lot of speculation on this. Da knew as much as anyone I suppose and told me all that he knew; but no one really knows why. It may tie in with Saint Patrick again. The religion. Jesus was born on December 25th. Seems there may have been some mercy in the cursing of the bloodlines; and that mercy is that the month of the birth of Christ grants a reprieve. But like all things? If there is human involvement there is also a loophole. A Blue in the month of December nullifies the 'break', if you will. Jesus was Divine, but dear Saint Patrick was 'one of God's foot soldiers' as you put it; so there had to be a balance. This year will be the 8th time I change in December since I was born. It will also be the last time it happens this century. The next one is nineteen years from now."

"Well damn the bad luck for this year; but at least it will be quite some time before we have to deal with it again." I said, and Kane chuckled softly.

"So it would seem."

"I still don't get it. You were born the 25th. Same as Jesus. So why did you even get the *Enhancement* in the first place? Seems to me like that would have made you of all people; immune."

"A lot of guessing about that as well, Love. Yes, I was born on December 25th. However, the *YEAR* I was born? 1863? There was a Full Moon that day. Or night. Some say that the audacity of being born on Christ's birthday is enough; others believe that the combination of the date and a Full that does it. Add my mother's birthplace into the mix? It is a recipe for disaster."

"Jesus, Kane. You sure got caught in the crossfire of an absolute shit show. It's like the entire Universe went out of its way to make sure that one way or another? You got fucked."

Kane grinned when I had finished my summary and shrugged his shoulders. He was a *WAY* better sport about it than I would have been. I'd have been pissed beyond compare, and for over a century it seemed.

"Maybe so. But just like the Decembers that I have 'off'? The universe sent me a mercy."

"What's that?"

"You."

That did it. I closed the space between us in three steps. The upcoming Blue month may have its hold on him in two days but right now I was the biggest, baddest and hungriest wolf around. And the Pull that brought it out in me was a shaggy haired man with amber eyes.

#

It was over an hour later when we emerged from the shop, and I was pleased to see I wasn't the only one slightly staggering out of the doorway. The half grin was once again on its natural residence and while I was exhausted, the sight of it blew on the embers of my sheer desire for him. Kane glanced my way and startled.

"Jesus, you cannot be serious." He said, and I can only imagine what my color revealed to him. "Even I need a moment right now. Please, my apologies if I fell short; but let me catch my breath."

I laughed as hard as I could manage in my depleted state, and Kane looked at me quizzically.

"Oh, good God! No way did you fall short. I can barely move."

"But your color...." He let the sentence remain unfinished.

"Oh, that has *ZERO* to do with what happened in the shop."

"Then what is it?"

I halted my steps and turned to face him. He was a sight; sawdust in his hair and up his entire back, and an expression of being completely lost. Once again, I found a deeper level of how far in love I could fall with him. His two favorite words came to mind, and he must have sensed it or seen my color shift because he raised his index finger at me in the now unspoken *'DON'T'* warning we both understood. I stepped closer and began to dust off his hair and shoulders. He grinned again as I did so, and I stopped.

"That. *THAT* right there."

"What?"

"That crooked half grin of yours. Jesus, Mary and Joseph; it kills me Kane. Every time. *Every* Goddamn time. There is no way I can resist it."

The grin had grown into a full smile at my use of his name, and it remained there.

"So? There ya have it. My fatal flaw." I finished, and his smile broadened.

"Your secret, is safe with me."

"Yeah, but you keep that grin up? *I'M* not safe with you."

"Thank you? I think?"

"You're welcome. And turn around; you have sawdust all over the back of your clothes."

"And you do not." He replied, and it was my turn to smile.

"That's because my back was never on the floor."

"Very true. But we should inspect your knees."

"Already dusted them off, knees to shins. I'm good."

"That? Is an understatement, my wife to be."

I have to confess; I liked the sound of that.

#

I had recovered enough after two cigarettes and thirty minutes of leaning against Kane's chest to consider venturing to the store. It was mid-November, and the air was not just crisp; it was cold. Still, he always sat with me as I smoked. His presence was warming in more than just shared body heat. When I had snuffed the second Marlboro Light, I patted his thigh.

"Let me go get the bird. Any other special requests? Besides an ample helping from aisle seven?"

"Only your safe and swift return. I can come along with you. I will if you want it."

"No babe, you have deadlines. I think I can manage this adventure on my own."

"There is not much you cannot manage, Diana." And the humming I felt as he spoke was a pleasure. Yes sir; this was all I would ever need. I got to my feet and Kane fell in to step beside me as I headed out to my Mustang. He kissed me gently before he reached and opened the car door for me. I scooted into the seat and he shut the door.

"Seat belt. And hurry home." I loved the sound of that word. Home. After a long time for me, and an eternity for Kane? We had managed to build just that. Funny how things happen that you never see coming.

"The biggest bird you can find." He called out as I backed out of the driveway. I waved and nodded. You got it, Kane. Biggest bird I can find.

#

I was no more than three-quarters of a mile from home when I spotted the hand painted sign on the shoulder of Route One. Chicks for sale. I had snapped my left finger up and turned the blinker on before I realized it. I travelled less than a quarter of a mile down the hard pack road when I found another sign scrawled in the same spray paint lettering. I pulled into the narrow driveway and drove the hundred feet to the house. I climbed out of the car and crossed to the front door, knocking twice on the oak. Less than fifteen seconds later it opened, and a friendly faced woman maybe ten years older than me answered. She smiled and stepped outside.

"You have the chicks for sale?"

"Why yes my dear, I do. An unexpected hatch just two days ago. We don't have the space in the coop."

"What breed of chicken?" I asked, and I realized I was giddy with excitement.

"Barred rocks of course! Hearty stock for these cold winters."

"I'll need one hen. Can you even tell when they're this young?"

"Of course, you can!" she said and laughed. "Come on honey, I'll show you how it's done."

I followed her to the coop. It was a good-sized enclosure; but she had been truthful. She had fifteen full sized hens residing in it, and any more would make it less a coop and more a Lawrence Jail overcrowding. Not if I can help it. She unlatched the door and stepped inside, motioning me to follow her. I did as she beckoned, but the sight of fifteen zebra chickens brought back the shower attack and I subconsciously flinched. In a nesting box less than eight inches from the ground was a large, striped hen. She fluffed her feathers as we approached, and blinked several times.

"Oh, just stop it Missy! Get. Shoo. Off with you now." The woman said as she waved her hands at the hen. It took a few seconds but the feathered mother finally did leave the box, and exposed her young babies.

I had never seen baby chicks before. Kane only had hens, and with no rooster around well there were no fertilized eggs. I stared down at them and grinned. They were ping pong balls of fluff and I was immediately in love. They were cuter than puppies sleeping with kittens. They rose up on their stick legs and milled about the inside of the box, tiny beaks opening and the sweetest chirps came from them. Little eyes blinking as they looked everywhere; taking it all in. My companion reached in and gently scooped one up. I was almost squealing with delight when she turned to me.

"This is how you *sex* a chick." She said, and with her free hand she gently grabbed both sides of the chick's head. I was horrified. Oh my God what was this sadistic bitch doing? She slowly lowered the hand that was supporting the chick until it was dangling, from its *HEAD*; between her finger and thumb. I was going to punch her dead in the face.

"See? This one's a rooster." She said, and nodded at the chick. No! I didn't *see*! All I saw was this adorable ball of fuzz about to get its head snapped off by a psycho closet chicken killer. What the fuck?

"His feet are up. A rooster is always a fighter, even this young."

I stopped and looked back at what she was doing. On closer examination, she was in no way hurting the little guy. And damn if she wasn't right! His little legs were raised up and his feet were almost to his chest, each toe curled as if ready to kick an opponent. A chicken version of a throat punch. I admired his spunk. She put him back in the box and gently scooped another ball of softness out. Again, she held its head between a thumb and forefinger and this time I watched its legs. They didn't rise up; in fact, they hung limp and lifeless. Oh my God she had killed it!

"Here's your hen, my dear!" she exclaimed, and I was stunned. She *JUST* murdered the poor thing! She gently slid her hand back under the chick, and once she did its legs became solid again in her palm. She let go of the tiny skull and the little lady was just blinking and looking around as if nothing had happened. Well I'll be damned! Even old sheepdogs have new tricks to learn. I smiled warmly at the woman that I had planned to pummel for poultry homicide not even a minute before.

"Did you only want the one?"

#

I practically skidded into our driveway fifteen minutes later then when I had left. Kane obviously heard my arrival and he was out of the workshop and across the yard in less time than it took for me to kill the engine. His eyes were narrowed and he scanned the road behind me. Satisfied nothing pursed me; he slowed his pace and approached the car with his head tilted slightly left in an unspoken question. He reached for the door and opened it for me. Gentleman through and through. Angus and Maureen had done well in raising this man.

"Is everything all right, Diana? You were not gone long enough to have made it to the grocery store."

"No. I didn't get there just yet."

"Are you okay? What happened?"

"Well? It's kind of a funny story. But I did complete my mission." I said, setting my shoulders back proudly as if I had just single handedly saved the entire city of Boston. Kane looked at me confused, but smiled despite it.

"Close your eyes and put out your hand." I said, and he eyed me suspiciously. After a moment, he smiled again and while still unsure; he did as I asked. He shut his eyelids and put his hand out. I reached into the pocket of my jacket and removed our newest flock member. I gently placed her into his much larger hand, and stepped back.

Kane opened his eyes and stared at the ball of softness and joy in his palm. It was a long moment that he stared down at her, but he eventually looked up at me. The amber was soft and warm, and a genuine smile had found its way to both his lips and his eyes.

"She is the biggest bird I could find."

Chapter Twenty-Six

Thirty-six hours ago, I was the more predatory of the two of us. I had pretty much attacked Kane in his workshop, and had then brought home a fuzz ball. Since then? I had braved a Saturday before Thanksgiving crowd in the grocery store instead of my intended Friday 'beat the rush'. I had successfully procured the biggest bird I could find and this time an actual twenty-one-pound turkey complete with trimmings; and made a cozy little nest and caged area for the ball of fluff I had placed into Kane's appreciative hand. Kane had been remarkably relaxed yesterday; he and Alejandro had completed all but one of the final orders and right on schedule.

Ahead actually, enough so that Kane had given the young man a few hours off early and slipped him an extra fifty dollars. In case he 'needed a pumpkin pie for his Mum' were his exact words and Alejandro beamed when he received it. It was his first job after all; and having been handed his first bonus had him walking with a new confidence. Yep. Someday, in the not too distant future; a young woman was going to find herself completely blessed if a young man named Alejandro falls in love with her.

I wondered about Kane's 'Mum'. Maureen. Did she see the same traits in Kane when he was younger? And did she smile inwardly knowing that between her warmth yet put up with no nonsense; and the lessons from Angus of 'all things manly', that in the future? A worn-out old sheepdog of a woman would find herself completely lost and somehow found when she fell in love with her son? While it would always be a little sad that I never got to meet them in person; their love and nurture and 'what's right is right' fingerprints were visible all over the six foot plus man I now lay beside in the early pre-dawn hours. Thank you both. You have no idea what a fine man he turned out to be.

Kane was sleeping peacefully; the smoothness of his breathing made me smile. It was a rare thing to observe him so completely resting. He was usually awake before I was and even if his eyes were closed; he was fully alert and in tune with me. It was wonderful to see him so relaxed. Even in his slumber he seemed to have that half grin just hiding around the corner and I reminded myself that Kane, this at ease; was far more important than my physical reaction to that grin and well *shit*! Just to Kane himself. I resisted the urge to run my fingers through his hair or nuzzle into his neck; he was *THAT* beautifully sound asleep. I closed my eyes and focused on the easy rhythm of his breath. It wasn't long before I fell into the same state of bliss, and I'm not sure exactly when I drifted off but I did.

#

The sky was beginning to lighten when I felt him wrap an arm around me, and it stirred me just enough to now indulge in both the wriggling closer to him and his hair in my fingers that I had denied myself a few hours earlier. It was a wonderful way to start a Sunday.

"Mmmmmh." I purred quietly as my nose found the crook of his collarbone and neck. Half draped across him; just lying together like this? It was the one place I knew I was safe from the world. His left arm gently pulled me closer against him. It was my favorite place to be.

"Mmmmmh." Kane replied and while the volume of it matched mine; the purr was not as gentle. I felt it within me, and it was a stronger hum than it should have been. I raised my head slightly and looked at him. His eyes were barely halfway open, and when I saw them I my breath caught. They were completely gold, and a hint of the iridescence was showing. Already.

My reaction did not go unnoticed by Kane. No, in fact nothing I thought or felt did it seemed but he had enough class not to corner me on whatever edge his *Enhancement* gave him. He really should have been a cop. He would know for a *fact* if somebody was lying, and all from the sound of their heartbeat. Hell of a talent! But then again; hearing people's heartbeats is not exactly one of those skills you can list on a resume.

"Are they glowing yet?" he asked softly. "I already know they are completely gold."

"How did you….." and I left the rest unspoken as a chuckle rumbled from his chest.

"Diana, this may only be the eighth December of my life that I will change, but it certainly not my first Blue month. Contrary to what you may think, Love? I *have* looked in the mirror."

"How? They were almost completely amber when we went to bed. Maybe a fleck or two of the gold, but they have never changed this fast Kane. Never." And his smile made one tug at the corners of my mouth. Damn he was irresistible. Almost…

"Don't. Do *not* say it out loud."

"And how do you know *THAT* as well?"

"Whenever any one of those three words you so enjoy torturing me with comes to your mind? You shift colors. And speaking of colors….yes my eyes *HAVE* changed this quickly before. You just have not been here to observe it before now. They have changed this quickly long before you were born. I told you. A Blue is the absolute worst."

I chewed on what Kane had said as I laid my head back down on to his shoulder. He was right, he *HAD* been going through Blue months long before I was born; and it made sense that he would know what happened to him and how quickly. After all, he had over a century to educate himself. I was considering all of these timelines and of course the wisdom Angus had passed to his only son, when Kane seized my hand in his. He was breathing heavier and there was a ragged edge to it.

"What? What's wrong?"

"You were running your fingers across my chest."

"Was I? Oh, I guess I was. A habit I've developed without realizing it. Your skin feels good. So, what's the problem?"

"It is driving me to the brink of madness."

"Jesus Kane, I'm sorry I didn't know it bothered you. I'll stop. My bad."

"It does *NOT* bother me Diana. It sets me on fire."

"And the problem with that is what, exactly?" I said, the Devil himself tugging at my words.

"It will *not* be a problem for me." He said, and the tone and manner in which he spoke told me this was no teasing verbal foreplay. I raised my head to look at him, and his eyes were glowing more than they had when he first woke. His forehead was glistening with droplets of sweat, and I immediately feared he was sick.

"Jesus, babe! Your half drenched! Are you all right? You catch a fever or something? What the fuck? You were sleeping so wonderfully not even two hours ago."

I tried to wrest my hand loose from his grip to feel his head, but he held it firm. I frowned as I tried again to get loose of his hold, but he was not having any part of it. I had known all along that despite my shit talking and threats there was not a damn thing I could ever *DO* to Kane unless he allowed it. *Knowing* it is one thing. Being slapped in the face with it in something as simple as being unable to get my hand free was another. I felt a simultaneous wave of anger and fear.

"Two hours ago, it was still the night of the New Moon. No moonlight reaches the Earth on that night."

"And?" I asked, still half attempting to wriggle my hand free. I am stubborn, and I am proud. It was useless and I knew it, but what can I say? I'm Irish.

"The sun is up. The New Moon is over. I told you that I would feel it immediately."

"Why won't you let go of my hand?"

"Diana, if I do? And you run your fingers across my chest again? I may hurt you."

"What? What the fuck kind of fucked up thing is *that* to say?"

"I asked for the biggest turkey you could find, correct?" he asked, his golden eyes glowing less brightly now but still reflective. I nodded my agreement. Kane closed his eyes and inhaled deeply. He released it, then opened his eyes again and looked at me. The gold had gotten deeper, and the half grin made its way to him once again.

"It is not just my appetite for *food* that is going to surge." He said, and the gold grew richer yet sharper. I remember the first time I saw that color and depth. The hens didn't lay one single egg for days.

"The sweat? That is from the sheer effort it took not to be all over you right now. It took *THAT* much. And there are still thirteen more days to go. Do you understand now?"

I nodded that I did, and I felt his grasp on my hand loosen somewhat. He glanced at me once more, and deciding I understood what he had warned me about; he let loose completely. He closed his eyes and sighed.

"I am sorry. It is not your fault, and you had no idea. I can't help it. Being this close to you? And this close to a Blue? It may tear me apart."

I felt something else grip me; and it wasn't his hand on my hand, and it wasn't Kane. Lucifer himself had shown up and when he did; he tapped my shoulder. I didn't even have to turn and look at him; I already knew I was going to listen. I allowed my hand to rest gently on Kane's chest before I felt the grin spread across my face. I ran my fingers across Kane's chest and down his stomach.

I'm not completely sure the order of what happened next, but when we finished some hours later? I understood exactly what John Cougar meant when he wrote the song *Hurt So Good*.

CHAPTER TWENTY-SEVEN

Four days later, I was staring in awe at the scattered remains of a Thanksgiving meal. There really were none; it was more an entire countertop of empty dinnerware. A stray fried onion or green bean in the casserole dish, a lick of mashed potatoes in the bowl; but the turkey was completely skeletal. Kane was not kidding when he said his appetite was going to increase. I looked over at him and smiled. He was stretched out on the couch, a flannel shirt over a T shirt and the ever present Levis jeans. Miraculously his stomach had not exploded from the volume of food he had consumed; I seriously have no idea where he put it all. He hadn't even undone the top button of his jeans. I couldn't believe he was still awake. The amount of tryptophan in his body would have knocked out an elephant. He was watching football; the first quarter of the Cowboys and the Redskins, and his eyes were completely open and alert.

And he thought *I* was amazing. I shook my head and smiled. Kane glanced in my direction and scowled, raising his finger in a silent warning; but he was grinning.

"Don't." he said, and I started laughing.

"How do you *know*?" I exclaimed, a giggle still present in my voice.

"I told you. Your color shifts."

"To what?" I asked.

"Pink." He replied, and I burst out laughing again.

"Really! Of all fucking colors? *Pink*?"

He nodded, and the grin became a full smile. His teeth were brilliant and large, and the reflective gold of his eyes danced as he watched me laughing. Pink! Hot damn! Now *that* was funny.

"Yes. It seems that when you think that I am 'cute', 'precious' or 'adorable', you color embodies that you are feeling girly."

"I didn't think that was possible." I snickered, and moved to clear some of the rubble of dishes from the countertop. He was beside me before I knew it, a gentle brush of his lips on my neck. He was moving fast; even by Kane standards. The Blue was indeed going to be one bad mother.

"Let me help. In fact, just let me do this. You cooked everything. Fair is fair. And at the risk of repeating myself? It was the most fantastic Thanksgiving dinner I have ever enjoyed. Everything was delicious. Thank you again."

"Really? I didn't think you liked it." I said, waving my hand toward the wreckage of empty tableware. He scanned the debris and chuckled.

"There's practically no need to rinse the dishes Kane; I think you licked most of them clean."

He smiled as his name hummed within him, and it was infectious. Pink or not; the man was adorable though I kept the word unspoken. He nodded his appreciation, and began to gather the scattering of casserole pans. I brought the turkey platter to the trash can, and looked at him.

"You want to chew these bones or anything?" I said, and was surprised to see the counter was completely cleared. In the time it had taken me to walk four steps, he had it done and had wiped it clean. Jesus, this was going to be one bad mammajamma for him; and it may put me in need of a hip replacement. Still; the house would be spotless inside of ten minutes. There were some advantages to his *Enhancement* outside of the bedroom. I grinned as I thought about the advantages inside of it as well.

"You are shifting red, Diana. Do not tease me."

"I am doing no such thing. You are hallucinating because of the massive dose of tryptophan coursing through your bloodstream. You probably need a nap." I walked back across the kitchen and placed the platter next to the sink. Kane looked me up and down, and grinned. The gold was rich and deep, and I didn't need any *Enhancement* to see the edge behind the color. Oh boy.

"No, I do not. But going to bed is not a bad idea." He said, and the smile took on the same gleam as his eyes. Oh shit.

"Kane, you can't be serious. We just got *out* of bed like two hours ago." I protested, but I felt a warmth rise in my skin. The way he was looking at me? Jesus. This must be what a rabbit feels like when a fox stares at it. While I didn't think I would wind up actually dead; he may just kill me yet. I took a half step backwards. I had waited too long; he had seen the shift in my color and was covering me with kisses and strong hands. I was backed up to the countertop and he pressed fully against me. I had to be glowing like lava because that is as hot as my skin felt under his touch. There was no escape, not that I wanted one; and I ran my hands through his hair. A growl came from him and he lifted me up and laid me across the counter.

"Jesus Kane, this one will not survive a Blue." I panted as he ran his hands down my body.

"I'll replace it. No projects until Monday." He rasped, and the intensity of what he was feeling thundered in my ribs. But will I survive until Monday? That was the last coherent thought I had before I was lost in the physical pleasures that Kane was visiting on me.

#

The post-game interviews were on the TV by the time I was able to catch my breath and form any semblance of thought. Kane was smiling warmly at me and his eyes were bright, and I just stared into them. They truly were magnificent. The glow from the Pull he was feeling was there of course, but the varying shades of gold were breathtaking. They were liquid metal, and each shift in them spoke volumes. He was incapable of lying from behind them.

"Are you able to smoke yet?" he asked, and I glanced down towards my crotch.

"I might be already." I said, and he laughed gently. His laugh was as honest as his eyes. God I was in love with this man!

"I would apologize, but I do not wish to lie to you."

"I'd know if you were anyway, Kane." There was the smile. I loved to see that, especially as big as his teeth were today. "My heartbeat and color might tell you things, but your eyes and the feel of your words tell me things too."

"I am very glad for that, Love. Very glad indeed."

"Help me up, would ya? I'm not sure I can do this on my own."

"You're welcome." He said, that half grin present again on his features. Damn. It was going to be a very long eight days. Thank you, God. I groaned as he helped me to my feet. He held me there until I was sure my knees would support me, and once he was satisfied they would do part of their job? He smiled and began handing me back my clothes. The kitchen floor had become an assortment of garments, as if somebody had thrown a hand grenade into the closet. Still; I was glad for his kindness. Had I bent down for my jeans I may not have been able to stand back up. I held the counter with one hand as I slid a leg into the denim. It was an effort. My fingers felt unevenness in the surface, and I looked down. Five long, deep scratches had penetrated the wood. I glanced to Kane's fingers. Both hands had dried blood flecks on the fingertips.

"Jesus Kane, are you all right?" He smiled, but the adrenaline had already dumped into my system. Thank God for it because it was the only way I could stand on my own. I grabbed his hands and examined them. Small spots of blood; but no wounds. I looked up at him questioningly. He shrugged slightly and grinned.

"What can I say? I was enjoying you. Very much so."

"What the fuck? Is that your blood?"

"Of course it is! I would never hurt you."

"There's no cuts, Kane!" and he smiled.

"There were. It is a Blue that's coming Diana; and a Super on top of it. I could probably heal from a gunshot wound in less than five minutes. Not that I have any interest in testing that theory."

"A *Super*?" I asked, and Kane's smile faded. He nodded and pulled his T shirt over his head.

"Explain, please." I said, and he sighed. He was pacing before he realized it. I had expected nothing less.

"A Super Moon. It is when the moon is closer to the Earth than normal. It happens from time to time."

"Well didn't we just get fucked in *THIS* trifecta!" I spat the words, and Kane stopped his stride and grinned at me. Sometimes I swear the man was a lunatic. That thought made me start to laugh. In actuality? He was! God, now that's funny!

"What is so amusing?" he asked, and I couldn't help myself. I told him what I had just thought. He joined me in the dark humor of the situation, and it was good to hear him laugh. When we had stopped, I looked up into his eyes.

"And what had you grinning? I don't see what would make you happy about a Super Blue in December. That's just some bullshit right there."

"You said *we*."

Perfectly, gloriously, fucked up.

The very definition of every great love story.

I was the luckiest woman on Earth.

CHAPTER TWENTY-EIGHT

Kane had refused to replace or repair, the countertop. While I had initially thought he was crazy; six days later I found myself smiling at the scratch marks. There were four different sets of them. Apparently, he *HAD* been enjoying himself. Not bad Jimmy, not bad at all. I moved to get another cup of coffee and my hips put my ego in check. Still two days to go. And nights. Shit. I smiled in spite of it. I ran my fingertips across the damaged wood. Kane had sealed the sites with varnish, but the ridges were still tangible. I giggled at my own insanity. There *really* was something wrong with me. He stepped through the door as I was finishing my laughter, and his eyes went immediately to where my hands rested. A devilish smile came to him, and the gold was deepening.

"Care to add to them?" he asked, and the vibration within me told me he was *not* kidding. I hung my head and scoffed.

"Are you going to *WHEEL* me to my car in two days when I have to go 'camping'?"

"I could call you a cab." He said, and the gold grew deeper still. Shit. I was saved by the telephone ringing. Thank you, Alexander Graham Bell; I might have died. Kane flashed me another smile before answering it. His teeth were enormous and so white they were almost glowing as much as his eyes were. I felt myself shift red. Damn. I was, in fact? Insane. Or at least a masochist.

"Hello." He said, his eyes on mine and the smile still lingering. In a blink the richness of the gold vanished as did his smile. His jaw set harshly and his eyes went so cold I actually shivered. He was beyond lethal. He was beyond frightening. Kane? Was terrifying.

"When?" he snapped. I was paralyzed. There was no warm vibration in my body when he spoke. His words drove a deeper coldness into me, and I began to wonder if it was possible for my blood to freeze inside my veins. I had worked outside at night during January before, and those shifts felt like a Miami day compared to the Arctic I was experiencing in our kitchen. My knees started to tremble, and scratches in countertops had nothing to do with it.

"Where?"

My hands followed suit with my knees. I was no longer paralyzed. I had crossed that boundary at his second word. I was now petrified. The thermostat may have been set on 74 but it sure felt like we were approaching absolute zero. Kane's body had gone completely rigid the moment his eyes had shifted, but his shoulders were now shaking. The pre-dawn morning outside the post office had nothing on what I was feeling right now. Thought, or my capacity to form one, had disappeared.

"On my way." Was all he said, and he slammed down the phone. I wanted to ask, but I had lost the power of speech. He exhaled sharply, dragging his hand down his face. He finally looked directly at me, and I felt every cell in my body stop. We were no longer approaching it; we had arrived. Absolute zero.

"Let's go." He said, and somehow even the frigid feel of his words was warm enough to unlock my body. I felt my heart start again, and my lungs had instinctively inflated once more. I shoved my feet into a pair of boots and grabbed for my jacket. Kane had already headed towards the door, and he stopped. He glanced back over his right shoulder at me, his hand on the front door knob.

"Jimmy? Get your gun. I'll meet you in the truck."

#

I yanked the door open and scrambled into the passenger seat, shifting the .357 in its holster as I did. It had been some time since I had it on my hip but it felt familiar; and my movements were so practiced it was automatic. The duty belt was still rigged out as it always had been. Any cop will tell you; you keep the identical gear in the same spot day after day. The location of the items remains constant and your muscles remember where to find them. This instinctive knowledge comes in quite handy when you're in the middle of a scuffle or and out and out melee. Your left hand *KNOWS* where the cuffs are, your fingers instinctively find the speed loaders. You don't even have to look or think about it; it's that automatic. This is what might, just *might*; get you home at the end of the day rather than on a gurney bleeding or being zipped into black plastic.

I hadn't even completely shut the truck door before gravel was spitting out from under the tires. I remained silent, and I looked over at Kane. His eyes were focused enough they could have cut through steel, and while it was scary it was not as terrifying as it had been moments earlier. Or maybe I had shifted back into Officer Jameson so quickly I had donned the armor of 'no matter how fucking scared you are you do it anyway' without realizing it. I returned my gaze to the windshield, and did not glance over at him again. Whatever it was, wherever we were going? I had complete and unquestioning faith in him, and in the knowledge that no matter what it was I would be right there beside him. If not in front of him. Kane may be *Enhanced*, but I was in love. That fact may have made me more dangerous than he was. Or at least a close second.

"Maria never came home from school."

The words hung heavy in the cab of the truck. Kane was barreling through town, and I understood exactly why. I had half a mind to mash my foot on top of his on the gas pedal. Maria was Alejandro's eight-year-old sister.

IS Jimmy; *IS*. You don't know that yet.

"How long overdue?" is all I asked. Oh yes, Officer Jameson was completely back and in full force.

"Forty-five minutes. But she is never late."

I nodded but said nothing. A wintry déjà vu crept across me. Almost a year and a half ago; a small for his age, thirteen-year-old boy named Timmy was also late for the first time in his life. And the last time. Fuck Lord, don't let *ME* be late this time too.

Kane had his hand on my knee before I knew it, though I never saw him look at me; and my peripheral vision was pretty damn good.

"What color?"

"Post office."

"Sounds about right."

#

Kane skidded to a halt in front of a house that given any other circumstances I would have described as charming. It was nestled back amongst now naked branches of what I took to be azaleas and rhododendrons, but a few evergreen shrubs still protected the cottage blue siding from the winter. I glanced up. There was maybe thirty minutes left of New England gray daylight. A quarter mile further down the road the landscape gradually shifted from cozy woods to the edges of salt marsh. Maria's bus stop was almost a tenth of a mile in the opposite direction. Forty-five minutes overdue was indeed reason for worry. Even as small a girl as she was would have been home by now. I was out of the truck and striding up the road in the direction she would have been coming from. My eyes scanned the tree line, watchful for a hint of movement. I studied the silt patches that were scattered on the rough pavement for her size four footprints, and for any that did not meet the same criteria.

It had been breezy that day, but not enough to have erased the evidence of her walk *to* the bus stop. I found three different places where she had stepped that morning. Based by the distance between each sneaker print; she took approximately a fourteen-inch stride. I also determined by one location I found her steps? Maria liked to skim stones. Her footprints had turned to face the edge of the pond, and tiny fingertips had picked up what I assumed were flat rocks. Her footprints showed she took two steps before skimming them. I stuffed that observation into my 'when we find her, I will come skimming with her' file; in the drawer of 'hope against hope'. I took two steps before skimming too. My heart thudded momentarily in my chest. Jesus God! Let us find her. And find her in time.

Kane was three feet away before I heard his feet on the gravel. He glanced my way but also studied the edge of the woods. I knew his senses were far sharper than mine and he was seeing, hearing and smelling further into the trees than I could. I glanced to my right and sank to my knees. He was beside me before they both met the ground.

"What?" his voice had softened somewhat, but the iron was still beneath the surface. I pointed to another silt section in the road. A size four track was visible, and this one was headed in the direction towards the house. Kane saw it and nodded his head. I watched his eyes as they lost any shred of humanity. He had spotted the same thing I had.

Not ten inches from Maria's tiny footprint, the front half of a work boot had also left its impression. An adult sized work boot. It was headed in the same direction that hers were. Judging by the pattern? It was a Timberland. I leaned forward and threw up.

#

"Diana? Are you okay?"

I nodded that I was and wiped the back of my hand across my mouth. I didn't have any mints, so a Marlboro

Light would be the only freshening of my breath. I lit one and drew deeply on it. I glanced down and was relieved to see that the deposit of my lunch was nowhere near the spot where the two footprints were. Thank God. I didn't want to be the one who fucked up the evidence. I nodded my approval without even realizing it.

"Cop. Through and through." Kane muttered, and I looked up at him questioningly. He was still rigid and on task; but the half grin he wore had genuine warmth behind it and I was never so thankful for anything in my life. For a split second? I felt a hair less terrible. It was not much, but based on the creeping darkness I felt surrounding us? It was exactly what the doctor ordered.

"Speaking of which, did the fuckers get here yet?"

"Not yet Love, but they are on their way."

"And you know this how?" I said, and felt the venom in my words. I wasn't really mad at Kane. I was just mad. And scared. Half-crazy with worry and dread. He flashed me a brilliant smile.

"I have excellent hearing, Jimmy."

#

It was almost a full minute before I heard the traces of the sirens Kane had already detected. When I did, I shot a look his way. His jaw was still set, but he gave me a quick wink. Yes sir Kane Woods; your hearing is above reproach. And even now, in the darkest of dark; he was concerned for me. Jesus Christ, I was the most fortunate woman on the planet. Ever. The briefest moment of 'okay' had come and gone as I saw the strobes of blue flashing through the trees. I stepped forward onto the road, standing between where the cruiser was coming and the small patch of sandy Earth that was the introduction to a tale I feared would end a tragedy. The trooper stopped when I raised my hand, and I pointed to the place where two contrasting footprints made the chilly evening seem even colder.

#

Almost a dozen more Staties had descended on the small town of Rowley before the dark had fully swallowed the afternoon; in addition to the local police and my former brethren from the Essex County Sheriff's Department. Kane had slipped off after the arrival of the first Trooper and I understood his reasoning. He now had a criminal record, and though I was 'retired'; he would not jeopardize my good standing with law enforcement by being seen with me. Yes, Angus and Maureen had done more than just a great job in raising their son. They had surpassed the bar.

I didn't have to see him to know that he was present. He could say my name or speak *TO* me from almost a quarter mile away, and I could feel the slightest of humming in my body. This was an unexpected facet of the destined lifelong mate, and one I was unaware of until this terrible night. While I had never imagined the possibility of it; its existence proved to be a handy thing especially in a situation such as the one we found ourselves in. I wondered if he knew it. I returned the favor, and I whispered his name out loud. A gentle vibration within me a few seconds later told me it was a two-way street. I'll be damned. Cosmic radio communication. Imagine fucking that.

Search parties of both blue and civilian were formed, and each group had a set direction to embark on. My band of six headed back towards town, skirting the trees and penetrating the woods about ten feet or so. Had we more bodies I would have pressed for twenty feet, but it was still a fresh search and I was thankful so many had arrived in such a short time. It was just shy of three hours since Kane got the call from Alejandro before I was on the edge of a line of six making their way towards town. We stayed even with each other; it was the most efficient way to perform a search, and the going was smooth but not rushed. Each member surveyed both the ground as well as the surrounding terrain. Somewhere in the midst of it; I felt more than I knew that Kane was covering five times the area we were and he was not missing a shred of anything. His senses were ridiculous on a normal day. Two nights before a Blue? And a Super to boot? Spiderman would be a blind deaf mute in comparison.

It had taken the better part of two hours to walk the road to the bus stop, and aside from the occasional matching sneaker tread of Maria's; all of which headed towards the bus stop and away from the house? No new evidence was observed. We had reached the end of the road, and I was the farthest right of the line. The T intersection was solid asphalt; there would be no pockets of sand to further assist us in what may have happened or which way she may have gone. I ran my fingers through my spikes and sucked in a deep breath of frustration.

Fuck! Just fuck! Kiss my Irish ass and Fuck all over again. I lit a cigarette and inhaled deeply. I had smoked it nearly full when my eyes came to rest on a something that froze my bones. I vaguely remember hearing the filter hit the ground. It sounded strange and echoed inside my head; though there was no reason for it to.

I don't remember anything after that.

Chapter Twenty-Nine

I sat up like I had been launched from a catapult and attempted to get to my feet. Strong hands seized my shoulders and gently pressed me backwards. I was clawing at the air and struggling to get loose; but to no avail. Why was it so bright out here? What the fuck? Who brought in the overhead lighting? About goddamn time! What kind of a mobile command was this? Half assed horse shit. Staties had to be in charge, dumb sonofabitches; my guys were *WAY* better at this. When I finally let my eyes adjust; I focused on my surroundings. I was inside of a building somewhere. The walls were white, and there were fluorescent lights on the ceiling. What the shit?

I shoved against whatever it was I was laying on with my right hand and swept my left arm across my chest to clear whatever it was that was obstructing me. My left elbow smacked against something solid. It was hard as stone, but warm to my skin. I looked to see what it was, and realized it was an arm. What the Hell? Where was I? I followed the arm left, and it met a shoulder. I continued my eyes journey and my breath caught when they settled on two radiating golden eyes and the biggest smile of blinding white teeth I had ever seen.

"Easy now, Jimmy. Easy." He whispered, and the love behind his hushed tone roared through my bones. Kane. He was here. Wherever here was? He was with me. It would be all right. I blinked several times and then looked around. I felt my eyebrows plunge towards my nose when I realized I was in an exam room in some sort of medical facility.

"How the fuck...." I began, and Kane shook his head gently. His smile was there, and it was a physical touch the way his eyes met mine.

"You collapsed in the intersection."

"What? That's some bullshit right there. I don't *fucking* collapse."

Kane angled his chin downwards and looked at me from the tops of his eyes. His eyebrows were arched and if I didn't know better; I would swear the right one was raised slightly higher than the left. Seems while the word 'indeed' had managed to find a home in my vocabulary; the right eyebrow move had found a toehold in his expressions. We were rubbing off on each other that was for sure. I found that I liked the idea. Okay, *FINE*! Maybe I had gone weak in the knees a time or two after a particularly good kiss from Kane or a marathon sex session; but I had only collapsed *ONCE*. One time! A pussy; that does not make. And besides when I did, it was because he had said the word.....

"Diana? Diana! Jesus Christ Love, what is it?" I heard the panic in his voice, but I felt my fear louder within me. I blinked and slowly looked at him. His eyes were blazing and he was focused solely on me, so much that if he stared much longer I'm sure my head would explode. I blinked again, and it all snapped into place and proper time.

"*The fucking truck*!" I roared, and I was moving so quickly that I had actually gotten a foot on the ground before Kane could react. *That* was saying something. Once he had again grasped control of me, he firmly pushed me back on to the bed. My mind was racing but the thoughts were razor sharp. The last thing I had seen was a faded red pickup truck with a ding and scrape on the bumper. It was parked not five hundred feet from where I had been standing. And the only other time I had collapsed? Well isn't *THAT* just a kick in the ass! The word Kane had used was *decay*. Funny how the sight of the piece of shit truck, *AND* the one-word Kane used to describe the smell of its driver; had the *EXACT* same effect on me. My stomach flipped as it all crashed down on me.

"Jimmy?"

It was a different voice than Kane's that spoke my name; but it was a familiar one. I slowly looked up at a State Trooper's uniform. Under the wide brim of a Smokey the Bear hat? Were the blue eyes of a nonsmoking Scotty from Lawrence Jail. I stared for at least ten seconds, and then I started laughing. I'm sure it appeared as the beginnings of hysteria, and it may very well have been; but of all the people I *never* expected to see? Scotty topped the list. And a Trooper? Holy shit!

"I will give you both some time." Kane said softly, and he slipped out of the room. Scotty watched his exit, and I knew Kane was more than aware that he was being observed. Scotty nodded once Kane had rounded the corner of the hall, and then he turned his eyes back to me. The blue of his shirt seemed dull compared to the brightness of his eyes, and I couldn't believe I was looking at Scotty. Damn! Funny world.

"You're all right then?" he asked, and stepped into the room.

'Yeah! Yeah man, I'm good. Probably just some low blood sugar kinda bullshit thing. You know I'm the worst about eating right."

He nodded, and stepped completely into the room. He glanced around, and quietly closed the door behind him. Satisfied no one was concerned by it, he then came over to the bedside chair and slid into it.

"Jimmy? I'm not gonna ask how Woods is here. I'm not even gonna ask why he's calling you Diana; I already know that answer. One look at him? And the way he looks at you? Shit, I don't need a gold shield to figure that out. The fact that he is calling you Diana tells me you feel the same."

Scotty paused, affording me the opportunity to argue his summary. When I didn't, he exhaled; looked to the door and then back to me. His eyes were brighter now, because the smile he wore was a genuine one; and its truth had found a way into the blue.

"I'm happy for you, Jimmy. I really am *HAPPY* for you. I don't care how he's here, or why; and I will never ask. God knows you more than deserve it. Aside from you? I'm the only one who knows who he is, and what he looks like. Or that he's even *alive*. It's safe with me."

"Thank you, Scotty. You have no idea."

"Nope! No, I don't!" he said, and laughed before continuing, "Nor do I want to."

We both laughed at that, and when we had finished, he smiled again and nodded his head in approval.

"How's the wrist?" he asked, jerking his head towards my left hand. I raised it to show him it was as good as new, and his eyes fell to the ring. He grabbed my hand and pulled it closer to his face for a better examination. He turned my hand slightly left and then right, looking at every detail of the piece. When he was done, he looked up at me and nodded his approval. It was my turn to smile, and he matched it.

"He designed it, didn't he? That's a custom ring." Scotty said, motioning his head slightly towards the still closed door.

"That he did."

Scotty's smile grew larger, and I felt a small giggle come from within me.

"Jimmy? My watch is finally over. I don't ever have to worry about you again."

We both laughed again. No truer words had ever been spoken. So long as I remembered to be patient and wait for the dawn to completely break before heading home? Scotty was right. He would not have to worry for me. Kane Woods would never permit anything bad to happen to me so long as he lived. And after one hundred and twenty-seven years? He was an expert.

"Statie, huh? Wow." I said, and laughter once more filled the room.

"Yeah, well? I didn't suffer a career ending injury."

#

Scotty didn't linger long; he seemed to sense Kane was probably dying an agonizing death outside and just down the hall. Scotty had a wife; and he mentioned that he could only imagine what it would be like to be this close and not able to be present if she was hurt. He opened the door and spoke louder than necessary.

"Well, Jimmy? It's great to see you again; and I'm glad that you're okay."

"Thank you, Scotty. It's been great to see you too."

Kane poked his head around the doorway before Scotty had taken a step out of the room. He looked at me ensuring I was all right; which I was. He stepped out from behind the wall and stood to his full six foot plus height. Scotty stopped and their eyes met. Both men had their shoulders set, and for the briefest of seconds I wasn't completely sure what was going to happen.

"I don't believe we've met. I'm Scott. I used to work with Officer Jameson. Three and a half years, before I jumped ship in April to become a Statie." Scotty said, extending his right hand. Kane grasped it and shook it firmly.

"I'm Kane."

"Kane. Nice to meet you, sir. Take good care of her."

"That is my plan."

"One I'm sure you will succeed with, no matter how difficult she makes it."

"It *can* be a challenge." Kane said, and the grin stole across his features as his eyes cut to me. Scotty chuckled slightly and nodded.

"Yes, it can. Still; something tells me you're the man for the job. And congratulations. Jimmy has a shiny new ring. I've never seen her wear jewelry."

"For some reason? She agreed. I am not stupid enough to let too much time pass; she may come to her senses." Kane said, and the grin became a full smile.

"I know what you mean." Scotty said, and held up his left hand for Kane to see the gold band that circled his ring finger. Kane glanced at it, and then back to Scotty's eyes. They nodded shortly to each other.

"I didn't give Susan more than three months to change her mind. Act quickly Kane, before it's too late."

"Advice I will follow."

Scotty turned back to me, smiled and made his exit. Once he had, Kane was right beside the bed.

"Scott was one of the ones who pulled me off of Martinez. There is *no way* he does not remember...." Kane said, and let his eyes wander to the now open and empty doorway of the exam room.

"Sure there is, Kane." I began, and the feel of his name made him smile and return his eyes to mine. "There is nothing for him *TO* remember. He joined the Staties in *April*, remember? You graced me with your presence in *June*."

"Jesus Christ. You cops are a scary lot. Thin Blue Line indeed."

"I have no idea to what you are speaking; my good sir."

"Jesus, I love you. How does a Christmas Eve wedding sound?"

"Perfect. But what's your sudden rush?"

"The marriage license is only good for sixty days. And I agree with 'Scotty'. I cannot risk you coming to your senses."

"Fine. Now that we have *THAT* settled; go find that prick of a doctor to release me. Or give me the AMA papers. Maria is still out there. And Georgia parks his truck just around the corner. Go Fido! Now, or so help me God I'm walking out of here in this johnnie. And not even *YOU* will stop me."

Kane raised his hands in the 'I surrender' pose once again.

"I do not doubt this. Not for a second. Get dressed; I will fetch the doctor."

Chapter Thirty

The sun was kissing the horizon as we got back to the street where Alejandro and his family lived. Kane was doing his best to appear calm; but the tapping of his left foot as he drove screamed of the Pull. He had maybe thirty-six hours before the Super Blue of a December swallowed him. While I admired his effort? One glance told me the depth of his struggle. It was twenty-eight degrees and Kane was sweating, and it had nothing to do with me. The sight of him on the kitchen floor after the Blood flashed through my mind's eye, and I shivered as I imagined what I may discover in two mornings. I shot a glance towards the sky. Keep him safe. That is all I ask. I will beg if You need me to.

Even in the dim light, his eyes were iridescent. Jesus, they swirled with every thought, feeling and sensation he experienced. It was stunning to watch, and I felt a pang of remorse that what he was experiencing was a far cry from anything happy. I'd have given my right arm for the gold to shift deep. The rest of my days in a wheel chair would a fair exchange if he didn't reflect the frantic desperation I was feeling as well. Kane had his hand on my knee before either of us realized it. We were so in synch with each other that it was as automatic as breathing. I looked down and smiled. My left hand had already found his thigh; a half second before his hand rested on my knee. Destined indeed.

The out of place faded red farm truck was in the exact position it was when I had 'collapsed' the prior evening. That made it even more out of place. Any decent neighbor would have joined the search. The truck had not budged an inch; a fact illustrated even more clearly by the silhouette of blacktop under it. A dusting of snow had fallen overnight, and no tire tracks combined with a crisp outline dictated he had not moved the vehicle. Maggot scumbag piece of shit. I had been too kind last month.

Even my vast vocabulary of swear words were at a loss. There simply weren't enough combinations to string together to even scrape the surface for the hate and fury I felt.

Georgia was involved. I knew it in my bones, as sure as I felt Kane's words. It was that rock solid, *KNOWING*. Every human being has been granted a 'gut' feeling, or reaction. For those of us who seek out being a cop? It is more than the average serving. The problem lies in this. You cannot present your gut as evidence. While it is rarely wrong; it is still intangible and an abstract force. The rules in a Court of Law require that any evidence is subject to be examined and scientifically tested by opposing counsel. Even a half snake defense lawyer is not going to admit they *know* their client is a maggot. A full-on viper? Oh Hell no. And yet, I *KNEW*.

"Kane, any sign of her?" I asked. He briefly smiled and tilted his nose through the cracked window that a block before had been rolled tightly shut. Seemed he too had the same gut feeling; though he never said a word. He closed his eyes and inhaled deeply. To the casual eye, he appeared to be trying to wake himself with the sub-freezing air. My eye was not casual. And I knew Kane and what he could sense.

"No. She is not close, or I would know it."

"Fuck." I muttered.

"Agreed."

#

The following twenty-four hours were a blur. The snow, while less than two inches, was just enough to have rendered the noses of the search dogs useless. Still, the K9s and their handlers crisscrossed through the trees; clinging desperately to the hope that in a sheltered spot where no snow had fallen the dogs might catch a scent. It was frustrating, heartbreaking and exhausting. When the sun rose the next morning? I was frozen, worn out and beyond sad. I was devastated. Most kids taken by strangers were dead inside of three hours. A pathetically cold fact, but a fact none the less. Maria had been missing for close to forty hours. While it offered a glimmer of hope to her mother, Alejandro and her two older sisters Isabella and Rosa; it strangled my heart. The lack of a body spoke of two things to me. One, we simply had not discovered it yet. Or two, which was worse; she was being held somewhere, and I tried to prevent myself from imagining what was happening to her if she was. I was not as successful as I had hoped. Bile surged and burned my throat, and it was sheer stubborn Irish pride that kept it from painting the snow. I coughed, and inhaled deeply. It was ragged.

"Drink this, Love." A whisper found my ear, and a warm mug of coffee was thrust into my numb hands. Kane assisted my cold stiffened fingers in wrapping around it, and I looked up into the soft golden light. I was about to drop where I stood, and he had sensed it. Yes, Scotty; your watch is over. The softness vanished as Kane scanned the tree line. A steely light filled them, and the air felt tropical in comparison to what I felt as I watched him. I swallowed the heavenly warmth of the coffee, and realized Kane had made it. Nobody could brew a pot like he could. And I knew *CAUWFEE*.

"Jesus. Thank you." I whispered, and took another sip. "I'm not even going to ask how you got it here still this hot. Your truck hasn't moved."

"I am sorry to disappoint, but Alejandro's mother does own a coffee pot." Was his reply, and he smiled as I followed his eyes to the house scarcely fifty feet away.

"Kane, on your worst day? You could never disappoint me." His smile flashed in the early gloom, and then faded.

"Diana? Today *is* one of my worst days. And I am taking you home. You can rest for a few hours, and then you must go."

I stared at him as if he had lost his mind. In my book, he had. All the marbles had escaped the bag. Go? Not happening.

"Are you out of your goddamn mind? Go? I don't think so. Not a fucking chance."

"I AM NOT ASKING YOU WOMAN!" he snarled, and his eyes were blazing a few scant inches from mine.

Even my heritage and last name quieted as I stared into them. It was the coldest inferno I had ever seen; and it chilled my marrow more than fifteen hours in the dark had succeeded in doing. I had never been comfortable with fear, but simply being afraid would have been a welcome experience. I teetered between terror and horror. I couldn't form a question; never mind muster my eyes into returning the fire of Ireland. His nose was practically touching mine, and for the first time in my life? I wanted to shrink away. Kane saw it, though I don't know if it was my color, my heartbeat or my eyes. Perhaps it was all three. Whatever it was; it softened him slightly.

He was still deadly serious, but realized how badly he had frightened me. A wave of guilt washed across the brilliant golden hues, but it was short lived. The resolve returned, and while less threatening it was just as strong. A thought formed in the midst of my fear.

"What do you mean, today is one of your worst days?" Kane never looked away, but his body moved as if he wanted to curl up and hide or run forever. His pupils retracted and then bloomed fully.

"It is December first, Diana."

"Is it? Well, yeah, so?"

"The Super Blue is less than ten hours away."

He caught my waist as my knees gave out. Third time's a charm, right?

#

I'm not quite sure how I got in the truck, but I was sitting, or more accurately? Slumped in the passenger seat beside him. He raised his right arm and pulled me into him, and even in my exhausted state the feel of his chest under my cheek soothed me. We had less than three miles to travel home, but the next thing I knew the truck had stopped in our driveway.

Somewhere in that short distance I had fallen asleep. Kane wriggled out from behind the wheel and was opening my door. I wanted to move, I swear to God I did; but my legs just were not cooperating with the commands my brain was sending.

Strong arms wrapped around me, and Kane lifted me from the truck. He kicked the door shut with his left foot and carried me into the house. It felt like only half a second had passed between the metal of the truck door striking home and my being placed gently on the bed. Ten hours before the Super Blue? Maybe my timing wasn't that far off. My clothing was being removed by gentle fingers, and I was lowered onto a pillow before I could manage a grin. Kane slid into the bed beside me, and while I knew there was no chance of him sleeping? The fact that he did made me inwardly smile. He pulled me to him; his arm wrapping around my waist and the warmth of him was a soothing balm my ragged body desperately needed. I was asleep in seconds.

#

"Diana? Love? You need to wake up."

The voice came from behind my right ear, but I felt it as much as I heard it. Kane was still wrapped against me; and I fought to stay asleep. This was bliss, and I was reluctant to leave it. He gently shook me, and a brief flash of anger travel through me. What? Jesus what? Just stop! Five more minutes wasn't going to kill anybody.

"I concur Lover, and would give anything to stay right where we are; but it is a luxury we cannot afford today." Fuck, had I actually said it out loud? A rumble of laughter from behind me finally brought my eyes to open. The red numbers of the clock glared at me. It was 12:05. Shit, was it noon or midnight? Echoes of Kane's words earlier resonated in my mind. *Ten hours until the Super Blue*. The fact that I was alive and it was a human arm around my waist told me it was noon.

"Kane I can't go. Maria…." I left the words hanging in the bedroom air.

"You have to. And quickly. Because I have to go as well."

I rolled over to face him. In all the months I had known him, I had absorbed every hue and kaleidoscope motion of his eyes. I had never seen this before. They swirled as if they had a life of their own, and there was no word to accurately describe the gold and reflective sheen they had. They were beautifully unsettling, and they pierced through me.

"What do you mean, you have to go?"

"There are search parties from here to the river. I cannot be here when the moon rises. I cannot risk coming across them tonight."

"Where will you go?"

"As far into Vermont as I can before my ribs start to hurt. There is a lot of forest that way."

"Kane, it's almost two hours to the border."

"Precisely. So get dressed."

#

It was a short good bye kiss, at least by our standards. No more than fifteen minutes. Kane was headed northwest to Vermont. It was a no brainer that I would head the opposite way towards Cape Cod. I smiled as I placed my overnight bag on the hotel desk to check in.

"Miss Jameson! How wonderful to see you again!"

"Thank you; it's good to be back."

"It was the moon on the waves, wasn't it?"

"It was that very thing."

"Same room as last time?" she asked, and I nodded. I smiled as she handed me the key. Scallops at the Ketch one more time. Hello, Hampton Beach.

CHAPTER THIRTY-ONE

I felt no rush to rise early. Kane had gone to Vermont, and it would be two hours before he even got close to Rowley. I watched the sun break the horizon and paint the sky in brilliant shifting strokes of orange and pink. After it had resumed its dazzling blue, I packed my toothbrush and finished my coffee. It didn't come close to a Kane brew, but it wasn't half bad. I inhaled the sea air, and thanked my friendly clerk for another fantastic night of silver waves.

"Will we see you again soon?" she asked, and I tilted my head.

"Never can tell what I'm liable to do." I quipped, and scooted down the stairs and towards my car.

It was less than forty minutes later when I crossed the town line into Rowley. Something felt wrong, and a squeezing sensation found my lungs. There were two State Trooper cruisers to my right as I drove in. The blue strobes flashed urgently, but the lack of a siren filled me with dread. Thirty feet further; there were two more cruisers facing the opposite direction. Their strobes flashed as well, but not in rhythm with the first two and it had a dizzying effect. I stopped the Mustang as I watched the dreaded yellow tape being stretched from a tree and in to the woods.

No No No No NO! This was *NOT* happening. I wiped my eyes; my vision had gotten blurry. Once it cleared, I spotted a familiar face under a Smokey hat. Scotty. I was out of the car and across the two-lane road before I knew it. The way his jaw was clenched told me everything that I didn't want to know.

"How bad?" I asked, and he shot me sideways glance before steeling his eyes on the horizon.

"It was a mercy by the time the cocksucker cut her throat. She was already bleeding out from the damage that twisted fuck did to her. The end was quick. The two days before; were not."

"Scotty, I have to see her."

"No Jimmy, you do *not*. I know it was a *HE* that did this. That tells you all you need to fucking know. Go. Be with her family. And your shiny eyed fiancé."

Kane! My God I had almost forgotten. The horror of knowing Maria's fate had let him slip from my thoughts momentarily. I nodded at Scotty, and though I would have loved nothing more than to hug him fiercely; I knew where he had retreated to. He was screaming at the top of his lungs in the tiny space all cops have behind a wall so thick no one hears a thing never mind sees it. No one, except for those of us who have screamed in the very same chapel; and still occasionally do to this day. I extended my arm and put my hand on his shoulder. He nodded curtly.

"I've got this, Jimmy. Her family will never see this."

"Thank you." I whispered, and he squinted his eyes and inhaled deeply. I turned back towards my car, and a tiny footprint in the snow caught my eye. It wasn't a size four sneaker print. It was the footprint of a little girl who had no shoes on. The dogs must have finally found her scent because paw prints followed her foot prints. There were several more of hers and they were not fourteen inches apart anymore. They were spaced maybe six inches now and they were uneven; evidence of her tortured journey into the trees. Blood streaked the snow between her staggering paces. It was a *HE*. And Maria had been bleeding out from the damage he had inflicted on her. I found myself trembling, but my knees were strong.

You *MOTHERFUCKER!* If there was a God in Heaven? He would let *ME* find this fuck and kill him. And if there wasn't? I was tired of being cold anyway. Eternity fireside; had its appeal. Internally, I found myself shrieking in the chapel next to Scotty's. Externally, I stiffened my shoulders and strode back to my car. I climbed in silently, drove slowly past the cruisers, and made my way home.

#

Kane's truck was in the driveway. Well Holy Shit there Mario Andretti! It was barely three hours past sun up. He must have stayed close to the vehicle while in alternate persona for him to have gotten home this fast. I glanced towards the house. The front door was shut, that was a good sign. Kane was inside and safe. I could almost taste the coffee. God knows I needed something warm this morning. My mind flashed to the footprints and blood in the snow, and I put my hand against the truck to steady myself.

The hood was cold.

I was across the yard and trying to open the door before I realized I had moved. It was being stubborn; no matter how hard I turned the knob it wouldn't open. What the fuck? I froze as the realization hit me. It was still locked. From yesterday.

Kane.

I had known fear; both before Kane and since. I had skirted horror, and even danced with terror. What I experienced in that moment had no word. It is the darkest of dread, times a million and that is only the surface. I had been cast down into some abyss miles below that. There was only one way out. I had to find Kane.

The front door being locked indicated he had not gotten back inside, but in the interest of being thorough I unlocked it and entered our home. The lights were off, nothing had been moved and there sure as fuck wasn't a pot of coffee brewing damn my bad luck. I checked each room to be certain and when they all revealed no Kane; I went back outside. My eyes scanned the yard. With the exception of a few chicken prints, the light covering of snow was undisturbed. Where the fuck *was* he? I forced myself to slow my breathing down. My pounding heartbeat might guide him to me but that wasn't going to be much help if I had a heart attack before he got here; and in that minute a heart attack was a very real possibility if not an imminent threat. Easy, Jimmy. Deep breaths. I shot my eyes towards the trees that guarded the path down to the river. The same path I had walked last summer as I discovered how to uncoil, if only in fractions. The same path that Rodan lay next to.

It wasn't a thought as much as I *KNEW* it. I sprinted across the thin snow and burst through the tree line. The branches were now stripped of their leaves; but ample evergreens were present and had afforded enough protection from the flurries to where there were only small pockets of white scattered on the ground. My eyes frantically searched for any sign of Kane, in a footprint or a paw print. Anything would have been welcome at that point. I found none, and that increased my fear level to Defcon One. I hadn't found him yet, but Kane was here somewhere. I knew it as surely as I was breathing. Speaking of which, slow that shit down Jimmy, don't stroke out before you find him. Thatta girl; deep inhale, slow exhale. Repeat. I coached myself through these simple measures as I expanded the perimeter of my search. The sound of running water reached me. While it had been below freezing for days now; the river had a pretty strong current and moving water was always slow to surrender to ice. I made my way towards the sound.

Fingertips were the first thing I spotted, and the nail beds were blue. *FUCK*! I hurdled over a fallen tree and was on my knees beside him. He was half in the river, from the waist down, and his feet were limp as the current tugged at him. The water, while still moving was no warmer than thirty degrees. Jesus Christ! I heard Ann's voice in my head.

He will finally die.

NO! Not now! I would *NOT* have it!

I grabbed onto his hands and pulled for everything I was worth. It was like seizing two icicles and the chill that shot down my spine had nothing to do with how cold he felt. Please Jesus, not Kane! Not now!

Maria was enough; more than I could take. Not Kane too! I strained every muscle I had and begged God for more strength. He granted it because I had managed to drag Kane's six foot plus body almost completely out of the water. I was panting and every sinew screamed in protest; but I continued my task. It was only after his toes were on dry land that I allowed myself to drop to my knees. Even then it was a fleeting rest. His fingers and lips were blue. Oh, *FUCK* No! *NOT* on my watch! I rolled him on to his back and horror smashed me when I realized I didn't see his chest moving. I pressed my ear to his chest. There was no movement and worse? There was no sound.

"NO!" I screamed, and pounded my fist on his ribcage. It wasn't an attempt at reviving him; it was the personification of a rage that stemmed from every awful thing I had ever seen. Dead kids. Broken bodies, small and grown alike. The carnage of July. None of it was as terrible as the sight of a deathly still Kane and the silence of his body. My fist struck again, and the sharp fire of what undoubtedly was a broken hand snapped me from the collage of horrible images. He was still not moving and he felt like ice.

Somewhere, my mind snapped to a thought. Fifteen and two. The ratio of compressions to breaths for one-man CPR. I tilted his head back, opening the airway, and shoved my breath into his lungs. They inflated briefly, and I straddled his hips. My palm was on the edge of his sternum, and I began to crush it as I counted aloud.

Searing flame shot up my forearm as I did; but I ignored it. When I had reached fifteen? I leaned forward and covered his mouth with mine. I forced the air from my body into his, and after the second breath, I returned my hands to the middle of his chest. I repeated the same count of crushing his breastbone, and two forcible oxygen exchanges once more. I was about to resume my assault of his ribcage when he sputtered a cough. It was followed by another, and a desperate choking inhalation on his part. I slumped over him, my forehead on the frozen Earth over his right shoulder. I kept my weight off him so that he could breathe, which thankfully he began to do a bit more regularly. He coughed one last time, and after he did the volume of air he drew in was deep and clear. His eyes moved behind closed lids, but they did not open.

"Kane? Kane! Can you hear me?" A twitch on his lips was the most incredible thing I had ever seen. He was still half dead, literally; but he felt his name enough that a smile almost appeared. Jesus, Thank You! I pushed myself up from the ground and whispered into his ear.

"You gotta help me Kane; I can't do this alone." Again, his lips moved, and his eyes fluttered slightly. I caught a flash of gold as one cracked, and it found my greens. The second snapped open and while he was back from the dead a scant five seconds; he focused on me. They narrowed and I can only imagine what the Hell I looked like.

"C'mon Kane; help me get you to the house."

I dragged myself to my feet, and yanked him to an almost standing position. He leaned heavily on me; and we stumbled our way back towards the warm fireplace and soft blankets. I had managed to get him inside and secure the door behind us. His head hung limp and he struggled to move but I didn't give one rat's ass. His fingers, while still cold had begun to return to a pink tone and his lips were a far lighter blue color than they had been on the riverbank. The bedroom was maybe twelve feet away, but I surrendered to my own bodily limits at four feet and laid him across the couch. I collapsed on top of him and it took every ounce of reserves I had to tug the two blankets down from the back of the couch. Both the knees and the bottoms of my jeans were wet and I didn't care. I covered him with me, and the two of us with the blankets; and delighted in the steady thud of his heartbeat under my ear. I was unconscious from utter exhaustion.

January 1991

The Super Blue

CHAPTER THIRTY-TWO

It was gray when I opened my eyes; which afforded me no insight as to what time of day it was or even if it was day. New England winters are six months of varying shades of gray; and there's not much difference between the lighting of dawn, noon and dusk. It is a stark beauty sometimes; at other times it feels dismal. I suppose what the circumstances you are in that particular snap shot of time in your life decides which way you describe it.

The first thing I focused on was the gorgeous fireplace Angus and Kane had built together. Had Kane opted to work with stone rather than wood? He still would have been every bit of an artist. The logs were mostly embers now, but they were glowing bright enough to tell me the flames had not long faded. One big breath on those embers and they would return.

Breath! Kane! I frantically searched beneath me with my left hand to feel for him, and my fingers failed to locate him. Panic settled on me and I sat up and swiveled my head in a desperate search for him. Jesus Christ! Where could he have gone? He had been more dead than alive by the time I had gotten him to the couch. The current state of the fireplace told me it could not have been more than three hours since they were lit. No way had he recovered *THAT* fast. The Blood had taken over a day for him to regain his feet; and this Super Blue made that look like warm ups.

"KANE!" I called out, and realized my voice was a scream. No matter, it was an accurate tone for the terror that had swallowed me. A flicker of movement caught my eye and he was beside me before I could even fully turn my head in the direction that he came from. I was wrapped in strong protective arms and pulled into his chest. A chest that had the most wonderful sound of breathing, and a heartbeat.

"I'm here. I'm here, Love." With every vibration of his words I felt was like Heaven Itself had thrown Its Gates wide for my entry. I was shaking as I clung to him and he pulled me closer still. I wasn't shaking from cold, nor was I shaking from fear. It took me a second, but it occurred to me that I was sobbing. Not crying; *sobbing*. The body wracking release of every fear and sorrow and agony you've ever known sprinkled with relief and joy and guilt for feeling those good things when so much awful lay around you. I don't know how long it went on. It could have been minutes or hours but when I was hiccupping my way out of it; I realized that however long it had taken? It was the desperately needed shower my soul finally got to take.

So much rancid had been washed away I was appalled that I had unknowingly carried it this long. My God, when had that happened? How had I not noticed it? Felt its weight?

"Okay. Okay." Was being whispered into my hair, the words punctuated by soft kisses. "That's good. Okay. Let it out. I'm here."

Yes. Kane was there; warm and breathing and each syllable he spoke I felt as well as heard. Jesus Christ, Thank You. There were times I thought I had been afraid. The truest fear I had ever known was the silence of his body when I pulled him from the river. I could live through most anything. But I would not survive losing Kane. Seeing him leaning on the hood of the Mustang in what felt like a lifetime ago had opened the door to this. I had stepped through, and was thankful every day that I had. That moment in July? The elation I had felt then? It was no more that the brush of a dandelion plume compared to what I felt when Kane coughed on the side of the river. My breathing returned to a more normal pace, and I squeezed him fiercely. A gentle chuckle came from him, and while it thrilled me to feel it in his chest? The exhaustion that lingered behind it concerned me.

"What time is it?" I asked.

"Just before dusk."

Dusk. What the Hell? That was one long ass nap Jimmy! Almost eight hours? That was more a solid night's sleep. I smiled and I gave him a tighter squeeze for a few seconds; then released it. Kane understood that was his cue to loosen his grip on me. When I discovered enough wiggle room, I raised up to look at him.

The gold was still in full possession of his irises, but it was not their metallic sheen that caught my breath. His skin was ashen, and there were dark circles under his illuminated eyes. I had never seen Kane look like this, not even on the kitchen floor after the Blood. He had been wrung out then that was for sure, but his flesh had a pinker tone to it that day. Today he looked like a man who had not slept in days, or one that had just gotten out of ICU. Right now? Kane was the image of Death warmed over; and my heart thudded twice when I realized that is exactly what he was.

"I know Love; I look pretty rough." He said, and even his half grin had a weariness clinging to it. I ached for him.

"Kane." I said gently, and he flashed the smile. "It's only been a few hours. Cut yourself some slack would ya?"

"It has been more than just a few, Diana. I have been awake for over sixteen." My mind was attempting to do the math, but it wasn't working. I blinked.

"Kane?" I asked slowly, and the smile remained, "What *day* is it?"

His smile faltered slightly, though I wasn't sure if it was the exhaustion he was feeling or the fact that he had to tell me the day.

"Monday. The third."

"Oh my God. I've been asleep for over a *DAY*? *AGAIN?*" I exclaimed, and Kane did a quick head tilt in an unspoken question.

"I do not know. I'm not sure what time you decided to nap with me. I awoke just before eleven last night. And what do you mean *again*? When have you done this before?"

"After I broke my wrist." I said, and raised my left hand to illustrate the occasion. The blanket slid from my chest to my lap when I did. Kane glanced at it and smiled softly.

"I'm glad that healed nicely. I told you the bones broke clean."

"Yes you did, my keen hearing fiancé." I said, and despite the grueling ordeal he had just been through? Kane beamed at his title.

"As much as I love hearing that word from your lips directed at me? I will be happier still when I trade it in for husband. Nothing will ever.... *AND WHAT THE FUCK?!?"*

Kane's sentence had morphed from softly spoken loving words into a roar. It was fury tainted with pain. He sprang up from the couch, yanking the blanket from me as he did. His eyes blazed; the gold a swirling cauldron of fear and rage as they scanned me up and down. His breathing was labored as if he had just run up a mountainside and while every muscle in his body was locked and hard as iron? He was trembling. I quickly glanced around searching for whatever danger he had seen. He dropped to his knees in front of me; eyes still frantically mapping me as he quickly ran his hands up and down my legs. Finally, we locked gazes.

"Your right *hand*!" He said, and his voice cracked in anguish. "What happened? Is the rest of you all right? Tell me! Please! Tell me now!"

"I'm fine! I'm fine. It's okay." I said, and he moved so quickly I didn't realize that he had until his nose was less than an inch from mine.

"You are *NOT* fine! That hand is swollen and four different colors!" He barked, and his eyes were boring into me. He closed them and inhaled, trying to bring himself back under some form of control. He released the breath, and when he met my eyes again, his had changed from rage to helpless resignation.

"You are hurt."

"It's not bad, Kane." I said, and for the third time ever, he did not smile. Instead, he hung his head and stared at the floor for a long minute. When he looked back up at me, the shine of the gold had changed again. It was a cold anger lighting them this time.

"And I could not stop it." He practically spat the words, and there was venom behind them.

"Because of this Super Blue, and *WHAT* I am. I was *NOT* there to protect you. I have lost two days of search time; and you are hurt." He was directing the venom at himself.

"Oh, fuck you! No, you *DON'T* Woods, no you don't!" I snarled back at him.

"Do *not* tell me *NO*. I was not there to keep you from harm." He fired right back. The bitterness he felt carried on his voice and in his eyes. I watched as the hatred for the *Wolf* part of him returned, and it was like all the progress he had made the past months vanished. "You are hurt, because of *WHAT* I am, and that silver *bitch* in the night that controls me."

He finished speaking with his finger pointed up, and he averted his eyes from mine as he sank into a crushing despair. I watched it overtake him, and a searing rage surged through me. Oh, you motherfucker!

"I am not hurt because of *WHAT* you are, you fucking thick headed Mick sonofabitch! I am hurt because of *WHO YOU ARE!"*

Kane snapped his head back up and locked his gold with my green. I'm sure they were close to as iridescent as his were; though mine did not carry the same questioning tint. He had no idea what I was talking about, and while I should have felt sorry for him that he had no memory of his time in *other* form? I didn't care. We had agreed, no more apologies; and he had broken that pact. In doing so he had tapped my primal bitch, and he was going to get her full force. He opened his mouth as if to speak, and I unleashed on him.

"*NO! NO!* You will *SHUT* the fuck up *RIGHT NOW*; and you *WILL* hear me!" I was half roaring myself, and so be it.

"*WHAT* you are is a wonderful man who occasionally, is not quite himself. *WHO* you are is the man I love no matter the form he takes. That Wolf of Ireland you hate so much is why you have lived one hundred and twenty-seven years. I broke my fucking hand doing everything I could trying to make sure you made it to one hundred and twenty-eight! And God willing many years after that! Because I won't make it a *DAY* Kane, not *ONE* single Goddamn day, if anything ever happens to you again!"

He had remained silent while I railed at him. He listened intently to every word I had hurled at him, and stifled the smile at the feel of his name but I saw the corners of his mouth curl slightly. What his features had kept hidden his eyes did not. It was a brief happiness, yet it was there all the same. The anger did not return to the gold; but a lot of questions were forming for him and they darkened with them, and I knew I was going to have to answer them.

"And before you even start asking any of those questions I see? Just remember this. You made a deal with me. No more hating yourself. And you broke it. So, just fuck you for that. I don't even blame God for that one. You did that one *ALL* on your own. Nice job, asshole."

#

Kane returned to the couch where I still sat with the second round of beers and two of the leftover pain pills I had from back in July. He handed me the opened long neck, and hesitated in giving me the tablets. I glanced up at him, and the metallic richness was dark with questions and worry for me.

"Jimmy, are you sure? You haven't eaten in at least twenty hours that I know of." I raised the longneck slightly in my left hand and grinned.

"Pork chop in every one. Gimme the pills."

"We need to get that taken care of." He said, eying my now multicolored right.

"No, we *should* get that taken care of. We *need* to talk. The fucker will still be broken tomorrow."

He began to put his shoulders back and insist, but I raised the index finger of my left hand from behind the bottle neck.

"Don't." I said.

Kane hung his head as a soft chuckle came from him and raised his hands; 'surrendering' once again. He was a wise man. He knew he wasn't going to win this one without physically dragging me to the hospital, and even one handed I'd have been fighting him the whole way. He gently placed the pills in my upturned right palm, and I tossed them into my mouth and swallowed half the beer. It throbbed a bit, sure; but nothing hurt as bad as the sight of him on the bank of the river. I shuddered at the memory, and finished the rest of my pork chop. Kane raised his eyebrows in an unspoken question, and I nodded that yes in fact I was still hungry. He got me another beer, and sat on the coffee table to face me.

"What happened to me?" he asked softly, and the gentle vibration I felt carried tenderness no vocabulary could ever convey. I sighed, and looked across at him. This? This was gonna suck.

"I *will* tell you Kane. And I am sorry to do it. A *lot* has happened; and it's not just about you. Though God forgive me what happened to you was the worst of it for me." The smile that he had when I said his name faded faster than I would have liked; but wishing and wanting something does not make it real. And in the Reality I was about to fill Kane in on? There were *NO* reasons to smile. None at all.

CHAPTER THIRTY-THREE

Awful is a powerful word. It is also adaptable. Something can taste awful, and something can be awful. Some things can also be awfully good. Awful is a pretty handy adjective, as well as a noun and even an adverb. Words that can be more than one part of a sentence are cool. Fuck was *FAR* more versatile. That word can be used as every form of speech, and sometimes it is truly the only word that will suffice. The reality I had just brought to Kane was not awful. It wasn't even fucking awful; both were too weak of a description. It was so bad I searched for a better word. In my search, I heard Ann in my head as clearly as if she were sitting beside me. It was *wretched*.

Kane had disintegrated when I told him that Maria had been found; and not in time. I had never watched another human being shatter before. We cops have that chapel behind the wall. We shatter too; but are not able to allow anyone to witness it because we still have a job to do and the surviving family to protect. Even when we 'fail' to prevent it, or get there in time; we still do our duty. Logic tells us that we did not 'fail'; we can't be everywhere all the time. That's logic; and logic flies right out of the goddamn window when you're looking at a raped and murdered child.

And maybe it should.

Watching another human being shatter is awful enough. Watching the man that you are in love with experience that kind of pain, and seeing the result? And you're the person who had to tell him what happened? Which is *WHY* he shatters? That?

That is *wretched*.

Kane had dropped to his knees in the middle of the living room, and while I was right down there holding him, crying *WITH* him as much as *FOR* him; I had that sense of failure and I couldn't shake it. And then? I got to play in the bonus round.

It had taken three more beers and a four finger pour of Jameson before Kane was reconstructed enough to even ask about how Maria's fate tied into my hand. Before he did; he slipped into the kitchen and returned with a beer for each of us and two glasses of that fine Irish whiskey. I noted that mine was not nearly as full as his was, but then again? I had only made it to stop seven while Kane had Drank the Ave. Twice.

"Diana, what happened?" he asked gently. "What happened that you broke your hand over me?"

I didn't exactly shoot the Jameson, but I took more than a hefty sip. I let it burn my lips and tongue, and inhaled as I steeled myself to tell him.

"I got home and the front door was shut, so I thought everything was fine with you and you were inside. But the hood of your truck was cold, and the door was still locked from when we had left the afternoon before. I came in but you weren't here and I was scared for you, so I went out to find you."

Kane nodded, and I shrugged my shoulders.

"And I did. And it's okay now. Your home, I'm home, and we are both all right." Kane stared at me a long moment and the gold slid to a darker hue.

"And?"

"And that's it."

The gold deepened, and then lit from within. He leaned forward from his spot on the coffee table and practically glared at me. Oh shit; he was pissed.

"Diana, you are not lying, but you are holding back far more than what you have said. Do *NOT* shelter me! I do *NOT* need protecting! You may be a sheepdog but I am *Wolf* if you recall! There is nothing that could have happened to me that can be worse than Maria!"

"Don't be too fucking sure about that!" I snapped. It was my turn to get pissed, though truthfully the anger was a façade to cover the fear that I had felt when I found him and still did.

"What? What could possibly be worse than *THAT*?" he was close to snarling and his voice had grown louder in both volume and the vibrations I felt. My anger rose louder than his decibels in both my ears and bones, and I stood up and yelled at him.

"You were fucking *DEAD*! *DEAD, KANE!"* and he didn't smile as he felt his name; he almost shuddered. It must have crashed through him. His eyes remained backlit with anger, and he narrowed them slightly.

"You are mistaken, Diana. I may have been unconscious or collapsed but there is no way I was..."

"DON'T YOU FUCKING DARE TRY TO TELL ME WHAT I FOUND!" I bellowed, and if my eyes matched my voice? They could probably set his skin on fire.

"You were half in the river, and your fingers and lips were blue! *FUCKING BLUE!* When I finally managed to get you out of the water and roll you over, you had no heartbeat. *NONE*! And you were not breathing. My hand? I broke it punching your chest!"

"Restarted me, did it?" Kane said and his tone still held an edge of temper.

"No, you fucking prick! Three rounds of CPR did!" I snapped, and his eyes changed brightness several times as he absorbed what I had just said. Kane's may have fluctuated; but I was sure that mine were still lasers.

I watched him as he wrestled with what he had *thought* to be true, and what he now *KNEW* to be true. He could hear my heartbeat and see every change in my color.

No matter how inconceivable it was for him? Kane knew it was completely fact. There was no lie in me. He finally looked back up to my eyes and there was a stunned guilt in them.

"I *died*." he whispered, and though he said it as a statement it held a whiff of question. His words, and the softness that he spoke them in, sucked any fury I had left from me. When it left so did the strength I had in my knees. I sank back to the couch and hung my head. Jesus I was tired. To the bones tired, despite my day plus of sleeping.

"Yes. Yes, you did." I whispered back. It was the loudest I could speak in my weariness. I mustered enough back up reserves to raise my head up and look him in the eyes. The gold was darkening and then flashing brighter again as he tried to comprehend all that he had just learned. I managed a half grin, and took his right hand in my left before I spoke.

"Please don't ever do that again."

#

It was scarcely ten that night when we made our way into the bedroom. It had been the night from Hell; and the massive emotional toll it had taken on the both of us kept us silent. I climbed into the bed and released a long sigh. I wasn't quite sure what to do, and there was nothing really left to say. I lay on my side with my back to Kane. The beers, Jameson and pain pills were taking their toll; or at least that's what I was blaming it on. Lord knows I wasn't going to acknowledge the fucking roller coaster of tragedy we had just spent three hours on. Oh no; Officer Jameson would not permit that. She was in her isolated tiny space behind walls thicker than any prison had ever built. She was screaming, but she was hidden from the world and everyone in it; Kane included.

He was beside me, but said nothing. His breathing was steady but had not slowed enough to where he was sleeping. I heard him inhale deeper than before, and a sigh that matched the weight and sadness of my own emerged from him.

I rolled over and put my mangled hand on his chest. His breath caught in a sharp but short inhalation. He put his hand on mine and then drew it back as if he had touched fire.

"Jesus Love, I am so sorry. I forgot. I didn't hurt you, did I?"

"It's fine."

"No, it is not. But it will be." He placed his hand gently on my forearm; far enough from the fractured metacarpals that it shouldn't hurt. It did not; in fact it warmed me from within. Officer Jameson was screaming in isolation where no one heard her. Jimmy may have been around someplace; but she was not front and center either. Diana was closer, and I could feel her strongest of the three; but even she was not leading the pack. A new pony had shown up today, and she was thundering out ahead of the herd. I hadn't realized she had even entered the race. A mystery, and the dark horse long shot because up until ten minutes ago? She had not made her move. She didn't break from the outside; she didn't charge up the middle. She simply realized how tired a six foot plus man was, and more importantly? She sensed how alone he was. Her move? She rolled over and placed her hand on his chest; refusing to leave him lonely. Her name?

The soon to be, Mrs. Kane Woods.

"Yes it will, Kane. And so will we."

CHAPTER THIRTY-FOUR

"You know Kane; I went thirty-three years without breaking a single bone. In the six months since I met you? I've broken two. You might be hazardous to my health." I said and laughed. I held up my now plaster encased hand to drive the point home. He looked over at it and then returned his eyes to the road as we approached the exit from the interstate. He smiled when I said his name, but there was tightness in his jaw.

"I'm kidding. Relax."

"Diana, I cannot relax when you are injured. The first broken bone was a blessing, but this second one? The blame lies entirely at my feet. I hate it."

"Stop it. You had no say in the matter, remember?"

"That is another thing to consider. How did that happen?"

"Shit Kane, I don't know but I don't ever want to feel like that again."

"When we get home, if you feel up to it? I would like to see where you found me. Would you show me the spot?"

I took a deep breath and considered it. The idea of going back to the location where I had found him lifeless was not an appealing one. One glance over at him ended my resistance. I could see the wheels turning and I knew he had too many questions for me to refuse. If I did? The man would never rest.

"All right. But I will not like it."

"Thank you." he said, and his hand once more came to rest on my knee. That made it a little more bearable. A little. Best I could manage at the moment. He made the turn on to the road that led to our house. Well shit. I sighed and he looked over to me.

"You do not have to, if it will be too much."

"Yeah. Yeah, I do. You will never let it go; and I won't have that hanging over us." He smiled as he parked the truck. His eyes were still completely gold, and the light within them was brighter.

"What?"

"You said *us*." I smiled and shook my head. Jesus, his happiness was infectious.

"C'mon. Let's get this over with."

#

It was a shorter distance to the river than I remembered. Three days ago; it felt like the Bataan Death March. Then again, three days ago? I was dragging a predominantly dead man back to the house. Kane was a solidly built man and he easily outweighed me by fifty pounds. Walking beside him now rather than supporting his weight made the brief walk almost pleasant. We had never walked in the woods together; and it would have been entirely enjoyable had the reason for it not been so dark.

We came to the turn of the path that led to the river. I stopped and my breath caught in my throat. My eyes focused on the spot I had found him, and the memory of Kane lying there filled me. I felt myself shivering and it had nothing to do with the temperature.

"Are you all right?" he asked, and the soft rumble of his words I felt conveyed his concern for me. I turned and looked up at him. His skin was back to a normal human color now; the gray tones had left while we slept last night and for that I was grateful. He still looked tired, but not as haggard as he had when I first saw him yesterday. The dark circles under his eyes were gone and the gold was full and shining. He looked *good*. He looked alive.

"I am now." I said, and smiled at him. He returned the gesture, and I seared every detail into my brain. Let *THAT* image replace the one from the other morning Jimmy; it is a far better one. He stepped closer and kissed me lightly. Oh yes, this was a far better memory to keep. When we finished, he studied my eyes. Once he decided I was in fact okay, he jerked his head towards the river.

"That's it?" he asked, and I nodded. He stepped back from me, and took two steps down towards the water's edge. I began to follow him and he glanced back to me, a little surprised.

"You are coming with me?" he asked, and I grinned.

"Of course."

He reached back with his right hand and took my left in his fingers and flashed a smile. The size and brilliance of his teeth still shocked me from time to time. God, I hope I never get used to that. It would be a *crime* not to marvel at that smile. I fell into step beside him and we made it to the edge of the bank.

Kane looked across the river to the opposite shoreline. The river was wide here; over seventy feet across and the distance combined with the current would make the swim challenging on a hot July day. On a freezing December dawn? It could prove fatal, and perhaps it had. I shared that thought with Kane, and he shook his head slowly, his eyes still focused on the opposite side. He seemed to be forming some sort of a puzzle; one he would try to assemble later. First, he had to gather the pieces. And that was why we were here.

"No Love, this would not be difficult for me the week leading up to a Full. The night of a Blue? And a Super at that? As Wolf? No. Something happened, but it was neither the river nor the cold."

It was a few minutes longer that he stared across the water. He finally pulled his eyes from that tree line, and gave me a quick wink before scanning the ground where we stood. I watched him absorb every detail and was reminded of how quickly he had done the same when I first met him. He was wrapped in a blanket, and I grinned at the memory. I had no idea back then of exactly how much he was capable of observing; my heartbeat and color included. His eyes stopped on one spot by the water and he squinted. He stepped over to where his gaze had locked and crouched down. I followed his movements and something shiny caught my eye. It was partially embedded into the soil, and had Kane not been reaching for it I would never have noticed it.

"What the fuck?" I muttered, as his fingers pulled it from the Earth. He hissed when he did it, and released it quickly. He waved his hand as if he had been burned but continued to stare at it. I focused on the object, and now that it was completely exposed? I recognized what it was. The signature mushroom shape of the metal could only be one thing. It was a bullet; and a hollow point at that. One that had found its target because it had expanded.

"It's silver." He said flatly.

"Get away from it!" I snapped, and stepped between Kane and the dangerous item on the ground. I shoved his shoulder backwards with my left hand to throw him from harm's way; and had he not been *Enhanced* he would have landed right on his ass. Even with the added agility that gave him? He almost did. The full impact of what had just happened jolted through me. He was *NOT* indestructible. That little piece of ore had just slapped me in the face with a new reality, and it was one I did not like.

Kane could be killed.

CHAPTER THIRTY-FIVE

Kane stared at the three bullets that sat on the kitchen table, and I watched the gold fluctuate as he studied them. He had located the other two within inches of where he had found the first one, and for obvious reasons I was the one to pick them up. The trio had expanded, which told me that he had been shot. Three times. I shuddered at the thought. A dark realization crept over me, and Kane sensed it because he shifted his attention to me. His eyes grew deeper when he looked at me.

"What is it?" he asked softly.

"You were *seen*, Kane." I said, and while he was clearly concerned for my worry, he smiled at the feel of his name.

"So it would seem." he said, and glanced down at the silver that had penetrated his body three nights ago. The weight of this knowledge did not escape either of us; and we didn't have to speak it aloud to know that he had been seen as *Wolf*. The fact that it was three silver bullets that he had been shot with could just have been a strange twist of circumstance. The use of silver tips was not unheard of for personal ammunition. I carried the very same rounds in my revolver. Still, I was never one to believe in coincidences; and I wasn't about to start now with a danger to Kane being present. Somebody knew what he was. And somebody knew what to use to kill him.

"I can't help but wonder how they got out of me." He mused as he focused again on the table top. I didn't like the sight of them, but until Kane had finished his questions they were going to remain in open view. He looked back up at me and saw my revulsion for them, and his eyes softened.

"We can put them away." He said.

"I hate that they're in this house; but the fact is that they were in *YOU* first? That is a big problem for me. A *big* fucking problem."

"I can see the wheels spinning in your head. Tell me your thinking on this."

"Kane; somebody knows about your *Enhancement*, and they knew what to use to kill you. My question is *why*. I don't know how those got out of you, when I found you there were no wounds to indicate you had even been shot. But three silver slugs in you sure as Hell explains you being dead." I said, and that final word sent a chill through me. Kane noticed it and was beside me before I saw him move. He rubbed my arms and nodded for me to continue. I inhaled deeply and shared my thoughts.

"Maybe they fell out when you shifted back. You said it feels like your ribs are being forced apart when you go *TO* Wolf. Maybe when you come *BACK* it is a similar thing. Maybe? In all that physical changing? They actually fell out."

"I imagine you're much bigger on four legs than either of us knows. I've seen your tracks, Kane. You are huge."

"Why thank you, Lover." He said, and his smile was not just from his name. I chuckled softly and shoved his shoulder. Truthfully the humor served to lighten my mood; if only for a few moments and it was a break he knew I needed. I enjoyed it as long as I could, but in the end; I circled back to the grim thoughts I had remaining that were unspoken as of yet. Kane saw when I did it, and ran his fingers through his dark hair.

"Go ahead. Finish."

"Even with what happened with Maria, somebody who 'accidentally' came across a wolf around here and shot it? Well they'd be talking about it, and people would pay attention. We have been to the doctor, the pharmacy, the grocery store and the post office. There's not many other places to go in town."

"And?"

"And nobody is saying shit. Not one word."

"Which tells you, what?"

"It tells me that somebody not only knows that you're *Enhanced*; they also know how to kill you. And they've known for a while or at least long enough to have gotten the proper ammo. And Kane? Their silence? That tells me one thing. They're hunting you." The smile he had flashed disappeared as he thought about what I said. His eyes darkened and grew cold when he realized I was right.

"The predator has become the prey." He said, and squinted as he considered that.

"Not on my watch, Kane. No sir." And my determination was rewarded by a brilliant smile of enormous white teeth. I paused to admire them, and exhaled a long sigh.

"You have more to say. Let me hear it."

"You never made it to Vermont, did you?"

"It appears I did not, though I don't know why."

"I don't know it for a fact, but I *do* know you." I said, and he glanced my way. "You stayed because of Maria."

"Jimmy, you don't know that. It was my idea to go. I had the truck keys in my hand when I walked you to your car. I watched you drive off."

"And then? What is the next thing you remember?"

"Waking up under you on the couch." He said softly.

"Like I said, Kane. I *know* you." His grin was short lived, and he nodded his head slowly in agreement. There was no way in Hell he would have left no matter his intention. Not while Maria was still missing. Any missing child would have been hard to leave. The fact that she was Alejandro's little sister? Considering the friendship those two had forged? It was an impossibility for him, and one I should have realized sooner. Kane was almost as protective of the young man as he was of me.

"We need to go see them. Alejandro, and his family." Kane said softly, and I wondered again if he could read my mind.

"I'll get my coat."

#

We climbed back into the truck six hours after we had parked it in the driveway at Alejandro's house. The family was beyond devastated; they were destroyed. I sat with the female members that remained, offering whatever comfort I could, but in the end? I felt completely useless. Kane and Alejandro had slipped off to the back porch shortly after our arrival, and when they returned several hours later both of them had wet eyelashes. I don't know what was said out there, but I hoped Kane had done better than I felt like I had. He started the truck and when we reached the end of the street, he turned right rather than the left that led us back home. His jaw was clenched, and he had a steely resolve in his gaze. I remained quiet beside him and gently put my left hand on his thigh. He relaxed a hair, but no more than that. He drove on for almost a half an hour and I had recognized where we were heading within the first ten minutes. He parked the truck and sighed.

"I need a drink." He said simply, and I nodded. Yes, we both did. And the Beachcomber was going to provide more than just the booze. It was going to provide Kane with the company of his buddy; one he needed desperately right now. The December air almost guaranteed it would just be the three of us, and as we stepped inside the place one glance around proved me right.

"Hey guys! It's awesome to see.......*what* the fuck happened?" Colin's greeting had changed mid-sentence. He had been happy to see Kane and me too I guess, but one look at us wiped the pleasure from the experience. He pulled three rocks glasses from the shelf behind him and poured healthy doses without even asking. Kane's was twice the volume of what his and mine were. Then again,

Colin and I had only reached stop seven. Kane accepted the drink and tossed more than half of it back in silence. Colin glanced to me briefly, and then returned his attention to Kane. He refilled the glass as if it had never been touched, and Kane slumped down into the barstool.

"Thank you, my friend." He said quietly, and Colin nodded.

"Of course. And I am." Kane looked up, and the contrasting eyes of the two men was something to observe. Colin had dark brown eyes and while they were normally cheery; tonight they carried genuine concern. Kane's were gold and glowing, and while usually backlit with happiness they were heavy with sadness this night. I felt out of place somehow. This was a 'man' thing for sure, and I found an excuse to leave them.

"I left my cigarettes in the truck. I'll be back." They were in my jacket pocket of course; no true nicotine addict ever leaves them out of reach but it seemed plausible. I slipped outside and inhaled the chilly sea air. It felt sharp in my lungs, and that brought me some comfort. At least *THAT* had remained constant. I wandered over to the truck and opened the door. I didn't want Kane to think I was a complete liar. I waited a few seconds before I shut it, and then pulled the pack from my pocket and lit up. I watched the two of them through the storm door window, and by the body language of each man; Kane was filling Colin in.

I lit a second as soon as I finished the first, affording them time; and my mind travelled to Ann.

He will need you in the most wretched moment of his life, and there have been many but this will be his worst. It will shatter you and test you. And what you do, in that moment and the days after, will determine both of your fates. I am here but you will not reach out to me. He will not reach out to his new friend Colin. Not until it's over, whatever it is.

I smiled as I observed them inside the bar. Well Ann, seems you were wrong. Kane did seek out Colin; and I seem to have reached out to you if only in my memory. Even an ancient soul and a Seer can be off a bit from time to time. I shivered, finished the cigarette and stepped back inside. Kane looked miserable, but better than he had when we pulled up.

Friends were a good thing to have. A very good thing indeed.

#

Two hours later we were almost home, and even in through his monumental sadness Kane had lightened up a breath. He had uncoiled, even if it was only a fraction, and I was thankful for it. We entered the town limits and the fluttering of yellow tape caught his attention. The blinker was on before I knew it, and he had pulled the truck to the side of the road. He snapped on the switch for the hazards, and started to climb out of the truck.

"Kane, no." I said, and he looked across the cab at me. The green of the dash lights bounced off the gold and they truly reflected not only the light but every raw emotion he was feeling. One look and I knew there was no stopping him. I sighed and nodded my head. He was opening my door before I knew it, and I stepped out without speaking.

The snow was littered with boot prints of varying sizes; as countless cops had swarmed the area of the woods where Maria had been found gathering every shred of evidence they could. The temperature had not gotten above thirty since that terrible morning, and the thin veil of snow was still present. The trail of her small footprints was clear, and I gagged when I saw that her blood was also. I glanced up into the tree branches as a fire of rage consumed me. Oh please, let *ME* be the one to find this fuck. There would be only one trial, and it would be mine.

The charge would be murder. I may have been 'retired', but my need for justice had not been informed of a career change. So long as I drew a breath; it would remain.

I dropped my eyes back to the ground and studied the tapestry. There were boot prints of course, and the tracks of Maria. Kane was examining them, and he focused on the tracks of the K-9 that had followed her final journey. He stood stock still for a moment, and I recognized the prickles of fear dancing along my spine as I watched him. His breathing had ceased, and when it resumed it was a strangled panting and he looked back to me. I have never witnessed agony like that before in my life, and I didn't ever want to see it again. The shattering of Kane when I had told him Maria's fate was nothing compared to what was unfolding before me. His eyes swirled and he was on the edge of madness. He sank to his knees in the snow and a wail the likes of which I had never heard before erupted from him. It teetered on another sound, and I suddenly realized what it was.

It was a howl.

The pain and loneliness that carried it pierced my heart as if he had stabbed me. It held the night for what seemed like an eternity. It was the song of complete despair, and the duration that it hung in the night brought tears to my eyes. I dropped beside him and wrapped my arms around him as he finished. He practically collapsed in my arms, and the shaking of his body bordered violence. He was sobbing, the exact kind of soul cleansing purge I had done when I woke up after my riverside rescue of him. I held him as tightly as I could, and hoped he was getting the poison out as much as I had. I kissed the top of his head as he released it, and stroked his dark hair. I glanced up at the stars and thanked the Big Guy for allowing me to be present when this happened. Kane stiffened in my arms and pushed back from me. I was stunned at his actions, and moved to pull him back.

"*No!* No. Kill me. *Kill me right now,* Diana. We both know three bullets will do it. This time, there will be no CPR. Do it. And use all six to be sure."

My head was spinning and I had no idea what my expression or color was, but I reached towards him again. He recoiled, and repeated his command.

"Kill me."

"What the fuck are you talking about?" I heard myself sputter, but the insane edge to his eyes held me still. He pointed to the ground with a fierce movement, and I followed his fingertip. He was pointing to a print in the snow. Yeah? So? The K-9s had found her. I scowled at him in confusion, and he pointed again. I looked down, and I stopped breathing.

The paw print was huge.

CHAPTER THIRTY-SIX

"Kane! KANE!" I was screaming his name once more in a forty-eight-hour period; and none of them had been during physical pleasure. He was still on his knees in the snow, but he was only present in his body. His eyes terrified me; the light in them a swirling mixture of excruciating pain and crushing guilt and he was drowning in it. My screams were my attempts to bring him back to me and thus far they were unsuccessful. There was no way he could not be hearing me; he could hear a whisper from me over three hundred feet away, and I was less than six from him and screaming for all I was worth. Kane was simply? *Gone.*

I moved towards him, and he absolutely did not see me. His eyes followed my movements, yes; but he wasn't 'seeing' anything from the bottom of that consuming darkness that had swallowed him. He remained motionless in the snow; he wasn't even blinking. Only the ragged movement of his ribcage was a visible sign of life.

I know where Kane went in his last rational thoughts, and it was worse than terrible. Ann was right. It was wretched. The agony from the day before had not even scratched the surface of what wretched truly was. My hand touched his shoulder and he finally blinked as he stared at it. He stayed like that for several seconds, and sprang to his feet and stepped back from me. He raked his fingers through his hair and turned his eyes towards me. I think he might have 'seen' me for half a second before he was gone again. This time, when he 'left'? He did so physically as well.

Kane could move fast; but he bolted off into the darkness beneath the trees with a speed that was almost impossible. I would have said it was except I had just witnessed it. It was like I had blinked and he had vanished. I stood in the same spot, my left hand still extended from when I had touched his shoulder, and I released the breath I had unconsciously been holding. It was shaky as it left me, and my knees followed suit. I listened as hard as I could for any sound of his boots in the snow and there was none. I was alone in the spot where Maria's short life had ended. I had been alone before and sometimes even in locations as tragic as this; but I had never felt what loneliness was until this very moment. Kane was gone, and he was *gone*; and I had no idea is he would ever come back. In both senses of the word.

Kill me.

That thought snapped me out of my daze and I ran back to the truck. My sprint was nowhere near his speed but I made it in three seconds. I yanked the door open and leapt inside the cab. I was driving before I had even shut the door completely, and the hazards were still flashing in the night. It wasn't proper Code 3 equipment but it worked; and the alternating lights had a familiarity to them. Had I not been so petrified I might have enjoyed it.

I reached our address and was relieved to see the only light on was the porch one we had left glowing for when we got back. I would have relaxed except I knew Kane could see in the dark. It was my comment about no outside lighting that had motivated him to install the porch light back at the end of the summer. I didn't park in the driveway. I roared that truck right up to the front porch and scrambled out of it as fast as I could. I threw the front door open and immediately headed into the second bedroom. I grabbed the top drawer of the dresser with my right fingers. The cast made things awkward but my urgency overcame the fumbling. I heard the heavy nickel slide in the drawer and almost collapsed with relief.

The revolver was still here. He hadn't thought of it yet. I had beaten him home. I made it in time.

Part of the departmental firearms training involves loading, shooting and reloading with your weak hand. Practicing that is designed to help you stay alive if you find your strong arm wounded and useless in a firefight. Without such training? Your gun becomes no deadlier than a brick you throw at your attacker, and a brick thrown with your weak hand to boot. I grabbed the .357, flipped the cylinder open and rousted the six silvertips from their beds and on to the dresser. One snap of the wrist and the gun was closed again. Unloaded thank Christ. I put it back in the drawer. I grabbed my speed loader case and shoved the stray six rounds into my jeans pocket. Reaching back into the drawer, I snatched the remaining box of ammunition out and crammed it into the jacket pocket. I was about to slam the drawer shut when I stopped. I grabbed the gun out again, and tucked it into the front of my pants. I had to get it out of the house. All of it. But I had no idea where to leave it. No matter; I would figure that out later. Right now? It simply had to be gone before Kane came back.

I quickly got back behind the wheel and backed out of the yard and onto the road. I heard gravel fly as I stomped the gas and the truck fishtailed slightly when I did. Easy girl; no sense in getting in an accident twenty feet from the house when you're trying to hide a gun out of his reach. I eased my foot off the gas, and the truck straightened as the treads gripped the hard pack and patches of pavement.

I forced myself to slow my speed, and my own breathing. I was out on the interstate before I realized how much of a panic I had been in. I ran a shaky hand through my hair and a giggle escaped me. It was based on borderline hysteria, but it was a welcome sound in the night. I tapped the knob for the radio, and pulled a cigarette from the pack with my front teeth. Driving with a broken right hand and trying to light a smoke is a bit challenging; but I managed and inhaled deeply. The familiar taste helped soothe my frazzled nerves further, and the next giggle was far saner sounding. I had done it. My moment of victory was short lived. Yeah, I had gotten the gun and the silver tips *OUT* of the house, but where the fuck was I going to ditch them? It's not like you can just toss them out on the side of the road. And I might need them back someday; though not for what Kane had just asked me to do.

Kane. My heart thudded loudly in my chest. Jesus! I had watched him submerge into true madness. The sight of the paw print beside where Maria had been found drove him to it. It was an enormous; easily twice the size of the other prints in the snow. There was no denying it. It was his. He had been there, and as Wolf. How or why I had no idea; but he had been. I know where his thoughts had taken him, and I couldn't really fault him for slipping from sanity. Kane had killed her. At least in his mind he had. And I was unable to bring him back no matter how hard I screamed for him. As alone, and lonely as I was feeling right now? It was nothing compared to where he was. Wherever he was.

Jesus. Just Jesus and fuck.

#

Even when you find yourself on auto pilot; there is Someone watching over you. I'm not sure which facet of the Holy Trinity had stepped forward and guided my journey that night, but based on my needing to stash a revolver and desperate need for a coffee of my descent? I'm going to lean towards the Cop; the Holy Spirit Herself. I don't know why I had suddenly decided She was female, maybe it was because I needed a Divine girlfriend in the moment, but She did not disappoint. I had parked the truck and killed the engine before I was even aware of where I was. I didn't just giggle when it dawned on me. I laughed. When I finished, I stepped out of the truck and entered the silver sided diner on Route 1 in Peabody.

I didn't dare hope it; but there she was. My stout, wise cracking, smart-ass waitress from three months earlier. I slid into the vinyl seat of a booth and absently scanned the laminated menu.

It was another one of those automatic things you do without any conscious thought. My eyes travelled the lettering without registering a word. A steaming mug of coffee was placed next to my left hand, and one whiff of it told me it was as Irish as Kane's parents. I smiled up at the matronly woman as genuine gratitude filled my weary soul.

"You're not a woman easily forgotten honey, and you look as bad right now as you did the last time. Maybe a little worse. This one's on me." She said with a wink, and left me to my thoughts.

She never missed a beat, and before I had even taken a sip, she was telling a trucker named Bill that his Peterbilt was the sorriest piece of shit this side of Connecticut. Damn disgrace the way he kept that thing, and her Daddy would be spinning in his grave if he knew she was even talking to him. I almost cried. I glanced up, and nodded my heartfelt thanks to the Courtroom above. The second Irish coffee had warmed my bones and eased my burden. The diner had quieted considerably since I had arrived, and I glanced up at the clock on the wall. It was four in the morning. No wonder it was so empty! I felt bad about keeping Helen here so late as her only patron, and I moved to stand up.

A warm hand with short fingers touched my shoulder, and another mug was placed on the table. She smiled gently down at me before seating herself across from me. Her auburn hair was clearly a dye job but somehow it was perfect on her. Her blue eyes usually sparkled with an untouchable humor; like she was privy to a joke only she knew, but when her butt hit the booth they slid to a more serious gleam.

"Whatever it is you need? I'm here."

I wasn't just wiping my eyes this time, I actually started to cry. This was *way* out of character for me; so much so that I questioned if I was still in fact Diana 'Jimmy' Jameson. Kane was the only other person on the planet that had seen me do this, and I was in love with him. To break down in front of a perfect stranger spoke to the state I was in. My thoughts were whirling. Kane was out there, somewhere; and he was 'gone'.

I had been confronted with a murdered child, a dead fiancé, and once I got him back? He had vanished into a place of such pain I didn't know if he would ever return. I was doing everything in my power to protect him from not only himself; but from whoever was hunting him. Fuck! He was tearing through the woods to God knows where, and there was somebody out there looking to kill him. And Kane *could* be killed; I had seen that firsthand.

"Miss Helen? You have no idea what that just meant."

"Maybe I don't. But you are not the only woman to ever look like that. And once upon a time, on a cold night just like this? Someone bought me an Irish coffee, too."

"Really? Who?"

"The biggest lug of a man who fills the floor board of his Peterbilt with fast food wrappers."

I burst into a laughter that teetered on hysterics; and she joined me in it. We howled in it, and I reveled in it. With all the fucked-up shit I had just been through? This was absolutely perfect.

#

It was just past seven in the morning when I parked Kane's truck in the driveway. The tires had left their evidence of my drive to the door in the snow, and I was saddened to see that it was still only my boot prints that marred the white blanket. Where was he? Jesus God; let him be all right. I climbed out of the pickup, now one .357 and silver tips lighter than I had been last night. Helen had agreed to hold the weapon for me, and when I assured her there was no body attached to it, she cackled and said she didn't give a rat's ass if there was.

"It'll be here when you need it." She had said, and slid it into her very large patent leather purse. I had no doubt it would.

The house was warm enough when I stepped inside, but it felt colder than the seventy-three degrees on the thermostat. Kane's absence was a deafening roar that made no sound. I was frantic with worry for him. He had been gone for at least nine hours, and I busied myself with setting up the coffee pot. It was never going to be as good as his, but it would have to do in a pinch. The temperature had dropped to the low twenties last night and he had been out in it. Even *Enhanced*; he was going to be half frozen. It would take some Jameson to get the chill out his bones when he finally got back. It was ready but I didn't turn it on. I wanted it to be fresh and hot for him, and I had no idea when he would come home.

Home. I glanced around me. It was a cozy house, and I had immediately felt like I belonged here. Looking back, the fact that I felt his words vibrate within me? I guess I did. But right now it was just a house. No matter how snug and warm it was? It was not going to be Home until Kane returned. Home was never going to be about a place, not for me anyway.

Home was about a *WHO*, not a *WHERE*. Jesus, where was he? Please. Please; let him be all right.

CHAPTER THIRTY-SEVEN

The lighter gray of a December day was slipping darker when I opened my eyes. Somewhere during the afternoon I had fallen asleep on the couch, and I sat up quickly. The house was still and quiet. The coffee pot remained in its holding pattern. It had been over fourteen hours and Kane had not returned. I was across the living room in seconds. I shoved my feet into my boots in the entryway and tied them as quickly as I could given the plaster handicap on my right. I was still bent at the waist and had finished tying the laces of the second one when I heard the doorknob turn. I froze as it opened, and Kane stepped inside.

I launched myself from my position, and crashed against him with enough force to stagger him backwards three steps. I wrapped around him, crying and laughing much like I had done that morning in July when the touch of his hand had assured me that he was alive and standing in front of me. Except this time Kane did not return the embrace; instead he retreated from it and was trying to pull me off of him. I fought his efforts but in the end, he peeled me from him.

"Where is it?"

He snarled the words; and it didn't take a detective to know he was talking about the gun. I looked at him, and the gold of his eyes were the coldest I had ever seen them. I shuddered as he stared at me.

"Give it to me."

I took a step backwards as the danger of the situation crept across me. He was deadly; but it was a lethality he directed at himself. For now. It took half a second before I found my skeleton, but once I did? I drew myself up to my full height and threw my shoulders back.

"It's not here." He knew it was not a lie.

"Get it. I will do it myself. One straight through my skull should do it."

"No."

His eyes blazed with a frozen rage I never imagined could exist. I wanted to shrink from it. I wanted to run screaming out the door and all the way to Providence. Every particle of me was terrified; but I stood directly in front of him and did not move. I didn't even flinch. We were locked in a Mexican standoff; and neither one of us so much as blinked. The air itself had gone still. It went on for what felt like hours.

"I killed her." Was all he said, and once the words were spoken the entire world returned to movement. He staggered slightly and put his right hand against the wall. He leaned heavily against it, and started to sink to his knees. I was beside him and supporting his body with a speed that was impressive even by Kane standards; though neither of us was paying much attention to that. He tried once more to remove me from him but I was not having any of it. One handed or not; I was a formidable opponent and protecting Kane, *from* Kane? Granted me a strength that bordered on Divine Intervention. He again tried to get away from me but I had him locked in my arms. This dance went on for several more attempts, and on the fourth he managed to get me half an arm's distance from him.

"I murdered a *CHILD!*" he roared, and his eyes locked on to mine. They were flooded with blind pain and hatred for himself.

Kane's head had snapped to his right; and I didn't comprehend what had just happened until I felt the sting in my fingers and the throbbing of my hand. He blinked at me as he returned to a position where he could face me directly. A red handprint was blooming across his left cheek, and he brought his fingers up to it. I had slapped the shit out of him. Stunned as I was that I had done it? I had locked on to something Scotty had said.

It was a mercy by the time the cocksucker cut her throat.

I hauled back and this time I didn't slap him. I *punched* Kane. My hand was screaming, but I drew back to repeat it. I was full swing when he caught my fist in his palm. It hurt; but not as much as actually connecting with his jaw. He stood in front of me; left hand wrapped over my right, and watched me as questions rose in him. His eyes still swam with disgust for himself, but there was a new edge to something within them as well. It was suspicion.

"You may have killed her, Kane. You may have." I panted. The last several times I had used his name he had failed to smile, and this occurrence was no exception. I found that I was missing that reaction from him. He hung his head at my words, and his shoulders slumped. It broke my heart. I drew in a deep breath and continued.

"It was a mercy if you did."

Kane buckled and dropped to the floor.

#

"How can you even *say* that?" Kane whispered from the near fetal position he had assumed once he hit the floor. "There is no *mercy* in the killing of a little girl."

So many thoughts and images flashed from my memory I had a hard time organizing them into anything remotely coherent. I was sitting next to him on the floor, and had managed to kick the door shut in the ten minutes it had taken him to speak. The house had warmed somewhat, and I realized that it was no longer just a house. We were both *Home*. I inhaled deeply and sorted through the jumble in my mind. This was not going to be easy to say, and it was not going to be easy to hear. But Kane had to know. And he had to hear it all.

"When Scotty and I got back to Lawrence that night, we walked into a scene that nobody can describe. What you did? You don't want to know the half of it." I said, and reached into my jacket for a cigarette. I normally smoked outside, but there was no shred of normalcy happening right now. I lit it and drew deeply before I continued.

"The officers were killed quickly, Kane. Instant. You tore out their throats."

I watched him flinch at my words, as if each syllable was a physical blow pummeling him. I hated speaking them, for that very reason. I'm not sure which one of us was in more pain. Rip the wound open and let the blood flow. Draw the poison out. That's the only way it will ever begin to heal. I reminded myself of that as I searched for the resolve to continue.

I found it.

"In the overall scheme of it? It was merciful. Somehow; that Residual you told me about? It was there. You couldn't stop what you were doing, Kane. But even in that? The officers really were the only innocents there. And that stayed with you, and you killed them quickly."

Speaking of the carnage is in no way *anything* I wanted to do. I hated that Kane had to listen to my description of what he had done as Wolf. I had tried for months to protect him from this knowledge. Now that I had started to tell him; I wondered if I had done him a disservice in my efforts to shield him. He uncurled slightly, and his shimmering eyes found mine.

"That, is what you call...*mercy*?"

It was my turn to feel like I had been slapped by the feel of his words; and I blinked twice but nodded yes. He squinted at me as if I had lost my marbles, and maybe I had.

"Compared to what you did to some of the others? Yes." I said with a finality that surprised us both.

Martinez. Organs exposed and intestines strewn across the cell. *Couldn't have happened to a nicer guy*. A grin born of a twisted sickness found my lips, and Kane spotted it. He slowly sat up and eyed me warily.

"Jesus, Diana. Right now, I don't feel like I am the most dangerous one in the room."

"Right now? You're not." I drew in the last of my cigarette and crushed it out on my bootheel. I exhaled the smoke and turned to face Kane straight on. This next part was going to suck. The absolute suckiest suck in of all Suckdom.

"I told you Maria had been found too late." I said, and Kane hung his head. I reached over and put my fingers under his chin. I gently raised his face until his eyes were even with mine, and I looked dead center into the metallic beauty of them.

"I didn't tell you *HOW* she was before she died. And I don't want to. But Kane? If you were the one who cut her throat? It was the most merciful thing you or anybody else could have done. It was quick."

It had been what felt like forever since I had seen him flash a smile when I said his name, and while he didn't smile right then either? The slight twinge of the corner of his mouth made my heart soar. Thank you God! Through it all, all this fucking wreckage; *THAT* was still there. He still felt his name when I spoke it. Here, in the blackest black of the dark; I had found a light. The broad beam of a lighthouse at a harbor's edge. It was the twitch of Kane's lips that would guide me to safety. And it would bring me home.

"I am afraid to ask, but I have to." He said, and I nodded my head slowly.

"She would not have survived her injuries. Not even if an entire surgical team from Mass General was there."

"Fuck." Was all he whispered, but it was all that needed to be said. The sick sonofabitch that had her? He had destroyed her. Her small body had lost so much blood there was no chance of saving her.

I didn't need to provide him with every gory detail, nor did I want to. Saying it aloud would have been too painful. Some knowledge is best left in silence. I leaned over and rested my head on Kane's shoulder, and he didn't try to escape my touch. He seemed to soften beneath me; and that welcoming gesture was the only brightness of this long, gray and terrible day.

"Even savage, Kane Woods; there is kindness and mercy in you. In the *Residual*." I said softly, and delighted in the feel of his arm wrapping around me.

I melted into it, and the frenzied past week washed over me. I was beyond exhausted. I was spent. There was nothing left; nothing had been undone, unsaid, or untried. The chips were all out on the table and the cards had all been turned.

A long sigh came from him, and I realized he was as used up and empty as I was. The bed was a welcoming thought. It was also twenty feet away. I relaxed and let my full weight settle against the man under me, and was rewarded with a gentle squeeze around my waist. A final thought crossed my mind, and I snorted the briefest of laughs.

"And you wonder why I said yes." I mumbled. He wrapped both arms around me then and pulled me against him. I closed my eyes.

It wasn't like it was the first time I had fallen asleep on the floor with Kane. Home is never about location. Home is about the company you keep. Right now? Home was on the entryway floor, and I was grateful to be there. I was almost asleep when I felt him slide out from beneath me. I feared he might be 'leaving' again, but my worry was unfounded and I felt Kane lifting me off the floor. He was carrying me, and I realized he was crossing the living room.

"Where are you taking me?" I asked, my voice groggy and barely a whisper.

"We have gone too long in places other than our bed. We both need to be there."

I laughed softly.
"What?" Kane asked as placed me gently on the bed.
"You said *we*."

Chapter Thirty-Eight

While it had taken Kane a week to fully recover from the Blood; the Blue had an odd effect on him. It was both a Blue and a Super. The Super had about killed him even without the silver that had struck him, but five days after I had found him dead and all the aftermath of Maria? The spring in his step had returned as if it was November thirtieth. It puzzled me how quickly he had physically recovered and when he returned from the store that evening? I asked him.

"Because it is a Blue, Diana. There will be no break in the Pull. No reprieve of the New."

"Wait, what? You mean all month you're going to feel it?" I asked, and Kane nodded his head. He looked almost guilty as he did it, and I exhaled loudly. "Jesus, you're going to be exhausted come January."

"As will you." he said, and the gold deepened to the hunger edge. Oh shit. Yes, I am. He stepped closer to me and his desire was almost tangible in the air.

"It has been a very long week." He said, and I realized his voice was lower. Deeper. It was bordering a growl, and the rumble I felt as well as heard confirmed it.

The hungry edge to his eyes shifted iridescent again; and despite feeling some trepidation to the impact on my hips I also felt a surge of heat. No doubt I had shifted one hundred percent red. The light within in his eyes grew brighter and he took another step towards me. Oh Jimmy, you're fucked now. In every sense of the word. He dropped the bag containing the Fritos and my cigarettes on the kitchen table but his eyes remained locked with mine. Kane could move in a blink, but his deliberate one step at a time approach towards me was far more unsettling than his speed ever had been. There was a flicker of fear in my spine as he took another towards me.

I felt exactly like a cottontail rabbit. I was frozen and I couldn't move. Then again, I'm not really sure I wanted to. It was terrifyingly erotic the way he was looking at me and moving towards me. He was still two feet away from me and my breathing was as heavy and jagged as if his hands were already on my flesh. He hadn't even moved closer yet and my skin was on fire. I was desperate to feel him but still could not move. He seemed to sense it, and the corner of his mouth curled up. This was not the crooked grin that had disarmed me so many times. This bordered on Kane licking his chops before he moved in for the kill, and I knew I was to be the target.

He took another step towards me, and it was agonizing how close he was but not yet touching me. Parts of me were pulsating, and parts of me were screaming. Most of me was praying for him to take one more step.

Kane standing there, was like being circled in the water by a large great white shark. I knew it was only a matter of time before he decided it was time to eat, and I couldn't wait to be served up. His eyes never moved from mine, and they shifted deeper in hue but more reflective. He came closer and I was trembling. My back arched as I felt his breath on my neck though he still had not physically touched me.

"God yes, Kane." I begged him in a rasp of a whisper. "Please. Do it."

He held back for another half second, but that felt like an eternity. My entire being was consumed with a need for him. It burned brighter in me than his eyes were lit, and I wasn't simply trembling anymore I was fully shaking. His teeth gently found my neck as his hands caressed each breast. A scream of ecstasy ripped from my throat as the orgasm thundered through me.

We were both fully clothed, in the middle of the kitchen, and he had done that to me. It didn't end there. It didn't end until near sunrise. Kane was right. I was going to be exhausted by January.

#

"I'm going out for the day." I announced a week later, and Kane looked over his coffee mug at me. He swallowed the last bit of it and nodded.

"Okay. I assume you do not want company, based on the way you said '*I*'." he said, and I smiled at him. He returned a smaller one, but it was sincere.

"It's not that I don't want you with me Kane," I began, and his smile broadened as he felt me say his name, "but it's hard enough to keep a surprise from you as it is. The whole heartbeat and color thing. If you're with me? It's not going to be just difficult. It's going to be impossible."

"Fair enough." He said after a soft laugh. "And I promise not to ask."

"Thank you. You are gentleman indeed." I said, and Kane chuckled and raised an eyebrow. I burst into laughter when I realized what had just happened. I'm not sure which one of us was more amused; me by his eyebrow move or Kane by my use of the word *indeed*. We had very much become an 'us'; and the adoption of some of the others mannerisms only drove the point home further. All the more reason for my needing to go out alone today. There were plans to be laid, and ones I did in fact want to be a surprise. That was no easy feat with us both being so in tune with each other even without his *Enhancement* advantages.

"Anything you need while I'm gone?" I asked, and he narrowed his eyes. He was suspicious, but he honored his word and asked nothing.

"Only your safe return."

"That's it? No samples from aisle seven?"

"No Love, I will venture out later for those. My selections will be far more than a 'sample'." Kane replied with a soft laugh.

"I don't doubt it. Your appetite is enormous this month. They'll probably have to restock the damn thing once you're done."

"And you had better make haste in your departure." He said, and the gold deepened as he looked at me. "It is not only my need for junk food that has increased." Jesus. The past week of Kane's 'hunger' had been exhausting, and by the way he was looking at me? Yes, I had better hurry. I smiled but chugged the remains of my coffee, and he grinned as he watched me.

"I'll be gone until the afternoon at the earliest."

"I will anxiously await your return, Lover." And the purr in my ribs told me he would be very happy to see me walk through the front door again. There was a pretty good chance he'd be dragging me into the bedroom as soon as I did.

"Jesus Kane, you may be the death of me yet." And the smile told me he felt his name. I returned it and rose to my feet. He stood as well, and opened the front door for me. As always, he escorted me to my car, and after a brief but intense kiss good bye, the driver's door was being held open for me.

"Hurry home, but drive safe." He said as I perched behind the wheel. "Seat belt."

"*Yes Dea*r." I replied and he flashed those brilliant large teeth at me as he closed me in the Mustang. I started it up and he stepped back, raising his hand as I backed out of the driveway and headed down our road. I was still smiling when I reached the end, and I turned left. My first stop had to be the Island, then straight to Boston, and I could work my way back from there. It was going to be a busy day.

#

"Well, isn't this a pleasant surprise!" Colin called out from behind the bar as I stepped into his establishment.

"And you're flying solo today! Oh God, what has he done? The usual? A one and one?" This is what Colin had affectionately named our Jameson and a beer traditional combination.

"Just a beer and yes, I am solo. Sorry to deprive you of your buddy this morning; but we need to talk." I said as I slid into the barstool. Colin turned back towards me with an open Coors Light and I raised my left hand. His eyes fell to the ring. A smile that could almost rival Kane's in size filled his face, and his eyes were dancing with joy when they met mine.

"*YES!* Yes, we do!" he exclaimed, and laughed. Despite my order of only a beer, two Jameson were poured.

"Colin! I have a busy day and a lot of driving." I said, but I was smiling right back at him. His happiness was contagious. No wonder he and Kane had become thick as thieves. They were men cut from the same honest emotional cloth.

"Jimmy, there is *NO WAY* we are *NOT* having this drink! Congratulations! I'm so glad that you said yes!"

"Wait, what?" I asked, the glass halfway to my mouth. "You knew?"

"Of course, I knew! He's been going on about it forever. Sat here many an hour drawing that very ring on hundreds of cocktail napkins. Probably went through two cases of the goddamn things before he got it just right. I wish I had champagne."

I sat there in silent shock. Jesus Jimmy, for a cop you sure missed every one of these clues! Colin raised his glass, and I followed suit.

"Besides," he said, and winked at me, "You made it to seven." There was no arguing that logic, and I smiled at Colin again.

"All right, but only the one. I have a busy day."

"Fair enough. The events leading to your cast will wait for another day then." He said, and clinked my rocks glass with his.

"Slainte."

"Don't sweat the champagne, there's bubbles in the beer. And Colin? This conversation? *Never happened*."

"I like it already. Whatever it is? I'm in."

#

Despite my assurances that I had eaten a hearty breakfast, Colin insisted on stuffing me full of fried mozzarella sticks before I left. It wasn't much of a challenge for him; as a purist I obviously had a deep affection for gooey melted cheese and marinara sauce. Kane had chosen well in his friend. Now it was my turn to go see mine.

Once again, my feet landed in the underground lair of awesome pizza and better friendship. A happy shriek to my left told me that Ann was working the bar. She dashed across the restaurant dodging both waitresses and diners alike, and grabbed me by both hands.

"Jimmy! The cast is a story I'm sure, but I'm *WAY* more excited by *THIS* hand!" she squealed as she held up my left. "Spoken about for centuries! I told you! Oh my God let me look at it! Come on!" she gushed as she dragged me to the bar.

"No pitcher today, Ann. Lots to do."

"I'm sure, but you *MUST* tell me everything!" she said excitedly, and began to pour a large glass vessel of 'whatever was the coldest'.

"Ann, I'm not kidding!"

"I know you're not! I'm simply not listening."

"Jesus, what am I speaking a foreign language? Nobody is today!"

"Shut up, Jimmy. You have friends. So does Kane. Colin and I will help."

"How do you even know.....?" I left the rest unsaid as I realized who, and what, I was talking too. Ann wrinkled her nose at me and stuck out her tongue. I nodded my head and laughed softly. I was glad I parked my car at Oak Grove and took the T into Town. I was going to need the train ride to sober up.

#

It was almost five when I stepped into the entryway and before I had even shut the door lips were pressed to the side of my neck. A gentle nibble followed, and any chill from December was gone in a flash. Jesus the man had an effect on me! I giggled, reached behind me and ran my fingers through his hair.

"Welcome home, Lover." He murmured into my skin, and I savored the feel of him wrapping around me. I felt more than welcome; I was thrilled.

"Did you get everything accomplished that you had hoped?" he asked, and I turned around to face him. I don't know how bright my eyes were, but Kane hung his head and laughed gently.

"All right, all right. I promised I would not ask."

"Thank you." was all I said. He raised his eyes to me, and they narrowed slightly. I felt my eyebrow raise, and he grinned.

"I'm sorry," he said, and my eyebrow went higher still. Kane released me and stepped backwards, resuming his 'I surrender' posture. "I can't help it; I have never seen you this color before."

"And that would be, what?"

"Purple. More violet than deep."

"Red and blue. Must be a blend of excitement and cop stoic." I said, and he laughed and nodded. I grinned at him, and he gave me one final nod.

"I will ask no further."

"Good, because I *WILL* lie. You'll know of course, but I'll still do it."

"I have no doubt that you will. You can drop the blue cop stoic; I prefer the red." He said, and stepped back towards me. He wrapped his arms around my waist and the crooked grin appeared.

"Besides; you have been gone all day. Whatever it is, you clearly have put much time and thought into it. I do not wish to dismiss your efforts."

"Well I certainly will not dismiss yours, Kane." I said, and his smile reflexively appeared. I ran my fingers down his chest. The gold of his eyes deepened and intensified as my palms made their way to his stomach. I gently tugged the T shirt up and felt his skin under my hand, watching the intensity and shifting glow of his gaze.

"If you are trying to distract me? It is working, Diana." He said, his voice low and thick with hunger. His breathing was faster, and mine matched it.

"Good." I whispered, and kissed him as my fingers found his belt. Kane spent the rest of the night 'distracted'.

The Lesser Blue

CHAPTER THIRTY-NINE

"Kane? Let's go out this afternoon." I said, completely out of left field. He smiled at me from across the kitchen, and cocked his head slightly. I returned the gesture and walked over to him.

"It's your birthday tomorrow; and obviously nothing is going to be open." I continued as I wrapped my arms around his waist. "We can go for a late lunch, so that places will be open still. It is Christmas Eve so they may be closing early; but I'd like to take you out for your birthday. Any place you want."

"Well, this is a surprise." He said, and I smiled. Oh, Kane you have no idea exactly how much of a surprise it is going to be. I squashed the thought, hoping my color didn't betray me. If I had changed hue he didn't mention it, and the fact that his eyes didn't narrow or shift light gave me hope that I had succeeded.

"So, where would you like to go?" I asked, summoning every shred of Officer Jameson to help me keep the secret. Only two more hours Jimmy; don't slip up. The man deserves it.

"I don't know. I have never been asked out on a birthday date. Or any date for that matter." He said, and I kissed his neck.

"What? With your good looks? No woman has ever asked you out?" I inquired, and Kane chuckled. His face flushed red and I giggled. Oh yes, he was.

"Don't. You are pink."

"And you are blushing. Which is adorable."

"Ugh." He said, and hung his head. The smile remained on his lips however and for as embarrassed as he was, he was enjoying it.

"C'mon. Let's even get dressed up. Not terribly mind you; but it is a special occasion."

"What special occasion?"

"It's Christmas Eve, and tomorrow is your birthday. And I get to spend it with you. Seems pretty special to me." I said, and his eyes glowed as he looked at me.

"My God Diana, what have I done to deserve you?"

"Pretty sure it's the other way around there, Kane."

His smile grew larger at the feel of my speaking his name, and the size and brilliance of his teeth was breathtaking. The gold was shimmering and reflecting every emotion he was feeling. The combination of teeth and eyes was marvelously offset by the darkness of his hair, and I was once again struck by how handsome of a man he really was. Rugged good looks that encased the most wonderful human being I had ever met in my life. Yep. The best Christmas present ever was standing right in front of me.

"Diana, I don't own any 'dress up' clothing. I work with wood and I have been alone up until July. Not much need for a suit and tie."

"Well, then it is a very lucky thing for you I have come along." I said, and tugged gently at his hand. His brow furrowed slightly as I led him into the second bedroom. His confusion grew as I stepped over and slid the closet open.

"Seems Santa hit our house first. A little early even." I said, and he peered into the now open door. The only clothing hanging in that closet was a button-down man's white dress shirt and a steel gray sports coat. Kane stared at the garments for an exceptionally long time and remained silent. I was beginning to grow nervous when he turned and looked at me. Any worry I had vanished when I saw the gold. They were beyond glowing; they were aflame and the hues shifted form and size as he took it all in. It went beyond happiness. This was joy; and I squealed inside like a twelve-year-old girl.

"You like it then?" I asked, and his smile exploded. He held my gaze for a long moment, and then slowly stepped towards the closet and removed his 'dress up clothes'. He held them at an arm's length and admired them. When he had finished, he turned back to me.

"Yes, I do. Very much so. Thank you."

"I stole a couple of your flannel shirts for an afternoon." I said, and he grinned.

"Stole?"

"Well? I'm retired now Kane, I can't say *commandeer* anymore." The grin spread to a smile as I continued.

"I wasn't sure of sizing; I've never bought a man clothes before. So? I stole them and brought them down to Syms in Peabody and the Sal in the men's department did the rest. I thought the jacket color would be awesome with your hair and eyes. In my defense, I did return the shirts to our closet."

"Thank you." he said softly, never moving his eyes from mine. Even without the destined lifelong mate aspect I would have felt the sincerity behind his words. Kane was genuinely thankful, and how much so surprised me.

"It has been a long time since I have received a gift."

That simple sentence slammed me as hard as a pile driver, and my heart broke for the briefest of seconds. Oh my God, it had been over seventy years since his mother died. She went six months prior to Angus' death. Since then? Kane had been alone. No Christmas presents, no birthday cards, nothing. Holy shit, the loneliness of it must have been awful! I vowed that he would have the merriest of Christmases and the happiest of birthdays from that moment on. And sprinkles of random 'for no reason other than I love you' presents and cards scattered throughout the year.

"Well? Go try them on!" I said, and kissed him quickly on the cheek. Kane hugged me tightly to him, and I was thankful for that. It let me casually wipe the tears from my eyes.

#

He stepped out of the bedroom and my breath caught in my throat. Holy Jesus! He looked amazing. And delicious. I gasped as he walked towards me, and the crooked grin he wore was lethal. He held his arms out from his sides and looked himself up and down, then back up at me.

"Is it all right? I only have jeans but I …."

"Oh…my…God." I quietly interrupted him, and his grin faltered for a second. "Fuck."

"What? I know I need a haircut, and…"

"You are the hottest thing I have ever seen. Holy shit! I'm gonna be fighting them off."

"What? Who?"

"Any women we come across. Jesus, Mary and Joseph. I might need to retrieve my gun. Or upgrade to an Uzi." I had chosen the jacket perfectly, and Sal had been spot on with the size and cut of it. Kane's dark hair and warm complexion were a good contrast to the crisp whiteness of the shirt, and the gold of his eyes was startling with the gray of the sports coat. The Levis he wore were the perfect amount of faded but not too light, and his black boots and belt tied the entire ensemble together flawlessly. I wasn't entirely sure but I may have started to drool. Kane blushed slightly, and there was no way cute, precious or adorable came to my vocabulary. He was devastatingly handsome, and every estrogen laced cell in my body responded to him. Complete alpha male and dashing. Jesus I was in trouble.

"I better step up my game." I said softly, and shook my head slowly. "Jesus."

"You are exaggerating Love, but I thank you for it."

"No. No I am not. Look at my color and listen to my heartbeat. I'm a serious as a fucking heart attack Kane you are dangerously good-looking." Kane looked me up and down, and squinted his eyes in a slight question.

"There will be no danger to you while I am around."

"No, but there will be a danger to you, *FROM* me. Blue month be damned; you might get hurt yet."

"The very best kind of danger or injury, Lover." He said, and gave me a quick wink.

"Jesus, let me go change. Shit I wish I had bought that 'little black dress'. This is going to be tough; trying to look like I even belong in the same room with you." I walked across the living room and stopped directly in front of him. I slowly looked him up and down, and when I met his eyes again, I shook my head. His eyes shifted darker and he pulled me to him, kissing me gently.

"Miss Jameson, you belong right beside me. You have both saved my life and brought me *to* life. I am completely in love with you, and I cannot exist without you."

#

I have had the occasion to get dressed up from time to time, but my 'dress up' wardrobe was scarcely more than Kane's was. I looked at the pathetic offerings of the closet, and muttered to myself about how I was going to have to go shopping. There were three outfits I had to choose from. An emerald green skirt and jacket, a purple and teal skirt and matching blouse, and a black skirt with red jacket. I opted for the last of the trio. The skirt was fitted through the knee but flared from there, and given the winter date I decided that was my best choice. I slipped into it and a black silk blouse, shrugged on the jacket and stepped into a pair of black flat boots.

I scanned my reflection in the mirror, and while I was not entirely satisfied it was the best I could manage. At least with the flat boots I'd have sure footing when the throngs of women began throwing themselves at Kane, and I'd be able to throw a punch or two. I checked my spiky hair; it would suffice, and put in a pair of red and black fan shaped earrings. All right, nothing to write home about, but at least I was presentable. I hesitated behind the closed bedroom door and hung my head. Shit Jimmy, you *REALLY* have got to think things through a little better! That is a prime specimen of man out there. Try to keep up! I leaned my head backwards and inhaled. Here goes nothing.

I turned the knob and opened the door.

Kane had his back to me and was reaching into the fridge when I stepped out of the bedroom. He stood up, two longnecks in his right hand, and I smiled at the sight of him. Jesus, he was *HOT!* Damn if he didn't clean up well!

"I thought we'd have a quick one here before...." Kane left the sentence unfinished as he turned to face me, and the unspoken conclusion of it had me immediately self-conscious. Oh God, this was bad. This was worse than bad.

No way can I even go out like this. Dammit I can't believe I didn't even *THINK* about buying *ME* something to wear. I really couldn't have gone all out and still kept this a surprise, but still! Shit! Shit, shit, shit! Jimmy you're an idiot! Of all the stupid assed things you've done in your life this has got to top the list! Ask a man out for a 'birthday date' and you don't even think about what you're going to wear. Jesus you *suck* at being a girl! I thought of ducking back into the bedroom and setting the outfit on fire. I almost reached for the doorknob when two hollow popping noises stopped me. It wasn't gunfire, and while I am sure I had heard the noise before I couldn't quite put my finger on what it was. I turned my attention back to Kane.

He was standing completely still, the fridge door still open but his hand was now empty. The longnecks had smashed on the floor, the beer hissing as it surrounded the broken glass. Nice. So bad he threw the beers down. I forced myself to look at his face, preparing for the disappointment I would find there.

His eyes were blazing, and the richest gold I had seen up until this moment. They brightened and deepened every half second, and he locked onto me with them. His mouth was hanging open, and I was completely baffled by his expression. The twelve-year-old girl in me wanted to run and hide, but I was not able to move from where I stood.

"I...uh? I didn't really think about what I was going to wear." I stammered. Kane stood stock still, he didn't even blink. I shifted my feet under the weight of his eyes, and my movement seemed to snap him out of wherever he had gone to.

"You are *stunning*."

I blinked several times as I let the words sink in. I had felt them rumble through me of course and I knew he meant every one of them completely, but I was having a hard time wrapping my head around the concept. I focused back on Kane. He was standing in the exact same spot and position; he had not moved as much as a hair. The only motion of him was in his eyes and they were fluid like the northern lights, except all the shades were metallic gold. I felt an unsure smile creeping across my lips, and my shoulders relaxed somewhat.

"We talking about me?" I asked quietly, still unsure of what had just happened.

"I most certainly am. Diana, you are the most gorgeous woman I have ever seen." I never saw Kane shift to pink, but I'm sure I was blushing.

#

We had decided on The Grog, a charming restaurant in Newburyport with the best pesto and bread I have ever eaten. Dining out, and dressed up? Was a completely new experience for us and I found myself liking it. We had gone out and grabbed a bite here and there of course, but an actual sit at a table, eat a meal 'date' was different. There was an intimacy to it, and even in a place full of people; we were alone. I don't think I ever took my eyes off of Kane, and he was definitely a sight to keep my attention. I made a mental note that this would be a more frequent event. The Grog placed us conveniently close to Plum Island, and I suggested we stop by and wish Colin a Merry Christmas. When Kane agreed, I smothered an enormous smile. Dear God don't let me shift purple now; I'm so close to actually pulling this off. I danced inside at the prospect of success, but externally I remained 'calm'.

When we pulled into the lot, there were only five vehicles there. Kane opened the truck door for me, and we had taken three steps before he noticed the handwritten sign posted on the storm door.

Closed for a Private Event.

He sighed and turned to me.

"Well, so much for that."

"Nonsense. We can just pop our heads in and say Merry Christmas. I'm sure Colin won't mind." I said, and tugged his hand gently. He nodded and walked beside me as we passed a large semi-truck that was parked on the side of the building.

"Why do I smell French fries?" he asked, and it took everything I had to stop the giggle in my throat. Oh, please God! Only ten more seconds! We reached the door, and Kane opened it for me, allowing me to step inside first.

The Beachcomber had been transformed into a magical blend of winter white, Christmas and the sea. The bar was lined with white candles and evergreen garland, and the smell of the balsam was heavenly. The tables had been moved to the side, save one long one that was draped in white cloth and was also adorned like the bar. Interspersed with the garland and lit candles were perfect sand dollars, and their flickering light danced behind the shells and set them aglow. I turned to look back at Kane. He had stopped in the doorway, taking it all in.

"Jimmy? I don't think this is the time to bother Colin. This looks like a wedding."

"It is, Kane. We had a date, remember?"

The smile he had at the feel of his name faltered for a second as what I said registered in his brain, and for that second my heart stopped.

My God, *had* he changed his mind?

The smile that replaced it was dazzling in its size and brilliance and when it did my heart leapt with joy; so much so I'm sure it was pounding in Kane's ears. I felt one almost as big crossing my face, and his eyes were positively on fire as he looked at me.

"Indeed we did, Miss Jameson." He said softly, and the humming I felt as he spoke was the warmest I had ever experienced.

"I'm fairly certain that is the last time you're going to be able to call me that; unless you've changed your mind."

"Never."

"Well? Then I guess we should get to it."

Kane's gaze was still on me when I heard movement in the room. There was no way he didn't as well, but his eyes never strayed from mine. The pure gold of them was startling, they remained illuminated as the color swirled yet remained constant. I knew who was there; I had invited each one personally when I 'went out for the day', but it was as if Kane and I were the only two people in existence. Everything else had fallen away, and all I could see was his eyes. That's all I would need to, everything he was feeling was intense and untarnished, and it was directed at me. I was bathed in love from him, and I can only hope he saw the same in my greens. I don't know what my heartbeat was telling him or what color I appeared, but my *HEART* was only saying one thing. He nodded slightly, and I knew he heard it loud and clear.

Yes, Kane Woods.

Today I become your wife.

Chapter Forty

The actual ceremony was brief; Colin's cousin Eric was an Episcopal priest and had agreed to marry us. Kane's parents were Catholic; but neither of us was so Episcopal seemed a fair compromise. Ann and Colin had outdone themselves with the décor; it truly was beautiful. Ann stood to my right, and Colin to Kane's left as we stood in front of the long white clothed table and listened to the words Eric spoke. Helen and Bill sat behind us, and Alejandro was grinning ear to ear as I prepared to change my name. I was elated to see it; the young man had not smiled since November. Eric finished the prayer, and turned to Kane. I watched a flash of darker gold cross the iridescence, and he stiffened.

"Diana? I didn't bring the ring." He said softly, and Colin and Ann both giggled.

"Kane, you're about to marry a woman who could've been an Eagle Scout." Colin said, and reached into his pocket. "She was prepared. I've had this for over a week."

Kane's shoulders relaxed and an embarrassed grin found its way to his lips. He turned to Colin and took the ring, a soft chuckle coming from him. He nodded twice, and cut his eyes to me. A quick wink, and the grin grew to a full smile, and much to my amazement? I fell deeper in love with him. I couldn't believe it was possible, but there I was in the midst of the freefall, and I was ecstatic in it.

I don't know which was more thrilling; hearing Kane say *I take you for my wife* or feeling him slip the platinum band down my left finger. It nestled against the engagement ring, and I'm sure my smile could have lit Boston. I thought I might burst from the happiness I felt, and I had to be the brightest red I ever was. Kane's smile was enormous, and his teeth were as brilliant as my color must have been in his vision. It was then that Eric turned to me, and I nodded. Ann stepped closer and placed the wedding band I had for Kane in my hand. He squinted his eyes slightly, and slowly shook his head.

"You are amazing, Diana." He said softly, and I smiled up at him. I could barely contain myself as I slid the platinum circle down his left ring finger.

"I take you Kane, to be my husband...."

#

"I don't care what your last name is. You're always going to be Jimmy to me." Ann giggled as she leaned in to me at the bar. I had been married for forty-five minutes, and this was the first time Kane had stepped away from me. I met her laughter with my own, and glanced across the room at my husband. He was standing with Colin and Alejandro, and whatever 'guy' talk they were having it was not enough to keep his eyes from finding me. He flashed a smile and winked. Jesus, I was in love with that man and everything about him.

"Oh yes. For centuries, Jimmy."

"God Ann, I hope so."

"Jimmy, who called the cops?" she asked, and nodded towards the door. A tall State Trooper stepped in, and I shrieked and dashed across to him.

"You made it!" I exclaimed, and hugged Scotty's neck.

"A bit late I'm sorry to say. Bad wreck on 95. Susan sends her love, and this." He said, and handed me a bottle of champagne.

"Oh, being at the scene with *THAT* in the cruiser must've been great!" I said, and we both laughed. Kane appeared at my side, and he smiled and shook Scotty's hand.

"I see you took my advice." Scotty said, and patted Kane's shoulder.

"Yes, I did. She can't change her mind now."

"Well congratulations to you both. But Kane? One look at Jimmy tells me she wasn't going to anyway. Wait, are we still calling you Jimmy?"

"Oh God, yes. My last name may be Woods now, but hey, Jimmy is eternal."

"Well, *Mrs. Woods,*" Scotty said, and it was the first time I had been addressed as that. I loved it. Scotty smiled as he watched my reaction, and out of the corner of eye I could see Kane. He was beaming. Scotty laughed and continued.

"Mrs. Woods, you look beautiful. I'm sorry I missed it, but as I said, my watch is finally over. And Kane? Look at her. She is glowing. Nope, she wasn't going to change her mind, but she does have a temper from time to time. Best you didn't make her wait too long."

"I have experienced that temper Scott. I agree. Besides; it is rude to keep a Lady waiting." The two men laughed after that statement, and Scotty turned his attention fully to my husband. I grinned as I thought the word.

"Oh, Jimmy wouldn't have waited very long. She'd just go out and get it done." Kane laughed heartily before answering.

"Scott? That is exactly what she did."

"I know. Jimmy may not be immortal, but she is a constant force of the universe. One to be reckoned with I warn you."

"I am more than aware." Kane answered, and gave me another quick wink. Scotty laughed and slapped Kane's shoulder.

"I'm sure you are. Well again, congratulations, and I am sorry I missed the actual ceremony. I hate to cut this so short, but I am technically still on patrol."

I hugged him again, and kissed his cheek. He blushed slightly, and shook Kane's hand once more.

"Go. Keep the streets safe for women and children." I said, "And keep yourself safe, Scotty. Thank Susan for us and send her my love."

"I will, Jimmy. I don't have to worry about you two." Scotty said, and glanced from me to Kane and then back to me again.

"You're the safest people on Earth with each of you watching over the other. The Devil himself would back away." He finished with a smile. He nodded at us both, and headed out the door, waving as he stepped outside. Kane watched him go, and then turned to me. It was the first time we had been alone together since becoming man and wife, and I studied every aspect of him. The slight touches of silver in his dark hair, the ebb and flow of the gold in his eyes, the creases at the corners of his eyes when he smiled. Every detail of him I seared into my memory, and he donned his signature half grin and took my hand in his and raised it to his lips.

"I never imagined this much joy, Diana. I did not know it could exist."

"I know exactly what you mean. *Husband*." I said, and Kane smiled.

"Would you believe me if I told you that I *felt* you say that?"

"Yes, I would. And I'm glad you do."

He stared into my eyes for several minutes, and I could not break my own gaze from his. It was surprising how easily everything and everyone else could slip from view when there were such moments of connection for us. We could have been standing in the crosswalk of Times Square when the ball dropped and I would not have heard nor seen a thing other than Kane. It was though we were wrapped in our own protective circle and nothing could touch us; and it was glorious. Kane again kissed my hand, just below my completed bridal set. I smiled and glanced at his adorned left finger, and he grinned.

"I love it. I had not considered that I too would have a ring, but I am proud to wear it."

"I asked Colin for the name of your jeweler. I had it inscribed you know. On the inside."

"Really? May I look?"

"Of course!"

"I had to ask. I did not want you to think that I wanted to take it off."

"Yes Kane, you can look." I said, and he kissed me gently before sliding the ring off. His eyes found the letters, and his breath caught as he read them.

"Mac Tire de Eire." He whispered, and he returned the focus of his gold to me. "Wolf of Ireland. You had it done in Gaelic."

"Seemed appropriate."

"It is *perfect*."

"That's why the wedding ring is platinum." I said, and ran my fingertip down the length of his nose. I winked and grinned as I continued.

"*Takes the sting out of it*."

#

If you bring together the right people, the smallest of gatherings can seem like the biggest of parties. Somehow? I had succeeded in doing just that. Alejandro, the youngest of the bunch, was completely at ease in talking with Colin and Bill. The teenager and the fifty-seven-year-old trucker were comparing fast food menus, and Colin was arguing his case for why Wendy's Frosty's were far superior to the McDonalds Shakes. Helen and Ann stood slightly off to the side of them; listening and commenting about the *fine cuisine* these men enjoyed, and laughing as if they had known each other for years. I stood beside Kane and observed it all, a smile permanently residing on my face. I glanced over to him, and his expression matched mine. He slowly shook his head back and forth and chuckled softly.

"What's so funny?" I asked, and he absorbed the scene before us a few seconds longer before turning to me.

"Jimmy? If someone had told me in May, that in December? I would be standing in the Beachcomber a *newlywed*? And with people I knew surrounding me? I would have thought them insane. It is almost unbelievable for me to be here."

I wrapped my arms around his waist and hugged him gently. He kissed my forehead and smiled down at me, and the size of his smile was rivaled only by his teeth.

"Do you remember the first time I brought you here?" he asked, and I nodded that I did. He looked over to our gathering of friends once more, and then back to me. The gold was blazing, and the flame that lit it was happiness.

"When we left and sat in the truck and I was staring out at the ocean. Do you remember that?"

"Yes. I asked you what you were thinking."

"Yes, you did. And I told you that I did not know."

"Yeah?"

"Love? I have been alone for a very long time. Having you love me was a miracle all in itself. More than I ever dared to dream. Even more so because you know *everything*, and today you still married me. But throw *them* into the mix?" he said, and jerked his head towards our friends, "It is overwhelming."

I rose up and kissed him gently, pulling him closer to me. His arms wrapped around me, and while the kiss he returned was not quite as gentle he remained under control. By Kane standards anyway. When we had finished; I was more than slightly breathless and we smiled at each other. It took me several seconds before I realized the room had gone quiet. Surprisingly, I noticed it before Kane, and I cut my eyes to our guests. Each one of them was watching us, and all of them were smiling.

It was Ann that started it. She let out a whoop and began to clap. The rest of the audience joined her in their appreciative applause, and I covered my eyes with my hand and began to giggle. I felt the heat of embarrassment flood my skin and I knew I was blushing. Kane hung his head and I watched his skin flush. This made me laugh, and in turn he grew darker red and chuckled. When he looked up at me, we both laughed harder, and each one of us raised a pointed index finger to the other in our unspoken but completely understood '*Don't*!'. Our matching actions invoked laughs from our friends, and inside of five seconds the walls of the Beachcomber echoed with happy people.

"Come on, my Mac Tire de Eire. You are a lone wolf no longer. It's time to be with your pack."

We crossed the few steps to them together, and were circled with genuine affection from each and every one of them. There was closeness between all of them, and they shared a loyal friendship for both Kane and me. When you bring the right people together, no matter how big the party? The gathering is also intimate. I was batting a thousand today, and the grand slam was the man I had just married.

Two hours later, after several toasts of my former last name were made in our honor and countless stories and laughter, Helen approached me. Bill stood back a step and made small talk with Kane about trucks, and I got the sense Helen wanted me alone. I took a stride left and she followed me, her eyes again sparkling with the knowledge of the joke that only she knew.

"Jimmy? Honey? I am so happy for you both. I knew you were crazy about that man; no way you couldn't be for him to have put you in such a state. Twice. In the middle of the night. After seeing you both together, I have no reservations about giving you my wedding gift." She said, and reached into her ever present large black patent leather purse.

She withdrew a box wrapped in silver paper adorned with two wedding bells covered in gold glitter. She glanced down at them, and the blue danced as she found yet another joke; one she shared with me.

"I had no idea they would match his eyes when I tied them in the ribbon." She said, and let loose a laugh that swept me up in it. The two of us were bent over at the waist inside of three seconds, laughing so hard that no noise came out. I waved my hands helplessly in the air and she stomped her left foot repeatedly, but still no sound came from our wide-open mouths.

The longer it went on; the funnier it became and the more we sank helplessly into it. I put voice to my laugh first, and once I did, she matched it in strength and volume. We must have looked like two completely crazy women, and neither of us cared. When I had finally regained enough breath to stand almost upright, I was wiping tears of the very best kind from beneath my eyes and she followed suit. I glanced over to Kane and Bill. They were watching us, each wearing their own version of a crooked grin, and Helen nudged my side with her elbow.

"Goddamn grins will be the death of us yet." She said, and I was afraid I'd be breathless laughing again. Oh, shit yes! She was right. Thank you, God!

"C'mon Bill, take me home and no stopping for any form of food that comes through a window." She barked, and hugged me fiercely. She kissed my cheek, and whispered.

"You two are gonna be just fine, baby. Better than fine. Your friend Ann, is on to something there."

Bill was shaking Kane's hand saying goodbye, and once he was done he kissed my cheek and wished me the best of luck. Helen was standing directly in front of Kane, and while he had almost a foot of height on her, she was waggling her finger at his nose. He had his hands shoved into his front pockets, and he was nodding and promising he would to whatever it was she was insisting. Finally, she reached up and scruffed his hair, winked at me, and instructed Bill drive her home. Kane grinned at me, and crooked his right elbow out. I slid my left hand into it, and allowed my husband to escort me to the bar for a drink and to join our friends.

Sometime later, Kane nuzzled his nose behind my ear. The feel of him pressed against me and the softness of his breath on my skin had me turning red again except this time I wasn't blushing.

"Ready to go home?" he purred, and I nodded that I was.

"Good. Then let us make our good byes. I very much want to be alone with you. *Wife.*"

I loved the sound of it.

#

"I *still* cannot believe you managed all of that." Kane said as he drove us back through Newburyport towards home. "And kept it a surprise! Well done!"

"I hope you weren't too disappointed. I didn't have much time."

"*Disappointed?*" he asked incredulously, and pulled the truck into the Mobil station. He parked but left the engine running so the heat stayed on. He did this for my benefit of course; his tolerance for the cold was far higher than mine. It was my good fortune that he also generated amazing body heat. It gave me an excuse to curl up next to him on chilly nights. Once the truck had stopped; he turned and faced me.

"Diana? That was the most elegant wedding I have ever heard of. The fact that it was ours? That tops the charts."

"Everybody helped, Kane. I didn't do it alone." I said, and his smile eliminated the need for streetlights. I found myself returning it and it was half a minute before I could continue.

"Colin and Ann really did most of it, although it was Alejandro that collected the sand dollars after that storm last week. He spent the entire morning last Sunday walking the beach to find them."

Kane hung his head for a moment, and then nodded before looking back at me. When he did, the glowing gold of his eyes fluctuated several times and I recognized the emotion behind each hue. Kane was truly moved by it; and that darker gold shifted lighter with pride in the young man. Watching those two shades flash like a strobe light was breathtaking, and I was hypnotized by it. As a man of character and honor? Kane was not capable of a bold-faced lie, and if he was it would be immediately obvious. Okay then. I might have my heartbeat and color to give me away, but his eyes were the clearest road map of all; at least to me. That knowledge eliminated so much bullshit from our lives. There was no lying between us. To even attempt it was just sheer stupidity, the other would know. So why bother in the first place? I silently thanked the Justice Court in the Sky. Kane and I had enough to deal with in our life together.

Eliminating the worry of lies was a kindness. I realized the shifting colors of his eyes had disappeared, and the single gold light now possessing them was one I recognized. I inhaled slowly. Oh shit. Kane had taken me for his wife. Now he was ready to take his wife. It was an idea with tremendous appeal for me.

"I think you'd better get us home." I said, and his familiar crooked grin held a hungry edge to it. "And by the way you're looking at me? I think you'd better hurry. I'd prefer *NOT* to consummate the marriage at the Mobil gas pumps."

"I would not tarnish the *consummation* with something so tasteless, Diana." He said, and put the truck into motion again. He was waiting for traffic to pass to turn left, and it afforded him a moment to find his 'inner scoundrel'. He cut his eyes in my direction and the grin reappeared.

"But I offer no promises that after our first intimacy as husband and wife? I will keep such self-control ever again. What you do to me? What I feel for you? There may come a time that you become my favorite indulgence in the middle of aisle seven."

#

We had just crossed into Rowley when the splotches of white began to strike the windshield. They were the big fat lazy snowflakes that every snow globe ever created tries so hard to mimic. Kane looked across the cab at me and returned the smile I was already wearing. Christmas Eve. We had just gotten married, and it was snowing. It was perfect.

"There's something magic about snow on Christmas Eve." I said, and Kane grinned his agreement. "It just feels *RIGHT*."

"Indeed, it does." He replied, and turned the left blinker on.

"Um, Kane?" I began, and he smiled at the feel of his name. "We live straight."

"I know, but as you said; there is magic in the air."

"Uh, okay..."

"Just trust me Jimmy."

"I do. Completely."

Kane maneuvered the truck down a paved portion of road that gradually disintegrated into a well packed dirt road. We had passed the last of the three houses on it over half a mile back, and still he drove on, pressing further into dense trees. The road narrowed into scarcely more than a country lane, and eventually the vehicle ran out of room. He parked and was opening my door in half a breath. I accepted the hand he offered me and slipped out of the passenger seat. He interlaced the fingers of his right hand with my left, and after a quick and gentle kiss, tugged my hand and motioned for me to follow him.
The soles of my boots were slick and not exactly prime walk through the woods in the snow foot gear; but as I

had said I completely trusted him, and I stepped beside him without hesitation.

We travelled a few hundred feet down a narrow foot path passing the thick trunks of ancient oaks and dense pines, and the one time my feet even hinted at a slip Kane had his arm protectively around my waist to prevent a fall.

The moon was past half full; the second full of December was seven nights out, and I could see enough even through the clouds to make out the way. I'm sure it was lit up like a runway for Kane and his incredible night vision. He could see in the dark of a new moon better than I could on a Full. We took three more steps, and the trees fell away as we entered into a large clearing.

I glanced around it in awe; I would never have suspected such a place to be here. It was completely silent, save for our breathing which formed clouds of vapor in the stillness. I looked over to my husband, and his smile was big and bright. The gold in his eyes shimmered; and even the steady and now much heavier fall of snow in the two feet between us did not distract from him. He kept my sole attention for half a minute; and then jerked his head towards the opposite side of the clearing. I let my eyes wander in the direction of his motion.

Maybe thirty feet away, almost to the opposite tree line, was a glow. It took me a second before I realized what it was. There were three candles burning. Candles; here, in the middle of the woods. For what? I was moving closer before I knew it, and once I realized it, I looked back to Kane. He was smiling, and nodded that I should continue across the glen. He followed me, but stayed a half step behind, as if he wanted me to discover this alone at first. Well, I trusted him, so I did just that. I carefully made my way across the two inch deep snow, and approached the soft and gentle light. A dozen steps and I was there.

What my vision beheld was so incredible; I crouched down in both disbelief and reverence. The three candles were in a 'V' shape, and in their center was a rustic manger scene. The figures were simple but unmistakable in their identity. Mary and Joseph flanked a hay trough made of slender branches that had been cut and tied together with what appeared to be vines. A barn roof structure covered them; and it shielded the baby Jesus and his parents from the falling snow. The thick white candles were outside of it and I realized they were domed in glass with vents on the tops and sides to prevent the glass from shattering. The candles were new; but everything else that lay before me was at least twenty-five years old. I felt tears begin to swell in my eyes, and Kane crouched down beside me.

"I discovered this the night before my ninety-third birthday.' He whispered. "Since then? I have come here every year to see if it is still here."

"Who?" I asked softly, never taking my eyes from the scene displayed before me.

"I don't know. It is only here on Christmas Eve. Tomorrow it will be gone. No footprints, no scent, nothing even *I* can detect. Not for thirty-four years."

"Kane? This is the most beautiful thing I have ever seen. Thank you."

"Yes. I agree. The most beautiful thing I have ever seen." He said, and out of the corner of my eye I realized he was looking directly at me. I shifted my feet so that I could look at him, and the warmth emanating from his eyes could have kept the Ice Age at bay for decades.

"Magic indeed, Mr. Woods."

"Of the very best kind...Mrs. Woods."

If ever the angels were to sing over this hidden precious manger? Their voices would never come close to the grace and peace I felt at the sound of Kane calling me that.

#

We pulled into our driveway some forty minutes later, and Kane as always opened the passenger door. I moved to step out, but he scooped me up in his arms and carried me across the yard. I laughed softly as he did it, and wrapped my arms around his neck and leaned into his chest. Once we reached the porch, he looked at the door, then to his left pocket, and then back to the door.

"You can put me down, Kane." I said, and giggled as he scowled at either me or the thought of it. Maybe it was both.

"I will do no such thing. Give me a minute, I will figure something out." He said, and I watched him run through at least six different ideas that he determined wouldn't work. It was adorable to watch; and I was thankful he was distracted enough to have missed my momentary pink color. I couldn't take it any longer, and began to laugh as I reached into his left pocket and pulled out the keys myself. I held the ring up by the house key, and he grinned at me.

"It's not supposed to be one doing for the other, Kane. It's supposed to be two doing it together, as one." I said, and inserted the key into the dead bolt. One twist to the left and the lock clicked open. I turned the knob to release the latch, and he shoved the door open with his foot.

"Sheer genius, Diana Jame....um, *WOODS.*" He said, and kissed me as he stepped over the threshold with me in his arms. Once inside, he kicked the door shut behind us, and kissed me once more before gently placing my feet on the floor. He ran his right hand through his snow dampened hair as he half grinned, and it was tinged with embarrassment at his slip of my name.

"It's going to take some getting used to, for both of us." I said, and gave him a quick kiss before running my fingertip down the length of his nose.

"It's only been seven hours. A nightcap to shake the chill from our bones?" I asked, and headed towards the kitchen. Kane fell into step beside me, and retrieved the bottle of my maiden namesake while I got us two glasses. He poured us a short one, and grinned as he raised it to his lips. I noticed his was equal in volume to mine, and arched my right eyebrow reflexively as I sipped mine. The warmth immediately coursed down my chest, and after a second sip it spread to my extremities. Kane did the same, but that grin still lingered.

"What?" I finally asked, and finished off the contents of my glass.

"Yes. Seven hours." He said, and emptied his as well. He placed it on the counter, and took the empty glass from me and placed it next to his. When he looked back up at me, that single gold light had returned to his eyes, and any remaining 'chill' vanished in an instant.

"That is seven hours too long, my *wife*." He said, and the richness of his voice rumbled through me. A powerful kiss was quickly upon me, and I was once again being carried through a doorway, but this one led to our bedroom. Indeed, there was magic in this night.

Chapter Forty-One

"Merry Christmas, Love." Was spoken softly behind my ear, and I smiled before my eyes even opened. Kane was wrapped around me, and the warmth of his voice was rivaled only by the body heat radiating from him. The *Enhancement* gave him some extra BTUs of that I was certain, and I enjoyed every second of it.

"Happy birthday." I murmured back, and he gently squeezed my waist tighter.

"The best of my life."

"So far. We have many more to come." I said, and he pulled me tightly to him. He held me close like that for a minute, then relaxed and kissed my neck.

"I'll start the coffee." He said, and moved to get up. I grabbed his wrist and pulled him back into the bed.

"In a minute." I said, and snuggled into his shoulder.

"Wow. This? Over coffee?"

"You bet your ass."

"I am flattered."

"Merry Christmas."

"Indeed it is, Diana. Indeed it is."

#

We finally climbed out of the bed twenty minutes later, and I changed up the order of my morning Trinity as the coffee brewed. Fluoride came first today, and caffeine and nicotine were commenced together, blessed with the creamy joy of Bailey's. Kane also topped his off with the liqueur, and we sat in front of the fire and enjoyed each other's company. I was leaning against his shoulder when I felt him start to shake, and I looked up to see what was wrong. He was smiling, and his teeth were astonishingly large and bright. The shaking was a laugh that bordered on a giggle, and it surprised me to see it coming from him.

"What?" I asked, and he permitted sound to find his laugh. When it subsided, that half grin appeared, and I was infected once again by it.

"Can I give you your present now?"

"Of course. But I will never want anything more than what I already have. I'm sitting here with you. And I already got the best gift ever."

"And what is that?" he asked, his eyes glowing under furrowed brows.

"Your last name."

"Jesus, Diana." He whispered, and I watched the gold swirl. Each distinctive hue of his eyes was as clear of a road map to Kane's feelings to me as my heartbeat and color was to him. Perfectly in tune with each other, so much so we felt each other's words though more often for me. For centuries. Ann was right. Yes, Scotty; your watch is over. Helen, you are right; there is no need to worry. And Alejandro? Learn from this man. You will never go wrong in your life. Colin? It is me that is not worthy, and it has nothing to do with Dorchester. Kane cleared his throat and took a deep breath.

"I am pleased you like hand me downs, because that ties in to your present."

"Kane?" I began, and despite the rising inflection of annoyance in my voice he smiled, "Do not *EVER* disrespect our family name again. You, or anybody else who does; will answer to me for it."

"Forgive me." He said, and bowed his head. When he raised it again, his eyes danced with humor. "I feel great pity for the next soul who does. It *certainly* will *NOT* be me. I know better than to tempt fate *twice*."

"Good. Now that we have settled *THAT*; go ahead with your present." I said, and Kane grinned excitedly. He practically sprang from the couch and scampered, I swear to God he *scampered*; to the back corner of the living room behind the Christmas tree. I was puzzled; there was nothing under the tree, no wrapped boxes, and I watched him with great interest. He reached his hand *IN* to the center of the tree, and removed a long cylindrical package from up against the trunk of it. Fucking genius! Hide it in plain sight! He damn near swaggered back to where I was sitting, and placed the tube in my lap. I stared at it for a long time, and then looked up at him. He was grinning, like a kid who had managed to fool his parents for the first time, and I returned one. The man was good. I had to give him that one.

"Wait! We need *libations*." he said, and in less than three seconds he was gone to the kitchen and returned with two Jameson's in his right fingers and two Bailey's and coffee in his left. Jesus, he had talents any maître d would kill for. I smiled and accepted the Jameson's, and he placed the mugs on the coffee table. It was a *COFFEE* table after all.

"Slainte." He said, and raised his glass. I tinked the rim of his with mine.

"Happy birthday." I retorted, and he smiled as we sipped together. Once we had, he glanced down at my present, and I grinned and nodded my head repeatedly.

"Can I open it now?" I asked, and the pitch of my voice revealed just how excited I was. His smile was enormous, and he said that I could. I tore into the green wrapping paper, and its shedding exposed? A tube.

I scowled at it, curious as to what it actually was; until I noticed a screw cap on one end. I undid it as quickly as my left hand would allow, and giggled as the whole 'lefty-loosey, righty- tighty' got confused with me using my opposite hand. Firearms training was one thing; unscrewing a cap was another story. I put the lid on the coffee table and tilted the case upwards allowing the contents to slide out. A soft cloth was wrapped around something skinny, and I hurriedly unfolded it. In my lap was two parts of a fishing rod. A fly rod to be specific; and a very old one at that. It was feather light and crafted beautifully. The cork handle had seen some use, but the entire piece was in exquisite condition. I stared at it for long moments, and when I turned at looked at Kane his eyes were brilliant but the light in them held a softness.

"When I snooped your driver's license? I came across some pictures in your wallet." He said quietly, but the humming in my body was not as subtle as his volume.

"All of the one's you looked the happiest in? Were with you and a dark-haired boy that grew into a man as you did a woman. And all of them, had a fish in them."

"Jimmy." I said, and Kane cocked his head, confused. I laughed as I realized the source of his lack of understanding. It *was* funny.

"No. That *IS* Jimmy. My older cousin, Jimmy. *James*, specifically. He taught me to fish, smoke and drink beer; all on the same day. I was eight."

"I like him already." Kane said, and grinned.

"Me too. The three most expensive habits of my life. I should send him a bill." I said, and Kane laughed. It was a good, honest laugh; and I swelled with happiness. Once he had quieted, I returned my attention to the fly rod.

"Kane," I began, and he smiled, "This is an incredible rod. Masterfully crafted, and quite old though it is in mint condition. Where did you get it?"

"It was my Da's. He loved to fish the river." Kane said softly.

There are moments when you think you could never be happier, and I had found that moment when I opened the fly rod and shared the story of my cousin and my eight-year-old self. And sometimes, those bright shining moments are the best you'll ever know. This was not one of them. I was thrilled at the gift of a fly rod that was for sure. But the knowledge that Kane had just given me his *father's*? Jesus. I was flying. No, I was soaring, and the enormity of it did not escape me.

I had been presented a legacy, and I was smiling through tears.

That is the very best place in the universe to find yourself in; and I was even more blessed for it because it was Kane that had brought me here, and it was Kane that I was sharing it with.

I closed my eyes and thanked the Courtroom Upstairs. I basked in the perfection of it, and after several moments I opened my eyes. Kane was grinning, and he slid a thumb under my eyes wiping tears.

"I am glad you like it." He said, and nothing more. Thank you again, Upstairs.

After finishing the remaining Jameson and the delicious Bailey's infused coffee; I rose from the couch and walked over to the pile of unopened envelopes on the counter. Kane followed my movement and as I began sifting through the mail, he sighed and ran his fingers down his face.

"Really, Diana? Bills? Now?"

"Shut up." I said, and sorted through the various letters. I stopped at a red envelope; and my smile, heartbeat or color betrayed me because Kane's frustrated expression shifted into an appreciative smile. It grew wider and he nodded his head approvingly.

"Well done, wife. Well done."

"Hide in plain sight. Although the tree trunk was a masterpiece." I said, and winked at him.

"The stack of mail was not an amateur move either." He said, and I crossed the kitchen and sat beside him.

"I'm a little afraid to give you this, because I'm not entirely sure you want it." I said, and his smile dimmed a touch before recovering. Its return gave me the courage to continue.

"It's ok if you don't. It is simply? An offer. It's pathetically small compared to Angus' fly rod. I'd apologize; but we are done with those. And unlike you?" I said, and cut him a feigned angry glare before I smiled and finished, "I honor that deal."

Kane dropped his head slightly when I said that, but then met my eyes with a certainty I had not witnessed before. The resolve behind the fluctuating gold had me dancing inside, and I hoped my color showed it.

"I cannot promise I will not fall short ever again, Diana. But I can promise that I will do my best *not* to."

"That is all anybody can ever ask, Kane." I said, and his smile bordered on blinding. "Merry Christmas. Or happy birthday. Whichever you prefer." I said, and passed the envelope to him. He gently took it from my fingers, and stared at it for several seconds. He looked back at me and the purity of what he was feeling painted his eyes and features.

"Thank you." was all he said, and though it was scarcely a whisper his body language screamed of his honesty. I nodded and motioned that he should open it. He obliged, and slid a finger under the glued flap of the envelope. Once it was opened, he removed the folded paper inside of it, and his eyebrows converged while he read it. A realization crossed his mind, and I watched as it dawned on him what the four by six piece of paper was.

He snapped his head up and looked at me. His eyes were wide and blazing, and I'm not sure if it was shock, fear, or joy that I saw. Maybe it was all three. The gold was shifting so quickly I couldn't really determine which emotion was foremost for him, and I realized I was holding my breath. I consciously made myself exhale, and while it was not as relaxed as I had hoped? It was better than it could have ended up being. Kane's eyes continued their strobe pattern; and I forced myself to sit still and meet his gaze. After an agonizing two minutes of silence, I spoke first.

"That is the renewal. It's for May. If you want me to refill it? Just leave it on the vanity counter and I will. Like I said; I won't think anything one way or another. It's just an offer."

"Diana? As always; there is never anything '*just*' about you, or in anything you do. But are you sure?"

"Not at all. And completely yes." I said, and any uncertainty I held vanished. I inhaled and cleared my throat before I finished.

"*Not* before May. Allow me some selfish indulgence. I want at least a year with you exclusively mine before. According to the Doc; it takes two months to completely clear my system. After that? All bets are off, so you have until May to decide."

I watched the flames in the hearth waltz, and appreciated the warmth from them. It was just before noon of Christmas Day, and it had been a morning of huge steps; the least of which was unfolded in Kane's right hand. What he held was the renewal prescription for my Tri-Levlen; my birth control pills. It was entirely up to him what would happen from there, and either way I had already made my peace with it. I wouldn't have faulted him for a second if I found that prescription on the vanity counter the next day. The thought of children was daunting enough for any couple. Factor in the risk of an inherited *Enhancement*? Well shit; this was not to be taken lightly.

I had been thinking about it and all of the possible consequences since Kane's proposal. I had been afforded time to think before I made my decision although it took me less than a day to decide.

A sound from my right seized my attention, and before I could fully turn that way a flare appeared in the fireplace. I watched the wadded-up piece of paper catch fire; roar, and then disappear into ash and smoke. I screamed with joy inside, but somehow Officer Jameson showed up and her cool professionalism rose to the surface of the moment.

"Are *you* sure?" I asked, and fully looked at Kane. He smiled brilliantly, and then let it fade into the beloved half grin that had disarmed me so many times before.

"*Not in the least*. And absolutely, *yes*."

Chapter Forty-Two

Six days later, a visibly upset Kane Woods watched me pack an overnight bag. He was pacing the kitchen and practically gnashing his teeth, and his frustration was bordering on anger. I was gathering the last of my personal items from the bathroom, and his constant motion took him in and out of my line of sight as he circled the kitchen. I felt exactly the same.

Six days was a pretty short honeymoon; but we had definitely capitalized on the time and my hips reminded me that we had not been remiss. I smiled at their ache, shoved my toothbrush in the bag and zipped it shut. When I peeked around the doorframe, Kane's back was to me and he was waving his arms in a silent argument with? *No one*. Our eyes met as he rounded another lap of the kitchen, and he finally stood still. His grin was sheepish and held a tinge of embarrassment. I started to giggle.

"Not sure who you're arguing with there Kane, but it doesn't look like you're winning."

"I am not. Not at all." He said, and hung his head. Even with his face down, I could see his face flushing, and my giggle expanded into a laugh.

"You're blushing again." I said, and he raised his index finger in an unspoken '*Don't*' without ever looking up. I laughed even harder, and eventually it wore him down because his shoulders began to gently shake. He dragged his hand down his face and lifted his head. The gold was more than glowing; it was an inferno but even in that there was humor and love. He smiled and shook his head.

"Jesus, even now; you make me laugh."

"Kinda have to, Kane. We can't stop it, so there's no point in getting all puffed up about it. And that *IS* exactly what you're doing, which is useless and we both know it. And still? You're doing it, and you're raging at something or someone invisible. Like *THAT'S* gonna change things? *NOT*. Sorry; but that's funny."

"I can't help it. Only a week since we were married and you have to go. It is frustrating and quite frankly? It is infuriating."

"Husband?" I said sternly, and he smiled though he knew I was serious, "It is a dance we have done before and will do again. So, *STOP*. Yes, I have to go. But? I get to come home after. I can't change it, nor can you. So just *STOP* sulking about it and having a borderline tantrum. You are far too old to be pitching a fit."

"I am not sulking." He said, and my eyebrow was arched the highest it had been to date with him. He nodded his head as he chuckled, and assumed his 'surrender' pose.

"All right; I am. And what do you mean, *far too old*?" he said, and the half grin settled on his face. Damn he was killing me with it.

"Anything older than five is too old for that nonsense, so just knock it off." I said, and the grin bloomed into an enormous smile. His gold in his eyes danced, and he narrowed them slightly as he gazed at me.

"What a mother you will be." He said, and that sentence stopped my heart.

"Do *what*?" I asked, and tilted my head slightly.

"Put up with zero crap; call it like it is. It reminds me of someone." He said, and I smiled and walked over to him.

"And what a fine job Maureen did. Her son is an incredible man. The perfect blend of gentleman and scoundrel. A girl never stood a chance." I said, and kissed him. He returned it eagerly, and his hands wandered my body.

"Kane," I gasped as he let me up for air, "Keep that up and we will be practicing for my motherhood." His eyes darkened and he grinned.

"Practice makes perfect." He said, and the rumble of his words shook me. It was just before three in the afternoon; less than four hours until moon rise. I raised his shirt and ran my hands across his middle; and the quiver of his stomach under my fingertips set me on fire.

"You don't need any practice." I whispered, and gently nibbled his neck. He tensed when I did so, and then abandoned any sense of restraint. We never made it to the bedroom; the couch was as far as we got. I was going to enjoy the 'practice'.

#

The sun was down and I was being hurried to my car. It was almost six at night. Kane was frantic in getting me to it; I swear he would have dragged me there and thrown me into the driver's seat had I hesitated another second. He leaned in and kissed me, and then quickly shut the door. I started the engine, and rolled down the window as the engine warmed up.

"My God Diana, I am sorry, but *GO*. It's starting, you haven't much time. I love you. *GO*." He said, rubbing his chest. His ribs were starting to hurt.

"I will. Give me your ring." I said, and he looked at me in startled confusion.

"Kane, you're going to change. I will keep it safe and return it to your finger in the morning."

He stared down at it for the longest moment, and then removed it from his left hand. He flinched as he took it off and my heart whimpered a bit for him. He hung his head and placed it into my outstretched palm.

"I love you, Kane Woods. See you in the morning."

"Return safely to me." He said, and I locked his eyes with mine.

"You do the same." I said, and shoved the Mustang into reverse. I backed out on to our 'road', and shot one final look at my husband. Kane was breathing heavier than normal and it had nothing to do with the reason for my later than usual departure. The moon was going to crest the horizon within the hour, and it was wreaking havoc on him. He managed a wave and I returned it before driving off. I turned left at the end of the road and while I had no idea where I was going yet, I didn't wait at the end of the street like I usually did. I could figure out a destination once I was safely away. I pulled into the parking lot of the post office, and lit a cigarette as I considered where to spend the night.

Tonight? Would be a challenge. It was New Year's Eve and there were not exactly a ton of open rooms in hotels or even motels for the night. Partiers were already booked in, and I considered what direction to even head. Boston would be impossible to find a room; First Night was a huge event and reservations were made six months in advance for that. Hampton Beach was out; they too had a massive party on New Year's and the same held true for any accommodations up there. Shit, I might spend the night drinking coffee in Helen's diner, and I laughed at the thought. There were far worse places to be, and even worse company to keep. Still; she would wonder why I wasn't with my husband. That was a question I did not want to have to answer; though I knew she would never ask. She had held a gun for me and didn't care if there was a body attached to it. But I didn't want to worry her about 'trouble in Paradise' even if the only trouble Kane and I had was not being able to keep our hands off of each other.

I had decided to head west towards Worchester; there were no concerts tonight as far as I knew and on the outskirts of the mid-state city I was fairly confident I could find a bed for the night. I rolled the window down completely and had my hand out of it to toss the cigarette into the snow. A faded red pickup pulled up beside my car, facing the opposite direction that my Mustang pointed, and my skin crawled as I heard his voice and accent.

"Well howdy, Miss! Happy New Year!" He said, and his smile was ridiculously false in its origin and warmth. The current temperature was twenty-seven degrees and that was a heat wave compared to what lurked behind his empty stare. I dropped the cigarette from my fingers, and his eyes found my ring finger. He glanced up at me, and the same reptilian smile he wore a few seconds earlier returned.

"Well now! It has become Missus, hasn't it? Congratulations! The fellow with the interesting eyes, is it not?"

"Yes. Yes, it is." I said, and pulled a magnificent portrayal of a giddy innocent bride from my arsenal of roles I can assume. I nodded vigorously and smiled, channeling my inner Valley Girl in the hope of concealing exactly how much I knew he was pure Evil. He may have bought my persona, but there was something within his that couldn't let him shut up. Or maybe? I played my role so convincingly; he didn't think I had an I.Q. over that of a carrot. Either way? He kept talking, and Georgia revealed more than he realized, and it terrified me.

"Yeah; his eyes. They see more than they should." He mused as he stared out into the trees behind the post office and in the general direction of our home. He drifted for a moment, and then focused back on me and the present.

"Seems this is the third time I've missed him. Hopefully, I won't again." He said, and the way he left that sentence hanging in the air made me shudder inside. Outside, I remained steady, and in his eyes? Goofy. Perfect. Goofy hides how much I heard him say, and it wasn't his words but the intent behind them. My stomach flipped twice and then sank.

"Well thank you, for your good wishes for us! If you will excuse me? It's New Year's Eve and I'm off to get some champagne."

"Of course! Of course. Don't let me hold you up. Missus......?"

"Yes sir; I sure am!" I said while smiling broadly, and I rolled the window back up. I waved, and drove away as quickly as I could without drawing suspicion.

My behavior and the timing of my words and actions must have worked, because as I glanced in the rear-view mirror his brake lights extinguished and he drove off in the opposite direction. He didn't speed nor did he leave too slowly. It was a normal departure; which is exactly why I didn't trust it one single bit. I knew I was dealing with a predator from the bowels of Hell, and I could only hope he was nowhere close to realizing the caliber of 'guardian' that he was dealing with.

I had done some undercover work in my time on the Sheriff's Department and playing Suzie the Boob gets you more information than your target ever realizes. They assume you're a giggly girl, and it is the ego that they can't resist. When scumbags think they are the smartest one in the conversation; they say more than they should. Who was I to inform them differently? Keep talking fucker; you're hanging yourself and don't even know it. Blondes may not always have more fun, but they get a lot more information than most realize. I waited for the truck to vanish from view, and then turned the Mustang around and headed out to the interstate.

I was merging onto the highway and replaying the brief exchange I had just had with *Evil*. Something was gnawing at me and I wasn't sure what it was precisely, but my gut was nudging me to examine every word that was said.

I'm not a rocket scientist by any means; I sucked at math but I wasn't a fool either. God gave me that gut instinct for a very good reason, and I listened to it. *Eyes that see more than they should.* What the fuck was that about? I mean, aside from the obvious that Kane sensed his 'wrongness' as much as I did? Where did *more than they should* factor in? A century of cop instinct flooded me, and I chewed on every bit of the conversation. *Seems this is the third time I've missed him.*

Suddenly my entire body went subzero, and the world went black. Or maybe it was my soul that had. I was conscious, fully aware and alert, but the terror I plunged into was mindless. I had no further human logic or thought. I had snapped into pure instinct and I sliced across three lanes of blacktop and on to the left break down lane of 95. I whipped the wheel left and plowed the sports car through the grass median in a severe U turn. I floored it and frozen turf pelted the windshield and lodged in the grill. I could give a rat's ass less, and I pegged the gas pedal down. The Ford fishtailed hard, and I almost lost it until the front tires bit into pavement. Once they did the rear ones followed, and I squealed them as I tore back onto 95 North.

Third time I've missed him. You *motherfucker!* I may have been on complete auto pilot, but one blazing thought cut through it all and lit my way home. *Third time*. I had only seen Georgia twice since the post office; once in Hampton beach and tonight being the second. You murdering fuck! The other '*miss*'? That? That had ended with Kane dead on a river bank. This redneck prick didn't know he had 'hit' that time; because Kane had survived. Oh, fuck you! Tonight, Georgia? If you come for him?

Tonight you will die; and I will be the one to kill you.

Chapter Forty-Three

The nose of the Mustang hovered at the edge of our road, and I was paralyzed. The moon had not yet risen, but it was dangerously close. I knew that the Devil that had come from Georgia was the one who had shot Kane; just as I knew he was waiting to try again. That baby raping fuck had sensed that Kane knew what he was and had tried to silence him. How he knew what Kane was I had no idea. It was nothing I could *prove*, but my bones screamed it and I put more stock in that than I did any 'evidence' that could be gathered. Sometimes? You just *KNEW*, and this was no exception.

I glanced east and while no outer rim of lunar had broken the horizon I knew there wasn't much time left. Fuck! Just like I 'knew' that this Confederate prick had put three silvertips into my husband; I also *KNEW* he had been responsible for Maria. Looking back? I had no doubt he was also guilty for the fate of the young girl found dead in Hampton Beach. Southern boys don't like the cold. If they come north? It's because they're running from something. I choked down bile while I wondered how many raped and dead girls were littered across Georgia. Maggot scumbag piece of shit, had been too kind.

I forced myself to let go of my rage at him for the moment. There was a decision to be made on my part; and it had to happen now. Kane was about to change. He didn't know what I now did, and I *knew* Kane was going to be hunted again tonight. Not on my watch you piece of shit. You gotta get through *me*, to get to *him*.

My revolver was at home. That was what Helen had wrapped in silver paper and golden bells. It was perfect and funny as well; but the fact that she knew it was no longer a danger for the weapon to be in the house was awesome. My problem was this. How do I get it, and then get away so that Kane didn't rip me apart in his *other* form but still stay close enough to protect him from Georgia?

My mind scrambled through twelve different scenarios, but in the end none would work, and I was running out of time. I had maybe fifteen minutes. I slammed the heel of my left hand on the steering wheel and rubbed my eyes. Shit! Shit, and shit! I had decided to creep south on Route One and wait two hours to be sure Kane had changed and was running through the woods, when movement in the trees caught my eye.

It was the shadow of a human moving carefully through the woods. I recognized the gait immediately. It was the stalk of a hunter. I didn't have to see the physique to know who it was and that there was no generosity for his visit. The car was fishtailing once again before I even realized I had stepped on the gas. I streaked up the road to our home with the lights off, and anyone following would not have known I was there because my foot never touched the brake pedal.

Earlier that month I had roared Kane's truck directly to the front door in an effort to get the gun out of the house. I had succeeded. Tonight? I screamed the Mustang across the very same yard and actually crashed it into the porch to get to that same weapon. I leapt out of the car and ran past the steam that wafted from what I presumed was now a destroyed radiator. I threw the front door wide open and bolted into the second bedroom. My wedding 'gift' had been returned to its domicile; the top drawer of the dresser and I snatched it up in my left hand. It was somewhat awkward when compared to my right, but not impossible or foreign. Thank you for the weak hand training Essex County! I checked that it was loaded as well as 'loaded' and yes was the answer to both questions.

I shoved the weapon in the front of my jeans, and jammed the speed loaders as well as remaining box of silvertips into my jacket pockets. I scrambled into the entryway, and my eyes were met by the first silver beams of a full moon breaking the horizon.

I froze where I stood, my eyes darting frantically as I searched for danger and my ears straining for any sound 'out of the ordinary'. For the longest of time, there was only silence save for the rushing of my blood and the raggedness of my breathing. I slowly reached out to the front door and closed it, ensuring that I locked the dead bolt. An awful realization drenched me. The front door might slow Kane as Wolf for a minute at best. If he was on the *outside*.

What was I going to do if I had just locked him *IN* here with me? I looked behind me slowly, half expecting the last thing I would see were huge fangs leaping towards me. The fact that it did *NOT* happen? That only intensified the fear. The house was dark; the fireplace had long since slipped to embers. For as much as I wanted the bright and warming tongues of flames? I knew better. No, if I survived tonight; it would be through the cold and blackness. I would not risk so much as a cigarette until after sunrise. No sooner had I thought that than I desperately wanted to smoke one.

It was going to be a very long night.

#

The moon had fully cleared the treetops when I relaxed enough and almost believed I had not locked Kane in the house with me. I still stood in the entryway, remaining in the exact position I had stopped in over an hour ago. My muscles were beginning to alternate between trembling and cramping and I knew that eventually I would have to move, but I fought it as long as I could. I was petrified that any movement on my part would focus every *Enhanced* sense Kane had directly on me.

If that happened? I would die; but when he changed back? The guilt would have him 'finally die' as well, and that fear was greater than the one I held for my physical wellbeing. An alarming thought skittered across my brain, and I did not like the way it felt or what it said. When Ann had said *finally die*; I naturally presumed she meant in a physical sense. Thinking about it now, bathed in the stripes of silver moonlight that streamed through the window of the front door? I wasn't so sure. Kane may 'die', but it may be just in spirit and heart. If anything happened to me and worse yet by his hand? He would be dead, but still breathing. Jesus Diana, be careful and be smart. *EVERYTHING* rides on what you do tonight. I remained still but my eyes were sweeping the windows; desperate in fear that I would see something, and that something would have enormous teeth.

Another half hour passed, and finally my body screamed loud enough that I had to move. I took a step forward, and my movements were stiff and awkward. Despite it, my muscles sang in relief and I released the breath I had been only allowing to shallowly fluctuate. I was mentally on high alert; and my instincts made my brain seem comatose. Every hair on my neck and head was straining as if the slightest movement would have them shrieking their warning. It was agonizingly quiet and still and I had managed two steps backward towards the kitchen. My ears detected no sound as I travelled, but then again? I couldn't hear a heartbeat from ten feet away.

No Diana; there will be no rest tonight. One slip, one tiny err on your part, and you both go down. The memory of Kane's eyes when I brought him to our surprise wedding, the way he looked leaning against the Mustang way back in the summer when I thought he was dead, his rapture at the front of aisle seven, and countless other moments of joy surged through my mind, and they gave me resolve. *Not* on my watch. This is only the beginning. I want *WAY* more than this.

Something solid was against the back of my thigh, and I realized I had backed up far enough that it was the kitchen table. My shoulders slumped in relief, and I carefully slid into the chair. I was stealthy when I did it, and I prayed that Kane was far enough away as *Wolf* that he did not hear it either.

I almost dozed twice after sitting down, though it was scarcely past eight in the evening.

Terror, all-consuming sheer terror, is exhausting. I was determined but I was no superhero that was for sure. I jerked my head up from my hand the second time and blinked as I tried to focus on what was outside. I scanned the windows; the moon had set the snow-covered yard aglow. Satisfied I was still alone, I returned my head to my hand. Jesus, a cigarette and a drink would be manna from Heaven, but there was absolutely no way I would risk either. Make it through tonight, and you have the rest of your life with Kane to enjoy such things. I concentrated on single minutes, and it helped stem the tide of being completely overwhelmed by the remaining seven hours of the Moon. Just over four hundred and twenty-five more times of doing this, and it would be done. I counted to sixty, and grinned my approval at my successful effort. Nice job Jimmy. Keep up the good work.

I had just completed success number ten and only had four hundred and fifteen more to go when a movement in the trees caught my attention. I narrowed my field of vision to the exact spot I had seen the flutter, and I waited for it to move again. It was several minutes I watched, and I was beginning to doubt myself when I saw a shadow peel from the side of an oak. I felt like I had been submerged in the Arctic Ocean as I watched a leg move from behind the trunk. Georgia was here, on the edge of our yard. There was only one reason he had come and that reason crushed any chill I had. White fury consumed me, and I was moving and at the door before I had realized it. It had gotten hot; not warm. *Hot*, though I did not sweat. I watched through the top window of the wooden door, and after a long minute he slid out from the side of the tree and stepped towards the house.

The revolver was in my left hand, but its weight didn't register until I heard the hammer cock back. In the solid silence those two clicks thundered, and I winced as I watched him. Judging by his continuing towards the house he had not heard it, though how was a mystery to me because it had shattered the stillness of the entryway and seemed loud enough to burst glass. The fingers of my right hand held the door knob, and I waited as I followed his stealthy approach to our door. It was an eternity before he had crossed halfway to the house and I heard my breathing. It was remarkably regular and steady. Jesus Jimmy; you are fucking scary. A grin found my lips. No, I wasn't scary. I was lethal.

Maria was one thing, and that conviction would rest in evidence. This hunt of his? Of my *husband*? The man I loved beyond any comprehension or rationality? *Fuck* you Georgia. No, there would be no trial. There was only one way this story was going to play out, and I felt the doorknob slowly shifting left. Twenty feet.

Even with my left; I'd have a good chance in this end game and he didn't even know I was here. The sound of Kane's laugh filled my thoughts, and it steeled my resolve. Bring it you piece of shit. It ends tonight. It ends *right fucking now*.

The cold night air swirled around me as I opened the door, but I didn't feel it. I stood in the dark of our entryway, and stepped forward to the threshold. The same threshold Kane had carried me across not one week earlier. Georgia had been scanning the road when I opened it, and by the time he looked back to the house? He was looking at the business end of a .357. He stopped where he stood, and I watched his breathing do the same. His gun was pointed down, and I focused on the center of his chest over both sights. He began to pant, and acted as though he was raising his hands to give up. To the untrained eye, that was what he was doing; except my eye was not novice. His shoulders shifted and set, and while he portrayed a scared man about to surrender? The slight shift of his spine telegraphed his intent to raise his weapon at me.

"Easy now. I mean no harm, Missus...." He began, and as his right arm began to rise I squeezed the trigger. Brilliant flashes of light were simultaneous with recoils in my left wrist and the pungent perfume of gunpowder filled my nose. I was momentarily blinded by the muzzle flashes, and I blinked several times to clear my vision. After a few seconds it recovered enough to where I could see his crumpled form on the lawn. There was a gurgling sound as if someone was deflating a ball just under the surface of the water, but the Evil did not attempt to rise. I still had more spots in my view than clarity, but I knew, and I *KNEW*, that I had shot well.

"Mrs. Woods." I snarled at him, and inhaled.
"Mrs. Kane Woods."

#

A humming within me jerked me from my trance. The revolver still had a coil of smoke rising from the barrel, so it had not even been two seconds since I had fired and introduced myself. The humming intensified, and in a moment of horror I realized what it was. It was Kane. I could feel him; lack of language had no bearing. Snarls or growls or whatever it was I felt it, and he was coming close and coming quick. By the time I slammed the door shut the humming had become a thunder, and it was getting stronger. *Fuck*! There was no way he wouldn't sense me. I snapped the dead bolt shut, and laughed as I did. Yeah, *THAT* will stop him. My mind raced and teetered on panic as each wave of vibration travelled my ribcage.

Well, this is where it ends. I'm dead, and in every sense of the word that matters? So is he. The thought of my demise was not so bad. Don't get me wrong; I wasn't welcoming it, but if there was one thing I knew? It was that Kane had the *Residual*. My death would be quick. Brutal, but quick.

Kane on the other hand would linger for decades if not longer; utterly destroyed and empty but still breathing. I glanced down to the revolver. Shit; had I fired all six? I had no idea. If not? Well at least he could do himself in if he chose to. I looked to the sky, and found myself begging the Heavenly Court for Mercy. I didn't ask it for me.

I shot one look over my shoulder and realized that Evil Georgia was moving. Well *FUCK!* I took a step towards the door to finish the job, but the crashing in my ribcage told me Kane was already here. I glanced skyward once again, and shrugged my shoulders. Fuck it; it's been a good run. And? *Thank You*. The last six months have made it all worthwhile. I'd do it again in a New York minute and a thousand times over; just to see that man smile. Hope to see You Three Upstairs in Court. If not? Well? The basement can't be that bad.

The basement! Holy shit! I had forgotten it! Since I had moved in I was aware there was a basement; Hell, I had wanted Kane to put the ECSD box down in it and he had refused. But I had not actually *THOUGHT* about it until just now. I shot another look up, nodded my thanks and raced to the door. His parents had locked themselves in there when Kane was younger and they were alive. *My father built them a fortress of sorts down there. Going out of town wasn't quite practical for them.* Even with a cast I opened the latch with ease, and I threw the door wide and clambered down two steps before turning and locking the bolt behind me. It was pitch black; no windows were there, and I felt my way carefully down the wooden steps.

My feet had reached solid ground and I finally exhaled. I had no idea where I was, but I knew that I was safe.

Angus and Maureen had weathered many a full moon down here, and I was oddly proud to be occupying the same space. The darkness was absolute, and I wondered how I would know when the sun had risen. I reached into my pocket and smiled when I felt the Bic lighter. Well shit! *Somebody* Upstairs favors me tonight. I spun the flint and the flame illuminated the six feet around me. I immediately spotted two candles and I lit them both, allowing their warm light to spread and reveal my surroundings. I held one up, and slowly turned in a circle, absorbing the sanctuary.

The walls were reflective, and at first? I thought they were mirrored. I stepped closer and ran my fingertips down the surface. It was cold, and smooth. I gasped when I realized why two candles threw so much light. The walls of the ten by twelve-foot room were *silver*.

I looked up and knew before I did that the ceiling would be too and I was not mistaken. So *THAT'S* how they did it. I swayed slightly at the cost of it, especially back in the late 1800s. How had two Irish immigrants managed to afford this? My thoughts immediately settled on Kane. Well shit! Of course, they would have found a way! Kane was their son, and no doubt they loved him, maybe as much as I did. I would have robbed a bank to build such a safe place, and for all I knew they had. I silently tipped my hat to them, and found myself wishing I had met them. They were my kind of people, and while the Catholic 'No you cannot be in the same bed together' mindset would have been an issue; it would have been a small one. I looked down to my left ring finger and grinned. And a moot point now, my in laws.

The basement may have been devoid of windows, but it was not soundproof. The scream I heard was a piercing horror. Kane had arrived it seemed and he had found Georgia. There was a single gunshot, and the scream morphed into a wail of agonizing pain. The sound went on for terrible moments, and was repeated again. It emerged a third time but that one was cut short and ended in a ragged whimper. I felt the smile occupy my features, and God forgive me I didn't resist its arrival. *Couldn't have happened to a nicer guy.*

I realized that a 'sane' person would think I needed a *LOT* of professional help, and perhaps they would have been right. But most sane people had not seen what I had seen, nor did they know what I *KNEW*. There was the legal system, and then there was *justice*. Fuck you, sane people; I'll take justice over the confines of the law any day of the week.

Another sound shattered the night, and its volume was something I not only heard with my ears but I felt it as well. The violence of it as it travelled through my body was similar to when you feel a thunderclap just over your head, but for me it was ten times stronger. It was so powerful that my joints give out, and I dropped to the floor as the strength of my knees fled. It flooded the night; destroying any corner of safety for any that heard it.

It was more than a howl; it was a celebration of blood and vengeance that had been dispatched by the fangs of a creature pure it its brutality. Oh yes, justice was swifter than the law, but justice was also terrifying. Mind numbingly so. It was an eternity that it filled the darkness, and I felt the edges of my sanity fray for its duration. I fought tooth and nail to retain it; and memories of a smiling Kane were the anchors to which I clung as it raged around me. Kane. Despite what was out there right now? Kane would come back and my need to see him again, to feel his touch and hear his laugh lent iron to my bones. I couldn't stand up just yet, but I had stopped crumbling.

The sound finally began to wane, and I was able to inhale. The crushing song had squeezed the air from my lungs and the breath I drew was as ragged as the first sputter Kane had made on the river bank four weeks ago. My God, had it only been that short a time? So much had happened it felt like a year had passed. The exhaustion of the past weeks settled heavily in my shoulders, and I glanced around the shiny room once again. My eyes found the far corner, and in it was a small bed. It was about the size of a full-sized mattress, and I smiled and closed my eyes. Thank you, Maureen and Angus. Your daughter in law desperately needed this. Kane's primal baying had ended, and I could move again. I crawled over to the bed and melted into its softness. I shrugged the blankets over me, and my head sank into the pillows.

#

I didn't remember falling asleep, but truthfully who ever really does? My eyes slowly opened, and I focused on my quarters. The room was still lit, and the metallic walls threw far more light than was normal for two candles. It was almost as bright down here beneath the house as it was in Kane's workshop on a sunny day with the fluorescent lights blazing overhead. I looked at the source of the illumination, and their length had disappeared by half. How long had I been down here? Shit, what time *WAS* it? I didn't have on a watch, and I realized I had absolutely no idea of how much time had passed. Fuck!

Worry began to tickle my thoughts, and try as I might I could not dismiss it. How would I know when it was safe to come out? If I came out too soon? The Wolf might still be patrolling nearby, and the Residual would zero in on me as easily as if I sent up a signal flare. And if he was close? I would feel his teeth on my neck before I would know it, and not in the manner I would enjoy. It would be quick, but it was not an option I wished to explore. No, I would sit tight down here in safety. Once Kane transformed back; I would hear his footsteps upstairs. The sound of two feet crossing the floor would be my signal of 'all clear'.

The peace I felt was fleeting. No sooner had I decided how this would end, I remembered the gun shot. Fuck! That spawn from Hell with a southern drawl had managed to get off a round! Had it hit Kane? I realized I was gasping for air and the fear swallowed me. Oh Jesus! Please God, no. I realize You are the Judge in the Courtroom, but for once let this be about Justice and *NOT* the Law.

The image of a lifeless Kane flashed behind my eyes, and I was strangling in terror. What if he was up there hurt? Or worse? Shit. Shit and fuck and shit again. How long had I been down here? I was pacing for several minutes before I even realized it, and once I did it didn't stop me. My eyes desperately swept the room for any sort of clock. A watch, anything that would shed some light on the passage of time.

Light. I glanced over to the pair of candles and studied them. Their length had shortened by half, and I focused intently on the tapered body of them. There were lines that girthed the wax, and the lines were evenly spaced apart. What the Hell? I stepped over to them and held one up. Four lines remained between the flame and the base. Its counterpart had the exact same markings. I glanced around the room once more, and this time I discovered a drawer under the small table that had escaped my earlier notice. I reached down and opened it, and easily a dozen more candles rolled in the compartment. I took one out and saw the same circles on it, except this one had not ever been lit. I counted the lines from wick to stem.

There were twelve. A flutter of hope rose in me, and I considered that I just might know the passage of time after all. I ran my fingertip down the dust that had settled on the wax, and each dip I felt as it crossed a line gave me more assurance that I was on to something. Or more specifically, my in laws had been on to something. Twelve lines. There were twelve hours of darkness most nights. Maureen and Angus had marked each candle in one-hour increments of burn time. My God, thank you! It was the greatest wedding gift any parents could have given their children! I was smiling through tears. Eight hours had passed since I got down here. The moon had been up for almost two before I did. That was ten. Only two more to go. Easy Jimmy, just breathe and do not think of what might have happened. You don't know anything yet. He is fine, the screams continued after the shot was fired. Kane had been strong enough to serve moon driven retribution on a child rapist and murderer. I insisted that I was right on this, and though my certainty was a lie, I clung to it desperately as though my very life depended on it. I smiled when I realized that in fact; it did. Jesus Kane, you have *GOT* to be all right. There is no way I will make it without you.

#

Watching grass grow, or watching paint dry are descriptions used for times that are far too long and boring; so much so that it becomes painful. Watching a flame nibble away at wax topped those two analogies, and it was excruciating how much time it was taking. There was only one line left to disappear, and I was practically exploding within the confines of the silver vault. I had ascended the stairs at least seven times; my hand inches from turning the knob but each time I returned to the basement. Eventually I took to pacing, and I realized that this was what Kane must have felt like back in July. Caged in cell thirty-two; he must have been half crazed in the small space and he had to share it with three other inmates.

My cell for the evening was larger and I was alone in it, but it still felt suffocating. I did not suffer from claustrophobia thankfully, but I was frantic with fear nonetheless. My fear was raking its talons on the outside of the door, and it would not relent until I could emerge and be sure that there was only *one* body on the snow-covered lawn. I realized that I should be planning how to cover *THAT* scene up, but until I knew Kane was all right it didn't matter. If anything had happened to him? I couldn't have cared less what occurred after; it would all be for naught anyway. Jesus *CHRIST*! When had one minute gotten three thousand seconds in it? Time was not crawling; it hadn't even stopped. I swear to God it was going backwards.

I was frantic and I knew it. To save whatever shred of mind I had left; I forced myself to sit on the bed with my back to the candles. My skin was practically crawling with my desperation for time to pass, and I scrambled for a way to stop my downward spiral. While the walls around me were silver, it was gold that reached me and stilled my spine. Kane's eyes, and each shifting hue and brightness, filled my mind's eye and eventually pushed everything else outside. I realized my breathing had slowed from a frenzied struggle for oxygen into the steady rise and fall of normal lungs. I felt the smile spread across my lips.

Once again; it was the light of Kane that had reached out across the harbor and was guiding me safely home. I closed my eyes and allowed myself to wander through the memories we had made in the short time we had been together, and the volume of them was overwhelming. I travelled back, recalling every span of happiness and every moment of anger, and each one flowed smoothly into the next. Not all were pleasant. Not all were terrible. But they all were honest, and they were real. The way we had learned so much about each other, and how we communicated both verbally and in silence was astounding, and I smiled inwardly as I realized I had managed once again to fall deeper in love with my husband, Kane Woods. Holy shit.

By the time I opened my eyes again, the flame had swallowed the final line in the wax and then some. I sprang to my feet and climbed the stairs two at a time.

My hand was on the doorknob and I stopped; straining my ears for any sound of Kane. There was none. I slowly opened the door, prepared for what I had no idea. Whatever I found; it was nothing so long as Kane was all right.

I blinked as the light of day reached my green eyes, and remarkably for once the light was not gray but bright sunshine and a blue sky. I snorted a laugh. About Goddamn time something blue was good! I scanned the house quickly and determined it was still secure from when I had locked the door last night. No, Kane had not come back in. I mentally smacked my forehead when I realized there was no way he could have gotten back in even after he 'once again became himself'. Diana you moron; you chained the door as well as latched it! Sure, he could shoulder it open on any given day, but this was the day after the *second* Full of December. Lord knows what shape he was going to be in today. I strode towards the front door, snatching my cigarettes along the way. I lit one inside; I didn't particularly care right now, and slid the locks open. I stepped back and the sunlight entered as the door retreated. It felt warmer than it should have on a thirty-degree morning, and I closed my eyes and absorbed it.

"Good morning, wife." Came from my right, and its sound was nowhere near as wonderful as it's feeling within me. Laughter erupted from me before I had even opened my eyes, and once I did? I found them looking into the shimmering gold that had rescued me from dark seas the night before.

"Good morning Kane, my husband." I said, and his smile was gigantic as I tag teamed him with the two words I *knew* he felt. "Happy New Year."

"It is the New Year, but I am not so sure it will be starting happily." He said, and cut his eyes towards the yard. I followed his gaze, and the scene displayed before me froze both my breath and blood.

I had seen firsthand what Kane had done as *Wolf* in Lawrence. In the Residual he had been quick to kill the officers, and in that same Residual he had been more *patient* in his dispatching of Martinez. What happened in Lawrence was a mere rehearsal to what my eyes now beheld. The yard was a masterfully painted tapestry of torturous revenge. Oh yes; justice had been served, and it had been served over quite some time it seemed. Unlike the jumbled assortment of body parts that littered the cell blocks back in July; this artwork was surprisingly intact. Limb wise anyway. The same could not be said of Georgia's viscera. It was strewn across the yard like garland swaged on eaves, and the breadth of space it occupied was staggering.

Somewhere, my high school mind recalled that humans had thirty feet of intestinal length. It seemed longer somehow once removed from its cavity in the abdomen. I probably should have been faint, or nauseous, but I was neither. God forgive me, I felt the smile returning to my face. A flicker of worry at Kane's reaction sparked through me, but it was silenced by a familiar thought. Jesus Christ; I needed professional help.

"Couldn't have happened to a nicer guy.' I whispered, and I looked to Kane with trepidation. He narrowed his eyes slightly at my expression, and I noticed a few flecks of amber were already returning to them. The Blue was over. We had survived it.

"I don't know which one of us is more frightening." He said softly, and gently shook his head. His eyes lingered on mine, and I heard myself speaking.

"Fuck this cocksucker.' I said, and jerked my head towards the remnants of Georgia. The snow had been painted red and pink, and a giggle was rising inside me. Kane stared at me a long hard minute. Slowly the half grin emerged.

"Fuck him, indeed." He said, and the amber flecks glowed as bright as the gold.

"C'mon. Help me get this shit off the lawn." I said, and he rose from the porch swing. It was only then that I realized he was completely naked.

"Shit Kane, I forgot." I said, and he smiled as he felt his name. "Let me get you something to wear. Jesus, you have got to be freezing!"

I darted back inside and grabbed the first clothing I could find. A flannel shirt, warm socks and the eternal Levis jeans were in my left hand. I snatched a pair of boots for him as I passed through the entryway. I had expected him to still be on the porch when I emerged, but instead I found him barefoot in the snow reaching down to pick up the destroyed body of a murdering pedophile. He grabbed the carcass under the ribcage; the absence of organs made it a convenient yet grisly handle, and Kane suddenly hissed and yanked his hand back.

"What the....?" He mused as he shook his fingers in the air. I dropped the clothes on the porch and ran over to him.

"There's silver. Be careful." I said, and stared down at filmy dead eyes.

"Silver? How?"

"This maggot fuck is who has been hunting you. He came again last night. So? I shot him."

"*You shot him?*" Kane sputtered, and he stared at me in awe. I didn't understand what he was so surprised about. Of course, I had shot him. More than once.

"Yeah. Weak handed though. I didn't finish him." I said, and kicked the vacant torso. I was never one to spit, but I did just that, right into the cavernous opening where his liver used to be. The absolute lack of guilt or remorse or even sorrow should have alarmed me; but it did not. Georgia, in all his Evil, had come to murder Kane. Because Kane knew just as I did, what he was. A child raping murderer. If I had shot a human being, I'm sure I would have been devastated, and the aftermath would have been beyond terrible. But I had not. I had simply removed a malignancy from the planet. And somehow, I sensed in my bones that the *REAL* Superior Court that was in session above me was okay with it. I hadn't gone *LOOKING* for him; that would have been murder. *He* had come looking for Kane; to commit that very crime. In the overall scheme of it? It was a wash.

"What do you mean; you didn't finish him?" Kane asked, and I realized that he had no memory of what had occurred. Kane had been *Wolf*. I hung my head and considered not telling him, but when I looked back up into his eyes the idea disappeared. I sighed, and told him everything. From my talk in the parking lot of the Post Office to the firing of the gun, right through every detail of screams and another gunshot and the howl. I left nothing out; not even the time markings on the candles. Kane silently listened to every word and for the first time?

There was no self-hatred in his eyes. He nodded once I had finished, and looked down at the one spot of snow that somehow still remained white. He stared at it for a moment, and I watched a smile creeping across his face. I felt my eyebrow arch and when he met my green eyes, the gold and amber in his held a certainty I had never seen before.

"It's not supposed to be one doing for the other. It's supposed to be two doing it together, as one." Kane had recited my words right back to me, and I felt my eyebrow drop back to its normal position. "It appears we have done just that."

"Indeed." Was my one-word reply.

THE END

Made in United States
North Haven, CT
06 November 2023